Looking back over the years I have always
Owning an inventive imagination, school essays were easy and writing letters effortless. Crosswords too are fascinating. Researching a clue, I regularly come across a titbit of knowledge that hides in my brain. Later it emerges as the answer to another clue or as part of my stories.

Most of my life, apart from children and family, art has formed a big role in my career. Trained in restoration of oils and watercolours, it was important when my husband and I had a picture gallery in the Midlands which my eldest son still owns. After we retired to Cornwall I began another career in writing. I was thrilled when my love of words reached a pinnacle as my books began to appear. First modern thrillers, then delving back in history I wrote another suspenseful story, the one you are about to read called Lethal Legacy. Enjoy, dear reader, enjoy.

The right of Isobel Kelly to be identified as the Author of this Work has been asserted by her in accordance with the Copyright, Designs and Patents Act 1998.

Copyright © Isobel Kelly 2008

All characters in this publication are fictitious and resemblance to real persons, living or dead, is purely coincidental.

All rights reserved. No part of this publication may be reproduced, stored in a retrieval system, or transmitted, in any form or by any means without the prior written permission of the publisher, nor be otherwise circulated in any form of binding or cover other than that in which it is published and without a similar condition being imposed on the subsequent purchaser. Any person who does so may be liable to criminal prosecution and civil claims for damages.

ISBN 978-1-905988-72-3

Cover by Sue Cordon

Published by Libros International

www.librosinternational.com

LETHAL LEGACY

ISOBEL KELLY

Libros
INTERNATIONAL

Libros International is like an extended family – always ready to give support. From Ken Douglas and Trevor Dalton who spearhead the company to Kelly Walsh and Philip Spires who create the right profile for publishing, I feel in safe hands. Special thanks to Dawn Harman and Carol Cole for their great welcome and last but definitely not least, Wendy McGuinnes is my kind of editor. Hard-working, helpful, patient and with great attention to detail, she sorts all the misplaced adverbs, adjectives and funny spellings that flow from my pen. She is a good friend. And finally to Dennis; his loving and generous spirit will be with me always.

CHARACTERS IN LETHAL LEGACY

Murdoch Macgregor born 1735 died 1792
Married – (a) Maeve 1770 – daughter – Marion born 1774
Married second wife Margaret 1779
William – Duke of Forres – son of Murdoch and Margaret born 1780
Married Sophie Rose – son – Giles
Giles – married Lily Fairburn – daughter – Lavinia Rose
Marion – stepsister – marries Alistair Macgregor who is a cousin – son – Andrew
Andrew Macgregor – marries Morag – their son – Merrick
Merrick Macgregor eventually marries Linda Rose
Lavinia Rose marries Ambrose Trevarron, Cornish mine-owner
Linda Rose, (Lindy) her daughter, is secreted away at her birth and reared by
Ellie and Jethro Barton, a Cornish mining couple
Lucien Rowley – Viscount, son of Lord Channing
Linda Rowley – his mother
Jennifer Rowley – his sister
Annie Gorland – housekeeper to Ambrose Trevarron
Betsy Polwen – cook to Ambrose Trevarron
James Walcott – solicitor
Amy Bunnion – midwife to Ellie and Lavinia Trevarron
James Lusty – doctor
Becky Lanner – neighbour to Bartons
Serina – gypsy
And others pertinent to the story

PROLOGUE

Murdoch Macgregor stood watching in horror at the edge of the crowd as the last of the male figures swung violently at the end of a rope and choked to death. Hell's teeth! What a horrible way to die! He gulped quickly as his stomach reacted to the impression of an agonizing rope held tight around his own neck. He had known these twelve men; all brave Scots, who had been determined to have the Scottish nation for themselves under Bonnie Prince Charlie. However, Charles Edward had lost; the Jacobite cause was lost and, for some of the rebels, there was only this ignominious end.

Murdoch, a tall eleven-year-old, moved hastily away from the group when a sudden puff of wind brought the stench of excrement to his nostrils, since most of the hanged had voided themselves as they died. This, to him, seemed the final degradation bestowed on them by the invaders. Not only had the English suppressed a rebellion but they had also murdered the pride of the Scotsmen. A motley crowd, sated with the spectacle and with nothing more to stir their curiosity, melted silently away to continue their lives; most of them aware they must guard every action from now on. For a savage and pitiless English yoke was hard set upon the necks of the defeated; the bravery of the Scottish nation, as they had once known it, was at an end. The words 'Long Live Bonnie Prince Charlie' would be silent from now on!

The young lad, all at once realising he was late, swiftly made his way to the stables where his father had left the horse whilst they sold the farm produce they brought to the Inverness market. He found his father hitching up the horse and in a sour temper both at the late arrival of his son and the fact they seldom agreed on anything.

"It's gie past time we were heading home, son. Did ye nae think o' the late hour? Whaw're ye been?" His father was, as usual, impatient with his son's absence.

"I saw the hanging, Father."

"Did ye now? And what did ye think o' it? As if I canna guess."

"Oh, that I shall never have anything to do with war or rebellions or - or politics."

"Oh indeed. So you say now. You've yet to grow up, my laddie."

"Yes, I'll farm. You'll see; I'll have the finest, richest farm in Moray one day."

"Laudable sentiments but a mite hard to live up tae when yer belly's empty and yer blood boils from injustice. You'll aye be like the rest o' us when you're older."

Deep in thought, on that day in 1746, Murdoch rode the thirty miles back to their small farm by the River Findhorn in Morayshire. He had meant what he said to his father. If he was really rich then nothing could harm him or the family he aimed to have one day; many sons in his image. How he would achieve it from the lowly position as son of a third son of the Macgregors of Forres was a crazy, far-fetched notion but still he planned and stranger things have happened.

He was a day past his forty-fifth birthday in 1780 when he stood on the ramparts of Forres Castle as the newly approved Duke. The impossible dream had come true.

"Ahem, your Grace, the jeweller is waiting," the servant said deferentially.

"Ah yes, I will be down directly. Take him to my study, I shall see him there. Where is her Grace at this moment?"

"In her boudoir, my Lord; at rest, I believe. Do you wish to see her?"

"No! I don't want her to be present. I'll see the man myself."

The retainer bowed and left to carry out his master's orders.

Murdoch continued gazing at the land beneath him, pleased with its meticulous order. He never tired of inspecting it for he had worked like one possessed for so many years to gain control of it all. Like a miser counting his gold, he cast his eye over the tilled fields, well-kept paths, stands of trees, the tidy cottages here and there where his workers lived and out to Findhorn Bay and the Moray Firth beyond. Fortune had been on his side throughout his early years. Following the death of his father from a stroke, first the eldest brother died without a male heir; then the second brother succumbed to illness, leaving behind a young, brainless idiot of a son to inherit the enormous estate.

James was a loud boasting braggart, given to strutting and crowing about his new inheritance. When he got involved in an unlawful duel with a courtier of King George II, the English Crown almost usurped the castle in penance. James, lacking wit and totally incompetent in the skilled art of swordsmanship, was at fault. He paid dearly for his cheek. He was executed.

Murdoch managed to get the law on his side and his entitlement to inherit the estate was upheld. He had sound cause at that point to thank his youthful vow that he would neither involve himself in affairs of a political nature, nor indulge in treasonable actions against the crown of England. He had been vilified on many occasions by his fellow Scots but when he had been tempted to help, he only had to think of the hanging to adhere grimly to his vow. Now he was Duke of Forres at last and his second wife was about to produce an infant. With God's grace it would be what he had always dreamed of, a son to follow in his footsteps. If so, he proposed to give her a fine ruby necklace to show his gratitude for her pain and suffering in delivering his son.

The Arab held out the gold chain towards Murdoch so that the central cabochon ruby scintillated as it spun in the light, the diamonds in the woven gold mesh surrounding the jewel adding their gleams to its radiant beauty.

"See, m'Lord, here is the catch. The locket will open to hold a picture or a snippet of hair."

"You have done well. It is quite magnificent; I intend it to be a family heirloom."

"You couldn't wish for a finer relic. It is a Burmese ruby and as rare a one as I've ever had in my possession. The 'Royal Orb' as it is named in your language, will adorn the breast of your Lady with beauty. I am most happy and deeply honoured that you will use it thus and will be pleased to serve you in the future." Elizar Ramirez bowed low.

His translation had omitted the last two words - 'Royal Orb of Death' was the actual name but why cause unrest in this infidel's mind? With profitable luck within his grasp he expected his patron to acquire more valuable jewels. He had been tempted to retain the ruby for himself, adding it to the small pile of perfect gems he was collecting for his old age but a tale attended the jewel that hinted it was evil. It had been passed from owner to owner after being stolen from its resting place in a Pharaoh's tomb. He had heard misfortunes seemed to occur to those who owned it. Elizar Ramirez thought the tale mere superstition, though he was not about to test it on himself. On the other hand, it was ideal to be used in his business as a fine jeweller of great repute and he hurried with the work so that the jewel would rapidly leave his keeping. That he was passing on ill luck worried him not at all. The buyer was of no great importance, so what did it matter?

Elizar bowed again. "Allah is praised, may you ever find favour with my work and be blessed with many sons. I shall be ready to serve you again should you wish it as I have many fine jewels to grace a lady's neck and increase your wealth." And may my coffers be full also, he thought.

Murdoch's heir, William, was born two days later, and Margaret was rewarded with the priceless locket. "It's yours to keep for your lifetime, my dear; after which it will go to the wife of every Duke when she produces her first son. I see it going down through our succeeding generations forever as a symbol of our greatness."

"Forever is a long time, Murdoch," said Margaret, who was inclined to be prosaic.

Irritated with her words Murdoch held out his hand for the necklace. "Let me have the locket back, my dear, so I may keep it safe for you. Our child needs all your attention for the present; you can wear it on suitable occasions until the next son comes along."

Margaret died a year later of the sweating sickness. Murdoch died in great misery in 1792 of a growth in his throat, which filled his waking hours with fear and his sleep with nightmares of being hanged. There were no more children, nor did Murdoch marry again. His son, William, a dreamy, colourless youth was barely interested in the estate, preferring to waste his time in trivial pursuits. He eventually wed a Lady Sophie Stewart, principally at the urging of his older half-sister Marion, by Murdoch's first wife.

She knew her brother to be weak and ineffectual and herself to be the only one who had inherited all her father's strength and love of the land. However, William was the heir; she was not deemed capable, so the law decreed, to run the estate or interfere in anything connected with it. She had to find a woman who would be strong enough for William, to guide and advise him how to protect the estates her father had toiled and fought for. So she found Sophie and then regretted it ever afterwards.

CHAPTER ONE

"I hope the devil has you tethered in hell, Giles! You are a blind, stupid fool!" The words echoed violently in the silent room as they were uttered in huge anger by Sophie, Duchess of Forres. She was a woman who had exhausted her brain trying to find a way out of the dilemma she was now facing. In despair she crushed the well-read letter to a remarkably unlined brow, though she was already past her fiftieth birthday. Her lovely face appeared to be at odds with harshness; nonetheless, she was no stranger to invective, having ruled a large estate with an iron hand for many years. Sitting gracefully at a Regency secretaire, she revealed an elegant figure dressed in a style that gave away her age, for she adamantly refused to put on the frills and tassels of the Victorian era, the heavy crinolines and bustles of whalebone and horsehair. Instead, she preferred the silks and gauzes of the Georgians, which were softer and more pleasing to wear, dressing to gratify only herself, dismissing the sometimes not so gentle criticism of close friends. When chided for her lack of fashion she would abruptly wave a hand and say, "I was born to soft freedom, the feel of silk against my skin, not heavy corsets that weigh one down needlessly. Without a doubt I shall die as I am."

The sound of voices echoing from the hallway made her recollect where she was and she hastily stuffed the offending letter in a drawer in her desk before composing herself in order to greet her granddaughter as usual with a cheerful face, though it cost her dearly to achieve it.

"Ah! Here you are, my love. Just when I was about to

wonder if your walk in the park had caused you to retire to bed with dire fatigue." Sophie smiled as she jested and Lavinia dimpled with a beam as she seated herself on a chair near to her grandmother and gracefully arranged her delicately pleated overskirt of sarsenet around her.

"Oh no, I could have walked for another hour at least but Prue was complaining of a stone in her shoe and becoming quite tiresome," she said, "and it was time I returned to see you, my dearest Grandmama." It was only a white lie, she told herself, so near the truth as not to matter. Her maid had found a stone in her shoe though she had shaken it out in a trice. However, she could hardly reveal to her grandmother that she had been dallying with Lucien once again for, in spite of the fact she had known him all her life, Sophie would not have approved of them meeting so surreptitiously. Indeed, she would have been furious at the subterfuge. The fact that Prudence, her maid, had taken a great deal of persuading to allow her to meet him without telling the Duchess was quite unusual for they both knew she was breaking her grandmother's rules.

"You're too soft with that maid of yours," Sophie said. "I'd have boxed her ears!"

"And a fine taking that would have caused in the park, with all to see me."

"Humph, I still say you are too gentle." Sophie gazed at the bouffant profusion of fair curls crowning the head of the dainty girl, as well as the deep green eyes, wondering anew how her self-opinionated, far from attractive daughter-in-law could have produced such a fine beauty.

"Fetch me my lorgnette, Lavinia, my eyes grow dim in this dreadfully poor light. Isn't it about time Frith lit the lamps? Drat the man, where is he?"

Smiling gently at the testiness, Lavinia obediently fetched her grandmother's glasses. "It is only mid-afternoon, Grandmama, would you like me to read to you? It will save you the trouble," Lavinia said tactfully, knowing Sophie's eyes were weak with age.

Sophie studied her granddaughter with fond yet assessing eyes. She has a willing heart, she mused, and she'll make a perfect marriage if only we can show her to the best advantage. Not the least like my son, thank goodness or his feckless wife.

Whatever had possessed the stupid pair of them to go sailing just when the weather was about to change she would never know, though by all accounts the trip was supposed to be brief; however, the boat was later found on the rock-strewn Scottish coast minus its occupants. Sophie hated the sea. She could never understand why anyone wanted go on it merely for pleasure. Enduring fierce, wet, and entirely unpleasant waves that ruined one's hair and clothes was not her idea of a pleasing pastime. Give her land and reliable shelter from the elements and she would never ask for more. Well, perhaps a bit more - like enough money to live on enjoyably in her accustomed style.

Fate had changed her life for the worse in the last few weeks. With the death of her son, Sophie found she had a sixteen-year-old granddaughter to raise and, not only that, she had been ousted from the home she had lived in since her marriage to the Duke. This would not have distressed her in the least, had her coffers been full but they were not. She was almost penniless. She barely had funds for her own lavish needs let alone sufficient to launch a girl into society. Sophie sighed heavily; then, putting away thoughts of what might have been if fate had not dealt her such a cruel blow, she tried gamely to concentrate on the conversation.

"Yes, Lavinia, you might as well. I will close my eyes while you read. I find it most soothing. One can concentrate exactly on the words and enjoy the story and, of course, the tone of the reader. At least you were well taught in that discipline and your voice is pleasing to listen to. I declare those two brats of Lady Carmichael sound like the screeching of a magpie, they are so shrill."

Or you may sleep, thought Lavinia, with a chuckle. Grandmama believes I am not aware how easily she falls asleep. Frith ought to be pleased I have saved him from her bad temper, which has lasted all day. Even I could not please her, though hopefully she is a little better than she was this morning. I quite thought Agnes would get her breakfast tray right back in her face; she was so cross; I was lucky to escape to see Lucien. Dear, darling Lucien. She sighed quietly not wanting to draw attention to her distress. It is such an age to wait until we are together always - when at last we can tell her the real truth.

Not that Sophie would be delighted to hear it. In fact Lavinia knew she would be furious despite the fault lying entirely with Sophie's bold and sometimes not so discreet philandering in Scotland. For even before her husband died, Sophie had taken lovers here and there until the time she had set her cap at a young Lord of her own age, whose estates marched with Forres and tried to tempt him. It was a stupid mistake. He was recently married and declined her advances in no uncertain terms. Though she was entirely in the wrong she never forgave him. After the Duke's death she declined to lose her title to a lesser being and carried on in London, much as before, only with greater freedom. After the death of her son she went back to Scotland to the castle in order to manage it. Almost immediately, she found her granddaughter had been allowed to mix with the Earl's son. Straight away her volatile rage knew no bounds and she banned any further meetings between them. However, young love has a way of surviving and Lavinia and Lucien Rowley thought they had found a way out of the problem. They just needed a little time to bring her round to their way of thinking.

Unfortunately the Duchess's swift move to London, taking Lavinia along with her, caught them by surprise. Lucien followed them as speedily as he could, but neither he nor Lavinia had managed an opportunity to talk with Sophie and make clear their future plans. At present what little chance they had to be together was fraught with danger.

CHAPTER TWO

It was small wonder Sophie was in a mood, for the past six weeks of worry had been enough to try the patience of a saint and she certainly was not that. Today's dreadful temper was brought on by a visit from her lawyer the previous evening, who unkindly conveyed the information she had already worked out for herself: that the death of Giles meant the title must definitely go to her cousin and there was no way she could return to Forres. There was nothing to be done about it, for the rights of succession were unbreakable unless there was strong evidence to rebut them and, even then, it would involve years of litigation and cost more money than she could afford. The removal of the Dukedom from her side of the family had to stand whether she liked it or not. Likewise the estate and the incomes ensuing from it were no longer hers. In short, she was not entitled to any Forres income or use of the family home in Moray because, following the death of Giles, it was discovered he had died intestate: there was no will.

Stupid, useless idiot of a fellow! Just like his father! Lacking sense all his life, he had left her destitute. It was particularly galling as she remembered reminding him to see their solicitor to finalise all remaining details following his father's death and make sure everything was in order. She had left for London to enjoy a change of scene presuming he had done what he was told and never bothered to check up on him, so she had to accept the blame as well, which was even more irritating. After the sailing accident, when the lawyers busied themselves with sorting out the tangled affairs of the estate, she discovered the horrible truth. By then it was too late.

Lavinia, due to a peculiar right of succession laid down so long ago by Murdoch, could not inherit the estate in her own right which made it doubly infuriating, as one could not argue with a dead man. Two dead men, in fact, for besides being barred as heiress to the property, Giles neglected to provide for her welfare so she was left without a penny to sustain her. Giles should have made sure his only child had more than a wardrobe of clothes and a few pieces of jewellery.

Now nothing was left from the wreckage save Sophie's town house in London, which she had inherited from her father, plus a small pension from a trust of her late husband. If there had been a son, Sophie supposed, Giles would have taken the trouble to ensure that the legal positions of both the children were clarified. Then she could have gone on living as she had done all her life and maybe made a better job of bringing up a grandson than was the case with Giles.

Sophie stirred restlessly, mumbling to herself as the burden of her thoughts irked her mind.

"Are you uncomfortable, Grandmama? Is the story to your liking? Would you prefer me to stop?" Lavinia eyed the Duchess with misgiving. She seemed sadly out of sorts.

"No, child, carry on, 'tis nothing." Sophie resumed her cogitation as Lavinia took up the story again, her modulated voice acting as a soothing background to the Duchess's thoughts. In hindsight, she could understand the train of events that had led to this awful state of affairs. Her lazy son had delayed meeting with the lawyers, just as he had delayed supervising the Forres estate until it became run-down and ruined, barely able to sustain the few people who continued to live and work on it. Despite nagging, he had ignored her pleas and she, in turn, had let things slide. It was no good at this point bewailing her disgraceful inaction which had helped to compound the present sorry state of affairs. Her mind travelled back over the years to a time when all the land around was fertile and extremely fruitful providing a good living for the estate workers. However, severe flooding in the summer of 1829 had devastated the area, ruining what in earlier times was labelled the Granary of Moray. Following that disaster, the local farmers had striven to make good the damage, but some, like her husband William, had wilted under the huge task. So much so that it contributed to his early death. Later, she tried to bring up her son with a sense of true purpose to his life, but even this failed, for he was completely self-centred, consumed entirely with his own pleasures to the exclusion of all else. Moreover, his early marriage brought nothing of real value to the estate, for his wife was useless and scatterbrained; nor had she a substantial dowry that would have helped financially; ending up producing a daughter instead of a son, and then refusing to contemplate any more children. They were no loss, Sophie decided, but the least they could have done was to make sure their only child had inherited monies to take care of her until her marriage took place. Sophie's thoughts continued to run through the irritating conversation she had had with her lawyer.

Lawyers! Bah! Nasty, conniving, deceptive people, so they were. They tied one up in bonds of legal jargon that made no sense to ordinary people. Not that she was ordinary. Never that! She was still a Duchess in her own right. At least, she pondered thankfully, no one could take her title away from her even if all else had gone.

"Well, Walcott, what am I to do? Have you any ideas? Since this news has come to us you've had weeks to work something out. So what does the new Duke say? Is he considering a pension for me as kin or, at the very least, provision for Lavinia?"

The lawyer ran his eyes round the huge drawing room of Sophie's London house. It needed refurbishment but, nevertheless, it was a most elegant room with an outlook on Wilton Crescent, which lay close to Belgrave Square. There would be plenty of people interested in such a fine, desirable residence he felt certain, not least himself. Then recovering from the daydream of living in a grand establishment, he fixed his attention on the Duchess, who was frowning at him in a most ferocious and decidedly alarming manner.

"I beg your pardon, your Grace; I was woolgathering. Admiring this house; indeed you have a lovely residence, you know, situated in the best part of..."

"We were not discussing this house, Walcott! Pay attention to the matter in hand!" Sophie said sharply, her patience evaporating in an instant at his tardiness. "What's to happen now? What of the future and Lavinia's coming out? Money has to be found for it. Is the new Duke in a position to help us? Come on, speak up, man!"

"I believe I can safely say no on that point, your Grace. The Duke has always lived in a modest fashion and has little money. He is also extremely dismayed with the chaos of Forres Castle and its lands. He feels most strongly that any person connected with the former Duke, a member of the family for instance, would be ill-advised to ask for help."

James Walcott recalled Andrew Macgregor's exact words, spoken with great acerbity.

"If those irresponsible thieves think they can loot an inheritance then ask me for succour because they've spent it all, then they must think me as addled as they. I do not wish to hear of them ever again. They must get on with their lives as best as they may."

Walcott decided then to preserve his own hide lest he lose the considerable income he had got used to and willingly agreed with everything his new employer dictated. Now he was in the unenviable position of dealing with the Duchess who had an unerring ability to dissect the truth from anyone ill-advised enough to try to hoodwink her; he was in for a nasty time unless he could smooth her temper.

"So you agreed with the man and think to advise me to sell my valuable house to live on the proceeds. You are more stupid than I thought."

As this was as near the truth as made no difference Walcott instantly denied her harsh words, swallowing anxiously as he racked his brains to convince her otherwise. "Of course not, ma'am, why, where else would you live? Certainly, we shall not consider it. We have to think of some other means…"

"Precisely. So, Walcott, what comes next? You are paid to think, not I."

"Your granddaughter is almost of marriageable age…"

"Yes, but finding a husband would cost money." Sophie interrupted brusquely, for once at a loss to perceive the direction Walcott was taking.

"It just so happens that a client of mine is searching for a well-born wife."

"Oh?" she said. "A few heiresses are in town at the moment but those with money have no looks and those without have no beaus. Has this man money?"

"First and foremost he is not well-born himself, though he is, of a certainty, rich. He has also, I fancy, been married before but is now a widower. If he finds Lavinia to his liking I do not feel he will be against providing a means of support for you as well."

"For me also?" Sophie took in the meaning of the last remark with some surprise. To have advanced so far meant things had already been discussed between the lawyer and this stranger. Her eyes narrowed in speculation as she studied the lawyer. "You would negotiate for us?"

Walcott bowed his head in affirmation. It was, after all, no different from the haggling he had do in litigation or court proceedings concerning money.

"Hmm, I can't say I like it. In some ways it smacks of selling my granddaughter and to a bourgeois at that! Whatever are you thinking of, Walcott?"

Walcott shook his head, raising a hand to deny the implication, whilst privately believing that he was right to suggest to the proposed suitor that sugaring the bait would encourage Sophie and bring her round to bartering the girl for money. Human nature is ever thus, he thought.

"No! She's been brought up to expect much better than that for her future. She comes from fine stock and I won't sully her bloodline to match her with a commoner."

"But what else can you do, your Grace? To try for a rich husband takes much time as well as finance. According to your means as of now…"

"Yes, yes." Her Grace was testy in the extreme. "I know the difficulties, I've been over the various means I have at my disposal. Not least to mention scanning the society columns in the papers to see who is eligible. I find there are few, disastrously few, men available this year. Certainly none with enough funds to take care of her in a fashion I consider essential. To launch her into society without a dependable chance of success is downright foolish and I will not consider spending foolishly. Yet to marry Lavinia off to a common widower - I am loath to consider it."

"You could do much worse, your Grace. She would surely not lack for comfort and you could probably insist on a few conditions in the marriage settlement."

"Yes, I could, I suppose." Sophie reflected on that last point.

"If you'd care to see the gentleman, it can be arranged. Most discreetly, of course. No hint of a meeting would reach other ears. It would do no harm, I think, just to meet, to meditate, perhaps, hmm?" He let the words die softly away; she was almost hooked.

She could always say no, mused Sophie and she would, if he proved unsuitable. She would know at once if it was out of the question; perhaps it would not harm to meet the fellow. "Very well! Arrange a time. Likely it's useless but I'll see what I'm refusing."

A meeting was arranged for the following day when Sophie usually visited a friend. Lavinia, engaged elsewhere, would not be told. No point in upsetting her for nothing, thought Sophie, knowing well that Lavinia would be upset, even though it was inevitable that a parting of the ways had to come at some point. It was, after all, her destiny in life to be wed and have children. Still, time enough for that if the fellow was acceptable.

CHAPTER THREE

"So you see, your Grace, I am a busy man with scant freedom for seeking a new wife. I have a fortune at my fingertips and no one to share it with. I want an heir. A son bred with my hardworking abilities yet laced with the best blood in the country. He will be a fine man if my plan succeeds and his mother will want for nothing, I assure you."

Sophie quietly surveyed the man with her sharp flint-like eyes that pierced Ambrose Trevarron through to his soul. The three were seated in Walcott's office engaged in battle. Already, preliminary skirmishes had been traded and the mine-owner was beginning to sweat a little. He was moderately dressed, not in the height of fashion, but presentable nonetheless. Not tall, he revealed his Cornish ancestry in his build, as well as the darkness of his hair and skin. He'd been open and truthful in his approach and she had been equally blunt in her own forthright manner so that a blush of anger crept under the skin of his face.

"You are not the gallant swain my granddaughter will be naturally hoping for."

"Who would, doubtless, be penniless?" The response was quick and acidic.

"She would, however, expect more than an ill-bred..."

"Careful, madam, how you refer to my breeding. I come from ancient stock. Oh, not titled, like you, but every bit as historic a race as your own." The words broke through bared teeth.

"Your Grace! Sir! Please! I'm sure you both have right on your sides." Walcott tried to smooth the hot feelings that were being generated in his presence. "Please let us discuss the issue at hand with gentleness and decorum. A marriage is a joyous occasion not a topic of acrimony! We can settle this so both of you are satisfied with the outcome."

The three of them resumed the discussion in quieter tones but steel had been drawn and, despite a final agreement, there smouldered, in the heart of one of the participants, a fierce brutal determination for vengeance which would be far-reaching and tragic in the fulfilling. No one would get the better of Ambrose Trevarron, nor ever had.

* * * * *

"But, Grandmama! It's absolutely impossible. I won't marry a stranger! I won't! Can't I just continue to live with you for the present? I promise I won't be a nuisance." Lavinia was completely heartbroken as she listened in horror to what her grandmother planned for her future. Immediately huge tears welled in her eyes and began to drop, unheedingly, down her face.

"Oh, child! If only it could be. But you wouldn't thank me for it later on. When I go to my Maker, all this goes too; the house and the frugal amount of money which is never enough. Soon we'll have sold all the fine pieces your grandfather bought for the house, then there will be nothing left. 'Tis true Ambrose Trevarron is not the suitor I would have wished for you but he is kind and you will be well taken care of. I've been told you will want for nothing. If your father was still alive, he would have chosen your husband for you. As he is no longer with us I must take his place."

"He is old! I want a young man! I want to marry Lucien. We are in love, he and I. I've tried to tell you…well… we plan to wed just as soon as we can."

"Lucien Rowley? Why he's penniless! No, child, I'll not see you married to a wastrel. He may be of noble birth but his estates are poor, he's worse off than we are."

"He's not a wastrel! It was his father who gambled. Lucien intends to work…"

"Work!" interrupted Sophie angrily. "What sort of work can he do? As for you – do you think to work like a skivvy alongside him? Think, child, what that will mean?"

"Grandmama, you don't understand! It's not like that," pleaded Lavinia. "We just want to be together. He'll take care of me. I love him and want to be with him!"

"Lavinia! Enough! The matter is settled. Trevarron is prepared to overlook the fact you have no dowry and you are barely past your sixteenth birthday, what more can you ask? Be reasonable, child. I am weary enough as it is. I have tried to do my best for you; a little gratitude would not come amiss!"

"Oh, I'm sorry, Grandmama, I'm not ungrateful, truly I'm not. It's just that, oh dear, it's so hard to explain. I thought with things as they are…to choose the path I want…" She ceased speaking as she caught the look in her grandmother's eyes, then gathering courage she burst out with the words: "I'll never love him as I do Lucien."

"Rubbish, my dear. Love invariably comes after marriage not before."

"But Cornwall is so very far from London, I'll never see you again!" Desperately, hardly knowing what to do or say, she pleaded on her knees before the Duchess, her eyes so filled with tears she could barely see.

"Of course you will, child! How could I bear to be parted from you forever? I'll see you when possible. Think of it, my dearest; you will be cosseted, live in luxury, cared for till the end of your life, unlike your poor Grandmother, who will have to live meagrely from now on." Sophie folded Lavinia in her warm, comforting arms in a vain attempt to soothe her piteous sobbing but it was a long time before Lavinia would finally accept she had no choice but to follow Sophie's wishes. "There, my poppet, it's not the end of the world," she said soothingly, "things will work out."

It was the end - at least as far as Lavinia was concerned.

She managed to escape several times to meet with the penniless Lord of the small estate close to Forres in Scotland. She desperately hoped he would be strong; would fight for her and plead their case but he seemed as stricken as she was. He had no idea what to do to help. The thought of facing the Duchess with their plans was as nerve-wracking to him as it was to Lavinia but, distraught as she was, she still continued to be with him, to love him whenever she could get away from her grandmother. "I'll think of something," he said, each time they met. "Don't worry, my love, we shall be together just as soon as I can manage it."

"I'm frightened my grandmother will prevail. Oh, Lucien, what can we do?"

His only answer was to take her in his arms and love her entirely to distraction. She, consumed with so much adoration that she was blind to the consequences, permitted him to take her to his heart and to follow the path he chose. Then Prudence, Lavinia's maid, suddenly realising she could be in trouble if she encouraged the illicit meetings any longer, protested that she would lose her job and thereafter Lavinia found it hard to get away. Nevertheless the deed was done and a tiny life was in the process of beginning. For the union between Lucien and Lavinia had borne fruit, thereby sealing their love.

When Lavinia discovered she was with child she knew her life was about to change for the worse for, now, there was no opportunity to see Lucien. Her maid turned adamant. She would tell the Duchess if Lavinia persisted. However hard she tried she could not change her grandmother's decision nor could she find the courage to confess she was pregnant. She was no longer free and all attempts to find an excuse to escape from the house and let Lucien know what was happening were frustrated, all unknowingly, by her maid and her grandmother.

CHAPTER FOUR

Lavinia soon found she was following her grandmother's orders powerless to protest without confessing all. Lucien had still not come to her rescue and she was filled with despair and an inability to decide what to do for the best. Furthermore it would have been unnatural indeed if she had not taken some small pleasure in the pretty trousseau her future husband bought for her. Even her grandmother was amazed at the generosity of Ambrose towards the girl. Perhaps, Lavinia reflected sadly, it might be for the better after all. A good future for her unborn child was vital. How could Lucien provide for three of them when he was so poor himself? As stricken and anxious as she was, she had inherited a strain of practicality that made her aware she no longer had any choice in the matter but must come to a decision on her own future. She took that decision in the knowledge that she had no other means of providing for herself.

After the wedding and the pair left for Cornwall, Walcott presented Sophie with a sizable sum of gold sovereigns which should, if she was careful, keep her from poverty until she died. The Duchess was taken aback in surprise. "There is just one condition attached to this." He held the bag of gold coins close, but out of Sophie's grasp. "One you have to adhere to if you want to keep this money."

"And what is that, pray?" She gazed at him with hate, aware of his insincerity.

"You will never attempt to see your granddaughter again. Mr Trevarron feels you will be a bad influence and he prefers his wife to have nothing more to do with you. I'm sorry, your

Grace, this is the stipulation. Do you want the money or not? This goes with the contract. It's your choice. If you take it you must do as he asks."

Sophie was shocked with the cruelty of the Cornishman. Perhaps she ought to have done more to make him like her. It crossed her mind that maybe she had made a fearful mistake giving Lavinia over to his care. As for the money, she did not think it likely in the circumstances, with the very long distance involved in travelling to Cornwall, that she would see very much of her granddaughter anyway so she might as well take it and enjoy her old age.

"Very well, I agree but you must give this locket to my granddaughter." She held a velvet wallet out to him. "You must make sure my granddaughter gets this without that cur knowing about it. I shall also want a keepsake and a letter from her as proof it's been delivered. Remember," she warned him, "he's not to know. Now if I may have a pen and paper I'll send a message to her. Surely you will grant me at least that boon?"

Reluctantly Walcott nodded. Still, he thought to himself, it was not as though he had had to promise the same thing to Trevarron, only to pass on his intentions. So, in spite of the fact he helped himself to quite a sum from the bag of coins he had given to Sophie, which Trevarron would never know about, nor the Duchess ever discover, he said, "And my reward for this favour?"

"I'll keep my mouth shut about your sharp scheming, my friend. A word in the ear of one or two friends could possibly ruin your business. I am aware of the devious means you have taken to achieve this marriage. Had I other sources to live my life as I have always done I should never have allowed this match. However it is done. I hope my granddaughter will benefit. Now the least you can do is to deliver this locket and my message. And remember – I will require proof that it has reached Lavinia."

Walcott stared at her in shock. Crafty old bitch! Despite all his machinations she still had the power to ruin him. Only now did he realise that he must go carefully for she would make a deadly enemy. He yet had to achieve ownership of her house. It would pay him to conduct himself with circumspection and follow her orders to the letter.

Sophie felt a moment's qualm as she relinquished the ruby locket, well knowing it was not hers to give away. She had brought it with her when she left Forres Castle. It should rightfully have belonged to the present Duke of Forres as part of his inheritance. Truth to tell she had not liked it and had only worn it the once to get a portrait painted to impress people. What did it matter that it was part of the estate? Her granddaughter would have inherited it from her mother in normal circumstances. Anyway, that was not achievable, nor could she ever take her rightful place as mistress of Forres. So, even if Murdoch, the Duke of Forres, had stipulated it should go to each Duchess when she produced an heir for her sire, well, what of it? She considered it just revenge for being ousted from her home. She would never tell anyone where it had gone but who knew what fate had in store? Maybe one day Lavinia's son would inherit Forres?

CHAPTER FIVE

The journey to Cornwall was tiring in spite of the Great Western Railway, which had replaced the stagecoach, thereby reducing the time of the journey from days to only hours. Lavinia, usually a talkative person, found herself too shy in the presence of her husband to do more than reply briefly to his abrupt questions. He too, felt a sudden gaucherie, was at a loss for words, which strangely angered him. It made him feel as if he were kidnapping a child, which he knew was entirely true in a sense, if one compared her age to his. He made no attempt to touch her on the journey, except for helping her up into the carriage at Paddington station, and he sat apart on the opposite seat to hers.

They ate from a picnic hamper which his London hotel had provided for them so they had no need to seek refreshments from either the stations they passed through or the buffet car attached to the train. Lavinia, who had scarcely eaten a bite on her wedding day, enjoyed the cold salmon and other delicacies from the basket, even accepting a glass of wine to wash it all down. She was grateful for what she took to be pure kindness on his part and wished the journey might go on forever and her marriage stay exactly as it was. When at last they reached journey's end, she was too tired to do more than seek the refuge of her room and, after a light repast on a tray, dropped into a deep, sound sleep.

Many hours later the sound of the door opening woke her as Ambrose entered the bedroom carrying a tray that held a champagne bottle and two glasses. "Aha, you are awake, my dear? How unfortunate for me. I was looking forward to waking you with my kisses." He placed the bottle and glasses on the table and lit the lamp. It cast a soft glow over Lavinia's fair tumbling ringlets, sleep-dampened, into tiny curls round her face.

She stared at him in sheer bewilderment, for a moment trying to recollect her new surroundings and then the grim reality of her position struck her with apprehension. All hope fled from her as she realised that, late though it was, he meant to exert his rights as her husband. While she had expected his advances she had thought he might wait until they had got to know each other better. "W-what time is it?" she asked, realising what a dreadful mistake she had made.

"Midnight. The right time to enjoy a glass of wine and other delightful pursuits. Come drink this, it will wake you up, restore your energy." He handed her a glass filled with the bubbling, pale amber liquid that tasted tart in her dry mouth.

"Are you not tired yourself? The journey has been long..."

"Not too tired to enjoy you, my fair beauty. I have no wish to delay my wedding night any longer. These last few weeks of waiting has increased my desire for you."

He ran his fingers through her hair, lingering where the curls gathered in the curve of her neck, then gently eased her nightgown off her shoulder until he could see the rise of her full breasts. Taking the glass from her limp fingers he loosened the tie at his waist and slipped off the jacket he wore; then abruptly, tossing back the bedclothes, slid naked into bed beside her. Without thinking, she instantly edged as far as she could away from him, her heart thumping with fright but reaching out his hand, he drew her towards him again with a firm grip. "No, my dear, we will not have any coquettish airs now. You were an expensive buy and I mean to have my money's worth. I will not be short-changed."

"You bought me?" Her eyes were pools of terror at his words.

"In a manner of speaking; shall we rather say - your grandmother sold you."

"I don't believe you! She couldn't – she wouldn't do that, she loves me!"

"Love has nothing to do with having money to keep oneself in luxury in one's old age. But never mind her; she is out of your life forever. You won't ever see her again. Your life is here with me in Cornwall, to give me an heir and be by my side to host the local gentry - as they are pleased to call themselves." He scowled momentarily and she guessed he deeply felt the lack of any blood kinship with the gentry. Money alone had failed to give him the entrée he sought to the insular clique of peers who held sway in Victorian England.

Her grandmother had warned her of this just before she left. It was one of the last morsels of advice the Duchess had given to her granddaughter before she left the house. Belatedly she had become stricken with remorse at what she was doing. Sending a child barely out of the schoolroom, yet brutally pitched into marriage with a total stranger was sheer cruelty, even if she knew Lavinia's manners and schooling would be equal to any occasion she would have to face. Nevertheless there were other things the child should have known, things that she personally did not feel able to discuss. Drat that stupid woman! Why hadn't her mother been there for Lavinia? Dead from drowning when she could have done something useful for her daughter and coached her in the delicate art of sex. In the end, Sophie soothed herself with the thought that she too had submitted to the intricacies of lovemaking without knowing the least thing about it beforehand and had survived and learned to enjoy other men as well.

Sophie's advice to Lavinia was brief but it held her firm when all her instincts bade her flee his touch. "Don't slight him, Lavinia. Men have funny ways. They like to think they are the biggest of the roosters in the farmyard and blood, or the lack of it, has a great deal to do with their pride. Take care."

"Come, my love, your husband wishes you to disrobe to see if the bargain is worth the having. I have been looking forward to this moment with eagerness."

Tears ran slowly down Lavinia's cheeks as her nightgown was pulled over her head and her body seized without pity. She didn't resist, for what was the use? There was no one left in her life to save her. The only two people she had loved had let her down. She had given her oath in this soulless marriage; only death would part her from Ambrose now. Her last hold on her past was broken as he entered her quickly without ensuring she was ready. She screamed with the pain of the assault as he forced his way in and he took it to be the breaking of her virginity. The sign of blood on the sheet the next day after her rape was further proof in his mind she was a virgin. When the doctor confirmed barely three months later that Lavinia was pregnant he had no thought in his mind the child was any other than his - but Lavinia knew.

Although only five weeks had elapsed between her lovemaking with Lucien and her wedding, her monthly courses, despite her continued hope, still failed to arrive. At first she had thought little, imagining it was due to her heartache at parting from Lucien but when she counted the days she soon realised what had happened. She had listened to gossip from the maids and knew that an early child was not unusual, so she gave the doctor to understand that the babe was conceived her wedding night. She also managed to avoid too close an examination by pretending a reluctance to undress before a stranger. He thought that she was just shy and that before she was finally in labour things would improve, so he did not insist but agreed with her that the middle of March should see the birth of an heir for Trevarron. Ambrose walked proudly as though ten feet tall. His ambition was finally to be realised. His son was on the way at last.

CHAPTER SIX

Daylight was slow to appear one winter's day in January 1851, sluggishly filtering through grey writhing clouds looming heavily over the Cornish landscape. Lashing down, cold rain-filled gutters and gullies and rushing in icy torrents off desolate moors, burdening every river to overflowing. The south-west wind moaned eerily through the bare branches of bent trees and buffeted the small, thick-walled cottages built to withstand the onslaught of the winter gales. The wise kept indoors if they could; only those who had vital tasks to fulfil ventured out to face the weather.

Amy Bunnion scurried up the steep, stony path to the Bartons' cottage, hugging a shawl close round her ears with one hand, while with the other she held fast to a heavy basket. Thank God, it was almost daylight, she mused, relieved she had had a good night's rest, without disturbance, as Becky Lanner opened the door to her knock.

"Jethro gave word then, bless him, he's a good man. Come in, Mrs Bunnion, this weather's not fit for a body to be out, but I've a herb tea all ready by the fire."

"How is she?" The midwife took the proffered mug gratefully, clasping her chilled fingers around its warmth as she sipped the welcoming brew.

"So-so." Becky made a face. "The pains are coming and going, some'at fierce one minute, then only just griping along the next. She bain't in a hurry though, I'll wager."

"How long she bin in labour?"

"Jethro said she started last night, slow like, he said, never told me till this morning as there warn't no rush, but I dassn't like the way of it so I told him to get ye here on his way to work. The longer she goes the more exhausted she'll be at end."

Amy finished her drink and made for the stairs. "Ye have things ready?"

Becky nodded. "Ellie's had 'em ready for weeks now, she's bin that anxious; after losing the last one she'm nervy like, I hope it'll not be the same again."

Amy frowned in her taciturn way, her lips tightly pressed together. "We'll just have to see what the Lord has to say, it'll be his wish that counts in the end," she answered in her usual abrupt manner though she was an angel of mercy towards her patients. Raking in her bag, she produced a small packet, which she handed to Becky.

"Make a mug of this, will ee, Becky, fetch it when I call. The raspberry leaf tea will help things along if she's slow, t'won't do her harm if all's well." She turned to the stairs and began forcing her portly body up the winding steps to the small bedroom above where a swollen figure tossed restlessly in labour. Going over to the bed she said softly, "How're you doing, Ellie, love? Yer water's not broke yet, so Becky tells me."

Ellie Barton turned glazed eyes towards the midwife. "No, Amy, this labour's just like the rest; happen I'm not meant to bear a live child."

"Course ye will, sweetie, don't ye fret now, thee will have a babby afore supper unless I miss my guess." Amy deftly examined the woman then called downstairs to Becky to fetch the tea before she began setting the room to her liking. She was almost done when abruptly and harshly penetrating through the drumming rain on the roof came the strident scream of a klaxon blasting its shrill warning around the parish. Becky had just reached the top of the stairs with the mug of raspberry tea and she and Amy stared at each other in despair.

"For God's sake, that's the mine! Oh dear Lord, Jethro's

down there!" Ellie rose up on the pillows as though to get out of bed, then sank back with a groan.

"Don't mind that siren. Thee's enough to get on with here, Ellie!" scolded Amy. "Jethro ull take care o' himself, but ye've got a mite of labour to go through yet an' ye need yer ease, my handsome, so let nature has its way." She reached for the mug of tea from Becky, eyeing her crumpled face. Amy remembered how she had lost her husband Saul only twelve months before in a roof fall. Ruddy mine, she thought, I bring 'em into the world and it takes 'em out afore they've hardly lived. Well, it is the Lord's doing I guess, but he ought to think of the sorrow he causes when he takes his people away.

Soon the two women were working hard to assuage the pain Ellie was suffering so acutely while rain continued to stream down in soaking floods, turning paths to muddy waterways, holding up urgent traffic and causing Wheal Rhodda to look like something out of a nightmare.

The scene at the pithead was typical of all mining disasters since time immemorial. Volunteers were coming and going, hoping to help with any proposed rescue. Anxious female kinfolk, shawl-wrapped against the rough weather, hovered in restless groups, seizing on every titbit of information. They hoped to pluck out news of loved ones caught hundreds of feet below them under a rockfall or, maybe, frantically choking from noxious fumes in the tiny tunnels, deep underground, miles from hope of rescue.

All at once a pony-drawn gig sped up to the engine house and a man stepped hastily down.

"'Tis the doctor!" The whisper flittered through the groups at great speed.

"Morning, Doctor Lusty, thanks for coming, we need you right quick, sir!"

"How bad is it?" James Lusty was no stranger to mining accidents.

"Eight under, I'm afraid." The pit manager lowered his voice as a hiss of despair went around the patiently waiting women as the dire news shocked them still further.

"It's a bad 'un, right enough. We've got two through to Level Nine, but ol' Tom Pedy's bleedin' so bad we'll not get him higher except with your help. The rest of the crew is still diggin' but I'm none too hopeful of more coming out; though be sure they won't give up trying."

Lusty groaned inwardly as he thought of the long dangerous climb down to Level Nine. After so many years of being on call he had gotten too old to cope any longer with the dirt and impenetrable dripping wet darkness lit only by the tiny candles of the men he would go down with. Men with no illusions about life, who continued to live midst the appalling working conditions and horrific dangers; never knowing from one minute to the next whether they would face death or see the sudden demise of a workmate, neighbour, brother or son. No unrealistic hope of sudden wealth influenced them and, for certain, no retirement pension diverted their grim view of the future. They were mineworkers, knowing only that they had to provide for themselves and their kin and they would continue until prevented by accident, illness, old age or inevitably death, although the latter came too quickly for some poor souls.

"Right, Sam, let's get on." Lusty entered the engine house and, quickly divesting himself of his clean clothes, slipped on working trousers and an old coat he kept for the purpose. Exchanging his own headgear for a mining hat, he placed an unlit candle on the front, then took up his medical bag in one hand, as he prepared himself mentally for the frightening task of descending many fathoms into the bowels of the earth.

CHAPTER SEVEN

Lavinia Rose Trevarron shifted uneasily on the sofa, glancing at the clock on the mantelpiece as she did so. What was keeping Ambrose? It was long past dinner time. The man had no thought at all for her condition, indeed no thought for anyone's comfort save his own. He wanted a son but failed to understand how wretched she felt, how she hated being pregnant. She would willingly surrender a year of her life if only she could go back to where she had been happy and carefree among those she loved.

She rang the bell lying on the small table beside her to summon the housemaid who, for once, appeared promptly, bobbing a curtsy to her mistress. Lavinia immediately lifted an arm for Nell to assist her, rising heavily with the weight of her late pregnancy. "I'm too fatigued to wait any longer for the master. Tell cook I shall have a tray in my room straightaway. Only a light collation, mind," she said wearily, making her way out to the hall to climb the stairs to her bedroom.

Nell sped back to the kitchen to pass on her mistress's orders, unable to resist adding, "The master will play pop wiv her when 'e comes 'ome. Thass the third time this week she gone to her bed and 'e doan't like it, you can tell."

"Well, the poor child's not fit for much; anyone can see that, save Mr Trevarron," retorted Mrs Polwen as she wiped floury hands down her apron. "Happen she's carried this babbie wiv sickness all through. I will be right glad when she's had it, poor soul. I hope she fares better when birthing it."

"Another two months to go, ain't it?"

"Yes, 'bout that," interrupted Annie Gorland, the bunch of

keys at her waistline giving away her status as housekeeper to the Trevarron family. "She may not last that long, she 'pears near her time now. Strange how time passes. Seems only yesterday they were wed. Now he's going to be a father. Hope he'll make a good 'un."

"Yes, happen she'll last a bit longer," continued Betsy Polwen, just as though the housekeeper had not spoken. "She ain't dropped yet. I allus knows when a baby's due..." Mrs Polwen aired her superior knowledge of childbirth but was momentarily quelled by a steely glint in the housekeeper's eye who was irritated at being made to look ignorant; when a knock at the back door diverted the ever present rivalry between the housekeeper and the cook.

It was one of the boys from Wheal Rhodda. He doffed his cap and spoke to Annie Gorland, his chest heaving for breath from his hasty run across the moors. "There's bin a fall at t'mine. Mr Ambrose says to send 'im some food. He'll not be 'ome fer awhile, so I'm to wait an' fetch it back." His eyes stared past the two women to the laden kitchen table where food had been held in readiness for the forthcoming meal. The cook watched as he swallowed the saliva that had quickly filled his mouth at the sight of more grub than he had seen in months.

"You dirty?" said the cook sharply.

"Not so's ye'd notice," quipped the boy cheekily.

"Then get thee in the scullery an' wash, then mebbe just mebbe, I'll gie ye a bite to eat while ye wait." He disappeared without a further word.

"Poor brat," Betsy voiced to no one in particular as she shook her head. "D'ye see yon threadbare jacket and torn trews? He's hardly a stitch a'tween 'im an' the weather. I don't begrudge 'im a bitta food to fill his skinny hide, the master'll not know, less'un ye tell."

"Go on then, I won't let on, the master'll not hear from me, I've never been one to carry tales, Polwen, whatever you might think." Mrs Gorland dusted down her dark serge dress as though to sweep the likes of a cook from her mind and with a disdainful toss of her head walked towards the stairs leading up to the hall.

"I'll inform the mistress he won't be home. I expect she will be relieved. Nell! Stop gawking and hurry up with that tray. Sooner you've served Mrs Trevarron the sooner we can relax and eat our meal. 'Tis as well she's off to bed, makes it easier."

Annie made her way up the stairs and through a baize-covered door into a large, well-lit ornate hall, from whence curved a majestic staircase to the first floor and thence in smaller circles to the second and third floor. It ended in a huge glass cupola which, in the daytime, cast light to the centre of the house. Ambrose Trevarron was very proud of his staircase. It had been designed for his renovated house and each time he used it he never failed to run loving hands over the fine mahogany balustrade or look upwards to the dome. He enjoyed the feeling of envy whenever he invited acquaintances to the mansion, for they always exclaimed at its magnificent design and congratulated him for being so lucky to own such a beautiful house.

"Luck!" he would roar. "There's no such thing as luck. Hard work's more like it. That and being wise with money. There's no waste in this household, I do assure you. No flagrant squandering here." The domestics could bear out his words, if they dare and if others knew how his wealth had amassed from the slavery of his mineworkers, they too kept their own counsel, for it was not wise to offend Ambrose Trevarron.

When Annie reached the hall Mrs Trevarron was nearly at the top of the first flight of stairs so, thinking to save her aching legs from a climb to Lavinia's bedroom, she called loudly from the foot of the stairs. "Oh, Ma'am! The master sent to say he won't be home yet awhile, there's been an accident at the mine. He has sent a lad to bring back his dinner."

Lavinia flinched sharply at the voice, one foot still in mid-air to mount the next stair. Startled, for she had been daydreaming again yearning for the life she had known with her grandmother and greatly regretted leaving. She turned her head quickly to see who was calling and her small hand, which was lightly holding the wooden banister which was rounded and polished to a dangerous perfection, failed to hold its grasp.

Lavinia had known fear before. At the time Ambrose raised his hand in anger to strike her when she refused his lovemaking. He had apologised soon afterwards but from then on she regarded him much like a dangerous dog with snapping teeth, one gave it a wide berth. This angered Ambrose more for, though he knew the reason for her scared withdrawal, he could not bring himself to make the loving advances that would soothe her distress. The gap widened further as her pregnancy became apparent and his lusting attentions filled her with disgust; then she shunned him as much as propriety allowed and insisted on her own bedroom where she could rest more comfortably.

As her frantic clutch slid uselessly from the rail, apprehension consumed her with fear and, before she could do anything to avoid disaster, her tired, ungainly body swayed and lost its balance. The dainty heel of her shoe, tangling in the flounces of her dress, was unable to find a hold and instantly she discovered the world was turning topsy-turvy as she tumbled backwards down the staircase. There was one loud crack as her head hit the banister and then a rustle of silk taffeta as she rolled the rest of the way to lie motionless on the hallway floor.

CHAPTER EIGHT

For a long moment Annie stood in sheer terror staring at the body, her leaping heart throbbing in her throat. Oh God, was it her fault by distracting her by calling out? What would the master say? He would be sure to blame her no matter what she said. Tearfully she ran to Lavinia and knelt down to take her hand. A sudden groan emerged from ashen lips as Annie touched her face and the housekeeper sighed with relief; thank the Lord she was not dead. It had been one dreadful fall. Annie gently shook her shoulder.

"Ma'am, it's me, Annie, open your eyes. Are you all right? Oh dear, please be all right, don't die on me! For God's sake, don't!" Lavinia did not respond to Annie's urgent calling so, unhappily, the housekeeper rose to her feet and, rushing to the servant's door, she yelled for Betsy and Nell to help. Together they managed to carry Lavinia up to her bedroom and there they lay her on a huge satin-covered bed and left Nell to see to the undressing of her. Then Annie and Betsy hurried back down to the kitchen where the boy was stuffing his face with bacon pie and quaffing a huge mug of milk.

"Look sharp, lad, Mrs Trevarron has had an accident, thee will have to let Doctor Lusty know. Finish yer meal quick and get him back here as soon as he can."

The boy stopped chewing and shook his head. "Doc Lusty's down t'mine, ee won't be up for ages yet. Not tonight or mebbe termorrow. The men are hurt bad down there."

"Lord save us! It'll take hours to get someone from Penzance and William has the carriage at the mine." She referred to the Trevarron's burly coachman.

"What about Amy Bunnion?" exclaimed Betsy. "I reckon she do know as much as old Lusty about medicine what wiv her herbal remedies an' all."

"You're right," said Annie recalling some of the treatments the midwife practised on people other than pregnant women. She was wise in the way of doctoring.

"Boy! Get thee over to Mrs Bunnion's, tell her she'm wanted urgent here! William u'll fetch her. Go on hurry up, will you, you munt waste time. We need her here quick!"

The lad shook his head again. "I gotta take Mr Trevarron's dinner, he's 'spectin' me soon as I can. He'll beat me sore if'n I don't get back soon.... Ow!" he yelled in sheer anguish as Annie boxed his ears. "T'ain't no call for that."

"Then do as I tell ee, first let the midwife know, then tell William he's to bring Mrs Bunnion as soon as possible. Mistress is more important than HIS stomach!"

"Either way I get it in t'neck," the lad mumbled as he picked up the basket of food then, as an idea struck him, he added, "I'll pass the message on - that should do it."

"Ye'll jolly well take the note yersel, ye young varmint, or thee'll never get another bite to eat here." Betsy added her words with venom. "Now get about yer business and if Amy Bunnion ain't 'ere in 'alf an hour I'll have thy 'ead on a plate!"

Not waiting a moment more in case of another cuffing the boy stuffed the last of the food in his mouth and vanished out into the fierce downpour. Betsy stood rubbing her hands with satisfaction. "There, thass got him going, now let's see how Mrs Trevarron is; I hope she's come round, that I do, poor lady." The two women were making their way up to Lavinia's room when Betsy remarked in a careless, offhand way, which didn't fool the housekeeper one little bit. "Thee didn't say how she come to fall down them stairs."

"No, neither did I, does it matter?"

"No, I just wondered, thass all."

"How does anyone fall down stairs? Yer foot slips and thass

that. Why did ye ask? Did ye think I pushed her?" Annie said tersely.

"No, of course not, ye weren't out there above a minute or so; just seems strange, thass all. She moves so slow, like and careful. Course wi' her size she couldn't help it."

"She was tired, cross with the master. Likely she just missed 'er footing, I don't know, do I? She was lying there when I got to hall. As she'm at t'foot o' the stairs I naturally assumed she had fallen down them. Satisfied?"

"Course I am, I was thinking about 'im. He'll go on something shocking if 'is son and heir ain't all right. Wouldn't like ye to get the blame or get sacked. We do all right together 'ere between us so yer need to get yer story right, so we back you up, don't yer."

"Let's see how she is afore we worry about being sacked, mayhap she just fainted in the hall." She was somewhat surprised at the cook's declaration. However, when Annie looked at the huge purpling bruise spreading down over Lavinia's forehead and the ashen look of her skin she could see things were very critical indeed.

"She ain't come round yet, though I've bathed 'er 'ead. All she does is groan. I don't like the looks of things, that I don't. Is the doctor comin'?" Nell stretched herself erect with a groan.

"Thee go down and eat with Mrs Polwen, Nell, I'll stay here with the mistress. I've already sent for Mrs Bunnion. Bring her up when she comes and keep yer calm. There's no call to fly into the rafters; the mistress u'll be all right, just had a nasty bump, thass all. Now off wiv ye both, I'll ring if I need ye. I'll eat later."

They retreated down to the basement kitchen most relieved to have the shocking matter handled by someone else. Ambrose's temper was such that neither wished to have the job of telling him of his wife's accident.

Meanwhile Annie carried on gently bathing Lavinia's forehead till all at once Lavinia gave a groan and seemed to draw her knees up under the covers. Startled, Annie watched for a moment then pulled the sheets back and putting her hand on the swelling curve of the pregnant stomach felt a taut movement. Incredibly, there was no mistaking the spasm of the swollen abdomen as the powerful muscles began the slow relentless task of expelling the contents of the womb. For, ready or not, nature had decided it was time for the birth and the unconscious woman could neither help nor hinder what was to come.

"Oh poor lamb! Now you're in labour! What am I going to do?" Annie rose to her feet and stood beside the bed aghast with terror as she gazed down at the prostrate figure. Now she was sure there was no hope for either Lavinia or the child, for none she had ever heard of had given birth to a baby whilst still unconscious. After a moment or two she recovered her wits and set about bringing Lavinia back to life, even resorting to pinching and shouting at her. However it was all futile; the young woman did not stir from her deep coma beyond emitting a heavy groan every now and then which seemed to coincide with the contractions of her body.

"Just as well we've sent for Mrs Bunnion seeing it's a midwife you needs." Annie spoke aloud to the silent room. "But if she doesn't know what to do, heaven help us all."

CHAPTER NINE

A loud banging at the door coincided with the final push from an exhausted Ellie to expel her baby. Amy swiftly gathered it up and laid it to one side before Ellie could ask its condition; then placed a ready cup of liquid at the woman's lips with the firm request to drink it up at once. "Ye're fair exhausted, lass, tak' this down quick, m'dear. It will make you feel better in a jiffy. Come on now, drink it all up."

"Amy..." Ellie obediently took a deep swallow and began again. "Amy...I haven't heard it cry. Is it dead?" Swallow. "Oh don't tell me it's dead, for pity's..." She drained the cup but before she had time to utter another word her eyes closed, her head dropped back on the pillow and almost at once she began to snore.

"Becky! See who's at the door, will you? While I tend to this." She bent over the little bundle lying on the bed as Becky flew downstairs to answer the loud summons.

"What the 'ell d'ye want? Tryin' to break the door down?" Becky gazed at the sodden figure of the young miner who was looking even more miserably woebegone.

"Mrs Bunnion's wanted up at t'Hall. Mrs Trevarron's been took sick, Doc Lusty's down t'mine, there bain't anyone else. Can she come quick?"

"How's she going to get there? Tell me that?"

"I'm off to t'mine to tell the Master, I'll send William double-quick. Tell 'er he won't be long, to be ready. Them at the Hall say it's right urgent."

"Well, I never! The cheek of the lad!"

"Who is it?" called Amy from the stairs.

"It's Bobby Garras from Nance Cottages, he says ye're wanted up at the Hall, Mrs Trevarron's been took sick, all of a sudden like, it appears to me."

"Could it be the babby's coming? It's a mite early. Tell him I'll be there as soon as I can. Has he a conveyance? I'm not walking up that there drive in this weather."

"Aye, he's getting William to come for ye so I'll tell him you'll be ready, shall I?"

Amy grunted an affirmative and then went back to the covered bundle on the bed. She took off the wrapping and looked again at the wizened little mite that could never have drawn a live breath. It had most likely died during the birthing or maybe before, she thought sadly. Ellie must have known it was poorly by the kicking, or maybe lack of it, within in her. No wonder she had been so apprehensive. Well, Ellie would sleep sound with the potion she had administered so promptly and when she woke she would be rested and more able to cope with the loss. Sighing heavily, Amy wrapped the babe up again and put it in her basket. No sense in leaving it for Ellie to see or Jethro to mourn over, they would have to get on with their lives as best they could without a child to lighten their days. It was God's will. Maybe they would be luckier next time though in her heart she very much doubted it. All she hoped was that Jethro was not involved in the mine accident. Ellie, poor soul, would have enough to grieve over without losing her husband as well. She finished packing then went downstairs and picked up her cloak and shawl from where they were warming by the fire.

"She'll sleep for hours with the brew I gave her. Just keep an eye on her, Becky; I'll see you later when I'm able. Ye're a good neighbour, lass. Ellie's lucky to have ye next door; she'll need all the help she can get when she wakes up from sleep. Oh by the way, I've taken the bairn if Jethro should ask."

Becky nodded, feeling a lump come in her throat; she was grateful for the praise but desperately sorry for the loss of Ellie's baby. "Poor Ellie had so wanted a child, she'll be right distressed. This will make her third try with nothing to show for it. She ain't the strongest of women neither; maybe she should let well alone and not bother with more babbies for her health's sake."

Mrs Bunnion nodded briefly then, as she heard the sound of the carriage, she said farewell and going quickly out of the door left Becky to ponder on her silence though not for long as her thoughts turned to Jethro. She hoped he was not involved in the mine disaster and hurt or maybe dead. Ellie would cope with the loss of her baby but not with losing Jethro. They were devoted to each other; just like her and Saul had been; hardly a day passed that she did not miss him. Damn that mine! And damn Trevarron for refusing to spend money to keep the mine safe.

CHAPTER TEN

Amy Bunnion struggled up the long, curving flight of stairs to the first floor behind Annie as she led the way, before arriving at Lavinia's bedroom door. She paused to take breath prior to entering the mistress's bedroom, gazing at the long wide corridor stretching out on either side. The stucco walls were lined with all kinds of pictures and finely worked pieces of furniture standing between the solid wooden doors that led to the many bedrooms. The floor was carpeted with an ornamental Brussels rug, which showed up well against the oak wood surround. A nightmare for the drudges who cleaned Tregender Hall, she thought, but supremely pleasing to its owner.

Once in the room Amy examined Lavinia meticulously. There was not any doubt she had started labour but, encouragingly, Annie said she thought Lavinia's depth of stupor might have improved for now she had begun to stir and blink her eyes. "What a dreadful thing to happen," she bemoaned to Amy. "Lord knows what the Master will say."

"Well, it's not your fault, is it? If a man will get himself such a big staircase he has to answer for the consequences if someone falls down it. That balustrade is like glass under the fingers. No wonder she fell, even if she was aware of the danger. I see she hit her head a right wallop. Mercy's sake, a banister is supposed to help you, not kill you."

Amy probed at the bruised forehead then quickly withdrew her fingers. Incredibly it felt like a fracture of the skull so she decided it was best left alone in case she did more harm. Surely the woman should have died with a blow of that nature? Unquestionably it accounted for the length of oblivion. The problem was - would she recover in time to deliver the baby? Not having the slightest idea at that moment, nor was she prepared to say, she hustled Annie downstairs to eat her dinner. "Leave things to me," she ordered. "I'll give you a call if I need you." Annie was more than delighted to go.

Several hours later, as Amy was bending over her patient dribbling a few drops of water onto the dry lips she was elated to see Lavinia's eyes open wide and fix themselves on her face.

"There now m'darling, how are you feeling? No, don't try and get up, just rest easy and all will be well. You are in good hands, lovey, and you'll be getting a nice surprise soon."

She spoke in the usual soothing manner she used for any patient who was terrified of the pain of childbirth knowing that her calmness would comfort their fright. Lavinia stared at her blankly then relapsed into a strange muttering that made no sense at all. Amy guessed the crack on the head was responsible for the delirium. Maybe the best thing was to get the birth over as soon as possible and by then the doctor would be on hand to treat the head injury. She rang the bell and asked for some hot water to mix a potion to hasten the labour. She was just administering it one spoonful at a time when a loud shouting from downstairs heralded the return of the Master of the house.

Ambrose Trevarron flung his topcoat onto a chair, yelling for the housekeeper as he did so. His loud voice and overbearing presence did much to frighten anyone who attempted to argue with him, though if they did, woe betide them, it was like spitting against the wind. Now Amy could hear him shouting for Annie or someone - anyone - to tell him what was amiss. She pitied the staff, though she expected they were used to his ways. She just hoped they would take the edge off his anger before he ventured up to the sick room or she would be hard put to be civil to him. When finally he came upstairs she was flabbergasted at his first words. "Haven't I enough to do with happenings at the mine? Lord save us, one would think I could have a little peace in my own home, for God's sake! What's amiss, then? I can't abide any more grumbling. If it's not one thing, it's another!" he snarled.

"Your wife has had a fearful accident as you can see. She's fallen downstairs."

"Always was careless, stupid woman. She's brought this on herself. Well, she'll have to get over it like the rest of us do. Let's hope she's not harmed the babe."

Unbelievably, he displayed not the slightest concern for the health of his wife, indeed he scarcely glanced at her. Instead, he eyed the small, plump midwife, neatly clad in a white voluminous apron, her shiny, black buttoned boots peeking from below her long skirts. She gazed at him warily, not exactly afraid, for she had exercised authority for too long to be overwhelmed by bullying but she knew when to keep a still tongue.

"How is the babe then? Do you think you can deliver him safely?" His eyes were like black buttons, hard and unfeeling. "No mistakes now, Mrs Bunnion, I want my son. He's to be healthy and all in one piece no matter what."

"I'll deliver the child all right, if it's possible, considering the extreme gravity of your wife's accident but one thing I won't guarantee is a son. That's in God's hands. You may have a daughter and if she's born fit and well it will be something to be grateful for." She watched curiously as he returned to the open bedroom door, gazed out into the corridor, carefully closed it then came back to where she stood by the bed.

"If it is female then you must put her down like an unwanted animal. I won't have a daughter! I want a son. My wife has strict orders to give me a son. She won't disobey, she knows the penalty. That's the only reason why I married her, to beget me a son."

Amy stood rigidly dumb with disbelief, her thoughts rioting in her head as she stared at the mine-owner, desperately willing her face not to show the contempt she felt. How could a man say that of his own flesh and blood? What was wrong with him? Was he mad? Hard and mean maybe, but she had never heard he was mad. She decided to keep her own counsel and see how things turned out. After all with his wife being so poorly anything could happen and she did not want to be put in a position where he could pin blame on her. For a moment she regretted hastening the birth. If things took a long time then eventually the doctor would be free to take over the case and she would be relieved of any responsibility. Nevertheless the deed was done and she would have to live with it and do her best. As for killing a healthy child - well she had never done it before and nobody would make her do it now.

CHAPTER ELEVEN

Amy was torn with compassion for Lavinia's struggles to deliver her child but felt in the state of affairs it was as well that she was off her head; she would never later remember the dire agony. She dare not give her a herbal pain-reliever as she would have done with her normal patients in case it had a bad effect with the head injury. Instead, after having the servants bring her all she needed for the delivery, she told them to stay out of the bedroom until she called, she could manage well enough herself. They were only too pleased to comply. It was late and they wanted their beds; so after all was put to rights and the master fed, the house grew quiet as everyone retired.

"Don't tell him!" Amy was startled out of the light doze she had fallen into as she sat beside the bed waiting for the labour to advance.

"What did you say, lovey? Don't tell him what?"

"If it's a girl. He'll kill me if it's a girl. He wants a son, damn him. But it's not what I want. He doesn't know the child is not his - whichever it turns out."

Amy managed to contain her shock with difficulty. What sort of a relationship had been going on in the Trevarron family? She had heard no gossip, no untoward events that would have occasioned such a confession. "Hush, lovey, he's not going to kill anyone. You'll have your son, I promise you." Amy's long experience with midwifery had shown her it was best to agree with a patient even when she was unsure what the outcome would be. If it turned out to be the opposite of what was wanted it did not matter. The important thing was not to upset or alarm the patient and cause further distress.

"I don't want a son; I want a daughter, a perfect little daughter just like her father. We'll call her Linda, won't we? Say you'll call her Linda - after my dear love's mother. It's a name like mine only a little bit different. But I'd like to add Rose to remind her of me. A little girl, that's what I want and that's what I'll have."

An hour later she got her wish and as Amy held up the tiny scrap of humanity to show her, she could see it was barely able to mew like a kitten and was minus the hair and nails of a full-term child but not far off for all that. A daughter right enough, but not the son her husband was waiting anxiously for. What on earth was Amy to do with the child?

Wrapping it up hastily in a small blanket she laid it to one side while she attended to Lavinia. The woman lay supine on the bed, her breathing slow and shallow, and the livid bruise on her forehead seemed darker than ever against the white face. She looked nearer to death than she had looked all evening. Amy gazed at her in apprehension and then was startled to hear her speak once more.

"You'll call her Linda?" Her lips barely moved.

"You know it's a girl?" said Amy, marvelling that she appeared in possession of her senses, though what the next hour would bring, she hardly dared imagine.

"Yes, I know. Hide her from him, won't you? He mustn't know she is born."

"Yes, I'll hide her." But how? Amy felt totally panic-stricken.

Lavinia waved her hand at the bedside cabinet and, after puzzling a moment, Amy pulled open the top drawer. "What do you want from here?"

"The package...it should be right at the back. Get it out; please...give it to my little daughter when she is old enough. It came from my mother and from her mother's mother. Now I want my daughter to have it. It can be sold if she wishes it or needs money."

Amy's searching fingers found a box, which contained a

heavy gold chain with a ruby and diamond locket hanging on it. She stared at it with awe, for she had never in her life seen anything quite so beautiful before. "I can't take that - they'll think I stole it!"

"No, they won't. My husband doesn't know of its existence. He would have had it away long since. My grandmother sent it to me. It has belonged to my family forever and he shan't get his hands on it. He hated my family. He wasn't good enough for them, you see. Nothing must go to him that is truly mine. This belongs only to my daughter. She is not his either so he will never have her, though I know he won't want her and might do her harm. You do see?"

Amy did not see but she nodded nonetheless. She began to ask the name of Lavinia's grandmother but Lavinia softly smiled, lifted her hand as though in farewell and with a deep sigh passed quietly into death. Amy stood like a statue as though turned to stone, quite horrified at the immediacy of Lavinia's death and the terrible burden she had just taken on; for now she had somehow to convince a man there was no child, let alone a son.

CHAPTER TWELVE

What was she to do? What crime was she about to commit trying to spirit a man's child away from him? If she was discovered, Trevarron would deny everything, would call her a liar for daring even to suggest he would have his own child done away with; there would be no doubt whose word would be taken in the end. While she cleared away the dirty linen from the birth, Amy's brain was working furiously, forming and discarding plans, trying to see a way out of the awful dilemma of what was to come; confessing to Trevarron he had a daughter and she had done nothing about it, she had not killed her as ordered.

Would he kill her? Or worse still, would he watch her do the awful deed? And what about her promise to Lavinia? Could she live with her conscience if she did not make an effort to do something but what? Then belatedly she recalled Ellie's child. Much earlier on she'd chided herself whilst being driven to the Hall, for bringing the little corpse with her. What good had it done to take it? Oh, she knew her motive had been to get the dead child out of sight of Ellie, but had it been right? Ellie should mourn exactly as if she had lost a living, breathing child, then go to the next pregnancy if she wanted to and however useless. Amy ought to have left the body for Jethro. Now she realised she would have the obligation of making sure it reached the church for burial. But her desperate thoughts flew ahead to a different purpose the child could serve. Could she substitute the two children and take the girl back to Ellie to bring up?

Playing God is not your responsibility, Amy Bunnion, mind your own business! What rights have you to meddle in the doings of other folk? You've enough to do in your life without taking on the responsibility of a child. She castigated herself with the futility of it all. Nonetheless, she had come to a conclusion that was worth considering in spite of everything in her nature that went against it.

A tiny whimper came to her ears and she quickly unwrapped the blanket and gazed at the little mite lying there. It moved its arms as though in protest and she gathered it up to hold it warmly against her. Poor little soul! How could anyone kill such an innocent babe? What kind of a father was he to even contemplate something so evil? With her mind made up, she washed and dressed the baby in a vest and napkin; neither would be missed from the huge pile left for her use. Squeezing a few drops of water between its lips she wrapped the babe firmly in the blanket that had previously enshrouded the dead child and then hid the tiny infant in the depths of her basket, praying the child would stay quiet. Quickly placing the dead baby at the foot of Lavinia's bed she covered it with a scrap of sheeting then, tucking the basket out of direct sight behind an armchair, she had a last look round to see if all was as it should be. Once satisfied, she sped out of the room to get Ambrose Trevarron.

Amy found him in the Library, stretched out before the ashes of a cold fire, an empty decanter of brandy on the floor beside him. He was in a heavy doze and it took several shakes before she was able to rouse him. He started up quickly rubbing his bleary eyes.

"Is it all over? You have my son?" he demanded gruffly.

"No, Mr Trevarron, I'm sorry to say your wife has died. The baby was born dead. You did have a son but sadly he was far too weak to take a breath. Come upstairs and see for yourself."

"My son is dead? How can this be? I told you to take care."

"Mr Trevarron! I'm not God!" Cross your fingers, Amy, when you say that, you'll rue this night for sure. She crossed her fingers behind her back and went on, "If a baby's born dead, it's dead, Mr Trevarron! There's nothing one can do. Your wife delivered well before her time. The little thing wasn't ready to be born and the accident didn't help."

"Yes, yes, I suppose so, but I did so want a son." He gazed at her in disappointment.

Why did he keep on about a son! His wife was dead for God's sake, hadn't he realised? She tried again. "I'm sorry about your wife, sir, it was all too much for her, what with the fall and all. I did what I could but she had this terrible head injury. How she managed to birth the child I just don't know. I'm sure the doctor will bear me out."

"Yes, yes," he repeated, reluctant to hear any details. "Very unfortunate of course but, most likely, sheer clumsiness was the cause of it. Now let me see my son."

Back in the bedroom Ambrose gazed down at the small figure of a boy-child who looked rather like a skinned rabbit. It had a thick fuzz of dark matted hair on a tiny skull and its skin was a dusky mottled colour. Altogether the corpse bore little resemblance to anything he had expected.

"Ugh! How dreadful! Is that a baby? I'd have expected him to look - look more robust. Cover him up! I shan't want to see him again. Get out now, your job is finished. Here - take this for your trouble." He thrust a couple of sovereigns into her hand. "Er - about my wishes earlier on - we don't need to mention I said anything untoward, do we? I, of course, wouldn't have let you dispose of ..."

"Of course not, sir, heat of the moment, I'm sure. Don't worry, I'm used to expectant fathers saying all sorts of things." Liar, thought Amy, he meant it well enough.

"Quite so." Ambrose thrust another sovereign at Amy. As she picked up her heavy basket and went to the door, he added, "She was always a weak woman, my wife. Poor breeder! I'll be choosier next time, eh? The gentry have no stamina for healthy sons!"

CHAPTER THIRTEEN

Amy could not answer she was so choked with spleen and the risk of discovery had turned her insides to jelly, so she got out of the house as quickly as her legs could carry her. Banging on the coach house door she roused a grumbling, sleepy William to take her home. Then, once his coach had driven away from her cottage, she hurried as best as she could up the hill to Ellie. Becky answered her knock with some surprise.

"Didn't expect you back this late," Becky whispered.

"How's she bin? Awake yet?" Amy enquired tersely.

"No, she hasn't stirred. How d'ye get on at Hall?"

"Never mind that. You know I took Ellie's babe with me? I wanted to keep an eye on her for I thought she might live. She's survived so far but she'll need a lot of nursing and Ellie will see she gets it, I'm sure." She opened the basket to show Becky.

"Is it alive?" She peered down at the bundle. "Oh! How strange, I could have sworn it was a male and had black hair and..."

"Course she's alive! At least she was last time I looked. Now all she needs is food. Ye were as distracted with all that knocking the minute she was born same as I was. Them as gentry don't pay no heed to ye when ye're engaged in difficult matters, if they wants ye then ye have to come running. The thing is there's no need to tell anyone I took her off thinking she might die, is there, Becky? I'll be a laughing stock hereabouts. Me with my know-how doin' a thing like that, I'd never hear the end of it."

"Depend on it! I'll not say a word. I'm only too pleased

Ellie's got a baby after all. She'll be over the moon when she wakes up and knows she's a mother."

Amy heaved an inward sigh of relief. She believed Becky was ever inclined to take things at face value and, for once, Amy was relieved at her unquestioning acceptance of the tale. Later she might turn events over in her mind and wonder about them but it did not matter. Amy would deal with that eventuality when it arose, if it arose. Now she was too tired to think and plan any more; all she wanted was bed.

"I'll go up and take her daughter to her." Amy climbed the stairs once more with Becky hard on her heels, not wishing to miss a moment of Ellie's reaction. Ellie was just rousing from the deepest sleep she had ever had and, as the bedroom was half-dark as well, she did not at first recognise Amy. She wiped at the flow of tears running down her face then cried out, "Oh Jethro, I'm so sorry, I've lost the babby again! I don't know what I've done wrong …"

"You haven't lost the babby, Ellie. Didn't I say everything would be all right? Well then, here she is! Your daughter! A mite skinny as yet but nothing a good few feeds won't put right. She'll be a beauty one of these days if she takes after her mother."

Ellie sat up enchanted to gaze at the tiny creature Amy placed in her arms, almost surprised at the searching mouth that craved sustenance. Instinctively she put her to a breast and was rewarded with a rapt feeling of joy as the child began to suck. "Oh, Amy, she's beautiful now, just beautiful; and here's me dreaming I'd lost her."

"What are you going to call her, Ellie?" said Becky, every bit as excited as she was.

"Why, I don't know, I somehow thought it'd be a boy."

"Call her something unusual, like Linda." Amy was casual but underneath her heart was beating wildly. How was she going to persuade Ellie?

"I ain't ever heard that name, but it seems ever so pretty. Linda Barton. A bit posh, ain't it, but yes, it sounds beautiful all right. I could call her Lindy for short, Amy?"

"Put a Rose 'tween the two and it'll sound even better. My second name's Rose," added Amy. "I've never bestowed it on one of my babes but there's always a first time."

"Oh! I never knew that!" exclaimed Becky. "You're a dark horse, Amy Bunnion!"

"Ain't I just." Amy's tone was dry. "Well, I'm off to get a bit of shut-eye. I'll see you tomorrow, Ellie. Becky will help you with the babby, won't you? Oh, I nearly forgot - have you heard from Jethro? Is he safe?"

"He's fine, Amy, only stayed on to help. He'll be home soon to see his daughter," Ellie said proudly. "My, but he'll be right taken with her; just fancy, a daughter. Never a boy that might go down that killer mine, but a gorgeous little girl for me. Jethro'll have to wait a mite longer for his son. Maybe next time, eh, Amy?"

Amy did not answer. She felt she had done enough in the last few hours to direct fate along another path. Only time would tell if she had done the right thing and avoided a murder or had she perhaps set in motion a destiny which would ruin a child's birthright? Reaching home she took out the ruby pendant and looked at it carefully. The locket was quite large because when she opened it she saw it contained a ringlet of fair curling hair and a picture of a woman; a tiny card written with minute writing that said it was Sophie Rose, Duchess of Grant Forres. Was she the grandmother? What was the peculiar story of Mrs Trevarron's childhood? The woman was dead now, so Amy would never know what lay behind it all. Sighing heavily, she closed the locket and wrapping it again in its velvet purse, she replaced it in the box. Before closing it she wrote the details of the births and the circumstances of their exchange in her precise script. If anything untoward occurred to herself she hoped Linda would inherit her grandmother's locket despite all the fuss it would cause. Amy hid the wrapped box in an old desk belonging to her dead husband and went to bed exhausted from her efforts. She would leave fate to do as it willed now, having done her level best to save a life. At least the little girl would be loved and cared for with the Bartons. From what she had seen of Trevarron's nature she doubted he had an ounce of love in him; in particular not one scrap for a girl-child.

CHAPTER FOURTEEN

Doctor Lusty descended the final ladder and began the long walk over rough ground to where he hoped he would find more than one man had been rescued from the rock fall. His legs and ankles were aching from the effort of climbing on one sloping ladder after another, all of them descending deep down into the bowels of the earth. His hands were torn for some of the ladders had splintered handgrips or broken rungs quite lethal to tread upon. Early on he had handed his case to one of the miners accompanying him, which enabled him to cling tighter to the hazardous mode of descent. The further he went down, the harder it would be to return. No wonder the exertion of climbing up, maybe a thousand feet or more 'to grass', was the cause of so many deaths from heart disease, quite apart from the life-threatening pulmonary illnesses caused by the ghastly ventilation and fume-ridden air. He estimated he must be near enough eight hundred feet down and he had to exercise strict control on his nerves at the thought of all the rock between himself and the open air.

If I get out of this place alive I'll never come down here again, he thought, not for the first time, though on each occasion in the past he had not hesitated to help his fellow man. They must get a younger man; I'm just not able to cope anymore.

"Let me give ye a hand, Doc, we have to crawl under the killas but after that we're nearly there, my 'andsome. It's a long ways down here, but the roof's high."

"Thank God for that small mercy; how you do this every day I don't know. You are bloody heroes! It can't be right to put up doing with this for a living."

Harry Hughie laughed at him, showing white teeth in the grimy exterior of his face. "Better than being penniless and having to beg for one's bread. My family wouldn't like that at all nor thank me for letting them to starve. Tell me where I'll get better work to support my kin and I'll be off in a flash."

"I guess I can't, Harry, and you look after them very well, man, and they're a credit to you." Lusty thought of Harry's five children, thin, undernourished. All dressed in old hand-me-downs, and mostly without shoes even on the coldest of days.

"I do my best, though I'd as lief have no more."

A picture of Harry's wife, Meg, came into Lusty's mind. Scraggy, shapeless and old before her time, beginning to lose her teeth from the pregnancies and poor diet.

"Come and see me soon, lad, after we've finished with this lot, and we'll talk, eh Harry? I might be able to offer a few suggestions, if you get my meaning?"

"Right, Doc, I do. Thanks very much, I'm obliged to ye."

Lusty was finally guided under a great hanging wall of slate held up by huge pit props which looked like a weird forest in the light of the smoky tallow candles fixed to each man's hat with a lump of clay. The bobbing lights gave a ghostly shadow-ridden view of rocky passages appearing at intervals where other lodes of tin had been mined over the years. The small group of miners and the doctor mostly moved in almost pitch-darkness, barely able to see the rough ground beneath their feet. All the while from around them, came the low-pitched sound from the earth as it creaked and groaned, ever moving as the world turned on its axis. The miners were used to the poor visibility and the noise but it filled Lusty with dread and he could not wait to get away from the fearful place and up to freedom and fresh air.

"The Doc's here, Tom; hold on lad, you'll be all right now. He's here to help you. Over here, Doc! He's still alive for you! Thank the Lord for His mercy."

The Doctor bent over the miner and tried to ascertain how badly injured he was by the light of his own and other odd candles that had been thrust into the rock on either side of the passage. His leg was badly broken for sure, but it also seemed that a narrow sliver of slate had penetrated his back and although he was bleeding badly none of the miners had dared to draw it out for fear they caused a worse haemorrhage. He worked on the man for well over an hour before he felt he was stable enough to be carried on a stretcher up the long appalling climb to the surface; he might still die when they got him up but at least he stood a chance. Down under the earth Tom had no chance at all. By the time Lusty finished, two more men had been found alive and he once more bent to the task of keeping them that way. The hours went by and soon it was apparent that no more men would come out alive from the fall. Wearily and disheartened that his fellow men should have to work in such terrible conditions for the benefit of just one man, he began the long arduous climb back to fresh air. Only to find that it was now the next day and he had been more than twenty-four hours underground. He ached painfully in every muscle from the tremendous effort of climbing to the surface.

Lusty was collecting his clothes from the engine house before making his way home for a bath and then bed when the man he had been thinking about with such deep anger came through the door.

"Ah, there you are!" grumbled Trevarron. "About time! I trust you're not putting in an enormous bill for going down pit; you should have waited till the men were brought up. Of course you know Tom Pedy died on the way up. It was a bloody waste of time, if you ask me. I needed you here! My wife has died and I've lost my son! Do you hear! You should have been up here! Not cavorting down the mine!" Trevarron hunched his shoulders as he shouted out his demeaning words, trying to intimidate the doctor. "So what do you say to that? It was all a dammed wasted effort! But you'll never learn, will you? You've no more sense than a village idiot!" Trevarron added viciously.

For a long hard moment Doctor Lusty stood with his back to Ambrose Trevarron wondering if the dirty hands he clenched round his clean suit would beat the arrogant mine-owner into a pulp; then, with a sigh, he realised he would do no such thing. For one thing he was getting too old; and what use would it be. The man was a despot; brute force would not move him but maybe logic and avarice would. At this moment, though, it would appear he had to deal with the unexpected death of Lavinia Trevarron. What on earth had happened? She was in perfect health when last he saw her. Tired of course, but then all pregnant women grew tired of carrying a babe. Apart from that discomfort there had been nothing amiss, nothing that is, that would cause her death. The only thing that ailed her deeply had never been in his power to heal. Nor had it been in hers once she was pregnant with a Trevarron heir. For he would have wagered Ambrose would rather have seen her dead before he would have allowed her to leave him. She was no longer important as a wife to him, only a body to carry a Trevarron son. Lusty was desperately exhausted but he knew he could not rest until he found out what had happened. Barely acknowledging Trevarron and ignoring the man's ranting, he finished dressing and went outside to find his horse and dogcart waiting for him. He went to the mare's head to give her the titbit which he always carried with him.

"She's bin well rubbed down and stabled, sir," said one of the young pit workers standing nearby. He had offered to care for the horse whilst the doctor was down the mine.

"Thank you, lad, she's a mite more precious to me than most things, I warrant."

Tossing him a penny he swung himself up into the cart and looked back at the mine-owner. "I'll be along soon. You'll get your report when I know what's killed her."

"Your neglect, that's what's killed her! You should have been topside. I'm not paying you a farthing for her. It's a bloody disgrace! You ought to be struck off."

The doctor, disdaining to reply, took up the reins and drove out of the yard, his brain, not for the first time, seething from all the sheer futility of life. Sometime later James Lusty scratched his head in puzzlement, conscious of the grit in his hair and the unwashed state of his body from the trip down the mine. He had finished the examination of the bodies of Mrs Trevarron and her son so he could record the cause of death.

He was surprised she had seemingly given birth to a full-term baby. He could have sworn she had been barely into her seventh month, if that, but the evidence before his eyes said otherwise. He could have been mistaken, for the child was puny, with little more than skin and bone to sustain him through what had been a traumatic birth. As for his mother, well she was easy enough to diagnose; a fractured skull from the tumble downstairs was all too plain to figure out. How she had managed to survive long enough to give birth was a miracle but then the determination of most mothers to safeguard their young was one of nature's first laws. He checked diligently on the deep bruising over her body, which was revealed in huge livid marks, standing out clearly against her white skin. Yes, it was all quite consistent with the fall downstairs. Except that was, for a sickle-shaped birthmark below her left breast on the upper ribs. Was it a family trait? He looked for a corresponding mark on the baby but saw none.

Well, at least Ambrose wasn't guilty of throwing her downstairs, he mused, not being there. Not that he would have put it past him with his temper but his alibi was sound enough going by the story the housekeeper had told. Funnily enough though she sounded quite guilty herself but he knew them all well enough to know there was no enmity between any of the women. Probably she was just still shocked at finding her like that.

He was conscious of wasting his time, of probing for things that were not to be found, trying to placate his sense of unease.

Drat it, man, enough is enough! he told himself sternly. A bath, then bed for you, m'lad, and leave the ghosts to their own devices, you've enough to do with the living, let alone worry about the dead!

He repacked his bag and strode from the room, relieved to be finished with the owner of the Hall. In a short time he would begin his retirement and seek peace and quiet, then he would be free of people like Trevarron. In that unthinking assumption he was mistaken - by a very long way indeed.

CHAPTER FIFTEEN

Linda was four when Ellie died halfway through a pregnancy that should never have been started. Jethro sadly mourned her then got on with the task of bringing up his beloved daughter with the help of his next-door neighbour, Becky Lanner. She was always on hand when Jethro was down the mine and the small amount she earned for this eked out a living she made from the selling of jams and pickles that were forever stewing on the battered kitchen range. Becky also sold knitted garments, which she worked on whenever she was not cooking. Redolent smells of tomato chutneys, raspberry jams, boiling vinegar, spices and herbs were a part of Linda's childhood, as was her father's sweet briar pipe and the coal tar soap he used to wash the dirt of the pit from his skin.

Surrounded as she was with love, Linda never really missed the woman who had fed her as a baby and brushed the blonde gossamer locks that soon covered the toddler's head in curls. Ellie had adored her. Each day she marked the small differences of her growing up, noticing eyes that changed quickly to a deep emerald green which were remarked on enviously by the rest of the village. Her slender hands and feet and soft creamy skin, so unlike many of the other children who came of badly nourished stock and suffered accordingly. It was this difference that caused Ellie to withdraw, rather self-consciously, from her good-natured friendships with other women and when poor health caused her to seek her own fireside, they did not bother to call round. Linda and Jethro attended her diligently until the end, aided by Becky whenever she could spare the time. After Ellie died, Becky was too busy with her recipes to mingle with anyone other than customers who bought her produce, or to see that Linda had companions; so Linda played by herself and rarely mixed with the village children. When she was five, Jethro, filled with ambition for his bright little daughter asked Martin Whitmore, the local minister, if he would teach Linda to read properly before she went to school.

"I want Lindy to learn all she can now she's lost her mother. The least I can do is give her what I've never had myself - I've the money to pay."

"Never mind the money, if this is your wish, Jethro, then I'd be pleased to help, but it is an unusual thing you ask of me. Everyone else in the village seems content to wait on the school teaching letters. But if it's just her letters you want her to acquire then why not have a go yourself." He stopped abruptly as he saw the slow burn creep up Jethro's cheeks and realised the man could not read or write himself. "On the other hand," he interjected swiftly, "my ten-year-old has an hour or two each day with me and ye'd be welcome to sit in and get the hang of how I teach, then you can help Linda even more in the evenings."

"Why not? I could do with a little more learning even if I am getting long in the tooth. Thankee, Reverend, I'm much obliged. You'm start as soon as yer able."

Tactfully Jethro was included with Linda in the lessons and soon, to his surprise, he began to grasp the rudiments of writing and reading quite well. After this, he was filled with more ambition than ever to encourage Linda's education. Linda swiftly overtook Jethro and she, in turn, tried to encourage him to make greater efforts. He was caught between his pride in her ability and succeeding himself.

The vicar was most amused at the intense rivalry, which sprang up between them. He used it to spur Jethro on to greater efforts but he knew the man would never catch up with the girl who owned a lively and imaginative brain that absorbed knowledge like a sponge; it made the minister pause many times to reflect on where she had inherited her abilities. Not from Jethro's family, he would wager. As for Ellie, he had never ever heard of her family being anything other than working class.

His son, Richard, although six years older than Lindy, often joined the group and soon became a firm friend of the girl who idolised him. Over two years went by in this pleasant fashion, which was, for Linda, a gloriously happy time. She continued to bask in the combined love of Jethro and Becky, though the latter could be sharp when she overstepped the mark and she grew apace both in size and knowledge. She caught up with and outstripped the other children in the village who had been born around the same time and no one would now guess how frail and tiny she had been at birth. Though still small in stature, she had filled out healthily and Jethro's pride in her knew no bounds.

The Reverend Whitmore was hard-pushed to keep up with the insatiable demands that his pupils made on him. Each vying with the other in competition to memorise all they needed to know. Linda also adored Richard, the vicar's son, and followed him all over the place whenever she could. Flattered with her attention, he was condescending, until he realised the intelligent little girl was determined to learn all she could. He took great pains in teaching her to swim, to shoot, and to set traps for wild rabbits and other small game. Each new pursuit she mastered was haled by young Richard and Jethro with pride, much to the dismay of Becky who chided them continually. "She's not a boy, Jethro, she'll need womanly skills afore long."

"She's a child, Becky; let the lass be happy with Richard, she bain't come to no harm with ee." So Becky let well alone and Linda ran free, except for the nightly homework with her beloved Jethro. Soon she surpassed him in everything but despite the difficulty Jethro had in absorbing the lessons some of them stuck and soon he found he was more aware of the pitiful and sometimes downright criminal practices that were being foisted on the miners. He began to protest, to ask for safer equipment; to condemn the lack of means for miners to climb the long distances to the surface, when they should have had automatic help like some other mines in the district. He was always questioning accidents, questioning everything, until at last Ambrose decided he had had enough of him.

Accidents were always happening at the mine; caused by old and dangerous machinery or perhaps carelessness of the pit workers. However, the miners knew there was more to it than just chance. For it seemed, no sooner did one of them grow resentful and make his voice heard in protest, he was struck down by a so-called accident and either lost his life, or was so badly injured he could no longer work again. Then he and his family were promptly ousted from their rented cottage to make way for another miner's family. After a while few people dared put their lives at risk by objecting to the vile conditions they worked under, so they continued to endure silently. After one particularly horrendous and tragic accident when a young lad lost his leg, Jethro went to the office and complained to the manager. "We need a new engine and a better pump. Men are dying by inches in that hellish atmosphere. Not to mention dangerous equipment that's too old to guarantee safety."

"Oh yes, and where's the money to pay for them?" Ever on the watch for trouble, as he swiftly emerged from his office, Trevarron was quick to respond to the complaints

"That's not my responsibility," replied Jethro tersely. "But if ee wants the kibble then ye have to protect t'men. Thee'll have a strike if ee dassn't," he warned.

The day Jethro was struck down with the runaway ore wagon Lindy waited in vain until it was nearly dark. "Come back inside the house, Lindy, you'll catch yer death o' cold out there. Likely your dad's been held up with a repair. He'll be along soon."

"Perhaps we didn't hear the hooter, Aunt Becky, maybe that's held him up?"

"Now, ye know that's not so, that there hooter can be heard everywhere. No, child, there's nothing amiss with the mine, ye'd have heard long afore this."

Linda was in a fever of impatience waiting that evening for Jethro to come up the hill as usual after his shift. They were due to finish some work set by Whitmore and she wanted to get on with it. After Ellie died she would always run down the hill towards him when she saw him, and be hoisted up on his shoulder for a ride up the hill. After he had washed she would dish up his meal that Becky had left in the oven and when he was finished they would share the lessons before going to bed.

"He's very late tonight, Aunt Becky, it's well past his time. Look the first star's out. Richard says that's a lucky star. It is, isn't it?" Anxious but trying not to show it she helped Becky take in the sweet smelling clothes they gathered from the clothes line.

"Well if it is, it hasn't shone on me lately; those berries from Trevassa Farm were past their best, I had to throw half of them away. Now, come on, Lindy, we'll wait fer yer dad inside, this night air bain't good. See it's getting dark and the dew's afalling."

"No. Here he is at last." With a sigh of relief Linda spotted the figure but, as it came nearer through the descending twilight, Becky felt a sudden squeeze at her heart. "No, it's not yer dad. It's Danny Duloe."

"Coo-ee, Mrs Lanner! It's about Jethro. He's…"

"Nooo!" screamed Becky. "No! I've Lindy here…"

Ignoring her warning Danny continued to yell. "He's dead! Can you believe it? Dead! They've got him at the mine…"

CHAPTER SIXTEEN

In a flash Linda swiftly evaded Becky's clutching hand and began racing down the hill past Danny Duloe who stood with his mouth wide agape and on to the village and the mine.

Becky ran after her, stopping only to berate the miner's boy who had been sent to deliver the news. "You stupid damned oaf. What did you come out with news like that for? All in front of the lass too. You know how she adores him. Get thee gone from my sight; you've no more brains than a bloody beetle!"

Linda, racing far ahead of Becky, ducked under a miner's arm and ran full tilt into the engine house. She stopped short against the rough planking stretcher which was set on two benches where Jethro had been laid out, still in his rough and dirty miner's gear. Linda was grief-stricken as she saw his twisted body, his limbs lying anyhow as if they belonged to a marionette doll; she took a deep breath of terror at the sight. Then lifting the edge of her skirt she wiped the smear of dust from his pale cheek. His face had not been marked in any way. It looked as it did when she often crept into his bedroom of an early morning, eyes still closed in sleep, face slackened and relaxed. For an instant she thought nothing was amiss until she saw the small trickle of dried blood that came from a corner of his mouth. Lifting her skirt again she tried to wipe it away but, having dried, it would not be shifted and a deep sob choked her as she said piteously, "Da! Da! Wake up! Oh, please wake up. Your supper's ready, an'…an' I promise I won't be better than you at my words. Da, I need ye. I love ye…please wake up for Lindy. Oh, Da, don't be dead. Please, if you love me, don't be dead! I can't bear you to die."

Quietly and tenderly they eventually eased her away from the dead man into Becky's arms. The runaway coal truck had mangled Jethro and nothing could have been done to save him. The men who carried him to the surface were grim with suspicions and grief. This was no accident. Jethro had been a canny man. He knew the ways of the mine; he would never have been caught with a truck like that. Becky walked back through the village with her arm around Linda holding her close to her side. From each side of the narrow street she could hear the villagers loudly talking, scarcely bothering to hide their views.

"She'm have to go to the orphanage in Truro," said one miner's wife.

"She bain't a soul fer 'er now," said another. "'Ceptin' Becky, course."

"'Er book learning' won't do 'er any good now; they only 'ire domestics from there," jeered yet another, jealous of Linda's superior brain compared with her own children.

"I'd tak' 'er in meself, ony I ain't the money to keep 'er," came a quiet voice.

Becky urged the girl along, also wondering how she could manage to keep the two of them when it was a job to make ends meet for her. Sales in the village were poor at best. Without Jethro's contribution she would find it hard to manage.

"I dassn't know what Betsy Polwen will make of this with Ellie being her sister an' all. She had a right respect of Jethro and a real taking with Lindy." Annie Gorland's voice rang out clearly. She had come into the village on her afternoon off to be met with the shocking news of Jethro's death. "We can't let the child go off to strangers."

Quite suddenly Ambrose Trevarron appeared in the doorway of his office and looked at the gathering crowd of villagers, his expression bleak, as usual. "What's all this then, got time to waste, have us?" His voice rang out silencing the whispers.

"We are discussing what's to happen with Lindy now that Jethro's gone. B'ain't no one else to take her in," shouted one of the spectators incensed at Trevarron's words. In the silence that followed the brave remark the sound of sobbing was very clear.

Trevarron stared across at Linda who was walking back home holding on to Becky's hand. The tears were running down her face. When she saw the mine-owner her body stiffened and she held her head up high, somehow reminding him of his late wife. "You killed my da." Her voice echoed clearly over the crowd who gasped and waited for Ambrose's reply but he stood silent gazing down at the eight-year-old child who faced him defiantly, her face a threatening thundercloud.

"You killed my da!" Linda's voice repeated, ringing loudly in the sudden silence. "You know the mine is awfully dangerous and the men get hurt all the time. Why don't you help them stead o' letting them die?"

"Hush, Lindy, you ain't no call to say that." Becky was in an agony of apprehension.

"Have so," responded Linda. "He was my da and he knew things were bad."

"Hush, Lindy love, let's go home. Your place ain't here, not right now." Becky's hands tried to urge the girl away but Lindy unexpectedly stood firm, looking straight at Ambrose with tears sparkling her huge green eyes. "You kill everybody who works for you if they argue with you. Why don't you listen to people when they tell you what is wrong?"

"Watch your tongue, miss, don't tell me how to run my mine."

"Well, somebody should. If you kill everybody you won't have a mine at all. My da just wanted to help with things that are wrong and now he has gone." Her lips began to tremble and she tightened them fiercely hoping not to break down in front of this awful man.

The murmuring of the watching crowd grew louder as they

watched the youngster hold her own against the mine-owner. "She's right, you know, mine's a bloody deathtrap!" cried a voice from amidst the throng.

Ignoring the cries of hatred, still concentrating on the child before him, something about her looks made Ambrose recall Lavinia even more strongly. It was in the way she held her head when she tried to defy him, in the straight line of her lips when she fought to get her own way. For a moment he mourned her loss then, as usual, shrugged the thought away. Yet it still persisted. It was the way Linda stood so proudly with her head held high on her slender neck just as his wife used to stand when she faced him in battle. Those times grew less frequent towards the end of her pregnancy almost as if the fight had gone out of her. With the objective foremost in his mind of begetting an heir and wholly conscious of the social gap between Lavinia and himself, he had solely concentrated on the former goal rather than making an attempt to love her, or at least to be a companion. If only he could have had a child of his own like this, dainty and beautiful, even in her poor dust-smeared garment. But she's not a son, his brain told him. Ah, but she'd have been mine, said his heart, admiring the way she had stood up to him. Then his brain leapt at the thought of another idea. With hardly enough time to think it through he did not hesitate.

"You have a right smart tongue in your head, young miss. I'll give you that. But you don't know it all. However, I've a mind to help. You've nowhere to go? Well, I'll take ee."

Stunned, the crowd stared at the hated mine-owner and a low murmuring filled the air. They knew he hadn't a charitable bone in his body so why was he offering? What was in it for him? There had to be some gain. Equally, there was no doubt, she would pay dearly for her bed and board. Likely he would gain a servant for free.

"Well! Speak up. Anybody else offering? No. I thought not. None of ye would give a brass farthing to help one of yer own. Well, my house is a sight better than an orphanage. She'll get good food and a roof over her head. When she's old enough to work she'll have a job waiting for her, I'll see to that."

"So she'll pay yer contributions back? Be a bloody slave, more like!" A low but clearly heard murmur came from the back of the crowd.

Ambrose's stare raked the crowd to see who was daring to heckle him but all he saw were faces full of animosity. "Get back to yer own affairs and leave me to mine," he growled, then with a quick nod of his head he beckoned Annie over to him and spoke his orders quietly. At once she went over to Becky and Linda and the three of them soon left the village and disappeared up the hill.

CHAPTER SEVENTEEN

Lindy Barton held tight to Betsy Polwen's hand as the plump, good-natured cook drew her into the large, warm kitchen below stairs at Tregender Hall. "Well now, lovey, let's find you somethin' to eat. That wind plays havoc with yer insides if'n they're empty."

"Now don't you go feeding' her up till she's a ball o' lard, Mrs Polwen." The acid tones of Annie Gorland startled the eight-year-old child and she shrank towards the shelter of Betsy's apron, hiding her head in fear.

"And don't you go frightening the little mite fore she scarce takes a step into my kitchen; she's my niece and I'll thank you not to forget."

"She wouldn't be here if I hadn't put in a good word, just remember that, Polwen."

"Go on with you, t'were master as says she was to come to the Hall; his conscience was stricken after all those happenings at the mine."

"Well, I suggested it, see, and in front of all them witnesses, he dassn't back down - leastwise not easily." Annie Gorland remarked complacently. "I'm not afeared of him and I'll speak out if I've a mind to."

"Huh! Have you ever known him do anything he didn't want to? He'd have backed down if he'd wanted."

The two women glared at one another as they began the opening lines to one of their squabbles. The exchange of words had gone on for so long it had become a habit.

"Please may I go home?" The small, quiet voice stopped them in their tracks.

"Not yet a while, lovey, you've come to visit here a piece; now take no heed of Mrs Gorland, she bain't mean no harm, she's just at that time o' life." Her eyes dared Annie to say another word and the housekeeper subsided with a loud humph for a brief moment.

"You reckon she's going to be all right on that truckle bed in your room?" Annie spoke to Betsy in a low voice as she watched Lindy tucking into some thickly buttered bread with a spreading of jam. "My room is much bigger," she added. "A truckle bed will fit in more easily than in that garret."

"Yes, she'll be right dandy, she's only a spit of a child and she won't take up any more room than a flea," Betsy responded quickly in case the arrangements were altered.

"Humph, kinda of dainty to be a Barton child, I notice."

"Now, don't you speak ill o' the dead, Mrs Gorland. My sister was always a bit frail, 'sides the child ain't done growing yet. She might get to look like Jethro a bit later on, though 'tis true she doesn't take after him now. Anyway's no good speaking o' them two, 'twill only upset her, and we'd best keep our tongues quiet for now."

Mrs Polwen looked down at the bent fair head of the child and said gently, "Drink yer milk, darlin' child, and I'll tuck you up nice and warm in two shakes in my room." Then shook her head as she saw two large tears slowly slide down from eyes that were wet pools of deepest green. "No call to cry, lovey, we're going to take good care o' you. Now look at that; see what Mrs Gorland's made you."

Lindy gazed at the rag doll Annie had produced from behind her back and with awed delight in her face gently touched the strands of yellow wool which were gathered in two thick bunches on each side of the head. The daintily stitched dress was made out of a scrap of dimity. Annie had been working on it for some weeks as a change from her normal needlework. She hadn't given a thought to what she would do with it but with Linda's arrival the problem was taken care of. It had only needed a stitch to complete.

"It's a girl dolly," Lindy pronounced gravely.

"Yes, so it is," agreed Annie, just as gravely.

"She's lovely. Is she mine?"

"Yes, if you want her, she's yours."

"I shall call her Victoria."

"After the Queen?"

"Of course not. I just like the name; anyway she doesn't look like the Queen, I've heard she's old. Maybe I'll call her Vicky. She looks like Vicky Penn at school."

"Is she your friend?"

"Well sort of. Anyway she has pigtails like my doll." She went to sit in a nearby chair by the fire where she inspected her gift with pleasure. Betsy and Annie smiled at each other. At least the doll had helped to ease some of the grief in Lindy's heart now she was an orphan. Between the pair of them they would try to keep her from mourning her loss too much.

*　*　*　*　*

Linda soon settled into the life at Tregender Hall. Normally happy and cheerful, she became more so as the weeks, months then years passed and she wove herself into the hearts of the residents of Tregender from Ambrose down to the gardener's boy. She was like a ray of sunshine in a house that had never heard much laughter in a very long time and those around her basked in the effervescence of friendliness and warmth. Even Albert Sithney, grumpy as he was, fell under the spell of her charm. Betsy Polwen no longer went to beg vegetables from him, she always sent Linda with her orders.

"He always gives you the biggest and the best, Lindy; I get the scrawniest to cook with. Don't know why he favours you but he surely does, my darlin'. Still, I ain't a worrying as long as we eat well and old grumps up there don't complain. Now, how about you do somethin' really nice for Annie? She'm ain't lookin' so good these days. Her legs are hurting' something awful again, I suppose. It's all them stairs, that's what it is." Linda would then do her best to get round the aging housekeeper and make her smile.

Every available moment she was off to the Reverend Whitmore for more lessons and out with Richard whenever possible. So the time passed happily for Linda and though she still thought of Jethro with great longing and sadness, her youth and vitality put her grief to rest allowing her to grow into a beautiful and intelligent young woman.

CHAPTER EIGHTEEN

The years passed and Linda grew used to the orderliness and discipline of domestic routine. She acquired the wisdom of running a house from Annie; how to cook and preserve food from Betsy; and how to make cream and cheeses from the dairy staff that came each day to work in the surrounding outhouses. She attended the local school and even had time to see Richard now and again. She was twelve and in the top class at school when she came home one afternoon and sat exhaustedly down on a chair in the kitchen without taking off her coat, allowing her satchel to slip anyhow to the floor.

Betsy turned away from the hot stove where she had been seeing to the boiling of a meat pudding for Trevarron's evening meal and stared at the girl. Her attention was drawn from the next task of cutting up greens to go with the second pudding, which lay in the warming oven for the staff meal. It would be served when Annie came back from the village after interviewing a new young maid for upstairs duties. The maids seldom lasted long but there was always a ready supply from the miner's daughters. The domestics always ate before the master as he was often inclined to be working late, and they had learned to look after their own interests first. "What's up, lass?" asked Betsy as she noticed Linda's face oddly stained scarlet with a peculiar, greyish white edging around her mouth. "You'm sickening' fer somethin'?"

"I've got a headache and I feel sickish." Then, before Betsy could react at her words and leap for a basin, Linda vomited on the floor.

"Great heavens, child! Why didn't ee head for the lav?

What's made ee so sick then, my darlin'?" Betsy held a basin under Linda's lolling head as she continued to violently throw up. Linda did not answer and, as she placed her hand on her forehead, Betsy was taken aback at the heat emanating from the feverish face and immediately she announced, "Come, my sweet, 'tis your bed for ee just as soon as ye can make the stairs. We'll have thee tucked up in trice. I'll give ee some of my special to settle yer stomach." She waited for Linda to protest; for her 'special' was quite the nastiest medicine there was, despite its efficacy to restore one back to good health. Betsy was at once alarmed when Linda did not object. The girl seemed oblivious of her surroundings and when she eventually got her to bed it was plain to see she was in a high fever and not aware of the cook or where she was.

"What did ye spill, Betsy?" said Annie when she returned to find Betsy mopping the floor.

"Lindy was sick the minute she came home from school. I dassn't like the look o' her at all. And what with all the sickness that's bin raging' in the village, I shouldn't be surprised if'n she's caught a fever from one o' them kids at school."

"I'll go up and see her," offered Annie immediately. "Ye'll have yer hands full down here getting his dinner, and I'm right peckish myself. I've been looking forward to my dinner all the way home. Anything I can take up for her?"

"Another bucket most like, and give her a drop o' water if ye can get it down. She'm burning up, she is. An' thanks, Annie, my 'andsome, I appreciate ye offering to climb all them stairs." She smiled gratefully at the housekeeper who nodded in return.

Annie was dismayed at the news for she had also taken time to visit a friend and been regaled over tea by the village gossip. There had been an outbreak of scarlet fever among the miners and several children and adults had already died from the disease. It had been brought in by an itinerant Wesleyan preacher who, succumbing to the illness himself, managed to infect quite a few people before he died. Coming upon the village as it did after a long and particularly bitter winter when people's health was at low ebb, the disease had scythed its way through the inhabitants with great intensity. The illness caused a mortality that they had not suffered in years. When Annie laid eyes on Linda she knew, without a doubt, what was wrong with the little girl. Linda had scarlet fever.

The meal that night was uncontrolled and haphazard for Ambrose; as first one then another of his staff went running upstairs to see to Linda. "What the devil's the matter with the chit, causing this fuss. I'd never have taken her in if I'd known she'd have all of ye in such a taking. What does Lusty say?" he growled at Annie.

"We ain't called him yet," she stammered in surprise knowing how Trevarron hated to pay for medical help. "T'ain't the measles or mumps, for she's had those. This is far worse. We can't get her fever down whatever we do; we've tried everything an' that's a fact. She's fair sick, Master, and I'm feared she is…" She paused, unable to say more.

Ambrose gazed at Annie Gorland with some surprise. He had known her for a long time, since her early widowhood and knew she could not generally abide children; perhaps feeling cheated, as she'd never had any herself. He had also, if the truth were known, taken a liking to the pretty child and often noticed her playing around the grounds of the manor. Betsy had, at first, kept Linda near by her then, as Ambrose made no comment, she had allowed her to play outside in the gardens.

"Get Lusty here at once, tell Sithney to send his eldest lad. He's a good fast runner, he'll find the doctor if he's in the village." Ambrose spoke abruptly. "Well, get a move on. What's the matter with you, Annie, do you want him or not? I could wring that bloody preacher's neck if he weren't already dead, the havoc he's caused amongst my men. Two of my best men dead and half the others aren't fit to scrape a bucketful of ore to save their lives. Nor will be for some days, I warrant you."

"Well, yes, but I thought…"

"Oh, get on with it, woman, I see well I'll have no order in this house until she's doctored." He ranted on at length then retired to his study when he noticed he was talking to an empty room. For Annie, shaking off her amazement, recovered quickly and went speeding away to get the gardener's boy to fetch Doctor Lusty. Heavens above, she had never known the old skinflint bestir himself for anyone else. Then the thought passed through her mind he might have had his own child to worry about if he had given a care to his wife. Did he sometimes have regrets, she pondered? If so it was no more than he deserved.

Trevarron had tried courting again, a young widow this time but the affair had come to naught and then he seemed to lose interest in remarrying, instead, devoting all his interests to the mine. There, he had enough worries to keep him solely occupied for things were continually going wrong and the miners were growing more and more restive with the delay in acquiring new machinery or making good enough repairs to keep the accidents at bay. Ambrose was a troubled man, for his London agent had recently died and the substitute was losing good orders. The mine-owner was in a quandary wondering whether he should change firms or stay with the firm he had always used, trusting they would improve. If that was not enough, there was the added burden of uncontrollable sickness in the mining village as well.

Two of his best workers had succumbed to the epidemic, while the rest muttered about "a plague being visited on the village for past sins". He had put a stop to that rumour by hounding out the scruffy parson who was preaching Methodism in the area. To cap it all, his own health was beginning to worry him. Not that he had caught the sweating sickness, for he was a fastidious man and kept himself clean, seldom mixing directly with his men but dealing through his mine manager with all the day to day problems. Pains in his chest seem to indicate only one thing: his heart was in trouble. He felt the cold threat of death go through him at the thought his heart might be weakening. At the same time, he felt it was beneath him to go crawling to Lusty, a man he had continually criticised. Time enough if things got desperate.

CHAPTER NINETEEN

"Well, well! What have we here?" began James Lusty in his celebrated bedside manner as he crouched beside the small bed wherein lay Linda. His hearty words fell on deaf ears and, as he took in the glazed brightness of her eyes, he realised that her high fever would make her oblivious of anyone in the small room where both she and the cook slept of a night. He pulled a stool over to sit alongside her, his heart still thumping from the long climb to the top of the house, where each of the servants had their attic rooms. Small and airless, they were either boiling hot in the summer or cold as charity in the winter but, nonetheless, it was their domain where they could sleep and gather strength to face another day of toil.

Lusty watched Lindy's fingers plucking at the sheet and the continual twisting of her slight body as the fever raged within her. Taking hold of one of her hands he felt the pulse racing frantically and had no need to count its clinical beat to determine she was a very sick child indeed for he had just left a family who had lost three children to the same fever. Desperately tired, having waged war against the illness for days, his spirits sank to a new low as he studied her face, noting the red glazed eyes and restless movements as she tossed back and forth upon her bed. He had always kept a watchful eye on the child since Ambrose took her in and over the years he was pleased to see how well she was treated.

"Take off her nightdress so I can see what the rash is like, Betsy, then get a basin of cool water and we'll sponge her down to reduce her fever." He pursed his lips and shook his head in dismay as Betsy did so. "She's scarlet all right, though some do say it is a good thing. It means the fever is coming out. If there's heat and no bright rash then well...it's when the rash stays inside that it is more dangerous." He paused as he put the stethoscope to her chest where he listened intently. Then he felt behind her neck and ears before examining her flesh in the faint light of the candle. Then he gave a start and peering down at Lindy's ribs said curiously, "Hold the candle closer, Betsy, what's this?"

"What you got there, is the rash bad?"

"No! I mean this." He pointed to a sickle-shaped mark under her left breast.

"Oh, she always had that. Birthmark, ain't it? I dunno how she came by it but the rest of her skin is clear with no blemish, she's only had the measles and the chicken pox. Weren't nearly so poorly with them neither. I hate to think what she's got now."

Lusty tried to recall when he had seen something similar before but at that moment he was too fatigued to remember. Helping Lindy to live was much more important. "It's the scarlet fever all right. We can only do our best and pray she will live through this night. Someone must be with her all the time, Betsy, if we're to save her. Can ye cope with that? Only it's a long trek up these stairs if ye have to fetch things. Is there a place downstairs where she can be shifted? It would make sense if she were near the kitchen. Save your legs. She'll have to be sponged down every hour to lessen the heat."

"I dassn't know if the Master would agree, thee knows whet ee's like." Betsy made a face.

"Perhaps thee could ask him? He'd not turn ee down if it might save her."

"I'll go and see him now. Likely though, he'll turn me down as well." Lusty grimaced ruefully, thinking of the past skirmishes he had endured with Ambrose. "I'm sure he hasn't taken notice of anyone since he was in short skirts. But there will come a day, oh yes, there'll come a day when he'll have to take notice."

"What do ye mean, Doctor Lusty? Do you know something we don't know?"

Lusty was about to answer when he recalled where he was and with a groan he rose to his feet and patted Betsy's shoulder. "You know, the trouble with getting old is one talks too much and does too little. Let's get on with making Lindy more comfortable, shall we? Give this draught to her and I'll ask your master to get her moved downstairs. See if she'll take all of it, every bit, 'twill help the fever."

Leaving Betsy to administer the potion Lusty made his way slowly from the attics, his mind, not as one would have expected on the coming argument with Trevarron but on the unusual birthmark on Linda's body. All at once, he remembered the occasion when he had last seen it. Trevarron's wife bore the same mark. He had discovered it when he examined her following her death after giving birth to a dead son. The boy had not inherited it, which was hardly remarkable. However, the weirdness lay in finding a total stranger not only having its like but it also being in the same place.

There was also the occurrence of the birth of a full-term child where a premature baby had been expected, which still puzzled him from time to time. I must have a word with Amy Bunnion, he muttered to himself. She was there at the time, she should know. Maybe I'm just imagining things. He shook his head as his suspicions rose once more to fret him, frowning with annoyance. For the life of him he could not say what was wrong but he would lay odds something was.

To Lusty's surprise Trevarron was most amazingly helpful and the two men spent some time discussing the best place to nurse the sick young girl eventually deciding on the back parlour, near enough to the kitchens but away from normal household traffic. Trevarron at once ordered Sithney, together with the stable boys, to help move some of the furniture. The room ended up with two beds, one for Betsy, who would be on hand at night and the other for Linda who was carried downstairs on a makeshift stretcher.

When all was shipshape and Linda had been suitably dosed and sponged again, Lusty went back to the study to see Trevarron. "We've done the best we can at the moment. It's up to nature to decide which way the disease will go. I'll be back later to see how she fares."

"Have a sherry before you go?"

Trevarron's offer startled the Doctor, so that instead of refusing he said, "Well thank you, Mr Trevarron, I will appreciate a drink to wet my throat. To tell you the truth, I scarce know when I last took food I've been so rushed off my feet with this epidemic. It has spread from the village, more's the pity, and with the wet, cold winter we've had, it's a wonder more people haven't caught it. 'Tis only with the mining group at the moment, living as they do in such crowded conditions. There will be a right outcry if it gets to the upper classes." Trevarron handed him his sherry grunting a brief acknowledgement. There was silence for a moment as the doctor quaffed deeply then he spoke again.

"This is fine sherry, sir, haven't tasted such a good one in years."

"Yes," answered his host carelessly. "It's from a small consignment I've had in the cellar. Nearly done, unfortunately, but that's the way of all good things." He sighed heavily and Lusty, always perceptive, caught the sense behind his words comprehending how lonely the man was. Perhaps, in spite of his great wealth, the doctor understood how greatly disenchanted he was with his life. Lusty thought of the previous family who had owned Tregender Hall. Who would have thought an upstart like this man could ever have taken possession from a family who had been established for so many years, they seemed set to stay for the next hundred or so? If it had not been for the weakest link in the chain, a youth and compulsive gambler unable to cope with losing so taking his own life, Trevarron would never have acquired the estate.

The young heir had not only spent his own life carelessly but had given over the lives of the local miners to a man who cared not a whit for their livelihood, their health or anything of use for the men, only the profits he could extract from their efforts.

James Lusty sipped his wine gratefully, though a tiny seed of jealousy induced a brief regret to cross his mind. How pleasant it would be to have money, to regularly enjoy sherry of this quality. Generally he dined very well, often on produce left by grateful patients in lieu of medical fees but most of them could not afford, or even if they could would never have dreamt of giving him, prime Malmsey. Casting the envy out of his mind he fixed attention on Ambrose Trevarron's next surprising words.

"You must give all your attention to Linda from now on, she mustn't lack for a thing. Betsy will break her heart if she dies, not to mention Mrs Gorland. She will get better, I trust, only…"

Lusty swallowed his surprise at the anxiety he could detect in Trevarron's voice and, seizing a rare moment of weakness, interrupted him hastily, "Undoubtedly if I've anything to do with it she'll recover in time; but if you're also worried about the deaths amongst the miners, well I have to say good food and decent housing play an enormous part in people surviving serious ailments. She'll not have lacked anything here, I presume?"

"Certainly not! I'll have you know my domestics can't grumble at how they're fed. Not that I tolerate waste. Oh no, them that waste better not show their faces in this house but we're all healthy, leastways up till now, that is." He rubbed his arm absentmindedly and Lusty noticed the faint sheen of perspiration on Trevarron's forehead.

Finishing his sherry the Doctor rose to his feet. "I'll just have a listen to your chest while I'm here; this damned fever is no respecter of persons. It's a devilishly quick striker when it's rampaging and to tell the truth I have never known it so bad."

"There's nothing wrong with me!" grumbled Ambrose with a disdainful shrug but he submitted to Lusty's probing examination without another protest.

"And how long have you been having heart pains?" Lusty said with a questioning frown as Ambrose buttoned his shirt.

Ambrose glared at him as though it was his fault. "Long enough, I suppose."

"Why didn't you tell me?"

"So you could fret and fuss around me. I don't need a keeper to mind my business."

"But you do need help. At least I can make things more comfortable for you."

"I don't want your pills and potions; they won't give me a new heart."

"No, maybe not, but I'll try and make the old one last a bit longer!" retorted Lusty, feeling irritated once again with the cantankerous mine-owner. If the man collapsed with a heart attack, he supposed he would lay the blame on him. That is, if he was still in a position to voice any complaint. Likely the condition would take him off.

"Are you telling me this one's not going to last long? How long? Come, man, I'm not a child that you should go tiptoeing around a straight answer."

"Neither am I God! He will be the one to decide. However, a little care in the meantime would not come amiss. Put your responsibilities to one side for a while and give your body a rest. Try not to lose your temper. Make sure you get plenty of sleep and let nature do its work. I'll make up a mixture which will steady things down and help to relieve the congestion. After that, sir, it is the Almighty who will govern the time and place when your heart gives up."

"I'll consider your advice. Meanwhile let's hope Lindy gets over this, I'd not like to lose her over a fever. Mind me well and keep sharp watch on her, Lusty."

"As I do on all I doctor around here. This fever is virulent. It's already taken the lives of some and there's no knowing how many more will catch it. Annie and Betsy have full instructions on how to keep themselves clean and you'd best be careful too. I'll do my best as always, Mr Trevarron, but as I say, it's the Lord who makes the decisions. Good day, sir, I'll be along first thing in the morning to see Linda. Betsy and Annie know what to do meanwhile." Without another word Lusty left the room.

Ambrose sat on for a long while gazing into the glowing heart of the fire, extraordinary images twisting within his head like the flickering flames. Some time later he retired to his study, where, after repeated attempts to compose appropriate words, he at last finished a letter to his solicitor which would be dispatched the next day with speed. He had never been a man to prevaricate with the truth; now his mind was made up he wanted to get on with his plan immediately. He would have preferred to go to London himself but did not feel up to the journey. Let the lawyer come to him, for which he was paid. Not that he had much time for the devious man anyway who, he had heard, was now living in the late Duchess of Forres' house in Belgravia. He would have to ask him how he had managed that little feat once his own affairs were settled and he could breathe more easily which, he hoped, would happen when the pressure was taken off him regarding the troublesome mine.

He went to bed feeling more light-hearted than in a long time. Lusty was likely exaggerating his fears about his heart. He might be mistaken. Then a familiar ache gripped his chest as he climbed into bed and he knew he would never shake off the malaise this side of the grave. He lay awake thinking of the past and the evil things he had done in an attempt to better himself, to raise himself from the dire poverty into which he had been born. He thought of Zelda, his first wife, then Lavinia and the awful thing she had birthed. Then he thought of Linda and felt an urge to pray to a god he did not believe in: Don't let her die! Please, don't let her die!

CHAPTER TWENTY

SCOTLAND

"Merrick! How wonderful to see you, son. Why didn't you tell me you were coming home?" Morag Macgregor, Duchess of Forres, threw her arms about her son in joy at his sudden appearance. "Och, lad, you are as thin as a whippet, I'll have Deirdre get some food right away. I canna have you starving the now."

"I've eaten well enough, Mam, though not as well as on your good wholesome fare." Merrick joked diplomatically so as not to hurt her feelings. "I'll wait dinner and have it with you at the usual time. For now I've a hankering for a glass of ale to quench my thirst, I've been riding for days it seems ever since we docked at Aberdeen. Where's Father?"

"Oh, he's in the Library. Probably asleep, I shouldn't wonder, he has just returned himself this forenoon; tired of course, with all the travelling. He had to go to London in the end to buy back the final piece of land that Giles sold off. Now the Estate is complete once more and he can rest easy. Oh, Merrick, you and your father have worked miracles these last eight years putting everything to rights."

"Yes, he mentioned in his latest letter he was on the point of concluding the purchase. It's taken the profits from this trip but well worth it to have you both so happy. Perhaps you can get him to take things easy now his ambition is fulfilled?"

They shared a knowing smile as she answered, "You know your father well enough now, if it's not one ambition it will be another. He will never stop striving for perfection."

"Still, it's not as if you need the money, we have more than we know what to do with; that's why I'm home for a while, I've decided to leave merchandising to those that need to go to sea and I propose to oversee everything from the shore. I'm tired of travelling; I want to settle down and..."

"Marry?" his mother interrupted him quickly.

He smiled. "Well, not yet, but sometime maybe. When I get round to it."

"Have you someone in mind?"

"No! So none of your schemes, my dear mama, I'll tell you when I am ready!"

"I'm glad you are not going back to sea, Merry." Her use of the name he had been called as a child stopped him short and he read the concern in her eyes which she always tried to hide from him. "I used to worry about you, especially when it got stormy, never knowing if you would be coming home." There was a sudden flash of tears then she cleared her throat abruptly and turned to leave. "Dear me, I must have a cold coming on; I'll away and order a tasty dinner."

He watched as she bustled off, sensing the deep dread she had endured every time he had gone back to sea. It had been a necessary evil for all of them these last years ever since his father had inherited the Dukedom. The Estate, after Giles had mortgaged every last acre, was in a sorry state. It had only been because of a small trust from William, the old Duke, which Giles had not been able to get his hands on, that enabled Merrick, at eighteen, first to buy a ship and its cargo, then to make a profit. From this early success he went on buying and selling until he had made a fortune for his family.

The wings of dark hair at his forehead were of a sudden tipped with grey these days and his mother noticed the lines of strain round his mouth, the new firmness that replaced the sweetness of his smile in younger times. He carried his considerable height with dignity, secure in the belief he had earned his place in the world by his own endeavours, for fate had not handed his riches to him on a plate. In spite of his sober mien, the curl of his lips showed he had not lost the humorous twist to his nature, which had endeared him to all who had been a part of his life until now. What the future would bring, thought Morag, was unknown but she hoped he would be happy in his new ventures and bring a bride home that she could love and accept into their tight-knit circle and who would love them in return.

Merrick, reflecting, thought only that he had earned a rest after the long struggle. He was going to take full advantage of the brief holiday before turning his attention to another lucrative pastime. At least he would find time to continue his love affair in London. Mistress Angelina would be pleased to see him again. This time he would not be rushing away to sea.

CHAPTER TWENTY-ONE

Later that evening, after they had dined and the two men were sitting at ease in the Library having a brandy before retiring, his father raised the subject. Leaning forward to tap his pipe on the hearth he said, "I heard some news from the solicitor who negotiated with the Duchess when I took over the Estate. He invited me to meet him when I went down to London. Obsequious fellow," he added distastefully. "Not someone I would ordinarily do business with; too full of his own importance to suit my way of thinking."

Merrick eyed his father without commenting, content to let him talk.

"However he had quite an interesting proposition to make. See what you make of it," Andrew continued. Merrick's interest sharpened.

"It appears he knows a Cornish mine-owner who has need of a partner. He is ailing, I was given to understand. Has no kin to pass the mining operation onto and needs someone to oversee the business until it is either sold or taken over by the partner. What do you think? Only you said you were tired of the sea."

"But not fool enough to go chasing down a mine," Merrick protested.

"I scarcely think you would need to do that; however it is up to you. Walcott's opinion of the profit is quite interesting. Of course one would have to go into the matter carefully. James Walcott had charge of the old Duchess's affairs, as you know. She's gone now; died some time ago I was given to understand, though I sometimes wonder what happened to my young cousin in the end. Lavinia Macgregor, you know? Probably she ended up happy with her lot but I sometimes question if I did the right thing. I never heard a word from either of them after I refused them help that time the Duchess called." He gazed into the fire for a moment musing on past memories. "I was so incensed with Giles mishandling the Estate I was ready to blame anyone connected with him. Forres had been Sophie's home all her life and, in the end, she got tipped out of it with no means of redress or help from me."

"Sophie? Oh, you mean the Duchess who was married to William?"

"Yes, she is the beauty in that huge oil that we have in the Great Hall. I was tempted to take it down and have your mother sit for her portrait but, truth to tell, the wall behind it needs replastering and I've never got around to doing half the renovating this place needs. Besides, I've got used to her being there; I believe I would miss her. In any case your mama is not interested in being painted, she says she's more to do with her life than sitting idle for the time it would take. It wasn't worth arguing over. So, to continue, she's your great-aunt, wife of William, who was son of Murdoch, our ancestor. Murdoch became Duke, instead of Chief, as a Scottish heir was once called before the English began their rule over Scotland. He was a demanding man by all accounts, far more intent on making the Forres Estate the finest in Scotland than caring for his people. He was respected but not liked and when he died there were few to mourn. Despite his ambitious aims for Forres I learned a lesson from his history."

"I'm glad you did, Papa, you've made a better Duke than any of our ancestors; all the people on the Estate worship the ground you walk on," Merrick said proudly, glad to pay his father a well-deserved compliment.

"Tch, son, you exaggerate my worth; I only treat others how I wish to be treated myself. Civility doesn't cost anything but it is amply rewarded. If, however, one makes an enemy and one has right on one's side, then one goes in hard and fast without delay to bring respect from those that procrastinate."

"I'll remember that little gem for I've always wondered when it was right to lose one's temper, especially when I've launched forth without thinking."

"The answer to that is never, merely pretend; then you will never lose the battle."

"But we are descended from a line of fighting and feuding Scots. 'Tis no wonder I've a hasty temper, now I know where it comes from." Merrick grinned widely at his father who laughed in wry amusement at this sally.

"I can bear witness to that, my lad. When you were at odds with me as a boy, you always made a most dangerous opponent. I didn't care to take you on too often."

"Then 'tis well I'm now full grown and can understand your teachings but, please, go on with the history lesson, Papa. For the first time in ages I've time to hark back to the past instead of fighting for the future. How did you learn so much about our forebears?"

"From old books in the castle and also talking to people. It's surprising how much the servants remember. Tales are passed from father to son down the ages. Anyway, where was I? Ah yes, I believe William and Sophie lived quite happily for some time until the flood; then the heart seemed to go out of William and he became morose and finally just wasted away. I think Sophie also gave up in the end, primarily after a difficult time coping with Giles who, it would seem, inherited all of William's slothfulness to the point of idiocy. Things must have got out of hand when Giles married a woman called Lily Fairburn, whom nobody knew. My father lost touch completely after that and we got on with our own lives. As you are aware your grandfather, Angus, was never much blessed with capital so we have always had to work hard for our living, sometimes eking an existence."

"But we've managed tolerably well, haven't we, Papa?"

"Yes, we have indeed. This is why I've kept silent on our family history, other than those details which involved us personally, especially as I blamed Duke William for being so feckless. Many others recovered from the flooding of 1829, why not him? At any rate he died as he lived, quite useless to the end. You see, William had a tendency to fritter away what he had inherited from his father, Murdoch, who made the Estate what it was: one of the finest, most profitable places in Scotland. Luckily for us, William had an older sister called Marion, daughter of Maeve; she married an Alastair Macgregor and they had a son called Angus; yes, he was your grandfather, hence our eligibility to inherit Forres.

"Marion was a very strong person like her father, but knew her brother to be quite the opposite. Having decided he ought to get married she even found a wife for him who also happened to be a strong woman. Whether she chose correctly I have reservations for Sophie was ambitious and greedy, quite unlike William."

"You mentioned a young cousin of yours?"

"Yes, Lavinia, I met her once when I went to London to let Sophie know how ill your grandfather was. I could have written to her, I suppose, but having heard of a London doctor who might be of help with his illness I knew I would have to approach Sophie personally to ask if she would help with the fees. Lavinia was there when I called on the Duchess. She was sweet and as well-mannered as one would expect from a gently reared child. Sophie was not. Quite the opposite in fact and, as you know, Grandfather died. I suppose I always blamed her for that though, in hindsight, I found out she didn't have the money anyway. Still, she could have told me the truth and been more gracious, it might have made things a little more bearable."

"Where is Lavinia now?"

"You know I meant to ask that question of Walcott but it went out of my head."

Merrick smiled fondly at his father before saying, "You did, after all, have other things on your mind, Papa; you must be feeling extremely pleased at how things went in our favour."

"That I am, Merrick, though I'm positive it could only be divine intervention that caused Grainger's downfall; that and cards. I never imagined I'd be so thankful for his compulsive gambling, for it enabled me to make an offer to get him out of trouble with the law as well as to pay back his cronies. Even so, despite his problems, he still struck a considerably high bargain. There was one point when I asked myself if I was mad for I found it hard to haggle with the man. Nevertheless I held to my objective giving as little ground as I could. But gradually my nerves began to collapse and I am certain I must have given away my eagerness to get the land."

"No matter." Merrick laughingly said, "My last cargo topped all expectations and we can meet the payment without default. The task is over and done with. What do you intend to do with the land now you've got it?"

"Well, I shall be draining some of the lower areas once I can get access to them for I've arranged for Redding to take on extra staff to clear the way through the fields. Then once we've that done we can control the water meadows and use some of them for barley during the dry season." The absorbing discussion of the Estate and all its affairs went on till the hour grew late; it was only when the last log suddenly crumbled in the grate that the two weary men yawned and decided to call it a night. Merrick, already at the door having bid his father goodnight, suddenly turned back.

"You didn't finish what you started to say. Do you wish me to go to Cornwall? It is not a path I would normally choose but I sense you have a feeling it could be worthwhile."

"Only if you want to, son. I don't aim to come between you and your plans for I've no notion of the outcome; it might be an interesting trip or it might be a failure; still, no harm done to find out. Why don't you see Walcott when you return to England? Perhaps you may glean more than me."

"I doubt it; you're a sly old dog when it comes to reading between the lines. I'll see how I feel when I am South and whether it fits in with my plans. In the meantime," he yawned,

"I'm for bed or I'll never rise tomorrow and Mama will be nagging us both." They parted company secure in the deep affection and respect they held for each other.

Merrick felt no urgency to join with his father in remorse over the fate of the former residents. He had not been a party to turning them out for he had only been a young boy at the time. Even if he had been responsible, the grinding hard work of his youth in an effort to reverse the evil scheming of Giles, would have weighed heavily on the side of his father. Before he went to sleep he reviewed the matter again. In spite of telling his mother there was enough money without needing any more, he knew this was not true. One had to be continually on one's guard protecting what one had and the only way to do this was to make the money work to replenish what was spent. Going to Cornwall, which, if he was honest, was the last thing on his mind, might conceivably be most profitable. He thought fleetingly of Angelina then turned his concentration to recalling his father's words, after he had told him he was leaving the sea.

"I believe we should diversify as much as possible now we are well-established. Spread our profits into different areas; mining is only one of them; machinery, transport, textiles, there's no end to the scope. Not that it will be me doing these things - it will be up to you if you wish to progress, to gain knowledge in the wheeling and dealing of industry..." Andrew smiled when his son interrupted.

"I know all about wheeling and dealing, Papa -"

"Yes, you do, Merry, I'm sorry; I forget you are not the child that once backed me with every penny you owned. Which you could have kept for yourself - the bequest was, after all, yours to do with as you willed. Instead you made sure your mother and I were safeguarded that we'd never want again. I have much to thank you for." Tears shone in Andrew's eyes.

"You know I could never have done otherwise - now forget the past, Papa, we have to consider here and now. You didn't answer my question. Do you mind that I wish to leave the sea and let a manager take over?"

"You don't have to ask me that, Merrick; you are man enough to make up your own mind. I am content to back you in anything you wish, oh, perhaps give a little advice now and then but my day for striving is over, for you must take up the reins and see for yourself what the future will bring."

"I'd still like to think you were by my side."

"So would I, Merry, so would I. Never fear, I will be there as long as you need me or as long as the good Lord lets me. Have faith in yourself, son, and take a lass to your heart like your mother, bless her, then you'll never go wrong."

Merrick frowned, Angelina Vallone was the exact opposite of his mother; how would they get on? Then as he drifted off to sleep he wondered whether Angelina would react adversely if he asked her to come to Scotland and marry him. He knew she loved him, but did she love him enough to leave her social round and make her life with him, have a family? The answer to that particular question would have to wait on his next visit to London and the rosy red lips that were waiting for him.

CHAPTER TWENTY-TWO

"Yes, these figures seem to show a reasonable profit, but it looks as though they've been steadily decreasing over this last year or two. Is the mine running bare?"

"My dear sir, it will never do that!" James Walcott interrupted quickly, comfortably at ease behind an elegant mahogany desk in the finely decorated Library in Sophie's old house. The restocking of the Library with finely tooled books had waited on his finances recovering from the refurbishing of the whole of the house. He had acquired the property in lieu of an alleged bad debt; supposedly fees due to him for services rendered to the late Duchess over many years. For an exchange of illicit cash, this had been easy to arrange by the commissioner who wound up what was left of her estate. Even so, his resources were stretched to the limit for a time with unexpected repairs. Now he gratefully inhaled the aroma of leather-bound books, which graced the hitherto empty shelves and blessed the profitable litigation that had quite recently come his way. Yet another sizable fee would be gratefully accepted for introducing Viscount Macgregor to the dour and ailing Ambrose Trevarron if he could possibly contrive it and would pay for other treasures he had his eye on.

"The pitmen always find another lode to explore, you may count on it. Cornwall is riddled with tin, copper, china clay and many other minerals as well. Better than a gold mine, wouldn't you say? For at least one does not have to deal with foreigners."

"Hardly, though I suppose it depends what one is looking for," allowed Merrick who felt, as his father did, that here was a man who would bear watching and very carefully at that. "On a different subject, my father required me to ask what happened to his cousin Lavinia. He forgot to mention her when he was last with you. I recollect my great-aunt Sophie is dead, or you would not be in this house, of course." Merrick paused, fascinated by the sudden pallor then the blush of red that came over the urbane solicitor's face.

Walcott's breath totally failed him for a moment then he inhaled only to end up in a paroxysm of coughing. It was a moment or two before he recovered his composure. "Ah you must excuse me...I – er – I suffer from gas – er – from digestive problems – the lunch, you know?"

"No, I don't know or care about your digestive problems. You were saying – about Lavinia?" Merrick responded sharply, his suspicions swiftly rising concerning James Walcott and wondering what skeleton was lingering in the old Duchess's history.

"Ah yes, to be sure, Lavinia. Well, she married, I believe."

"You believe. Don't you know?"

"Well – yes, she did marry."

"To whom?"

Walcott swallowed hard. Suddenly he had a very bad feeling about this questioning and where it was leading. "Ambrose Trevarron," he mumbled, no longer able to stall.

Merrick stared at the man, caught for a moment out of his depth, his mind racing rapidly over the words. "What! You mean this – er – mine-owner who needs a partner?"

Walcott nodded weakly. What on earth could have possessed him to approach the same family, for God's sake; how could he have imagined they would not find out?

"When did they marry?"

"Er – let me see, it must have been about the time your father became the Duke."

"What made her marry a Cornishman? Surely it was an unlikely match? How did they meet? The Duchess, as far as I am aware, had never set foot in Cornwall."

"Her Grace could not afford to bring her granddaughter out in the manner she would have liked to. Unfortunately Lavinia did not have a dowry, so…" Walcott shrugged his shoulders. "We had to make the best of what was available."

"We? Meaning you and Sophie?" A slow burn began deep in Merrick's chest.

A young girl, scarcely on the verge of womanhood palmed off. To what or whom? All of a sudden his family blood rose in a heat. He had been ambivalent about the details of the mining business; he had merely followed his father's suggestion to enquire a little more deeply. Now he knew he would go to Cornwall, if only to trace his father's cousin. Instincts told him there was more to the situation than the solicitor revealed. There was also the matter of Walcott's ownership of Sophie's house. His next step was to enquire into the legal basis behind that. At least the solicitor his father took advice from these days had a good reputation and would ascertain the facts. He had fixed an appointment with him to deal with other matters so Merrick would add this latest enquiry to the rest.

CHAPTER TWENTY-THREE

The household crept on tiptoe with hushed voices while Linda's temperature climbed steadily over the next two days. James Lusty was assiduous in his attention and determination to win the battle. When, after two night-long vigils, in the early morning of the third day he saw sweat beading Linda's forehead, he knew they'd won the first fight and, God willing, they would see her through recuperation. As Linda slowly improved and became mobile Ambrose suggested she should be taken to his summerhouse for a short time each day to enjoy the springtime sunshine and warmth. Taking advantage to rest, as advised by Lusty, he soon found he could conduct a conversation with Linda, which was far more adult than he would have supposed.

"You are looking better, child, than a week ago," he remarked one day to Linda as he relaxed in a nearby chair. "You are losing the pastiness of your illness; no doubt the sun has been good for you."

"Thank you, I am feeling much better. I trust you too are benefitting from having to rest?"

Startled, Ambrose glanced sharply at her from under beetled brows. These were not the words of a commoner. Even her voice was gently modulated to pleasing tones.

"What makes you think I am resting? I can sit in my Orangery if I like without all and his wife thinking I'm ailing."

"That's true but you must know there are no secrets in this house or in the village come to that, so everyone knows that I've been ill and everyone knows that you are taking a rest, though I'm certain they will not know exactly why you are taking a rest."

He caught the question in her voice as she paused to let him expand on his health and chuckled to himself after declining to answer. Instead he continued to study her profile as she bent her head to the book on her lap.

The sun, shining through her golden curls, threw into relief the high-boned cheeks and tip-tilted nose. There was nothing of the Barton family in her face he decided and then he caught his breath as he clearly saw whom she resembled. Lavinia! Suddenly he perceived what he should have known all along - she was as like his wife as it was possible to be. Rising abruptly he made an excuse to Linda. "I have some work I have to see to. I'll see you this evening for dinner. Make sure you rest well this afternoon." He strode swiftly out of the room. Linda took no notice; Ambrose was often brusque, sometimes leaving her without a word. Once outside, Ambrose called for his horse to be saddled and changed into riding gear before setting out for Amy Bunnion's cottage.

For once, she was at home, as there was no imminent birth pending. So, taking advantage of the good weather, she was working in her small front garden. She eyed him warily, then put down her weeding fork to greet him with an offhand politeness, suddenly feeling a cold wave of alarm run through her body.

"I won't mince matters, Mrs Bunnion," Trevarron began abruptly. "I want the truth of the matter. That obscene object I saw that day my wife gave birth - was it my child?"

He knew! Amy shivered with fright. Could she go to prison for what she had done? Well, best get it over with, bad news only got worse from keeping. "No, it wasn't yours."

"Then my wife had a daughter and because of what I said to you, you were feared I would harm her. You gave her to the Bartons to bring up, didn't you?"

Quite mystified at the elation in his voice she nodded. "Thank Christ for that!" Ambrose voiced relief. "I knew it!

I've always known it. One can always recognise one's own child."

Amy opened her mouth to refute his words but he held up his hand to stop her.

"Yes. I know you are concerned this has come out now but don't be. We both made mistakes so the less said the better. As far as I am concerned we shall go on as before."

"What will go on?" Amy cried. "Are you telling her or not?"

"No, I cannot undo the past and suddenly say she is my daughter so I intend to make her my ward. Only you and I will know the truth and I am sure you will not want things to be made public?" Ambrose was quick to interrupt.

Numbly she shook her head. She had tried not to interfere but the fates had decided otherwise. As long as Linda did not suffer because of her silence what harm could it do if she kept quiet over the fact that Linda was not his daughter? He would only wreak his vengeance on the child if he knew his wife had married him while she was carrying another man's child. It was no worse than the lie she had already committed. To suffer an agony of conscience over one more lie was nothing. At least she would not undergo any lawsuit because of her actions and the girl would be cared for, she guessed, a great deal better than she had been before. Amy decided to say no more; Linda was still young. She would tell her the truth when she was older and could understand the complicated circumstances.

That same day Ambrose sent for Betsy Polwen. "Linda is recovering well from her illness, isn't she? I can't believe she was so poorly only a short while ago."

"She is that, Master, I'm grateful for the care she has had, you've been right kind..."

"Yes, well I've decided to take things further. Linda is very intelligent and I do not want to see her waste her life or return to that village school where she can possibly catch goodness knows what dreadful illnesses. I want to send her to a good school, have her taught the niceties of life; in short, Mrs

Polwen, I'd like to make her my ward as she has no direct kin. There are to be no more domestic duties for her. What do you say to that?" Ambrose eyed her in his usual grim manner as he spoke.

"I doan't know what to say, sir, accepting it's real kind of you, sir. I suppose it's up to the lass to agree. Can't imagine she'd turn down an offer like yours."

Linda, when she was asked, agreed that she had been happy at Tregender Hall and was equally happy to go to a good school and learn more.

"Don't imagine it is a gift, child. You will be allowed the chance to pay back my indulgence. When you leave school you will work for me in the mine office. Your teacher tells me your reading and arithmetic are well enough to beat the best in the village and that is as I thought. You continue to do well and I shall be proud of you."

"Am I to stay here?"

"Yes, of course, where else would you go?"

She forbore to answer him directly, for her pride would not let her acknowledge that she would be destitute without his charity, so instead she said, "May I ask a favour?"

"What is it?" Ambrose growled, feeling he had not got the best of the conversation.

"May I read the books in your Library?"

"Hmm, they are not childish books, miss. You will not be able to understand them." Indeed Ambrose rarely took one down himself for most of them were far beyond his own comprehension. He had purchased them as a job lot when the house was rebuilt and he scarcely knew what was on the shelves. Still, if the chit wanted to find out her ignorance it could do no harm. "Read them if you want to but mind you put them back in exactly the same place or I shall forbid you take them down. When you have read something I shall test you on it."

She smiled at him, not in the least put out that he was trying to assess her ability. "Perhaps you would like me to read to you now? I read stories to Aunt Betsy and Mrs Gorland, which they both enjoy. Before I was ill I was engaged in Jane Austen's Pride and Prejudice which is most involved and exciting. I would be most pleased to begin again for you if you like so that you may enjoy your rest."

Now how, thought Ambrose, did she know I was bored with nothing to occupy myself except mining details? "Very well, no doubt it will give you practice, child, but take no heed if I drop off to sleep." But he did not go to sleep. Instead he looked forward each day to further readings and the joy of being with the girl he thought of as his. Moreover, when Linda's voice grew tired, he would take over and read a chapter or two himself. This went on for another month until Doctor Lusty proclaimed both invalids to be much recovered and it was time for Linda to resume her studies and attend the school in Penzance where he had enrolled her.

Ambrose had been pleasantly surprised at Linda's reading ability. It was so good he took great pleasure in finding books she could enjoy. Many times Mrs Polwen came to fetch Linda for her lunch to discover them to be deep in discussion over some volume or other and be told sharply to bring a tray of food so they could carry on undisturbed.

"I don't like it, that I don't," Betsy said one day to Annie. "He's taking 'er out of 'er natural course in life; she isn't never really gonna be more'n a servant an' I don't hold wiv all this h'edication. Course I know she's the brightest one in her class at school. But this new school she's goin' to are sure to find out she ain't proper quality."

"Try telling 'im that, if'n you dare," retorted Annie. "Best leave it, Betsy, he'll get tired soon enough an' when he feels better he'll be back to the mine anywise himself, an' she'll be forgotten." However, Annie was wrong.

All at once, Linda was set on a path of cultured grooming when she was enrolled in the Academy for Young Ladies in Penzance; paid for by Ambrose, who also provided the clothes for this new position. She was taught dancing, music and deportment as well as the three Rs. She also learnt how to defend herself from the jealousies of those girls who deemed themselves above the level of one who had been raised as a mere servant. Even being the ward of a wealthy man counted for little. It was much the same as the envy she'd endured from the miners' children which she had learned to cope with in time.

CHAPTER TWENTY-FOUR

Months passed and the headmistress, who had at first been doubtful about taking Linda, quickly realised how bright and naturally good mannered she was and tried her best to turn a blind eye when Linda was driven to fight back. This caused problems for Linda with a few of the girls, angry that she had a defender. She was very quickly labelled 'teacher's pet' and villified all the more. However she loved to learn and despite problems managed to acquire a great deal of knowledge along the way.

Every year the school put on a play or light opera for the parents and kinfolk of the girls. It was well patronised by local people who enjoyed a night out. The drama that year was 'Erminie', a comic opera in two acts, which was light enough for the uneducated but gave, so decided Geraldine Tench, her girls something to get their teeth into. Quite youthful, considering her senior role, she was a forward-looking headmistress; quite sure she could raise the standards of the girls and give them something to strive for other than marriage. Elder daughter of a colonel in the army, well educated and travelled, she had started her school primarily for officers' children but this had amazingly expanded into the local gentry as her fame spread. The place was in great demand for young ladies and naturally Miss Tench chose the best. At present she was engaged in deciding on the most appropriate for the leading role in the opera and was quite torn between Linda, with the clearest voice and the most comely figure, and Abigail Tresillian, who although word perfect, had bulging blue eyes in a fat face with a figure to match. Nor could she attain the high notes that were required for perfection.

Her mama was a patron of the school which, in spite of its apparent achievements, hovered between breaking even and imminent bankruptcy. Unfortunately Miss Tench, clever though she was, was no match for a bursar who was plotting to make his fortune at her expense.

"Well, Miss Tench, you'll appreciate I've gone to a deal of trouble to find the best material for the gowns and I've also managed to find those who are happy to make up the costumes," said Lady Tresillian. "As it is my daughter's last year with you it is the least I can do. Her younger sister is so looking forward to following in her footsteps one almost feels one plays a large part in seeing that the school continues to survive."

"Oh, I trust it will," said Miss Tench weakly.

"Of late, my husband, concerned with banking duties, of course, has expressed his dismay with the accounts, but we know you'll survive, won't we? We will pull together famously. But you must make sure the main parts of your opera go to those that will best help you. The 'riff-raff'," she emphasised with a shudder, "have no part in this production unless they are servants or just one of the assembly. Thus all will know exactly how they stand, don't you agree? People have to know their place and keep to it."

Miss Tench had no choice but to comply. For Lady Tresillian had made it very clear there was no contest. It was Abigail for the main role or no opera and indeed no school. Sadly and very much against her will Miss Tench knew she had no option but to decide against Linda. Except the day that Linda learned she was relegated to being merely in the chorus was devastating. She came back to Tregender in despair.

"Oh, Aunt Betsy, I know the part, I know every word, every note. Miss Tench said I was really good. Even those that don't like me very much said I was the best one to play the role. Abigail was given the part because her mother's a snob and she's a lady and she hasn't been brought up as a servant…"

"No more'n you 'ave, young lady. But I knew no good 'ad come o' pampering you an' sending' you to a posh school. Blood will out, so it will, the gentry will never let you beat 'em even when you can," Betsy stormed angrily, as much upset as Linda.

"What's all the noise? I can hear you yelling upstairs. Polwen, kindly explain why Linda is crying." Ambrose stood at the top of the stairs leading to the kitchen quarters truculently demanding to know what the devil was up. Betsy obliged, getting more and more vociferous by the moment.

"Hmm! Is that all? Dry your eyes, Linda, and make sure you are word perfect when I come to see the play. I should hate to think my efforts are wasted."

How he managed it Linda never found out. Nor did she know that the bursar was instantly sent packing and, out of the blue, Miss Tench began to look happier. Abigail left the school and her sister went elsewhere but no one minded about that for Abigail was a prig of the worst kind and many in the school had suffered at one time or another with her tongue and vindictive temper. The opera, needless to say, was a great success and Linda, for the first time in her life, tasted fame as the applause echoed loudly throughout the Hall. Ambrose, basking in the many congratulations that came from all sides, began to plan the future.

CHAPTER TWENTY-FIVE

Before he left for Cornwall, Merrick paid another visit to the solicitor to complete his objective. Despite close questioning concerning his previous meeting and the surprising facts of which he had become aware, Merrick found it difficult to make James Walcott reveal all the arrangements that had taken place between Sophie, Lavinia and Ambrose Trevarron. He could not contradict that it was a cooperative agreement and perfectly legal as far as the solicitor was concerned. It had gone exactly as the Duchess required. Why rake over the old coals of events that had happened so long ago? Realising he would get nothing more out of the wily lawyer, Merrick changed the subject to enquire how was it that Walcott was living in Sophie's house.

"As I understand the way of things, though I may be wrong, not being a lawyer, the house was to revert to the Forres Estate on the death of Sophie, Duchess of Forres. So can you tell me what legally happened? For I don't see the house listed amongst our property."

Walcott swallowed hard then stuttered, "It - it - was t-taken in lieu of d-debts."

"Oh? What debts?" Merrick's voice took a harder note. "Were we notified?"

Walcott spread his hands depreciatingly. "Her Grace had little jobs for me to do."

"Yet you told my father that you took no further interest in the late Duchess after he became the Duke. I also spoke to Sophie's former bankers and they too confirm that after a sum of money was paid into her account she lived within her means until she died. There were no debts, were there? It will be easy to prove once I set the law in motion. I believe the result will be a considerable prison sentence pending the charge - for fraud, would you say? Unless, of course, the wrongdoer were to - leave the country - for instance?"

James Walcott knew when he was beaten; there was nothing more to say. He had taken a gamble thinking it was easy to get away with - and lost. With a sadly regretful glance round the room at his treasures and the books he had collected so carefully, he muttered, "When do you want me to go?"

"Why now, of course!" Merrick said it in the savage tone of one who resented being pushed too far and was not going to allow any further delay. In fact he was so angry that if it were left to him he would as soon kill the scoundrel as let him go.

Giving a groan of anguish Walcott rose to his feet. "I'll just pack a few things…"

"You will go now, just as you are, taking nothing."

"But…how will I live? I need some money…my clothes…"

"It does not concern me, any more, I suspect, than it concerned you that Sophie and her granddaughter were given bad advice. I suggest you go lest I change my mind and have you arrested or maybe deal with you in a more violent way, as I've a mind to."

Despite thinking with sorrow of the gold in the safe, Walcott scurried out of the house before his Lordship changed his mind and set about him. He knew he had been wrong but that did not stop him wanting revenge for the way he had been vanquished.

CHAPTER TWENTY-SIX

Linda was turned seventeen the first time Merrick made her acquaintance on his second trip to Cornwall. It was arranged he would stay at Tregender Hall during this visit. There were decisions to discuss and preparations to make following Merrick's first inspection, which included plans for the installation of a new engine tower, engine and hoist, which would facilitate the movement of men and ore to the surface. William was waiting at Penzance station as he arrived. The coach seemed cool and comfortable after the long dirty journey from London.

"Master Trevarron do say I fetch ee to the Hall, zurr, ee won't be long. Called to the mine ee be. Sent 'is 'pologies but the 'ousekeeper'll mak' ee right welcome. An' Cookie, she'm squarely 'andsome wiv' her food, so she is." He prattled on unceasingly, pointing out local views and items of interest as they travelled through the countryside. Merrick, wearied from the tedious train journey, brightened considerably at the prospect of good food and a warm bed. And though it took him a little while to understand the coachman's thick Cornish accent, his ready ear and years of consorting with sailors from all parts of the globe soon picked up the gist of the conversation. That he was in a mining area was unmistakable, judging from the particular style of engine houses dotted around the countryside and tall chimneys, pointing their brick finger to the sky. Close by there was always a huddle of grey granite cottages, which invariably housed the labour force of miners and their families, surrounded by moor and rock outcrops.

Cornwall had once been completely wooded but now whole forests were being quickly denuded for pit props and for the making of charcoal which, combined with saltpetre and sulphur, made gunpowder; a product vital for the defence of the realm.

Merrick was smilingly welcomed at Tregender Hall by Mrs Gorland, for Ambrose seldom had company these days and it made a nice change to have a guest in the house. When Ambrose told her of the expected visitor there had been much bustling, extra cleaning and commotion to make all ready for his comfort. On his arrival she cast a sharply penetrating and inquisitive eye at him as she asked, "Would you care to see your room, sir, or wait in the Library for Mr Trevarron. He is not expected to be long but he will send a message if he is delayed. Perhaps I can get you some refreshment?"

"I'll wait in the Library, thank you, and yes, a glass of sherry will do nicely."

He was standing gazing out of the long windows of the Library at the neatly edged lawn that led past statuary to dense shrubs which protected the area from the prevailing west winds when a girl strolled across the wide terrace. She had been tossing a ball for a terrier, which gambolled at her feet, begging for just one more throw.

"No, Tam, enough, I'm tired. Heel boy, it's time we went indoors."

Merrick heard her clearly through the glass as he studied the attractive girl before him. Who was she? Quite obviously part of the household or she would never have walked so familiarly around the garden. Ambrose's daughter? Hardly, especially after learning in the early days of the partnership that his father's cousin, Lavinia and her baby had died in childbirth. The mine-owner had been taciturn with the explanation and Merrick tactfully did not enquire further. Perhaps he had an older daughter? In which case why hadn't William mentioned a lady of the house might greet him?

Walcott, naturally, had been singularly lacking in

information, saying he was not informed of the personal happenings in the family, his role was strictly with the business, but Merrick recalled he had specifically mentioned there were no male heirs, hence the seeking of a partnership. The girl could easily be a daughter, he thought, as he watched her move out of sight round the house, his interest stirred in spite of her youth. As the wind blew her grey twill skirt against her body he could see how it outlined the slender figure and the way she carried herself. She had neither the looks nor the bearing of a servant girl though Merrick was puzzled by the plainness of her outfit of twill, which fitted tightly over a white blouse. Ah, of course, it was a school uniform. He remembered reading that some schools required conformity. In that case she was almost bound to be a daughter of Trevarron for no village maid would ever attend a local school in uniform.

The explanation came at the dinner table to which Linda, to her surprise, had been asked to attend. Although she had been in the habit of dining with the mine-owner when she was on holiday from school, he had never requested her to join him when he had guests, for these tended to be men of some local substance who fostered their business activities close by.

Merrick noted the barely masked shyness of the maid when Ambrose introduced her. "This is my ward, Linda Barton, the daughter of a colleague who unfortunately died some twelve years ago leaving Linda orphaned. She has made a home here since that time and now she has left school we are planning the next step that I trust will be happy for both of us. She has been educated to a reasonable standard, even more than is usual for London society Misses, so I am given to understand from those that frequent the capital." Ambrose went on to express an air of disdain for the current aristocracy. He spoke as though they were to be deplored rather than envied. Inverted snobbery, Merrick noted, his innate perception studying the mine-owner and curious at the odd look of perplexity that flitted over Linda's face. Was her future being settled without recourse to her wishes? Had Trevarron found a husband for her she disliked?

Merrick noted the tiny frown on an otherwise smooth brow and sensed Linda was disturbed with the turn the conversation was taking. Although her attention appeared to be directed at her plate, Merrick could see she toyed with her food instead of enjoying what was a pleasing meal. Then Linda raised her head and stared openly at him and, all at once, he found he was looking at her as if at a well-known face. Each feature seemed familiar, almost as though he had gazed at her face so many times before. Her fair hair, parted centrally, was swept back into ringlets caught in place behind each ear, framing an elfin face lively with curiosity. She gazed intently at him, aware of his fixed scrutiny and blushed delicately, her eyes brilliant with a lustre of polished emeralds in the candlelight. His gaze dropped to her lips. The top lip curled into a perfect bow, the bottom lip was full and sensual. It would be a lucky man who took this girl to wife, he reflected, then almost shuddered in surprise at the erotic thoughts passing through his own head. How ridiculous! This child was just a schoolgirl even if she was on the verge of womanhood. He had Angelina to consider, why, he had almost proposed when he had last seen her before he left London. Yet he hadn't! Why not? The feeling of unease returned once more to disturb his thoughts.

Angelina had kept him waiting for a long while in the small salon of her London flat after his arrival and then had rushed in to greet him, flustered and pink, her bodice awry and with tumbled curls. "Darling! How very unexpected! I believed you to be in Scotland. Why didn't you send word you were coming? I was resting, my love. The soirée given by the French Ambassador last night was dreadfully boring in spite of the opportunity to use my native language. Indeed, I have to declare I am becoming so Anglicised I scarcely recognise myself. It's all your fault, my darling. You've finally converted me."

Merrick had not given the occasion a thought until he was on the train to Cornwall, then replaying the scene in his mind he recalled the distant slam of the outside door while he was engaged in kissing Angelina. It could not have been the maid for she had left on an errand no sooner had she let him in, after saying, "Madam is at home, please to wait in the salon." He had been too overwhelmed with Angelina's lovemaking thereafter to take notice or even care but now he wondered. He recalled the tumbled bedclothes and unruly mess strewn around the bedroom. If she had only lain down on the bed for a brief while to rest surely it wouldn't have been quite so disorderly? Perhaps it was someone she didn't want him to see? Was she lying to him about her affections? Was he simply a lover she dallied with?

Reviewing the whole matter realistically he could understand that she would not have stayed at home waiting for his brief appearances between voyages. Her nature required constant love and attention so, if he was not around, she would go seeking elsewhere. Nevertheless this was a woman he had determined to be his wife. He had planned to take her home to his parents who, he now realised only too well, would be appalled with her style of life and would shun the idea of accepting her into their family. Even though he had never been denied a thing in his life he knew Angelina would never find any fondness in their eyes; truth to tell, his own eyes had lately opened to the fact that to marry her would be wrong.

CHAPTER TWENTY-SEVEN

"Ah, how splendid!" Ambrose rubbed his hands as he surveyed the third remove; a brace of roasted ducks garnished with fruit sauce. The butler was placing jugs of gravy and bowls of vegetables on the table before refilling the glasses with wine. He was not a constant resident in the house but hired for the occasion when Ambrose entertained.

"My cook has a unique way with roast duck and her sauces are most delicious." Ambrose spoke with rare good humour. At last he was nearing the point when his plans would bear fruit. "I'm sure you are famished after the journey, come fill yourself, we shall have plenty of time later for our talk. And you, Linda, eat, child; you have hardly touched the fish. Mrs Polwen will be upset at your tiny appetite. She will think you do not like her cooking."

"Do you live in London, sir?" she asked shyly, striving to change the subject and wishing herself anywhere but dining with the two men that night.

"I keep a small pied-à-terre but apart from my parents' home in Scotland I have no home of my own. Roaming over the world for so long I have never felt the need to have a permanent residence. However, the time has come for me to settle down, to make a new life, and live in one place instead of many. Maybe it will be London, but I've yet to make up my mind and the future is uncertain. Travelling down to this part of the world has enabled me to discover more of this country than I've previously had time for. It may well be I shall look for an estate and enjoy some rusticating."

"Ah, and maybe you'll be thinking of marriage, milord?

Best thing for a man, eh?" Ambrose was quick to interrupt. "Just where my thoughts were turning as well. Oh, it's not too late for me to father a son, ye know?" he interjected quickly. "It's still in my mind to do so, despite our arrangement. Of course it will be many years before the lad might be of an age to inherit his share of the mine so ye need not worry about the partnership, we shall keep things as they are. But at least the terms of our alliance leaves each of us free to back out if necessary. Not that it is of any importance at present."

Crafty old devil! So that was the way the wind blew. Put my mine right, then farewell partner. Merrick had been aware of this clause but as sufficient compensation at market value prices would be due the departing partner he felt it had been worth the risk. But marriage! For God's sake, the man must be sixty if he's a day! (In fact Ambrose was fifty-five, though it was true he looked far older). Tumultuous thoughts cascaded through his brain like a flood as Merrick contemplated the legal aspects that would emerge. Who was he going to marry? Had there been any gossip? He tried to recall any conversations that had arisen about Trevarron or even a hint the man was contemplating matrimony. All he had ever heard about was the arrogant meanness, the reluctance to do anything for the miners and the swiftness to oust out anyone even daring to ask for mercy.

The miners had come to realise very quickly that Merrick was as opposite as one could get from the older man. In consequence he had learned more of the workings of the mine, the dire sufferings of those who had to go underground and even about the day-to-day lives of their families. When the miners found out he was encouraging Ambrose to mechanize the pit, with the latest lifting gear for men and ore, their loyalty to him rose a hundredfold. Not one hint of his wild thoughts reached his face as Merrick carried on calmly eating his dinner but again he noticed that Linda seemed subdued, had lost the spark of animation which had encouraged her to join in the conversation; then shortly afterwards she excused herself and left. Had she been upset at the turn the dialogue had taken? Perhaps she was worried about Ambrose taking a wife? Being only his ward she would have to rely on his generosity to give her a home or possibly find her a husband.

Merrick found plenty of reasons thereafter to see Linda, using his relationship with Trevarron as an excuse. By this time he had found himself a comfortable lodging place in Penzance, also a horse, which he kept stabled close by. This enabled him to have easy access to the mine and to visit the Hall. Soon they were on amiable terms and he looked for a welcoming smile whenever he visited. However, he kept his emotions under strict control and neither by word nor deed did he let her know he was other than a business partner of Trevarron. Just why he should act in such a restrained manner when all his senses made him want to court Linda openly puzzled him, except for the fact he knew he was gaining her trust and goodwill. Inwardly he railed futilely, for Ambrose never gave him the slightest opening to make clear his interest. As each day passed he racked his brains to find a way to raise the topic.

Reticence was not a quality of Merrick's make-up and he chafed at forbearance. Ambrose had more than once accused him of interfering in problems concerning the mine that were not his business, so venturing into a personal relationship and actually having to ask Ambrose if he could court Linda went against the grain. Matters went on like this for some time, until there came a day when notice arrived that Merrick was urgently needed in Bristol docks to sort out a problem with a cargo that had gone astray. One of his ships had not made landfall at its appointed time and was presumed lost at sea in a storm or perhaps even boarded by pirates. Vowing he would resolve matters one way or another and openly seek permission to make his interest known to Linda when he returned, he reluctantly had to leave the situation as it was. The shipping dilemma would not wait on courtship; it had to be dealt with immediately which meant informing the insurers and letting the relatives of the crew know. There was always hardship involved when this happened and it was his practice to quietly help where necessary.

CHAPTER TWENTY-EIGHT

James Lusty was at long last arranging his retirement, for his practice had finally been bought by a newly qualified physician by the name of Jonathan Paul Fyfield, MD. He was London-trained and as full of himself as any bright young man with all his future before him could be. As soon as he was settled in, the young doctor put up and polished his handsome brass plate, donated by a loving aunt, after successfully passing all his exams and gaining his degree; nailing it to the crumbling wall of the old surgery where Lusty had practised his profession for more years than he could remember.

"It's not the cleanest of places, is it?" remarked Fyfield dryly, brushing his jacket where it had swept dust from a rickety shelf. "I shall have to change a few things here, I fear, or it will be almost impossible to achieve sterile conditions in a surgery like this."

"You may try," answered Lusty. "But you won't get it elsewhere, leastwise no place I know of in this part of Cornwall. Yet, people do manage to live in spite o' the dirt." He wondered how well Fyfield would get on when he had to make a trip down the mine; perhaps have to amputate a man's arm or leg under appalling conditions that took not the slightest heed of antiseptic measures. "I shall be here for two more weeks if you need to ask anything. Then I'm off to live with a widowed sister near Worthing. I intend to enjoy my retirement to the full for I have surely earned it after all these years. As for you, young man, I wish you well. Folks round here are hard to get to know but once they do they will be good friends. Good day to you, sir; enjoy your vocation."

Lusty closed the door on the new doctor but not before he caught a glimpse of the zeal in his eyes. I was like that once, he pondered sadly, where did it all go? How many years of preaching cleanliness and decent living? How many deaths from disease and malnutrition have I seen? How many babes died before they reached their first birthday? Talking of which, he reminded himself, I must say farewell to Amy. Strangely I haven't seen her around lately. He rubbed his hands over his face wondering whether to sit and snooze in his armchair for a while then chided himself for being lazy. He would visit this one last time and say goodbye. Now she had given up the midwifery he had not given her as much as a passing wave. Ah well, times change, the old ones have to give way to the new, I suppose, he muttered under his breath as he drove the pony and trap through the village to where Amy lived in a tiny thatched cottage on the edge of the moor.

At first there was no answer to his knock and he was just about to leave when he heard shuffling sounds and Amy opened the door. For one awful moment he thought he was facing a stranger then he realised that the gaunt, grey-haired, aging woman with a bright yellow cast to her face was indeed Amy. "I'm so sorry, Doctor, I didn't know it was you, come on in."

Startled, Lusty doffed his hat and entered the cottage. "Good day to you, Amy, I was just passing and thought I'd have a word. I'm right pleased to find you in."

"I'm glad to see you, my handsome, that I am. Don't often get out these days. Sorry, but I cannot move so fast now. Often visitors have gone before I get to the door, but now you're here, will you join me in a cup of tea?"

He nodded and sat down. "Gladly, m'dear, gladly."

The small living room was tidy but a faint odour hung on the air, which caused him to frown, not primarily with distaste but with an anxious knowledge of its likely cause. "I haven't seen you around lately, Amy. Of course I've been quite occupied myself in arranging for the new doctor to take over from me now I'm fixed to retire. At last I can see an end and with much thankfulness I can take a well-earned rest. But never mind me, how are you? It's a long time since I've seen you. Have you been hiding away?"

"In a manner of speaking I suppose, since I handed over the midwifery to that nurse who moved into Penberthy's old cottage. She's making out right well. As for me, I've not felt up to gadding around. I've been intending to have a word with you anyway, so I'm glad you've called. I've bin doctoring myself for some time now but my remedies are not up to things the way they are. But I don't need to say more for I can see you know what I'm getting at?" She handed him a mug of tea and returned to sit down in the well-used chair by a small glimmering fire, cringing as she did so as a swift pain raced through her body.

"Where's the trouble, Amy?" Lusty demanded.

"It started low down." She touched her belly. "Then in the last two weeks the pain has bin some'at cruel here." She placed her hand gently across her midriff. "Liver, ain't it? This yellow's bin coming out on my face last day or two. All I want is some'at for the pain. You can't do any more for me; I know that only too well. The trouble took a hold of me without me paying much attention until it was too late."

"Why ever didn't you come to me before, my dear, when I could have helped?"

"Could you have cured me?"

"That I couldn't say. You know it's not always possible." He sounded grieved.

"Then I'll say it for you. There b'ain't a chance you could have done ought, so don't ee fret, Doctor. I knew what I had ages ago; I've made my peace with the Lord."

"Oh, my dear friend, I'm so sorry, so very sorry." Lusty, for all his training in dealing with death, felt helpless and inadequate with Amy's blunt acceptance of her fate. He did not question her self-diagnosis for he knew that, unqualified as she was, she had an inborn sense of knowledge and working experience of the human body that very nearly equalled his own. Yes, she would undoubtedly know by now there was no hope.

"As I say, don't fret. I've had a good life and I don't regret one bit of it, save maybe I'd have liked a bit longer." She smiled and he could see how the bones of her face stood out in severe gauntness, the yellow tinge to her skin even more apparent.

"I'll make you up something that will help with the pain, my dear, and of course I don't need to warn you if you overdo the dosage, it will be dangerous." A look passed between the two friends that spoke volumes.

Amy nodded, her eyes brimming with tears. "Thank ee, James; I knew I could depend on ye to help at the last. Now there is one more thing ye can do for me and that is, hear my confession, if you will?"

"Your confession!" Startled, Lusty wondered for a moment what she meant. "You are never Catholic, are you? If so, it's a priest you need, not me."

"No. I've been Methody all my life an' I'm not going to change now. No, James, this is different. I can't die without knowing whether I've done wrong in a situation I had to face many years ago and whether I've got to put things right or leave things to fate. You must advise me, there's no one else I trust more."

"Well, I'll try," replied Lusty still confused.

Amy went to a desk in the corner of the room. Taking out a box, she removed a velvet cover and held up a necklace that sparkled in the firelight. She handed him the letter enclosed within. "Read this," she instructed him. "Then you will know what I'm talking about."

Lusty read her concise explanation of that night at Tregender Hall and taking up the necklace opened the locket and studied the picture. "Good God! It's Linda!"

"No, it's not, but she is like her grandmother, isn't she? It's her miniature you are looking at." Amy corroborated his exclamation with a smile. "And one has to admit she grows more like her mother, as I recall, the older she gets."

"Like her? She's the very image. Why didn't I see it before? Does Trevarron know who she is? More to the point, does he know she's not his daughter?"

"Yes, he knows she's Lavinia's but he took it for granted she was his as well and I didn't have the courage to say him nay. He knew he couldn't say anything but I suppose he's tried, in his own way, to treat her as a daughter. At least she's getting well educated."

Lusty shook his head in amazement at the twists of fate. Life was never straightforward as he had learned so often but this situation beat everything he had come across so far. "This solves many of the questions I've puzzled over with Mrs Trevarron's death and the fact that Linda has a birthmark on her body very similar to one I saw when I examined the body of her mother. I've racked my brains at the connection. Now I know, it seems so simple; why I didn't put two and two together amazes me." He shook his head again. "Having confessed, what is it you want to do?" he continued. "Are you thinking to tell Linda about her birth and how she was given to the Bartons? It won't exactly thrill her to find out she could have been disposed of soon after her birth. Except she was very happy with the Bartons and adored Jethro."

"Yes, I'm still in two minds considering if it would be the right thing to do. I've always kept an eye on the child right from the time of her birth and, apart from when Jethro died and her future was chancy, she's always been cared for by someone or other. Trevarron's looked after her all these years and there's no call to say he won't see her safely married to make a life and be happy. But these last few weeks I've had dreadful thoughts. What if I did wrong all those years ago? I deliberately changed things for everyone, you know."

"I can't see what else you could have done under the circumstances."

"I've deprived the child of her legal future. Will I

suffer hellfire for interfering?"

"Amy Bunnion, of course you won't suffer hellfire! Why, you have done more good in this world than evil. What if Trevarron had harmed the child? What would your conscience have been like then? No, my dear, you did the right thing, so don't give it another thought. But I agree with you, it's now we have to think of."

Lusty sat back in the chair cradling his two hands together while he pondered the dilemma. It wasn't the girl he was thinking of but Ambrose Trevarron. In spite of the influence of his new partner, Lusty could see no actual change in the mine-owner. He was still a despot and when Macgregor left the area to see to his other business affairs Trevarron usually sought to bring back his old dictatorship. The doctor was surprised, in many ways, Ambrose had not exacted a tribute from Linda before this. Yet he had paid for her keep and schooling, not to mention her clothes. What was the old skinflint up to?

"The trouble is Trevarron might take things amiss if he gets to know that Linda is his wife's daughter but not his. She's no kin apart from him saying she's his ward. I'd bet a king's ransom he's not so much as made things legal and adopted her officially. Of course he ought to have a will but knowing him he'll have it tied every which way to make sure he gets the best bargain and whether that will include her is anybody's guess. If it comes out that she definitely is not his then he may toss her out and hang the consequences."

The lengthy deliberations of the midwife and the doctor were eventually resolved when they came to the conclusion that Linda should be told so that she was free to choose her own destiny. They also agreed that nothing would be mentioned to Trevarron, at least for the present. Accordingly, a message was left at Tregender Hall that Mrs Bunnion would be pleased if Linda paid her a visit.

"She'm right poorly, Lindy," Betsy confided when she passed on the request. "I've put together a few choice morsels she might find tasty. Don't forget now, tell her if she's needing any help she only has to ask, though she's a right independent body for accepting favours. Like as not she'll not accept any. Funny she wants to see you?" she went on. "Course she did birth you, so maybe it's to do with that?"

Linda left her to mutter to herself and chivvy the new maid into getting a move on with chores. Strange, thought Linda, the maids never lasted long in the house, a new one came every few months. When she mentioned it to Betsy she had been abruptly told to mind her own business. So, taken aback with the rejection, she had not asked again or noticed the search had widened considerably as local girls did not apply.

CHAPTER TWENTY-NINE

"Sit you down, girl, I'm pleased you managed to get here, I haven't seen you in a long time." Amy leaned back carefully in her chair, hoping the tiny dose of opium she had taken would be enough to see her through the talk with Linda. She had not wanted to blunt her senses or be unable to think straight but she feared the pain when it came gnawing at her insides like a red-hot poker. However she had so little time left to put her affairs in order she had to make the effort. Amy put the basket of delicacies to one side after she had exclaimed over the sending of them. It was sad as she knew they would hardly be touched; her appetite these days non-existent, for most times she could scarcely keep barely a mouthful down before she was sick but never mind that; how could she begin? All her attention was riveted on the girl as she pondered her words. How do you turn a person's world upside down and tell them they are someone else?

"Lindy child, I'm not long for this world, so afore I go I have a keepsake for you and a tale to tell which maybe I should have spoken of before but somehow it never seemed the right time. The years since you were birthed have flown by and at each point in your life as it changed I wondered whether the time was right. Forgive me if I've done you wrong in not speaking up before but it has been a hard decision to say something even now." She stared curiously at the girl as she began her tale.

Linda looked back at her with puzzled eyes but she remained silent wondering what she was to hear. Whatever Linda imagined it certainly was not what followed. When Amy ceased to speak and, in turn, sat silent waiting for Linda to ask questions, Linda was numb with sheer disbelief; all she could think of was Ellie and her dear Jethro. They were not her beloved parents after all! She swallowed a sob of unhappy longing for the two people she loved best in the world, even though Aunt Betsy and Annie Gorland had been substitute parents for so long. What a dreadful thing to find out after all this time. Who did she really belong to now?

When Amy could bear the silence no longer she took out the necklace and handed it to Linda. "It belonged to Sophie, your great-grandmother, so I believe, at least that's what your mother said when she gave me this for you. I am so sorry it's taken so long to tell you. I've looked at this necklace so many times and wondered what I should do. I blame myself for not saying something earlier when Jethro died. But you were taken up by Trevarron and..." Her voice died away at the look on Linda's face. She could tell she was very angry about the meddling in her life.

Linda undid the locket to gaze at the face within. The portrait was beautiful, the heavy jewels surrounding the locket obviously valuable but it did not make any difference. The woman could be anyone; a stranger, not a relation or one who had loved her and cared for her. She could not feel a scrap of the emotion she would have felt had she been looking at a picture of Ellie or Jethro. "What do you want me to do now?" enquired Linda, still numb from Amy's revelations except for a strange anger that coiled around inside of her that her whole life had been make-believe, she was an imposter.

"What do you want to do, my dear?" Amy had feared tears but not this icy reception of her story. Remorse hit her again as she thought of her past actions.

"I don't think I want anyone to know. After all, if it's true, I'm a bastard. Or if not, then I'm Mr Trevarron's daughter. I can't think which is worse. Oh, he's been very kind to me but I could never think of him as a father. It's bad enough being his ward."

She shuddered briefly. "No. We'll say nothing, Mrs Bunnion; let us keep it a secret between ourselves for the present moment. I'm happy as I am, and I don't really want to change my life again. As for the necklace I'll hide it away until I make up my mind what to do with it. It might be better to return it anonymously to the family. Likely it is an heirloom. They will be glad to have it back."

"An heirloom that was bequeathed to you, Lindy, don't forget that."

"It's not something I'd wear. In fact I don't even like it very much. I'll keep it for now but as far as I am concerned it's not mine," said Linda, so positively that Amy knew she would never change her mind. In some ways she was glad of that. She had never felt at ease having the jewel in her possession. Despite its beauty she had always sensed a malignancy about it and was glad it was going from her keeping. Shortly after that Amy bade farewell to Linda well knowing she would never see her again. Soon she would take her last and strongest dose of Lusty's concoction and sink into the final oblivion that she craved.

Taking a short cut over the moors Linda slipped into the Hall by a side door without seeing anyone. She went straight to her room where she locked the door. She wanted to evade detection in case asked what was in the parcel, now she could hide it and no one would be the wiser. Before she placed it in the armoire, which stood in a corner of her room, she took out the necklace to look at great-grandmother Sophie's portrait, sadly wishing it had been her own mother's picture. Mrs Bunnion had said her mother greatly resembled the grandmother but there was no way that Linda could relate to a possible resemblance. Even the heavy jewels meant nothing to her beyond a wish she could return them to their rightful owner and possibly make contact with a family that until now she had no idea existed. As she slipped the necklace back in its pouch she saw some stitching had loosened and she tugged on a thread which unravelled as though it were meant. At once the lining of the bag opened and a fold of paper showed within.

Linda felt something momentous was about to happen as she carefully pulled the paper from its hiding place and found it was a letter. It was momentous. More than that, it was positively earth-shaking. Her spirits sank to their lowest ebb as she read. If the letter was true she was without doubt the bastard of a man who, it appeared, had deserted her mother. Nobody could be so cruel, she thought, to do such a vile thing. Then she realised what this meant. How was it possible to marry Richard Whitmore with the stain of illegitimacy hanging over her? He would be utterly ashamed of her when he got to know and there was no way she could hide things. His parents, particularly his mother, would never forgive her if she married him without confessing her dreadful background.

As for herself, to spoil the deep friendship she had had with her childhood comrade would break her heart. In the years they had known each other he taught her to swim, to shoot a pistol, to study and excel in reading, writing and even mathematics. They were allies and up until now she knew she could confide almost anything to him. But this? God almighty, how could she tell him she was as good as a foundling? Especially after his last words before he left for college.

"When you are eighteen we shall be married. By then I shall have finished college and become a vicar like my father. He is hoping to retire so I may qualify for his living, then we shall make a life for ourselves and be happy. Will you wait for me? I suppose I should mention it to Mrs Polwen, as she is your aunt, but there is time enough to let her know. We will keep it a secret between the two of us."

Shyly Linda smiled at him, her face aglow, already portraying the qualities of beauty that would blaze into existence when she was older. "How wonderful to marry my best friend. Aunt Betsy won't object; you know how she dotes on you. Be assured she will be delighted and so too will Mrs Gorland. I could not be happier to accept your proposal, Richard. I will wait for you."

"What about Trevarron? Last I heard he was saying that he is your guardian. Have you agreed to this? I don't trust the man and never have; he is devious and full of ulterior motives."

"Well," Linda said doubtfully, "he has paid for my schooling and my clothes but neither he nor Aunt Polly said anything about him being my guardian, only that I was to be his ward, whatever that might mean? What is a ward, anyway?"

"Oh, you goose, Lindy! It means exactly the same thing as being his daughter. You have given him the right to run your life, to act as your parent."

Linda stared at Richard aghast for a moment then she laughed uneasily. "Don't fret, Richard; I'm sure he just means to be kind. We got on well when I was ill and later convalescing. He won't stand in our way when the time comes and he knows my mind is made up. You'll see; it will be fine."

Richard did not feel the same confidence but knew he was not in a position to offer for her at that moment. He must work hard to gain his qualifications and be accepted by the ministry before he could officially ask her to be his wife. Despondent, he began his college training with deep gloom but after receiving two letters from Linda that were cheerful and most supportive he settled to his work in a better frame of mind and replied happily that all was well with him.

As this ran through Linda's mind like scorching acid she asked herself, What was she to do? How could she manufacture a family who would be acceptable to the Whitmores, who prided themselves on being upright citizens? As for Trevarron, what was he up to? Surely he didn't intend her to marry a stranger? Did he know of Richard's intentions and approve? How she wished she had someone to talk with, to help her sort things out. Aunt Polly was no use; she blew with the wind. Perhaps she would just wait and see. Maybe things would work out – surely they couldn't get worse. Or could they?'

CHAPTER THIRTY

"He dassn't want no other place laying, the other gen'lman ain't stoppin'. Shall I set up, Missus Polwen?" Polly sniggered to herself as she saw Linda's face.

"Not stopping?" Linda exclaimed in dismay; she'd been hoping that if Ambrose had a companion she need not join him over dinner.

"Well, doan't matter, less fret for us." Betsy's voice was tart as she saw Linda's disappointment, misreading it entirely. Damn me if she ain't sweet on a furriner, a Scot from Lord knows where, she mused. Merry hell and high water, tha's all we need; he more'n a touch too high for t'lass, even if she is a looker. She frowned crossly and her next words were sharp. "Change tha' dress then get a pinny on an' help or nobody u'll eat dinner afore nightfall."

"He only said lay for one," interjected Polly who was secretly jealous that Linda was able to dine with the Master and be waited on as if she was society.

"Thank heavens for that, I can eat in the kitchen," said Linda who dreaded facing Ambrose that evening. Why did she have the odd feeling he already knew of her birth? Amy had said nothing when she told her she wanted to keep the thing entirely secret. Then her eyes had taken on a shuttered look and she had ushered Linda out in some haste, or so it appeared to her now, thinking back. If Trevarron knew then maybe there were others; perhaps the Whitmores knew and that was why she had sensed Mrs Whitmore had never really liked Richard having her as a friend. Oh, how complicated life had gotten all of a sudden, how she wished she could go back to the days of old when there was only Jethro, Becky and Richard to love and her days were filled with happiness.

Dinner had been over some time and Linda was in her room when Polly knocked on the door. "You're to change and go upstairs, Master wants to see you. At once, he said." Polly spoke abruptly, pleased to give her enemy an order even if it was only second-hand. She stared at Linda's downcast face revealing misery. Stupid girl, she doesn't know when she is well off. Now if it was her. Abruptly her dreams were cut short as the door was shut in her face after a brief acknowledgement. Behind it Linda groaned in despair. This was it. Amy must have said something to Trevarron after all.

She could think of no likely reason he would have sent for her at this time of night. The meal had been over ages ago; the household ready for bed. With her stomach coiling in apprehension, Linda put on a moiré silk dress and matching slippers, then throwing a fragile lacy shawl about her shoulders, walked from the back wing of the house through to the Library where Ambrose usually spent his evenings. When she came into the room, Ambrose was standing in front of the fire gazing into the flames. He turned as he heard her, his gaze taking in the slender form in the pale pink dress, her curled hair caught in matching ribbons on each side of her face and an enquiring, almost fearful look in her eyes. How strange, usually she was bright and cheery, although recently, she had appeared downcast and quite unlike herself. Likely female megrims, he thought, remembering Lavinia and her wayward moods. Briefly Ambrose scowled, and then his lips lifted in a smile of welcome which, as usual, did not quite reach his eyes.

"Ah, Linda, my dear, here you are at last, come, sit by the fire. We've something to discuss you and I – I hope you are ready for some good news?" Oh she was, she was! Her heart leapt in eagerness that Richard had asked Ambrose for her hand and he was agreeable to the idea of them marrying.

"Linda," he began. "Quite a few years have gone by since

your illness, when we sat in the sun and read to each other. I formed an idea even then, though you were still very young and today I see before me the results of that idea." He paused, studying her afresh. "You have grown into a beautiful woman, educated and accomplished – at least for the meagre society we have in these parts – able in every way to assume your role as a wife. A wife who is fit to marry into one of the best families in the land. It'll be a union that is extremely important to me; recompense, one might say, for the way you have been cared for. Your rescue from the Poor House wasn't achieved without substantial expense, you know. As my – er ward – it follows that you must be as willing as – say, a daughter would be compliant, in return for all the care she has had. In short, my dear, I wish you to be agreeable to Lord Macgregor and accept his offer of marriage."

"He – he's offered marriage?"

"Let's say – I have suggested it and he has not disagreed, on the contrary, he is thinking it over." Linda, unable to comprehend, was overcome with shocked horror. Dear God, this was really dreadful, quite the last thing she had expected. What about Richard? Dear, thoughtful Richard, he had warned her Ambrose was devious, that he had never trusted him. But to marry Lord Macgregor? A stranger? Ambrose must be mad if he thought she was going to obey. She was pledged heart and soul to Richard!

"No, I don't want him! I – I, that is, Richard has already asked me and I've agreed!"

Carried away by his eloquence, Ambrose did not at first perceive his overture had fallen on very stony ground. As her whispered denial reached his ears it struck him at once how aghast she was, how all she could do was to shake her head from side to side.

"Richard Whitmore! Do you mean that sanctimonious mealy-mouthed pretence of a man whose only ambition is to be a vicar? He'd no right to offer you anything!" His tiny eyes suddenly narrowed. "What else has he offered you – or taken?

What else, damn you, Linda?" He started towards her with all the pent-up fury in his heart and with a roar of rage his disappointment boiled over like lava pouring from a volcano. Swiftly he grabbed her arms wrenching her out of the seat. She flinched backwards but he held her firmly against him. "You hussy! You ungrateful slut. Have you slept with him – that no-account preacher who thinks he owns the world? Have you – have you?" He shook her till her teeth rattled. "I'll have the truth from you if I have to beat you black and blue!"

"No-n-n-no! Leave me alone!" she managed to gasp, suddenly as angry as him. "Why should I sleep with him or anyone else? Take your hands off me, you bully! You don't own me, no one does. I shall do as I wish, marry who I want to!" she screamed back at him.

"That's where you are wrong, my girl. You do belong to me. I am your real father and your mother was my late wife! There! What do you think of that? You're mine, you hear! You are my daughter!" Christ! It was out in spite of himself. He had been resolved to keep quiet, to let things unfold when he had Macgregor where he wanted him.

"On the contrary, Mr Trevarron, you are quite mistaken." Suddenly and quite coolly Linda found the courage to challenge him. "My mother was with child when she married you. You are not my father, someone else is. She left a letter with the facts."

"You are lying!" he hissed at her. "I was told the true story by Amy Bunnion. She delivered you, then for some extraordinary reason – she's likely mad – exchanged you for the Barton child. It was much later I got the truth out of her."

"It was because my mother wished it so. And because you are not my father. Don't you understand – I'm not your relation, you are not my guardian? Aunt Betsy is the only one who has a right to look after me and give permission for me to marry."

Twin spots of colour on his cheeks blazoned in rage. "In that case, if you won't marry Macgregor and we are not related then it's very simple, you will marry me!"

"You are mad, completely mad." Linda stared at him aghast; utterly taken aback at this new turn of events. In all the years she had lived at Tregender Hall she had never imagined he could act this way towards her and yet, had not her intuition warned her?

"That's where you are wrong. I've always wanted a son. Your mother couldn't give me one, but there is nothing to stop you taking her place. I've bought and paid for you just like your mother before you. She thought to short-change me and evade her duty but no one is going to gainsay me about you. Polwen is my servant and so are you, my girl, whatever you think. You will both do as I say or Polwen will be thrown out of this house to starve. I'll see to it that she never gets a job anywhere. Do you want that to happen, miss?" He stared viciously into her shocked eyes knowing he had won. She would never allow Betsy Polwen to be treated so badly.

"Now, I'll show what I mean, I'll make you understand!"

CHAPTER THIRTY-ONE

Betsy never knew what made her go up into the main hall that night. Normally at the same hour she was to be found in her rocking chair close to the banked up fire of the range, either sewing or reading the penny dreadful magazines that she loved so much but the day had been traumatic. Her senses were raw enough to unsettle the familiar routine. Whilst it was seldom a habit for Trevarron to send for Linda after dinner, Betsy had taken little notice until the kitchen clock chimed the hour and she realised it was getting late and it was time to retire. Before she knew what she was about she climbed the stairs to the hall and was outside the Library door at the very moment when Linda screamed in appalled outrage. Without a moment's hesitation, Betsy flung open the door and burst in the room to find her beloved Lindy struggling angrily with her employer who was obviously intent on trying to rape her. Linda was sobbing, imploring him to leave her alone but the strength of Ambrose was gradually overpowering her and slowly she was being forced to the floor.

"Get off her, you rancid dirty dog! Leave my babe alone! Isn't it enough you misuse the young chambermaids? No wonder we can't keep 'em long; they leave frightened out o' their wits. Why you ain't got any o' them pregnant afore this, I'll never know," Betsy howled, beside herself with rage, as she sprang forward and began pulling Linda away.

"Get back to the kitchen, woman, where you belong and mind your own bloody business and I'll tend to mine." Ambrose was in such a rage he scarce knew what he was doing or saying. "Stupid cow, I'll have you out of this house first thing in the morning!"

"I'll have you know she's my niece and if ye don't get yer 'ands off her this minute I'll fetch a constable straight away. See if I don't! Come, my pet, come to Aunt Betsy. There, my beauty, don't cry, I'll not let him touch ye again. Nasty evil-minded villain, I'll see you in jail so I will! Just because you're rich don't think your money will save you!"

Ambrose came to his senses at the word constable. It would not do for his sins to be found out, or any investigation of his morals, let alone anything else, for he suspected the law was just waiting its chance to pin something on him. He had been dealing with more than the mine for some time and was no stranger to the local criminal fraternity. "Go on, take her, but you're out of this house, first thing in the morning, you hear, and without a reference! I'll make sure you end your days in the workhouse!"

"See if I care, you old lecher!" Betsy put her arm round Linda to draw her away.

"Just a minute, Aunt Betsy." Linda paused on the threshold of the door. Without warning a direful memory had surfaced in her mind, her brain tossing it from the depths where it had festered a very long time. Ambrose had talked of his plans covering many years. "Did you have Jethro killed?" Her voice was strained, hard.

Ambrose stared at her before replying, intrigued at her newly found maturity. He had foreseen this promise in her so long ago when she was a child. He knew then, if he could foster it, he would have a perfect woman, fit mate with his strength to give him the son he had always so ardently desired. The news that she was his own child had taken him aback but ever resourceful he had thought to use her to his advantage in another way by marrying her into the aristocracy. When Linda refuted his relationship, he gloried in the fact that he could do as he once had planned so long ago.

"So what if I did? I'm not admitting to it, mind. You've benefitted a thousandfold. You'd have been a miner's daughter, a miner's wife, and a toothless old hag at thirty. Is that the life you would rather have? No, Linda, what you're offered is much better than anything else you will ever get, so you have a choice. It's either Macgregor or me. Take your pick. Do you understand me?" Trevarron stood there truculent to the last.

Linda stared at him, her eyes filmed with unshed tears. This man – this monster – had murdered her beloved Jethro. How could she avenge the man she had always thought of as being her father? Ambrose was clever; no wonder his men had never managed to get the better of him. Could she? It was hardly likely, but she would have a damned good try. For now she needed to get away, to think.

"We'll talk of this later, I'm tired; we shall go to bed, Aunt. To sleep, I trust quite undisturbed?" she added glaring at Ambrose Trevarron, her eyes hard as stone. He stared back then nodded. He had won, thank God. He was right, she was an intelligent woman. She knew which side her bread was buttered. She would choose him without doubt. He could read people like a book and was seldom wrong. Relieved that the commotion was over, Betsy led Linda back to the kitchen where she made a soothing drink for them.

"You'll sleep alongside o' me tonight, my pet. I wouldn't put it past that swine to go prowling round again in spite of his promise. But u'll get more than he bargains for if he comes up in the attic, that he will, as God is my judge," she said with feeling.

"No, Aunt Betsy, I'll be fine. He won't try anything more tonight, not now you've said you would fetch the law. Still, Constable Penwick would think twice about facing him in a rage." She shivered in memory. "I'll lock my door, I promise. You go to bed. You've enough to do looking after Annie. He won't sack you, he will never want to be left with a sick woman and no one to feed him or take care of his house. He'll not be able to hire a soul from hereabouts to look after him as you've done."

Deliberately, Linda kept her voice lightly impersonal as though the last dreadful hour had merely been a troublesome interlude. Inwardly her nerves were torn to shreds, as she could hardly believe her so-called benefactor could have turned on her like that. Her intuition now understood he had always been like it and only her girlish innocence had protected her from his wickedness. Smiling gently at Betsy, she gave her to understand that all was well with her niece and the morning would bring calm and understanding. Betsy, exhausted by now, was more than happy to seek her own bed and let the dust settle. She agreed without further resistance to allowing Linda to sleep downstairs. She would have felt differently had she known what Linda was planning.

CHAPTER THIRTY-TWO

When Merrick left Tregender Hall to return to his lodgings, he flung himself onto his horse and took off along the drive, ignoring everything save the thoughts rolling around in his head. Trevarron was after more money, that was plain enough and he would lay odds it was not to improve the mine. To that end would he sell Linda to anyone who would provide the wherewithal? No. It had to be more than just that. There had been a distinct inference that he wouldn't be averse to marrying Linda himself. But why should he burden himself with a wife at his age? The trouble was, he admitted to himself, he had no idea of the kind of association there was between Trevarron and Linda. Why had he made her his ward? According to Linda she had no relative except Betsy Polwen. Ambrose had stepped in and given her a home when her father died. Why? The man had never struck him as being benevolent and after the gossip he had heard he was positive that no generous motivation had entered into the agreement. The man had his agenda worked out and somehow Merrick was afraid it would not do Linda any good. Yet, until he had the facts, he could do nothing. Well, let's get the facts. We'll start first with Tom Spenny.

Merrick had noticed Spenny was oddly reticent to talk about his employer when he began to ask questions about the workings of the mine and, even more so, about Linda. What did he know about Jethro's death? Was he somehow involved with it or was he the culprit? Merrick eventually managed to track Tom down in the backyard of his cottage, just outside the village.

The door was answered by Tom's wife who told him, grumpily, Tom was likely shutting up the pigs they kept there. Either that or he had gone to the local tiddly-shop for a jar of ale. She did not care where he was.

To Merrick's relief he came across Tom closing the gate which led to the sties. He grunted a surly welcome to Merrick and stood waiting to hear what the partner wanted. Without preamble Merrick said, "Tell me about Jethro Barton."

"What's to know? He's long gone," Spenny said tersely.

"Yes, I know, but what made Ambrose Trevarron take over the rearing of his child?"

"I dunno, no one else offered. She'm an orphan. 'Twas either him or poor 'ouse."

"Is that a fact?"

"I'm tellin' ye, ain't I?"

"So what happened to Jethro? How did he die?"

"I told ye afore, he got 'it by a coal truck."

"Deliberately?"

"Course not; he'm liked by everyone. 'Twas an accident, anyone 'ud tell ee that."

"There have been many accidents in this pit. In fact it has a bad reputation for being accident-prone. And not just ordinary accidents; ones that often prove lethal."

"How do ee know that?" Spenny's eyes flickered anxiously.

Merrick knew he had touched a raw spot. "One hears things from all sorts of people."

"Yes, well, one dursent take notice of all ye may hear. There's a lot of spite in t'village. If one has one ha'penny atop another there's allus some who'll point a finger."

"At you, maybe? Come on, Tom, I'm not out to get at you. My aim, as you know, is to restore safety to the mine. If wealth is to come out of it then it should be for the benefit of everyone. You, me, the miners, their families and so on. Do you want me to walk away and leave you to Trevarron? Let things go on as they have in the past?"

"You wouldn't do that, would you?" For a moment his face

looked bleak and scared. He had been spared doing Trevarron's dirty work while Merrick had been around and he was loath to be used again; if Merrick went then Tom would have no choice.

"Trevarron and I do not agree how to run this mine. Of course it's his mine to start with, I'm just a comer-in, and he has the final word. But if I'm adding money to improve the conditions then I have to know what is going on for it to be worthwhile."

"You wanna ask 'im how he got the mine."

"What do you mean? Hasn't it been in his family a long time? It is what he told me."

"No sir, it b'ain't. He won it from young Lord Trevarron playing cards. T'ain't his name neither though he said he was a distant cousin, said he would adopt the name as it made it easier for the locals, them being used to it, like. The young Lord shot 'isself after losing the property. Daft bugger! He'd only just inherited from his Da, but he was a crazy gambler, he'd bet on a falling leaf if somebody took 'im on."

"Oh, that does put a different light on things. Tell me, can you keep a close button on your lip?" Merrick said sharply wondering if he ought to trust Spenny.

"None closer. I'd not keep this job if it weren't so, but I b'ain't up to any dirty work, if that's your purpose. I'm nearing retirement if I'm lucky, and I've had enough of…" He paused, staring back at Merrick with a frightened look on his face.

"Doing Trevarron's dirty work?"

Spenny did not reply for a moment, uncertain how to answer, but the honest look in Merrick's eyes reassured him and he decided to be truthful.

"If I 'ave done it, I b'ain't doing it no more."

"I want to marry Linda Barton." Cautious as ever, for some strange reason he decided to put it that way. It would not do to let Spenny know of Trevarron's plans.

Tom pursed his lips and whistled anxiously. "Tha's taking

yer life in yer hands, sir. T'master wants her 'isself. I seen the signs long ago. He's waiting till she grows up."

"Is that why he had Jethro killed?"

"No, Jethro was causing unrest in the mine."

"Aha, you do know something, Tom! No, don't say anything more. When the time is right I'll get you to repeat your story but when you do I shall have obtained immunity for you. There is such a thing as being coerced into crime. I've no doubt this will act in your favour. In the meantime, will you warn me if he does anything out of the ordinary? I'll see you well paid for your information."

"I dassn't want payment, I'll do it for free this time. I wants rid o' that villain. To tell ee the truth, I'm right glad ee come forward. I was at me wit's end wiv worry. I got the rest o' the village on me back; I'm caught between them and him."

"Listen, I can't go back to the Hall at the moment for I've business elsewhere. Can you get any facts to me as to Trevarron's intention with the mines? There's no one else I can ask for I'm sure he keeps a still tongue in his head. He trusts you, 'tis likely he'll tell you about his plans. Come to that, I am trusting you too. You must make up your mind which side you are backing for you cannot serve both of us. I'll be fair with you but not if you think to play both sides against the middle."

"I won't let ee down, sir. 'Tis a first time in many years I've felt safe wiv a person. Don't leave us; you'll be the making of this mine and the village if you stay. T'men 'ave respect for ee. Already they feel safer trusting you."

"Thank you for your confidence, I'll do what I can for all of you, but if he tries to get me out, the law will uphold him as legal owner," Merrick warned.

"Don't we miners have any say? We work bloody pit for a stingy pittance. Who takes our side? The law's always against us working folk as far as I can see."

"Collectively you have a voice; though if you were to strike I've no doubt he'd starve you out. No, Tom, let's do things peaceably and wait and see. Meantime, I suggest you mend your fences with the village people and gain their trust. You need them on your side in case things get nasty. Keep in touch with me?"

"Aye, sir, I promise I will, as soon as I hear anything."

Though the news that Tom Spenny brought Merrick the next morning was anything but welcome: Linda was not to be found; overnight she had run away from Tregender Hall.

CHAPTER THIRTY-THREE

Once back in her room, Linda began preparations for retiring to bed in case Betsy came back downstairs to check on her. She only took off her dress and hung it up, then donned a large nightdress, which hid her undergarments. The silk pumps were returned to the wardrobe and stout walking shoes that she would have on later were discreetly tucked under the bed. A small valise, which she had purloined from the storage attic, was packed with a change of underwear and a dress and toiletries, then slid alongside the shoes. Another dress was readied to slip into and a heavy cloak completed her provision for leaving. Lastly she reached for the velvet case, which she had secreted at the back of a solid mahogany armoire which stood in a corner of her bedroom.

The chest held china and silver, hoarded for decades from the Trevarron family for, although Ambrose had gutted and remodelled the Hall, he kept the old furniture to restore a look of antiquity to the house. Linda did not mind the armoire remaining in her room, as she loved its carvings and polished sleekness. Despite the urge to look at the contents, she had not touched the case again lest Betsy caught her at it. Betsy never gave a thought to knocking on Linda's door before entering for, having brought her up since a child, a locked door between them would have been unnecessary.

On opening the case Linda gasped anew at the locket's glowing beauty. Fine gems gleamed in the candlelight, emitting a prism of colour that flashed round the room as the chain swung gently in her hand. The locket itself was quite large; the gold filigree edging that was inset with many diamonds looked almost like delicate lace. Whoever had crafted the work was a master in design. She pressed a tiny catch and the lid sprang open. At once her great-grandmother's face stared up at her. If only she could speak, thought Linda, I would know my mother's past and how to reach my family. That is, if there are any to reach. It seemed impossible to imagine at that moment she was about to do just that - to run from all she had ever known in her short life to find to whom she really belonged and face danger and, perhaps, disappointment in her quest. With a sigh she replaced the necklet in its case then picked up the letter and opened it. Who was Lucien? Had he been married and unable to marry her mother? In that case, how had her mother started the baby within her? A blush rose to her cheek at her straying thoughts. It would appear she had so much to learn about life. She had never entered into the usual girlish gossip with school friends and neither Betsy nor Annie had ever spoken of personal matters. She knew she was woefully ignorant of the facts of life. Maybe this letter would reveal more. With yet another sigh she began to read.

Tregender Hall.

My dearest Lucien,

If you get to read this letter I shall be dead. I have had, just lately, an overwhelming sense of approaching doom. Some might call it mere fancy, pregnancy fears and fusses. I know otherwise. Don't mourn me, my love, for I feel fate never meant us to be together in this life. I do not blame you for leaving me to my fate knowing of your responsibility to your family. Yet if our position had been reversed I would have followed you to the very ends of the earth. Sadly, I was forced to undertake this pretence of a marriage to a stranger, a cruel, hard stranger, who thinks only of obtaining a son; nothing else matters. He is consumed with this ambition which I know cannot, nor ever will be, fulfilled. Take our offering instead - your daughter - for I am sure I will have a girl. Ambrose will never want a daughter, particularly as she is not his. She is yours, my darling, only yours, our love was blessed with fruitfulness.

Somehow I shall arrange for you to have her, I do not as yet know how. Will you name her after your mother, whom I have always loved? She did once love me, I know, when my own mother neglected me so badly. I am ever in her debt for that kindness. How I hate my grandmother for taking me to London and then arranging this vile marriage. She has no idea of the wrong she did me. Care for Linda Rose and love her, tell her about me.

I love you, Lucien, forever yours. Lavinia Rose.'

Linda clasped her hands around the note, gazing up at the ceiling in an agony of grief, willing herself not to cry but, unbidden, the tears slid down her face to splash on the paper. Her poor mother, how she must have suffered. Had Lucien rejected her? Was she made to marry someone? It certainly seemed like it. Yet her mother never stopped loving him, so maybe he had not deserted her after all. As far as Linda was concerned her mother had loved and wanted her. How wonderful it would have been to have known that so many years ago. Linda clenched her fists in frustration. This letter made it all the more imperative she find her kin to unravel the mystery of her birth. One thing she was sure of, she owed nothing to Ambrose. He must have treated her mother as badly as he had treated everyone else she knew of, including her this dreadful evening. She was not going to wait to be forced into marriage as her mother had been, either with him, or this austere Scot. No, she would escape tonight and hang the consequences. Anything would be better than remaining to be a victim.

CHAPTER THIRTY-FOUR

Tregender Hall looked the same on the outside as it had looked when first built. Square-set, granite-faced with large Georgian windows set almost to the floor at ground level, with stout inner shutters. The same granite was used in the high walls which extended on either side of the house, inset on one side with an arched gateway that led to the carriage quarters, stables and servants' area. The other side had a matching archway filled with a gate of iron filigree through which could be seen part of the landscaped garden. Inside the house, pokey rooms and long corridors had given way to comfort and space. Opening the roof to insert a glass cupola, thereby bringing light into the very heart of the house and designing a central spiral staircase beneath had been an achievement. It had even, if only temporarily, brought a kind of popularity to Ambrose, hitherto shunned for his outrageous capture of the Trevarron property through the notorious game of cards.

The ensuing death of the young heir had added further spice to the sordid episode but Ambrose had gauged the curiosity of the local gentry very well. They would make peace in return for an invitation to his sumptuous house. He was not mistaken. However, he basked in fame for only a little while. Once the prying eyes had been assuaged the local people were satisfied not to return. The house, with all its finery and decorations, was the subject of many a tea party's gossip. On the contrary the owner of it meant nothing; he was only an upstart after all and socially one who would never be cultivated for his charming manner.

Ambrose, once rejected and shunned, withdrew; his

overweening ambitions to integrate with the Victorian aristocracy had been thwarted. Instead, he concentrated on making his mines pay as much as they would yield before turning his thrusting aspirations towards acquiring a son through Lavinia. Failing that objective and a couple of abortive attempts to gain another wife, his warped mind evolved yet another scheme; to rear a child so grateful she would do as he wished.

This plan, it appeared, tottered on the brink of failure due to his crass misreading of the situation. Once again he berated his violent temper. Hellfire! It has let you down time and time again. Do not let what happened to Zelda occur again. Not if I can help it, he growled to himself as he got into bed, but Linda will never be allowed to leave me, I know that now. I won't let her marry Macgregor, she'll marry me. She'll be my wife and only mine. It's my last chance to have my own son. I can't let her go. I won't let her go! If I have to commit murder again - I won't let her go.

CHAPTER THIRTY-FIVE

It was simplicity itself for Linda to raise the window and slip out into the grounds to make her escape. Her only fear, at two o'clock in the morning, was Tam hearing her steps as she headed for the moors behind the house. The house was surrounded by gravel and it was all she could do not to make a noise as she picked her way carefully through the garden and on to freedom. When she was about a mile away she heaved a sigh of relief. Not a sound disturbed the night air save a hunting owl from the location of the village. She had decided not to go in the direction of Penzance for that was the first place they would look for her. Instead she was heading for the north coast and the village of Zennor. With luck, she would pick up the coach coming through at dawn from St Just. It would take her far enough up-country to pick up a connection for London. There, she was convinced, lay all the answers to her background. She only hoped the meagre funds she had saved over the years would be enough for her fare. After that, who could tell what would happen?

Linda guessed she had taken a wrong path when, after trudging up a short rise, she saw she was too far over to the left and would have to skirt Mulfra Hill to reach High Kerrow before dropping to Zennor. A short way further over on the left she could see, in the light of the moon which was three days off full, huge stone boulders standing in a rough circle. The Nine Maidens! Her heart fluttered in her chest like a caged bird as she stared at the huge monoliths: featureless, immovable. One could truly believe that these prehistoric stones were once maidens who had been cast into granite for some unimaginable folly, to dance forever on the windy heights of Cornwall.

Suddenly aware she was walking through a land of giants and pixies, ghosts of sailors drowned in the sea below or miners from the surrounding pits, she took fright and turned quickly to race across the moor seeking a path that would lead her to Zennor. Oh please let me get there safely, she prayed! Her reckless flight took her heedlessly over rough ground of gorse and heather, marsh and stone. As used to the moors as she was, she had never been out late at night, or so far away from home. The rock, which lay in her path, was small and well hidden but large enough to catch her foot and trip her headlong to the ground. Hitting her head on another stony outcrop was the last thing she knew as everything went black. The bag, clutched in her hand, went flying into the undergrowth and Linda lay as still as death on the Cornish hillside.

She awoke to find herself being shaken and jostled in a rickety cart that seemed to find every bump and rut along the stony path. Sitting up gingerly, for her head was aching like fury with every lurch of the cart, she squinted at her surroundings.

"Aaah, youse wiv us then? Thought ye'd never wake up. Powerful long sleep ye've had. Reckon nature has her way o' healing. If I'd a known ye'd take so long I'd have stayed in me own van; thass it, up ahead, I got yin o' the lads driving it. They left ye on the cart in case ye snuffed it. Easier to toss ee out, see?" the voice said matter-of-factly.

Linda gazed at the small, brown wrinkled face of the woman who sat alongside her, in blank dismay. Where was she? She knew she was supposed to be elsewhere but where? Her confused brain, still suffering from the effects of the fall, refused to help her.

Groaning with pain she lay down again on the coarse sacking which disguised fat shapeless bundles beneath her.

"You ain't gonna die on me? If so, thee best say quickly,

afore Matthias gets madder than 'e is already. He dursent take to strangers; picking ye up goes agin the grain wiv him. If it warn't fer me he'd let ee lay till the crows 'ad took ee, so make like thee's alive or ee won't be setting at me fire tonight."

"I'm all right; but my head aches fit to burst. Where am I and who are you?"

"Me?" she cackled a spurt of mirth. "I'm Serina, Serina Boswin. Who are thee?"

After a long pause Linda sat up again and frowned before staring blankly at the old woman. "Oh dear, I don't know – I can't seem to remember anything at all. Not who I am or what I am doing on this cart. Oh dear life, my mind is completely empty." Who was she? Where had she come from? What had happened? All she could see in her mind was blackness. Not a shred of memory to give a clue of her past life.

"You have a lump on thy head which termorrow will be black an' blue. 'Tis likely the cause of yer memory failin' ye. Doan't fret, child, 'twill come back to thee afore long. Lie there and sleep. I'll tell Matthias ye ain't gonna make crow's meat after all." With that she hopped off the cart with a sprightliness that decried her age and scurried to the front of the small procession winding its way through the moorland. The sun was hidden behind low cloud but Linda sensed it was approaching evening. Had she slept all day? How far had they travelled, these people, whoever they were? Then without knowing quite why she was not more shocked, she knew a band of gypsies had picked her up. All Betsy's dire sayings streamed through her brain. As far as Betsy was concerned being taken by gypsies was only barely second best to being taken by the devil! Yet Linda felt sure they meant well, they had not wanted her to die on the moors. At least Serina seemed to be of that mind. She had yet to meet Matthias!

A small coppice, with a nearby stream having a fast run of water from the moors, was used for the campsite of the gypsies that night. The old woman tried to interest Linda in a plate of stew; but she shook her head listlessly then greedily drank the offered mug of water. Serina gave her a blanket and pointed to a mat by the small fire and she lay down thankfully again and tried to sleep, her headache throbbing too much to let her do anything else. Around midnight the old woman woke her with a quick nudge to her shoulder. She jumped in terror and sat up.

"Shush, luv, you'm fazing the camp wiv thy racket; here drink this." She handed the girl a mug. "Reckon you'm gotta fever. Thass all we need, ye wiv a fever, thee's just like a chavvy wiv croup, keepin' us all awake. Matthias won't like it one bitty..." Linda took the mug and obediently swallowed the bitter brew which tasted somewhat like other nasty brews that Betsy now and then concocted. Within a short time her fright lessened and she shook off the nightmare that caused her to twist and moan in her sleep. She had been dreaming that Ambrose was chasing after her and no matter how hard she tried to run he was reaching out his hand to grab her. His hand was on her shoulder when Serina had roused her. Thank goodness it was only a dream. "I'm sorry I'm a bother," she apologised gratefully to the gypsy woman. "My head still aches but I think I am better than I was."

"You sleep, my conya, the drink will help ye. It will soothe the pain."

All at once Linda felt a cool, gentle hand stroke her forehead and she drifted off to sleep while the gypsy woman caressed her gently. Poor frashed chavvy, she'm runnin' from someone that's a fact. Soon as she's well, I'll ducker the cards and read her fortune. She'm a strange one to find. She could have been my Sara lying there 'cept she's fair as bleached linen. Oh Sara, I wish thee was here to comfort me in me old age. She sighed deeply then climbed the stairs of the Vardas to her own bed.

CHAPTER THIRTY-SIX

The dark-skinned old woman eased the pipe from her lips and accurately aimed a gobbet of spittle at the small fire that lay between her and a fair-haired girl busily tending a cut on the bottom of her foot. She watched it hiss momentarily and disappear, then as the burning wood settled, causing a shower of sparks to leap into the night air, she commented, "Kettle's still hot, best tak' a bowl o' water into' Vardas an' wash yer dirty self. You ain't had no water near you'm since we picked you up."

"There's scarcely been time, has there?" replied the girl defensively. "I had no idea that gypsies were so disliked, those dreadful people at that last village were really hateful, I was sure they were about to kill us." She finished cleaning the last of the grit out of the cut and, rising, went to fetch a bowl from the nearby Vardas. Filling it with warm water from the old blackened kettle that steamed beside the embers, she carried it carefully inside the gypsy caravan and placed it on the floor.

"There's soap an' a towel ont' shelf by the door. Call me when yer done an' I'll fetch ye a cleaner rag to wear. Those you'm got on will have to be burnt else ye'll likely be recognised if'n they come after ye. D'ye reckons they will? Only Matthias don't take to any strangers as a rule, especially if'n they bring the law on us. He done ye a big favour as it is, takin' ye up along o' us - not but what it ain't a bit o' my fault an' all, you'm being all terrified out o' yer wits. I reckon we'll have time tonight for ye to tell me what scared the very marrow from yer bones." The gypsy woman rose awkwardly, her old body bent and creaking with the ache of rheumatism that was gaining on her year by year despite the remedies she took to ease the pain. Too many wet winters and not enough sun, she thought wearily, as if nature had turned her face away from her people. Why was it she was forever recalling the old days when the sun shone with warmth and life was worth living? When Davie was alive to love and thrill her to the depths of her soul. Abruptly she shook her head - dratted old memories, sign of age that was all they were to her now. The good days were long since gone. She shrugged them away even as she climbed the steps to the caravan and pushing open the door entered the tiny cabin.

Her eyes took in the slight form that stood naked and shy before her. Gone was the dirty tear-streaked face, replaced now with a clear unblemished skin just faintly dotted with a powdering of freckles on the dainty retroussé nose. Her eyes shone darkly black in the moonlight coming through the tiny window but Serina knew they were as green as new spring grass, with pale flecks of gold in their depths. Her graceful form, on the verge of nubile womanhood, portrayed the swelling pink tipped breasts, slender waist and long curving thighs that gave great promise of the amazing figure it was destined to be. Serina was fixed in sheer amazement, and then she recovered and slammed the door,

"Move over, dearie, I'll find some togs for you in that chest. I gotta pair o' slippers that might fit ye and we'll put some salve on that cut o' yourn, don' want it to turn bad." She found herself gabbling to hide the shock that had overtaken her when she saw the naked girl. For pity's sake, the girl was quality, damme if she ain't, she thought. If Matthias saw her now - he would get rid o' her for sure, and then in an instant she knew he would not - he would want her for himself. God almighty, the tribe had to be caught in the uproar that Berta would cause if she realised Matthias was straying.

"You got lice?"

"No! I haven't!" cried the girl indignantly.

"Only I don't hold wiv lice," said Serina, ignoring her

outburst. "Because we're gypsies don't mean we're the scum o' the earth. Keep yersel' clean an' keep healthy, that's what I say. Here's a comb, take it through them tangled curls, then ye'll have to cover 'em up wiv a scarf, won't do to let all and sundry know how fair ye are." She rummaged in a chest while she spoke, hauling out first one garment then another till she said, "Ah, this will do ye," and held up a dark brown velvet skirt against the girl. "Here's a top to go with it and I'll loan ye a shift till your'n is dry. Now, m'girl, what are we to call ye and what kind o' story are ye to tell Matthias when he asks us, which he will do when the camp reaches Launceston? We'll be staying over in Dutterton Woods. We gypsies are safe there; the local people don't treat us like nasty vagrants and felons to be drummed out of a village with sticks and stones as happened today. They'm having more respect for us'n."

Linda thought of the angry people in the village they had passed through that morning. Much of the fuss had been instigated by one man but soon the rest of the village turned out to drive the gypsies away from their midst. Their normal plan to sell clothes pegs and lace was rebuffed and the evening's supper was very meagre indeed with no money to spend on food. Linda, who had lost a shoe when the tribe panicked, ran in terrified disarray from the vicious blows the villagers were heaping on them. The deep cut, caused by a sharp stone underfoot when she attempted to leap onto the moving caravan, was painful but at least she had avoided being hit with a cudgel.

"How old are you, miss?"

"Seventeen. Well, almost eighteen," Linda said shyly.

"Why, yer a woman full-grown, I took you fer a child. I was married with a babe at my breast when I was your age. An' as proud of my Davie as a cat with a bowl of cream. Ye need a man's love to bring a spark to yer eye and a blush to your cheek, my 'andsome," she jested with a wry grin. "So, miss, what's yer name?"

"I'm called Lindy at home; my full name is Linda Barton."

"Them are posh names. Where are ye from, Lindy?"

Linda hesitated. Rank terror, rising like bitter gall in her mouth, overcame her as she stared back at Serina all of a sudden afraid that the old woman would send her back.

"Don't worry, I ain't gonna blab on ye." Immediately Serina perceived the cause of her anxiety. "So far as I'm concerned yer a free spirit, 'tis Matthias who will want to know, so I'm just preparin' ye. Come back to the fire now yer dressed and we will sup a hot drink while ye tell me yer story, this night air is not good for my aches. I need to be warm." They seated themselves back at the fire and when the old woman had a cup of hot herb tea in her hand she smiled at Linda and nodded for her to continue.

Reassured, Linda said, "I come from Trewren, I've lived there all my life."

"The mining village north o' Penzance?"

"Yes, I was first in the village, and then I lived at Tregender Hall."

"Who are your folks? I ain't ever heared o' prime quality by the name o' Barton round there." The old woman fetched an old pipe from a pocket and proceeded to fill it.

"The Bartons were my…" she paused, quite overcome with deep sadness at her recent discovery, the shock of learning she was not the true daughter of Jethro and Ellie Barton after all. "My…they were the people who adopted me when I was a babe."

"Who were your real parents then?"

"I'm not sure. You see, I never knew my own mother; she died when I was born, but I've only just discovered who my real father is. That is, he is not the man who took me in when my …father …. when Jethro Barton was killed …the man who thought he was my father. Oh dear, it is so frightfully mixed up. I hardly know myself let alone try to tell you."

"Well, who took you in then from Tregender, if I might be so bold as to ask? God's truth, child, it's like pulling teeth to get your history. How are we gonna decide what to tell Matthias, if'n you don't tell me first?"

"Ambrose Trevarron. He owns the Hall now, though I heard tell he won the place through a game of cards. The old family who had it before are long since gone."

Serina drew in a shuddering breath as she heard the name of Ambrose. It wasn't a familiar Christian name in these parts. Was it possible it was he? Quite likely, she reflected, for he had always been sharp with cards. She'd known him rook many an unwary victim. His disappearance from the tribe when they had been travelling in the north had caused a stir especially as nobody heard of him again in gypsy circles. He could have fled south to Cornwall to escape retribution but she had always presumed he had headed for London and maybe taken a ship abroad. So, after all these years, was the devil raising his ugly head? Well, she had lived long enough to know that the wheel turns and what goes around, comes around, what goes up, must come down, but she had never expected to hear his name spoken of in this fashion. Especially to hear he might have bred a child as fine as this, why it was scarcely possible.

"Why do you look like that? Do you know him?"

"Once, long ago, I knew an Ambrose, or more correctly my sister's child knew him. Too well I fear, for she died of knowing him. But never mind all that. Why did ye think he might have been yer father and was that the reason ye ran away?"

"No!" Linda hung her head in shame and a tear ran down her face. "If it were only that I could have borne it, for we got on tolerably well together. Instead it's quite different. First he told me he was my father and I must marry the man he'd chosen; then because I had only just found out the truth I told him he was wrong, we were not related. After that he got furiously angry and said I would have to marry him instead!"

"Hell's teeth! It must be him! I knew him for an evil villain and it sounds as though he is little changed! No wonder you ran, child, t'would be like runnin' from the devil himself.

Hush now, dearie, dry yer eyes and tell me the story right from the beginning, for I'll never rest this night until ye do. Just keep yer voice low for the camp is at rest now; we dassn't disturb them or Matthias will be wondering what we are plotting. As 'tis, mayhap we'll go inside the Vardas so I can rest on my bed while ye can sit in my rocking chair. My Davie bought it for me at St Germans Fair one year when he was flush with money; it's been a fair comfort over the years since he died. But what am I saying, it's your'n story I want to hear, so up in the van wiv ye where you will tell me all that's happened in your short life."

So Linda told her story exactly the way the woman who had brought her into the world had told it to her. She couldn't know all of it, of course, but her lively mind had filled in some of the gaps from odd remarks she overheard while she was growing up. When she finished Serina gave a deep sigh. "Well, if that doesn't beat all the tales in the world for sheer peculiarity."

"Don't you believe me?" Linda begged.

"Oh, I believe you, it's too strange a tale not to. Trouble is, what will Matthias believe? He's the one we have to convince so that you can stay wiv me."

CHAPTER THIRTY-SEVEN

Linda was on her knees beside the small, gently glowing campfire, which cast a haze of fragrant oak wood smoke into the still air. She was preparing the meagre wild vegetables that Serina had given her, in readiness for a jogray or gypsy stew. She was beginning to learn quite a few Romany terms and no longer felt a stranger in the gypsy camp. Serina had gone to seek a bit of meat to cook with the vegetables, hopefully large enough to provide them with food for at least two days. Linda helped where she could but for safety's sake had taken no part in the foraging or the selling of gypsy goods outside of the camp. Nor did she mix or talk to anyone around her; more than conscious of her lack of knowledge of the gypsy customs and tribal speech.

"Best keep yer head down, luvvy, till we see what's best to do fer yer future," Serina directed, aware that Linda's presence in the camp was looked on with great disapproval. Linda was in favour of that attitude as her mind was still in turmoil over the recent events in her life. Intent on her work she did not see anyone approach until a pair of huge black boots unexpectedly stood beside her. Swiftly she raised her eyes to the huge figure wearing them then, with a gasp of fright, she scuttled backwards in an effort to reach the Vardas when the man spoke.

"So you are the stranger we picked up a week ago?"

She nodded warily, knowing at once it was Matthias. Her fright subsided a little when she saw he did not look quite so menacing. Rather than huge he was a tall, well-made man clothed in thick togs that made him look bigger than he was.

His beard was grey though his dark hair was only lightly flecked with silver, and jet-black eyes shone in the brown of his face.

"What is your name?"

"L-Linda Barton." Oh where was Serina? Please hurry back.

"Hmm, is it your real name?" He tried to peer at her face, which she kept low, hidden beneath the scarf, scarcely raising her eyes to look him in the face.

"Yes, of course." she said defiantly. Truthfully she could lay no claim to any other.

"And why were you running?" he went on as though she had not spoken. "From the law? Or has your master thrown you out of his employment?"

"None of those things. I am an orphan and I am seeking a trace of my own family."

"In the midst of the Cornish moorland?" His voice held a hint of quizzical humour.

"No, I tripped and hit my head. I was going to Zennor to take a coach for Bristol."

"And then?"

"Get from there to London somehow." She shrugged as though careless of her fate.

"Where were you living before this bump on the head?"

"I think that's my business, don't you?" Now the defiance showed itself openly.

"Ah! The mouse roars." His eyes glinted suddenly with icy steel. "Anyone who stays in my camp becomes my business, missy, it will pay you to remember that," he retorted angrily.

She wondered if she had gone too far in view of Serina's warning that he was a person to be afraid of. "It's only that my head is in a muddle. From the bang on it, you see. I was not aware this was your camp. I have scarcely found out who anybody is apart from Serina."

"Hmm." He stood silent for a moment gazing down at her then swiftly, before she could avoid it, brought the stick he was holding to the tie at her neck and with a quick jerk flicked the scarf off her head. Instantly, in wild disorder, blonde curls and ringlets fell about her shoulders, changing her appearance in an instant from a cowering slip of a child into the radiant beauty that had sought to hide. "Your head holds more than disarray, it seems, why do you seek to hide yourself from us?"

"Well," she faltered, "you are all dark while..."

"You are as fair as a lily. Are you well-born?"

"I don't know." She did not know so it was hardly a lie. Oh, Serina, hurry back.

Almost as though she had heard Linda call for her, Serina made her appearance.

"You've been hiding a gorgio child. Why didn't you tell me, Serina? You made her out to be a Didecoi which is plainly not true."

"Isn't she?" Serina played for time, her brain working frantically for Linda's sake. She could not determine the mood he was in and did not know how to act for the best.

"Oh, Serina, Serina, don't mistake me for a Pikie, we've known each other much too long. You'll have had her story out of her the first night, if I'm not mistaken; now I want the truth, so out with it. Tell me all you learned from her."

Before Serina could say a word Linda interrupted. "'Tis all true and just what I told her. I was running off to find my family. I was a maid in a big house back o' Penzance. The Master...well he tried..." Her face flared with embarrassment, scarce knowing how to explain Trevarron's attack on her. "It wasn't right so I left in a hurry. I only had a brief notion I belonged somewhere else. It seemed better than what I had to face where I was so..." She shrugged. "I lost my way over the moor and I was running because I thought I'd miss the coach..." She stopped, unable to think of what else to say.

"Ah! I see. Did he succeed?" Numbly she shook her head and he laughed. "Stupid man!" He laughed even more as she glared at him with her huge green eyes ready to brim with tears, though whether in anger or shame he could not determine. "I like you," he announced, his face still creased in a smile. "Come to my supper fire tonight, Serina; bring this fair gorgio with you...without her scarf this time. She has a beauty I shall enjoy while we are eating." There was a pause as he considered the girl still kneeling in front of him. "No, let her wear it. We have one or two young men in the camp that would fight to the death for her and I have a mind to keep her for myself."

"But you can't...what of Berta?"

"Ah yes, Berta. What of it? She has learned to turn a blind eye over the years to my weaknesses. Why should she change now?" He turned away and strode off towards his own Vardas. Linda and Serina could hear him chuckling as he went whilst they sat and gazed at each other in dismay.

"Well, he likes you; that's one good thing," said Serina with a sigh. "Perhaps a bitty too much for our comfort, or yours, my conya. I must think what to do. Carry on cooking the stew, it will keep till termorrow; thank the stars, for tonight we'll eat better'n a king." Without another word she climbed up into the van and Linda heard her rummaging about in boxes for quite a while until all was quiet and she presumed Serina was asleep.

When she had the pot of vegetables and meat cut and cooking to her satisfaction she found a mat and lay down before the fire and tried to compose her thoughts. So what if Matthias had taken a fancy to her? What could she do to protect herself from him taking over her life? She supposed the only option she had was to run away again. Surprisingly she was loath to do that. She would miss Serina and her fund of folklore and wisdom. From their quiet talks she had learned much of the world around her that she never knew had existed outside the walls of Trevarron. Serina had spoken of the Ways of the Road and the Romanies that trod the Ways; herbal cures which amazed her; cooking on an open fire; sheltering during the bleakest of weather. In fact, Linda realised there was a wholly different way of living that was free and simple. Except for the violence which erupted now and again from those people who did not understand the Romany way of life.

"Thass why we keep to us'n and move in tribes fer protection. We'd all be hung from the nearest gibbet if we dursent."

"Surely not!" Linda cried out. "Don't people know you wouldn't harm a soul?"

"Trouble is, my lamb, there's some o' us as bad as they're painted. Like nature itself. There's good and bad in everyone, an' it's the hedge crawlers that do us down."

"Hedge crawlers? Who are they?" Linda was intrigued with the name.

"They're the scum o' our race, more's the pity. The cheats and swindlers, horse thieves, con men and women come to that. As I said, scum! Ye find one o' them in yer vicinity it poisons the whole area. That's the good thing about Matthias, he don't stand fer no double-dealing from anyone. He guards his tribe well. Sharp as a blade he is to turf 'em out - most like wiv a blade a'tween their ribs."

"He kills people?" Linda burst out in dismay.

"Shush! Course not. At least not fer anyone to find out. Keep a still tongue in yer 'ead, miss, or I'll not say another word."

"Oh I will, I promise. Don't stop talking to me. I have so much to learn and there is no one else to teach me. I appreciate your kindness, I do," Linda begged tearfully.

"There, dearie, I won't leave ye by yerself. Yer good company. I ain't ever talked so much in my life. Now fetch a brush and I'll do yer 'air. Can't 'ave ye looking like a winter 'edgehog, now can we?"

"What does a winter hedgehog look like?" Linda giggled at the old woman's sardonic scowling expression that was bordering on amusement.

"Hedgehogs roll 'emselves in dry leaves when it gets cold so they have a good warm blanket round 'em. Come spring when they gets moving it takes a while to rid 'emselves of the leaves and they look kinda like a tousled brush." She stopped, her eyes glinting with mirth as peal after peal of laughter came from the helpless girl.

"I don't l-look l-like a h-hedgehog."

"Not if we brush yer 'air, ye won't! But just now I'm sayin' yer the spitting image of one! Damn me if you ain't!" Still chuckling she proceeded to brush Linda's hair till it shone like gold then coiled it back under a carefully secured scarf. "There, my girl, that'll do you for tonight. Keep your face low and sit back from the fire. With luck Matthias will forgo his foolish plan and leave you alone."

And if he doesn't, contemplated Linda, what am I to do? Where shall I go?

CHAPTER THIRTY-EIGHT

Once again Serina's rummaging produced a clean skirt of pale blue cambric and a muslin blouse with embroidery round the neck. A wide shawl covered her shoulders and the coloured scarf that held back her fair tresses matched that of her eyes.

"'Tis as well you are tidy, just in case Matthias wants ye to show yer 'air," said Serina, confident that she had no need to worry that Matthias would upset his wife and family by taking the girl for himself. However, in case she was wrong, she considered fighting hard for the right to treat Linda like a daughter and to keep her close. On the other hand she knew Linda must fulfil her destiny and the cards she duckered for the girl showed she had a long way to travel before she found her real love and happiness. It appeared that way did not lie with the gypsies but how it would come about was beyond her powers to see at that moment.

"But where am I to go?" Linda asked the old gypsy after she had told Linda her fortune. "Or is this the long journey from Penzance to Launceston? If it isn't, how am I to know what to do? How can your cards say I must travel, but not where or how?"

"Bless ye, childling, this ain't but a mile or two, compared to the long road ye'll have to travel. Ye'll find not one but two loves when ye reach journey's end."

"Oh! Won't that be complicated? I'm not greedy, I only want one love."

"There are all kinds o' love in this world, Lindy. One might be yer sweetheart, and t'other might be anyone. Ye just relax, ye'll know soon enough, I warrant."

Linda retired to her bed after the reading, realising that the old gypsy had said all she was going to say, though it still did not give her any answers as to what she ought to do. Was she to leave as soon as possible or stay longer with the tribe?

Deep in thought Serina lay awake for a long time dismayed at the obstacles that seemed to strew the path of this young maiden until eventually she would reach the loving happiness that Serina wished for her.

Linda sat by the fire after she was readied for the forthcoming meal thinking over the enormous changes that had taken place in her life since she had been born. Nothing had stayed the same for long and, according to Serina, those changes were going on for a long time to come. Where would she end up? Where was safety, a family of her own, and some dear person whom she could trust and love? She was out of reach of Richard; he would not know where to find her. Would he want to? He would undoubtedly take notice of his mother and by now the whole district would know she had run away from the Hall. There was no way, with that scandal around her, that Richard, or his mother, would contemplate having her in their home let alone agreeing a marriage with Richard.

CHAPTER THIRTY-NINE

The last rays of the sun were turning the sky to a deep rose as Serina and Linda made their way to the glade where Matthias and his immediate family had parked their caravans. A large fire, encircled with boulders, was burning brightly in the centre of the surrounding ring of Vardas that housed his relatives. Matthias was seated there talking to his brother and eldest son. A little way off, women moved around more cooking fires and Linda could see a number of carcasses that were being turned on spits over coals.

"Come! Sit here with us; the food will not be long." Matthias waved a welcoming arm at the seat beside him then pointed to another across the fire for Serina. She scowled as she sat down, unwilling to leave her young charge so close to the dangerous man.

"Tell me of your master? Is he rich?" Matthias was eager to draw Linda's history out of her for his instincts told him it was unlikely she had been born into servitude.

"I suppose so. He has a big house and land and he also owns some mines nearby," Linda answered evasively, wondering how much she ought to tell him.

Matthias curled his lip. "Yuck! How can one spend one's life underground! Out of the sun and fresh air? I would rather die than go down a mine, wouldn't you, Zac?"

His brother nodded and spat in the flames. "Worse'n prison, I daresay, though I ain't bin in neither, nor ever want to."

"It depends on whether one has enough money to live and bring up a family," said Linda as she gazed into the flames of the fire with a sorrowful expression on her face. "There are so many people who live on the edge of starvation in Cornwall that to have a job, of any description, is a prize worth having. I expect you've gone hungry from time to time. That village we passed through on our way here, the people treated you badly and you suffered from their unkindness. Supposing every place you went to treated you the same way? You'd starve and your children would die. Any job that paid for you to live would be welcome, don't you think?"

"The child has a point, Zac." Matthias gazed at Linda with new respect. "So you are not just a pretty face, you've had schooling, haven't you?"

She nodded. "Yes, I've been taught well enough, and I appreciate kindness. Serina has looked after me exceedingly well but I owe you much gratitude for allowing her to rescue me."

Matthias smiled and nodded, pleased with her thanks and even more pleased with her polite manners. He ran a knowledgeable eye over her body and felt a yearning to touch the fair skin that held an attraction for him. Then Berta, his wife of many years, came up behind him and thumped a bowl of stew on the upturned log beside his leg. The gravy splashed out and the hot liquid sank through the cloth and burned his skin.

"Watch what you're about, you clumsy rackley! You nigh burned the skin off me."

"Then watch what you're about, my Chal, you pay too much attention to things that should not concern you." Berta stalked away quickly having left Matthias in no doubt she knew of his wandering eye and was giving notice he had better beware.

With a swift curse under his breath he picked up the bowl and then motioned the others, who had also been served, to begin eating. There was silence for a little while as hunger was assuaged, then gradually the conversation began again. Linda, unaware of the silent war that was going on between Matthias and his wife, was intrigued with the unusual dishes she enjoyed that night. She moved over beside Serina and, even though she was a light eater, she sampled many of them at the urging of her gypsy mentor who quietly explained the ingredients and how they were cooked.

"Aunt Betsy ought to be here. She'd love these different recipes," she enthused, without thinking of the listening ears.

"You have an aunt? Then how come you were running from your home?" In a flash Matthias interrupted their conversation.

"It's a little difficult to explain," Linda began.

"Then you must gather your thoughts, girl, for tomorrow you will give me a full and truthful explanation; I require no less. But now we will watch the dancing, for they are ready to begin." As he spoke Linda noticed several of the young women had gathered in a wide space and the opening chords of a couple of musical instruments were already beating out a melody. Moments later the women were whirling sinuously in time to the music and the onlookers found they were swaying to the throbbing sounds that filled the glade. Linda had never heard such strange thrilling music before. It made her want to get up and dance with the young gypsy girls and twirl and pirouette like them. She felt an unusual heat come over her and a deep throbbing run through her body. She was not to know that her eyes gleamed with excitement or her lips were parted and quivering with anticipation. Nevertheless the eyes watching her took note of her actions and pondered their next move. Matthias knew he had to rid himself, temporarily, of Berta and Serina knew she had to stop him.

CHAPTER FORTY

Tregender Hall was in frantic turmoil. Ambrose strode outside to the stables in a furious temper, tossing orders to Betsy, as she stood in the hall, wringing her hands in frightened dismay. "See the place is well-ordered before I return. Get the doctor to Gorland if she's no better – or we'll get a new housekeeper to replace her! You are all a lazy lot of good-for-nothing idiots that you can't keep an eye on a girl to stop her wandering - but she won't have gone far - I'll have her back shortly, you'll see, and she won't escape me a second time, you can be sure of that." His voice faded out of earshot and Betsy gave a sigh of relief, then jumped with a loud squawk, as Annie's voice sounded in her ear and she turned hastily to find the housekeeper behind her.

"Makes a devil of a noise, don't ee, the miserable ol' tyrant. I hope he don't find her, poor lass," she croaked roughly, as she clutched a blanket around her shoulders.

"Annie! For God's sake whatever are ye doing outa bed. You are not well enough to come downstairs. Don't fret; I'll see to things, he won't have no cause to grumble." She put out a hand to help Annie Gorland to a chair.

"I don't mind admitting me pins are shaky but I'm alive, which I did not expect to be las' week, I can tell ee. Help me to the kitchen, Betsy, there's a love, and make a pot o' tea that ye can stand a spoon in. I bin lyin' upstairs listening to all the shouting. Can't stand it no longer. What's bin goin' on while I'm abed?"

A little later the two women sat in the kitchen one each side of the fire while Betsy related all she knew about the sordid affair of her employer trying to rape her niece. "But how was I to know she'd take it into her head to run," she continued. "A girl who bain't bin further'n Truro in all her life. Course it were 'is doing - trying to get at 'er last night. If I ain't bin there – the Lord only knows what would 'ave 'appened – the dirty dog! An' so I told' him straight, I did. Fetch the law, I will, if'n you don't leave off of pestering my girl. He was so furious he might 'ave killed me!" she said dramatically.

Annie shook her head with concern as Betsy went on, "He stopped quick nuff, I tell ee. Ee bain't a fool, ee knows I'd do it too." She took another slurp of tea before studying her companion with keen eyes. "Reckon I'll fetch Doctor Lusty to ye today. I doan't trust that new yin. Master gave me leave an' Lusty bain't left yet. He'm awaiting fer Mrs Bunnion to go. She won't be long neither. She'll likely slip away soon. She got Becky Lanner staying to nurse 'er, poor soul. She'n Becky always hit it off, thank goodness. Now up to bed wiv ye, my girl, and I'll get one of Sithney's boys to run to the village. Good job he 'as a brood o' young 'uns or I don't know where we'd be for errand boys." She stood up wearily then helped Annie upstairs before returning to sort out the day staff that were just arriving.

Ambrose, for some strange reason known only to him, disliked a large number of people around him at the best of times and would only tolerate the two prime domestics, a young parlourmaid and an immature skivvy, for dirty work, to live in the house. The rest of the workers came as required daily, to char or do dairy work or to add to Sithney's labour force when he and the under-gardener were hard-pressed. William, the coachman, had a nephew in training but arrangements were strictly conducted between himself and Trevarron and had nothing to do with the main house. Two stable lads came up daily to see to the coach horses and Trevarron's hunter, though the latter was getting fat through lack of exercise. Today, however, the horse would have all it could manage while Trevarron was engaged in the search for Linda.

Halfway through the morning Betsy looked round for Polly to run to the dairy for her, then decided it was quicker to go herself. She had always been quiet on her feet, despite her size and the two girls in the dairy were too intent on their gossiping to hear her enter the cool dark building where butter, cheeses and clotted creams were processed.

"So there I was, standing in the butler's pantry twixt dining room and study, where you can hear every word, when I heard the master ask 'er, plain as the nose on yer face, it were." Polly paused, relishing the moment. She liked nothing better than being the centre of attention and here was the ideal moment to be listened to. Kate stared at her with her mouth open.

"Go on, Polly, ask 'er what. Hurry up, I gotta get on, or Polwen u'll be after me. Ask her what? You'm hold onto the gossip like you want payin' for it."

"Why to marry 'im, course, dunderhead! Oo, ain't it romantic? But what does the silly chit do but say no to everything. I reckon she wants to take 'er time. I'd grab 'im quick afore he changes 'is mind, if it t'were me. But thass not the half o' it, there was a right rumpus over it, Polwen hushed it up o'course. Wouldn't you know, Lindy gets all the luck and I only get Andy Truswell from the 'tater farm? I tell ee, some folks dassn't deserve the luck they -"

She stopped abruptly as the cook, now standing right behind her, aimed a hefty clout which hit its target with a loud thwack on the side of her head. Giving out a terrified bellow and clutching one bright red ear, Polly, giving a horrified yell, escaped further retribution by ducking swiftly under Mrs Polwen's arm and fleeing in desperate haste to the house, sobbing as she went.

"You want one an' all, Kate, fer listenin' to gossip?" When the young dairymaid quickly shook her head Betsy said, "Right, I don't want to 'ear owt of that stupid Polly's ramblings, got it? One word outsider 'ere which I find repeated in the village an' yous can whistle fer yer job! There is more'n enough talk around that there place about things that don't concern them so I don't want any more, see?"

"Not a word, Mrs Polwen, honest. I never heard nothin' that I'll ever pass on. I swear it. I'm just doing me job like always. She came out to me. She bin doing that all the time, y'know. Course I never pays no heed to 'er mutterings, an' never have, honest, I won't say a word."

"See ye don't. Now, what did I come in here for? Aah yes, a pint o' cream afore Lizzie whips it away for the cheese-making. Where is she, by the way?"

"Nipped out to fetch the chives fer the cream cheese; down by the greenhouses, I 'spect. Flirtin' wiv Halwyn, I suppose, stead of doing what she's supposed to. An' he's bone idle, too, I dassn't know how Sithney stands 'im."

"Lizzie hear owt from Polly? Well, you see she don't from you, unnerstand?" She eyed Kate with a baleful eye as the dairymaid nodded swiftly then got on with her work. Betsy rubbed her hands over her face when she returned to the kitchen. Hellfire and parsley sauce, she groaned to herself. Linda had run away to escape the Master's clutches and here she had been thinking it was Macgregor who was after her. What signals had she missed because she had been far more concerned with Annie? Now she came to think of it, there had scarce been time for Linda to fall for Macgregor. No, it was all that old swine Trevarron's doing. Whatever Polly had heard was all on his side. She'd give him what for, making up to her Lindy. 'Cept, of course, Linda wasn't a baby any more. She had the right to marry whomever she chose, but never that Macgregor, he wasn't her class at all, she'd be miserable in a month. Ah well, she mused, all the anxiety at the disappearance of Lindy would not get her chores done. So she hastened to get the dishes out for the meat pies she would produce for the evening meal, thankful she had prepared the beef the evening before. She was hard at work when Doctor Lusty tapped on the back door but, shaking flour from her fingers, she opened the door with a smile.

"Oh, Doctor, I'm that glad to see thee. Annie's bin so poorly this last week. That there new doctor just gave 'er a bottle of medicine, nothin' else…"

"Has the medicine done any good?" Lusty's tone was dry as he eyed her piercingly.

"Well, yes," Betsy allowed reluctantly, "but o' course, she'm would have felt better wiv restin'. I made sure she kept to her bed without fail."

"Doesn't matter what has been responsible as long as something has worked – now tell me – what did you want me for? What else has gone wrong?"

"Well it was partly to look at Annie an' work yer old magic to get 'er better. But really I wanted you to know Lindy's disappeared! Run away, she has! The Master's fair screeching with rage because of it. And it was his fault that started it all. He was trying to…well, you know. If I weren't so feared for me job I'd still go to the law and turn him in. He's a right swine and always has been, especially with the young maids. Why I could tell you many a tale…"

"You don't need to, Betsy. I've always had a good idea of what has gone on here. But back to Lindy. Have you any idea where she might go?"

"No. She doesn't know a soul barring us. She's just running scared and Lord knows what harm she'll come to now. All because of that dirty dog…"

CHAPTER FORTY-ONE

Doctor Lusty listened to Betsy's rambling tale with a degree of patience acquired over many years but, when she repeated herself for the fourth time, he called a halt. "Right, Betsy, I think I have all the facts now. I'll just slip up and see Annie then I shall go home to give the matter some thought."

"The question is why, Doctor? She was happy here; there weren't no call to run off. Me an' Annie would have protected her against that - that evil man."

"Yes, well, that evil man, as you call him, is your employer, don't forget. What will you do if he throws all of you out? No, Betsy, keep your counsel for now. Leave it to me to sort things out. I fancy I know a little more than you do, but I want to think about it. No good comes of rushing our fences; I've often heard you say that."

He smiled as she quoted more clichés then, before she really got going, he took himself off to the upper regions of the house to see Annie.

"How do you like our new man, Annie? He looks to have done you a power of good. Why, you are better than the last time I sounded your chest and that was, let me see, the winter we had all that influenza. Four or was it five years ago?"

"I do feel better, I admit. But he's not the same as you. He's too young for a start."

"Time will cure that, won't it? In thirty years someone will be against his retirement for exactly the same reason." They both laughed merrily.

"I can only agree with Doctor Fyfield. You can get up now, but take things easy. See him as arranged and take his medicine. Yes, it's horrid, but medicine doesn't do you any good unless it tastes dreadful." He drew an answering smile from her. "Look after Betsy as best as you can, she is worried to death over Lindy. There is no need to fret. The girl has a good head on her shoulders; she'll be fine, I'm sure."

He took his leave and went back home for a rest before carrying out his intention of visiting Amy. He felt bone-weary and old. Retirement can't come too soon, he reflected, or I'll never live to enjoy it. His confident remarks to the women did nothing for himself. In truth he was as concerned as Betsy about the fate of Linda but for entirely different reasons. Had she taken it into her head to go looking for her family? Lusty groaned in pure frustration. Why had he left it to a sick woman to tell Linda? He would have made a better job of the whole affair himself and perhaps given her guidance. Deep in thought he turned to his bookcases and rummaged for sometime before he found what he sought. Dunderhead! He should have done this an age ago but his head had been full of leaving things straight for the incoming doctor. Slowly he leafed through the pages of the book before giving a sigh of satisfaction as he reached the place he sought. As he read further his pleasure turned to surprise. Well! Who would have thought it? Fate had never ceased to amaze him in the past but never more so than now when he needed all the help he could get. It wasn't that Lindy might have gone away with Macgregor but the worry was, supposing she had not!

Lusty knocked on the door of Amy's cottage and saw the curtain twitch before Becky opened the door. "Come in, James, I was just making sure it was you before I answered the knock. She's just dropped off -" Becky nodded her head at Amy's bedroom door. "I need a word with thee afore she rouses. She's not getting much sleep. No," she said hastily, "it's not the cancer; it's her mind that's giving her trouble."

Dear God, what now? Lusty said to himself. "What do you mean, her mind?"

"Well, it's her conscience, see. Over swapping the babies.

She can't make up her mind if she done..." She paused at the look on the doctor's face.

"What swapping of babies?" he exclaimed striving to keep his face blank.

"Don't tell me you dassn't know what I'm a-talking about. I was sure you'd know, thee are cleverer than me, I'll be bound. I knew plain as day - she went off that day wiv a boy an' came back wiv a girl. Stands to reason she don't magick one outa thin air. Course it were the Trevarron child. He'd bin prating about a son long enough. Whole village knew he was a right daft loon about it. Reckon Amy thought he'd do a mischief to the little'un if she were left to his tender mercies."

"Did Amy know you knew?" James was curious.

"Nope, I figured if she had wanted to tell me she would've. So I never said nothing an' neither did she, 'cept now, in her ramblings. Lindy's his child, ain't she?"

James, marvelling at Becky's powers of restraint, decided to tell her the rest. "No, she's not Trevarron's, she's the daughter of his late wife and a former lover before she came to Cornwall. Why Lavinia Macgregor married Trevarron we'll never know now but the baby was definitely not his. Lavinia evidently hoodwinked Trevarron completely and so did Amy come to that."

"Thank God. It's always concerned me she had some o' his blood running through her veins. Amy knows all of this? About Lindy not being Trevarron's child, I mean?"

"Oh yes, she does, but she doesn't know that Lindy has run away from home - I've just heard the news myself. Trevarron went crazy and tried to molest her."

"There! And I was just about to ask you if you could persuade Lindy to come again and say she forgives Amy. The poor soul will die in peace if she does. Amy's fretting how Lindy took the news; thinks she was angry wiv her. It was bound to be a shock for Lindy 'tis natural, but I'm sure 'tis no more'n that, she was always a level-headed child."

"I'd persuade her willingly, if I knew where to find her. I

think she's gone to trace her family. Which is a great pity for she won't know what I've just discovered today; on my very own bookshelves. It's a book called Burkes Peerage!"

Becky looked blank; as well she may, for no one of her status would know of a book listing all the peers, baronets and knights in the realm. First compiled in 1829 it was a recognised authority on British aristocracy with family pedigrees. James acquired the book together with a number of medical books bought at a second-hand bookshop on one of his rare visits to London; he had barely glanced at it since then and it remained forgotten until he had been presented with the problem of tracing Linda's whereabouts.

James read the list of the Forres family from the time of Murdoch and his surprise at finding the last name in their section of the register – Merrick Andrew Macgregor – was startling to say the least. A cousin of Linda's? No, perhaps second cousin but still part of her family. Praise the Saints! Now all he had to do was find Linda and reveal that her cousin, Merrick Macgregor could lead her to the rest of her family. Then a sudden thought struck him. Wouldn't it be wiser to tell Macgregor first? Perhaps he might not want to become associated with Linda? Taking leave of Becky he mounted his horse and sighing heavily he turned it towards Penzance.

Some miles away, on the moorland overlooking the North coast, Trevarron watched Tam nose back and forth trying to pick up Linda's trail. His inspiration to use the dog had paid off. The girl hadn't gone to Penzance as he might have supposed but had headed North – to avoid pursuit most likely, he muttered to himself. You are not so clever after all, young miss, I will come across you before too long, I'll wager, if this dog knows what it's about. He's got your scent; he'll track you down. "Come on, you stupid animal, where is she? Find Lindy, go on you mangy hound, seek, damn you, seek!" he screamed at the dog. A short while later, her valise was discovered in the bushes but not a sign of the girl. The dog was hauled away, protesting, from a small outcrop which he insisted on licking; seek as he might the trail was cold and Trevarron was left to fume and dance in rage.

He raged still more when he examined the bag. It was almost beyond belief that Linda had a necklace in her possession which was so valuable. Had she stolen it? He examined it with great care; particularly the miniature picture it held; recalling his stormy meeting with the late Duchess and also seeing it rest around her neck. He had envied her possession of it and wondered why the Duchess had not sold it if she was short of funds.

Somehow she had got it to his wife and now it was in his hands. Excellent! He would never need to go cap in hand to get more money from Macgregor or to offer Linda in exchange. The sale of the necklace would allow the funds he needed to pay his debts, and he was determined nothing would stop him taking Linda for his wife.

A ripple of cold wind off the sea chilled his cheeks as he stood silently racking his brains on the hillside. Where was Lindy now? What the devil had possessed her to flee from him? Surely she knew he wouldn't really hurt her, not if she obeyed him. He turned and looked at the three men who had come with him to search as they stood to one side with the dog, as if unwilling to share his dark thoughts. The cool wind brought a whiff of pungent wood smoke, probably from a cottage. Out here in the breeze it brought back memories best forgotten.

He recalled fires in the open, a woodland fire; a campfire and the people round it – of those who lived their lives perpetually in the open air. Gypsies! As his mind took the thought, his eye unexpectedly caught sight of broken bracken where a cartwheel had rolled over and crushed the fronds. Searching further he saw the deep print of an unshod horse in the damp earth. Of course! Somehow, quite amazingly, she had been picked up by a band of gypsies. He didn't know which tribe, or where they were at this moment, but he could hazard a guess where they were going. When they reached their eventual destination, which would probably take them a day or two of travelling, he would be waiting for them. God help them if they did not have Linda with them. Oh yes, my girl, I'll have you yet, wherever you think to hide!

CHAPTER FORTY-TWO

James Lusty tracked Merrick to a small inn by the harbour where he had gone to eat a solitary meal and think out his next move. Merrick was surprised to see the doctor and though desirous of keeping to himself politely asked the older man if he would join him.

"Yes, I'd be pleased to, if you don't mind," Lusty replied. "I have chased all hither and yon today with scarce a bite to eat and I'm right famished. What I have to tell you can be said as well over a good meal as anywhere else. And I'm in good company."

The meal, when it came, was beefsteak and oysters covered in suet pudding oozing with gravy. Merrick watched the good Doctor put away at least half of his share in a very short time, together with a tankard of porter, before saying gently with a humorous smile, "You had something to tell me?"

"Dear me, bless you, sir, you'll think me so rude to neglect you like this. Puddings have to be eaten hot, you know, or they don't taste the same. Dear me, no. However, it has taken the edge off my appetite so I may go more slowly and can talk to you. Carry on with your meal while I order more porter. You'll join me, of course?" Merrick nodded and he called the waiter over to refill the tankards, ate some more of his pudding then wiping his lips, took a long draught of porter.

Merrick patiently carried on eating. Probably the old chap had just come to say farewell, taking advantage of begging a meal at the same time. Merrick did not mind but he wished the doctor would say what he had come for then leave him in peace to think his own thoughts.

Where had Linda gone? Not that it was his affair. He had been on the point of turning down the mine-owner and asking point-blank questions of his own; such as where had the monies disappeared to that had been expressly provided by him for renovations to the mine workings. For Trevarron had asked for a large sum in return for allowing Merrick's courtship of Linda. A marriage was mentioned but it struck Merrick that if he was to produce enough money Trevarron would not care if he married or not. Therefore, what did he want with so much money? He should have more than enough to live off comfortably if he never worked the mine again. Was that it? Was he going to take off to a warmer clime to retire? Well, he will not by my assistance, Merrick decided. To hell with the lot of them, he had had quite enough of mining anyway. Also he had heard that the bottom was dropping out of the business, now overseas mines were producing more minerals than the Cornish mines had ever produced. He would be wise to get out while he could. He was so full of his problems rolling around his mind that he barely listened to the doctor's opening words.

"Mr Macgregor, I have something of great import to tell you of the young woman who has been living at the Hall. Namely Linda Barton."

"Linda? Yes, what about her, I heard only today she left suddenly. Do you, by chance, know where she is?" Merrick lifted his head to frown at Lusty.

"No, I'm afraid not; I had hoped you would know, considering all the village gossip connecting the two of you. There's little that happens here that is overlooked, you know."

"Well, I don't know," Merrick said curtly. "As for gossip - folk will prattle at anything. And, in truth, there has been nothing to prattle about. Has Trevarron sent you?"

"No, sir, the less I have to do with that man, the better. Now attend me while I tell you what I know. It's a long story so bear with me while I start at the beginning."

Intrigued with the doctor's serious tone Merrick forgot his meal and concentrated his attention on Lusty hoping he might pick up a clue to Linda's present whereabouts.

"You have or had in your family, she may be dead now, I warrant, a lady by the name of Sophie, Duchess of Forres. Correct? Good. She had a granddaughter called Lavinia, who was once wife to Ambrose Trevarron."

Merrick nodded intently, all at once becoming immensely intrigued.

"Lavinia had a fatal fall near the end of her pregnancy and died but not before she was delivered of a child who was supposedly born dead." Lusty paused then to take a swallow of porter and review his next words.

"Yes, Trevarron told me both she and the child died. But this is only idle gossip, Doctor; get to the point if you will, sir." Merrick hated rambling tales that led nowhere.

"Patience, sir, I'm telling the story from the start. The child he saw was not his after all. Lavinia gave birth to a daughter who was spirited away by the attending midwife for she feared that Trevarron, in his desire for a son, would harm her. Ellie Barton, Jethro Barton's wife, had a stillborn son that same evening who replaced the girl-child, then, unknowingly, Ellie brought Linda up. Though how this took place without a soul being aware is quite beyond imagination." Lusty still baffled shook his head.

"Then Linda is...confound it, man...is she part of my family? Devil take it, Doctor, are you sure?" Merrick felt quite dazed as he took in Lusty's words, at once realising the significance. "This is one incredible story. But I am going to need proof it is true."

"Lavinia told the midwife everything before she died. She also left Linda a valuable locket, which had belonged to her grandmother. The back of the locket and the clasp was chafed so I imagine the Duchess wore it often enough to be recognisable to her family. Inside, is a picture of the Duchess and a lock of hair."

"Is the locket faced with an enormous ruby, set in gold mesh laced with diamonds?"

"So I believe. At least from the midwife's description it would appear so."

At Lusty's nod Merrick whooped with elation. Diners nearby, startled at the noise, smiled at his huge grin. "Of course! Why didn't I think of it? I remember the locket from a portrait of Sophie, which is in our home in Scotland. Looking at Linda I was always surprised at how well I knew every line of her face – how familiar she seemed. Clearly she is a descendant of the Duchess. But it is to be hoped she's not inherited that woman's nature which was avaricious in the extreme!"

"Aah!" Lusty was delighted with the effect his story had on Merrick. Now he knew he did not have to worry about Linda's future. This young man would take care of her and return her to the family she had lost through no fault of her own. That is, he qualified mentally to himself, if it was possible to find her quickly with no harm done and most certainly before Trevarron could lay his hands upon her. He hoped, for Linda's sake, they did find her in time for he did not trust the man not to harm her. He had long known him as a cruel man who would take revenge for the slightest thing. If it came to a point of law, he wondered who would win the battle to claim her. Surely the law would take more notice of her real family over any claim by Trevarron?

"Where is she now?" Anxiety took over from elation in Merrick's mind as he questioned the doctor. "Why did she run away? Was she searching for her relations?"

"I don't know, but if she has gone to look for her family then I imagine she will go to London to trace the Duchess. I have a deep fear that Trevarron will be asking much the same question, though he knows nothing of the relationship between Linda and his wife. No, he will merely think she has run away from him. After all, his attempt at rape is not beneficial for good relations. He will want to make peace with her."

"What did you say? He tried to rape her?" This time the bellow of rage from Merrick drew murmurs of dissatisfaction from his fellow diners and a waiter hurried to the table to see what was wrong. "I'll kill that man when I get my hands on him!" He rose to his feet too angry and impatient to think of finishing his meal.

Swiftly the doctor placed a restraining hand on the arm nearest to him, urging Merrick to remain seated, at the same time waving the waiter away with the other, giving a reassuring smile. Then, turning to Merrick, he said, "Gently, my boy. Nothing can be achieved if you go off half-cocked. Indeed making threats will bring the law down on us. We have to use that same law to help us. Trevarron, I suspect, has skirted the law too many times for them not to be aware he is devious. He has but to put a foot wrong - if you get my meaning? Relax. Someone in the village might have seen her; by this time tomorrow, I will know. If you want to do something useful see if you can get something out of Tom Spenny about Trevarron's movements. It's always useful to know what the enemy is up to."

"Don't worry, he'll keep me posted."

"You sound very sure. He's Trevarron's man, heart and soul, of course. He'll never say anything straight out but he might let something slip."

"He's my man now, he got tired of doing his master's dirty work, he wants to retire."

"Aah! You have been busy, I see. Well let us keep that snippet quiet for the present moment. I do not believe in letting the right hand know what the left hand is getting up to. You enquire at the station to see if she left by train and I'll get in touch as soon as I hear anything from the village. Where will I find you?"

"Possibly at the mining office with Trevarron. He'd thought to bribe me by giving me Linda in return for a great deal of money. I am about to disillusion him. He won't find it easy to answer all the questions I am going to ask him. I'll also be having a quiet word with Spenny if it can be managed."

"See you don't arouse Trevarron's suspicions, he's as fly as any maggot in a dung heap. Keep your head if anything is said about Linda. You are like a pot with the lid fast on – ready to blow with steam. You must keep a check on your rage or we will fail at the first jump."

"And you are as full of metaphors as a fable book. Don't worry; I've been in worse situations." With less to lose, Merrick reflected. This time it was about a member of his family and also Linda's safety and happiness. He would find her and take her back to his parents where she would be looked after and given a new life. It would please his father to think he had rescued a daughter of Lavinia's. He would find her a husband … abruptly he frowned at the idea. Who would be good enough for her? Just for a moment Merrick felt savage at the idea Linda would be possessed by some other man, then remembered he had decided he was much too old for her, too jaded with hard experience and the knowledge of other women. He required a wife who would turn a blind eye to passing forays with the gentle sex or to put it bluntly, a wife who was compliant in bed, would bear his children and leave him free to conduct his business affairs and do as he pleased.

CHAPTER FORTY-THREE

When dawn came it was overcast; the wind blew strongly from the west with rain in its teeth when Tom Spenny arrived at the pithead the next morning to count the men into work. Each miner looked up at the sky as he began his shift and Tom knew a silent prayer was offered that each would see that same sky, whatever the weather, come nightfall. The harsh sound of coughing, hacking and spitting filled the early dawn, mainly from lungs, diseased by toxic air that was barely breathable at times, especially in the deeper parts of the mines. The men, crowding in, were all ages, and some just young boys of seven and eight. They would do the fetching and carrying of tools and props and push and pull wagons back to the ore-carrying skips where they were hoisted to the surface.

The pitmen were responsible for all the shaft pump work as well. It was often cold and mainly wet work and most miners detested working in the shaft. Few of the skilled miners would undertake the chore if they could avoid it so it was left to the young and old men who were not part of a team.

Once the men disappeared below, a collection of young girls and married women with children, old enough to help, arrived at the pithead to work on the ore being sent to the surface. These workers were known by the Cornish name of "Bal Maidens" (the word 'Bal' meaning mine). The money they earned was essential to a mining family to complement the often-poor wages of the menfolk. The group sorted the ore into various piles, depending on its content, before it was sent to the smelters. It was hard, rough work and those that worked the ore tables invariably had raw, chapped hands from handling the broken rock. Tom had just settled the women to their tasks, in charge of two overseers, when Trevarron arrived on the scene. "Everything all right, Tom?" he growled as usual in a curt voice. "Got them all down?"

"Yes, the men are on their way but pump's out o' action an' sumps flooded. I got Carew and Davis workin' on't engine an' I've cleared bottom level. Be an hour yet afore they rig clack valve and start up again."

"Why the devil wasn't it checked last night? That's what you're bloody paid to do. Do ye need me to do your thinking for you? Get Sweeting and Buckley on it as well. They won't hang about - not while they're losing dosh. I want that pump going sooner than an hour."

"Things wouldn't fail at all if one had the proper machinery," interjected Merrick, as he entered the office, arriving just in time to hear the conversation.

"Oh yes, it's easy for you. Spend more and more money that's all you can prate about. I want to make it, not throw it away. The machinery's fine. It's them that use it!"

"So you waste their efforts by not having the equipment to do the job efficiently. I call that being bloody shortsighted. You'll get twice the profit out of these mines if you are prepared to install safe engines." Merrick had held his temper in past exchanges with difficulty but this time he was not going to back down. He could see there was no alternative but to have a showdown with his partner. "But there, I've said it often enough, explained it till I'm blue in the face. Now it's up to you. I'm thinking of starting afresh on my own account anyway and, as you are not using my money for improvements, I'll have it back and put it into something worthwhile. I cannot deal with a partner who is backward in thinking. Sometimes one has to spend to save."

"Who says I'm not improving?" Trevarron was quick to interrupt. "I'm not rushing hotheaded on your say-so into something new without thinking long and hard about it."

"For God's sake, we've been thinking, enquiring and

investigating modern methods for six months and more. You either do it or I go. It's your choice. It's now a make up your mind time for I'm not dancing to your tune any longer. Partner!"

All of a sudden it hit him, so rare an event he could never remember it ever happening before; Trevarron realised he was caught in a cleft stick. If he told Macgregor to go, he would have to return Macgregor's money, which he had already lost to gambling. Indeed, more than that, if the truth was known. On the other hand, if Macgregor stayed then Ambrose knew he would never end up with Linda. That was if he found the girl, of course.

"You are right, sir! We'll install the engine of your choice. Off with you to London and order it straightaway! By the time we're finished remodelling this place we'll have the most modern pit in Cornwall, I'll be bound. Well, man, what are you waiting for?"

For a long moment Merrick stared at Trevarron as he took in the words. Why the extraordinary capitulation? What was the mine-owner up to now? Ah, of course, he wanted him out of the way. Now it was Merrick's turn in the cleft stick. If he left, what was that devil going to get up to? Yet he couldn't afford to pass up this hasty surrender. What was he to do? Then it came to him that he could use the newly developed telegraph office at the station to bring his manager, in charge of his London affairs, down on the next train. He would use the man to oversee the order from the engineering firm who would supply the new engines. He had already explained what was needed and had their estimate so the order merely needed confirming. He would stay in Cornwall himself to see what the wily mine-owner would get up to next; at least until he could leave the situation to take care of itself. However, he was not about to explain all that to Trevarron; the less that man knew, the better.

"Excellent! I'm glad you've decided at last. I'll get straight on it, oh and Tom, if I'm needed, get word to my lodgings in

Penzance, they will know where I'll be found." On the spur of the moment it was the only way he could think of to tell Tom he would still be available. He hoped the man would understand and act on it.

"Needed for what?" growled Trevarron, glaring at Spenny once Merrick left; his suspicions, ever on the alert, were aroused. He had a strong sense which had rescued him from trouble many times. He had known, for some while, Tom Spenny was becoming more reluctant to do his bidding but it was a different tale if he had actually gone over to the enemy. Accidents could happen to all sorts of people - they did not have to be miners.

"I dunno, boss, perhaps he thinks we can't manage our own affairs. Things we've been managing long before he arrived. Gotta nose on him like a ferret, probably worried about his share of the profits. D'ye need me fur anything else, ony I gotta get that damn pump sorted out?" Spenny's voice was surly, giving nothing away as usual.

Trevarron nodded and Tom Spenny left the office and headed for the pithead. Inwardly he was quaking jelly. He knew Trevarron of old and guessed the mine-owner smelt a rat. Right daft bugger, he muttered to himself. Macgregor might just as well have shouted it out to the village as say that to t'Master. Talk about dropping me in the shit. Old 'brose would suspect his own mother if he'd a mind to. I'd best watch my step, wouldn't put it past him to 'ave a go at me, especially now Macgregor's gone off; but two can play at that game. If he tries to take me then God help him for I'll come back hard as I can on him.

CHAPTER FORTY-FOUR

Tom Spenny, arriving at the top of the shaft, had just begun climbing down towards the pump to see what stage the repairs had reached, when all at once, the ground leapt up and shuddered under him. "Christ, what the hell was that?" he yelled to the man just below him who was standing on a platform alongside the idle pump.

"I dunno. Could be a fall but the only news an hour ago was water's climbing fast..."

His last words were lost as all of a sudden a huge blast of air roared up the tunnel shaft beneath them, almost unseating Tom from the ladder. He clung with all his might to the framework until the vibration had settled then called out, "You okay, Pete?" There was no answer, for Peter had been swept from the platform down the mineshaft. Cursing the fate that held him bondage in this most awful of jobs, he climbed wearily back to the surface to organise some kind of rescue for the injured mineworkers. He also had the job of letting Pete Carew's family know that he must be dead.

It was well after midnight before they got the pump working and drained enough water to find out what had happened. Apparently an old shaft, long since abandoned, had filled up with water before breaking loose into the eighty-fathom level and, in no time at all, had filled the shaft up to twenty fathoms of depth below the pump engine.

As it gushed violently out to find a new level, it sent a blast of air screaming through the mine which blew out most of the miner's candles; thus adding terror to the horror of the catastrophe as the men struggled to find their way out of the mine in pitch darkness. Five miners were drowned that day. Others had almost miraculous escapes, particularly the sump men who were not in their usual place at the shaft bottom as a result of the pump failure. If they had been there they would most certainly have been drowned but, instead, they were repairing timbers in the shaft at thirty fathoms when the inundation had occurred. Work in the mine ceased until all the damage could be assessed.

The whole mining hamlet mourned together with the families of the dead men, for the one day the mine was out of action. If they did not work they did not eat. Furthermore, accidents were so common that it was rare for men to reach forty without some dire event overtaking them; a number died even before they were thirty from accidents or disease or falls from ladders, due to dizziness, brought on by heart strain. That was not all. Just as many deaths also occurred in the mining parishes, among the families, from typhus and other endemic fevers caused by poor sanitation and overcrowding. To stay alive was a lottery that few won.

Yet despite the hazards, poor food and squalid hovels, young boys learnt the trade alongside their fathers and developed skills which produced fully-fledged miners, almost before a boy was out of his teens. There was no other way to earn a living other than to leave home and trust to finding a job elsewhere. With no savings to tide a man over until he gained employment, it was an impossible task so people stayed where they were and put up with hardship and a virtual serfdom under the hand of the mine-owner.

By the following day Ambrose decided he required his manager too badly to get rid of him. The mine needed constant supervision and, whatever doubts Ambrose had of Tom's loyalty, at least he knew he was good at his job. He did not care if Tom was trying to free himself; one word from Ambrose and he could be arrested for any number of crimes that Ambrose could prove against Tom if he had to. He knew it would not be necessary in his case, he only had to use the threat of blackmail for the man to come to heel. All that would keep for another time; Ambrose was after bigger game. Now that Macgregor was out of the way he was going after Linda. If his guess was correct, the gypsy tribe should have reached Launceston for the Annual Horse Fair. He vowed he would find Linda or, at least, discover where she had gone.

"Now the pump's working and we're back to normal see you keep it that way," he growled to Tom Spenny. "I'm taking a few days off."

Tom stared at him curiously. "Where can I reach you, if necessary?"

"Oh, I shan't be gone long, though my business takes me up-country. I'm sure you'll manage things till I get back. I've a mind to visit the Horse Fair at Launceston; I need to replace my hunter and two of the carriage horses are getting old so it's as good a chance of finding a bargain there as dealing locally here. I should be back next Monday at the very latest."

Tom grunted at this news, it all seemed logical, except that Trevarron was not a logical man and he hated to go far from his property. What was he after this time other than to search for Linda? The gossip over her disappearance lasted a short while in the village then people had other things to think about, but Tom was aware Trevarron would not let the matter rest there, he was after the girl, Tom would bet on it. There was not a thing he could say or do about it, the man was his own master after all but it was unfortunate that it should come at a time when Macgregor was away. He put the matter to one side while he got on with the difficult business of overseeing the mine and did not give another thought to it until late evening when he was able to leave the mine and go home.

CHAPTER FORTY-FIVE

Launceston Market was a swarming multitude of people by the time Trevarron arrived on the scene. Mist and torrential rain over the moors had delayed him beyond endurance, streaming down so hard that paths and roads were awash like rivers in spate. Sparing his coachman for once, he had allowed them to stop at an inn on the Bodmin road but when a meal was placed in front of him he had cursed his own folly, for the food was rank and inedible. Tossing the plate to one side he had roared for brandy and spent the rest of the night by the fire consuming large quantities of the liquor until the weather abated. When, at last, they took to the road it was past noon and Ambrose was in a furious rage with a sore head from the liquor and the aggravating delay.

They had not gone far when, suddenly, the coach slewed to one side as a front wheel hit a deep rut and jerked free of the axle. More hours were lost as they sought help from a nearby village to replace the wheel. In the end Ambrose spent the rest of the night in a villager's cottage, which pleased neither party. The occupant, because Ambrose was a surly guest and too mean to pay much for the lodging and Ambrose, because he fretted at the hindrances that baulked him at every turn. As he got more and more angry he vowed he would take it out on Linda's hide for causing him so much aggravation.

Once they reached Launceston he left William to organise a safe location for the coach; then, giving him instructions where he would be found, told his man to follow on afterwards. Free to make his own way he sauntered along close-packed lanes of stalls set out for selling farm produce, fairings, food and drink, herbs, medicines, sideshows and jugglers, in fact every conceivable method to part a man from his money. Ambrose ignored all of it as he headed in the direction of a campsite way beyond the stalls where horses waited to be sold.

"'Ave a look at this one, milord, he'll carry ye anywhere's ye wanna go. A prime two-year-old, strong as a mule he is, just try him, sir, you'll not regret it." That and many cries from other hustlers went unheeded as Ambrose strode purposefully across the meadows to the banks of the Tamar which passed through the forest of Dunterton to where he knew the tribe would be camped. He was not wrong. The smell of a fire and the sound of children playing led him straight there. Pausing momentarily in the trees his mind went back to earlier days when all he knew of life was a gypsy camp, poverty and hardship. He had got himself out of that situation soon enough with his able wits, and ambition had carried him a long way up the social ladder but not far enough yet. He needed the girl to help him to do that. Close in his footsteps followed William, ever alert to protect his master.

CHAPTER FORTY-SIX

Tom Spenny was tired and hungry and saddened by yet another accident. A young lad of nine had lost his foot when he had fallen in front of three coupled trucks full of ore on their way to the skip road where the ore was hauled to the surface. By the time the boy had reached the surface and the doctor called he had gone into shock and had died from the injury. Tom mopped the last dregs of gravy up with a wedge of bread and sank back in his chair, belching approval of the food. He and his wife were often at odds with one another but he could never fault her cooking; the stew he had eaten was quite delicious. Now all he wanted was to turn in and have a good night's sleep, so he could cope with what the next day would bring. He sat idly picking his teeth as he wondered when he would be able to get the news to Macgregor that Ambrose had departed for Launceston, if that was his purpose, though knowing him it was probably to somewhere else entirely. His thoughts went back to Macgregor's words in the mine office when he had left them to go to London. He did not take the man for stupid so was he trying to tell him something that he might not want Trevarron to know? Conversely, if Trevarron thought that Macgregor was out of the way, maybe that was why he was going to search further afield to find the girl? If Macgregor knew he might do that - well he would just pretend to go away. So, if that was true, then he would find Macgregor in Penzance and he had better get off his butt and go there. He would not be able to leave the mine tomorrow that was for sure. Oh hell! He thought of his bed and groaned. Why he had ever got mixed up in these dreadful affairs he would never know. He sighed and rose to his feet. "I'm off out, Lizzie, don't wait up for me, I'll be late."

"T'ain't yer night for beering, Tom, an' ye'd best not be whorin' neither. Where ye going? 'Tis late enough for bed, so it is, and that's where I'm bound directly."

"I ain't beering, an' I ain't whorin', I've mining business if ye must know. Now shut up! If you've a mind for bed then get there and quit askin' foolish questions," he yelled irately before slamming the door behind him.

Merrick was about ready to turn in when Tom arrived at his lodgings. He had suffered a fruitless day waiting for news from the doctor which was not forthcoming and racking his brains to find a suitable excuse to go to the Hall and speak with Linda's aunt, the cook. Of course she was not really her aunt after all. Mrs Polwen would be devastated at first, then possibly very angry at being misled. Not that she would vent her anger on someone who would shortly die herself for that, according to Lusty, was Amy Bunnion's fate. Nevertheless she would likely take it out on him if he were so bold as to enquire where her beloved 'niece' was. Tom's appearance was welcomed eagerly and Merrick took him immediately upstairs to his small sitting room.

"Launceston? For horses? What the devil does he want with horses? There's nothing wrong with his carriage horses. He told me he purchased them six months ago. Where do you think he is off to? Why didn't you get word before?" Merrick railed angrily.

"Cos I've a bloody mine to run, as if ye haven't noticed," Tom yelled back at him. "Today and yesterday have been bad enough to make me jack the whole bloody lot in. We lost one o' the young 'uns today. One o' the wagons ran over his leg an' he bled to death, poor sod. Do ye think I'm made of stone not to care?"

"Why the devil you employ children down there, I'll never know," Merrick yelled back. "It's bad enough for men but young boys must find it a hellish nightmare."

"It's allus been that way, since afore my day, an' they take home their pay same as the rest o' us, of course, while they're learning to be a miner. It's needed bad at home, don't forget. As soon as a child's able to walk and grasp the basics they are put to some use. It's a fact of life in mining. There's no room for pampering when you're starving."

Merrick shook his head in resignation. "So Trevarron is heading for Launceston, is he? Well, I'll just have to track behind him and see where he ends up. I'll leave at first light. Let Dr Lusty know where I've gone and - oh hell - I'd forgotten about my manager, he's to order the new machinery for the mines. If you hang on I'll give you a letter allowing you to collect the wires that come in for me at Penzance Station. If need be, wire me at Launceston as to what's happening and I'll do the same for you. In the meantime, keep your ears open for any news of Miss Barton. I don't trust Trevarron one little bit. He's a scoundrel and I'm going to unmask him the first opportunity I get. Luckily for me I've learned enough of his evil doings to save me from making a blithering fool of myself and loaning him more money. I don't know what he has done with the first lot but there is no evidence of it in improvements to the mine."

"Nor will ee have told of the gambling he is partial to," Tom retorted. "It got him a fine house and living. Now he'll take you for every penny he can wangle out of you. He likely thinks that as it worked the first time why not now. Watch your back, m'lord; he keeps a knife in't top of his boot, not to mention a derringer in his waistcoat and he's devilishly handy with both."

"Then we are quits. I never go abroad without protection, more particularly in this country. The roads are alive with footpads and all manner of light-fingered gentry so one needs beware. I've not travelled the world without knowing a thing or two."

Spenny grinned. "I'd give much to come wiv ee. 'Tis a pity I've got to stay here. Think of me when ye stick 'im and go as deep as you can."

"Now wait a minute, I'm not about to stick anyone, at least not unless they go for me first. You bear that in mind, you bloodthirsty villain!"

"Aye, zurr! I knows yer a gent, I was only funnin', it's me that has the score to settle. He's run me ragged for so many years; I hafta get free o' him."

"Be patient, you'll be free one of these days, I promise, you are not the only one, Tom; half the village is in the same boat. See to the mine, lad, I'll be back when I can. I'll train it through to Liskeard then hire a horse and ride north from there avoiding best part of Bodmin Moor. I should be on Trevarron's heels if he's taken his coach. William's not an out-and-outer at the reins. He'll be slow over Bodmin Moor. There is always the mist to contend with."

"That reminds me," Tom interrupted quickly. "William sticks closer to Trevarron than a limpet. He guards 'im like a babbie. If'n ye can't see 'im don't be misled that ee ain't around. I've known him creep up and fetch a skull breaking thump o'er a man's head when ee wasn't looking. He carries a wooden axe-handle in one o' his pockets that'll split a man's noddle open. All the miners hereabouts go in fear of him, that's for sure."

"Thanks, Tom, for the warning. I'll take good care to watch my head and keep my weapons handy if I catch up with those two. Now I'd better get off. I only wish I knew where I was going and what to look for. It's strange that Trevarron is off to Launceston. If he had been heading for London I could understand it. Why would Linda go there? She could have caught the coach through to Bristol and then gone on from there up to London."

"Perhaps she got a lift, there be plenty of people going to the market. Gypsies for one, they are always back an' forth the length of Cornwall…" He paused suddenly as his mind took in possibilities. There was a moment's silence as the two men looked at each other, speculation growing in their eyes. Has she been picked up and given a lift, thought Merrick. Has she been spirited away, thought Tom, his natural dislike of the Romany race coming to the fore.

"The tribes usually gather in Dunterton Woods for the Horse Fair. I'd try there afore you go on to the market in the main town, it's even nearer Liskeard," Tom said gravely. "Watch yer back and be careful. Gypsies will do you down if they get half a chance."

"Tom, you're a gem. How would you like to leave mining and work for me? I could do with someone with your knowledge in another business I have in mind."

"Nah, I'm getting too old. Not but what I'm a tad tempted. Go on, off withee, I'll see you when ye get back. Ye'll have changed yer mind by then." He laughed and swung away through the door. Merrick could hear him still laughing as he went down the stairs. Maybe he'll not laugh when he knows I am serious, he thought.

CHAPTER FORTY-SEVEN

Merrick caught the first train out of Penzance at dawn. There were two goods vans on it as well as the carriages for passengers, which suited him very well as he had decided to take his horse instead of trying to hire one at Liskeard and maybe encounter a problem. He loaded the animal into the guard's van and spent the trip comfortably seated in a carriage instead of riding 'hell for leather' across the Cornish moors as he would, otherwise, bound to have done. Gazing out of the window he reflected on the changes in the county, his shrewd brain already making plans to capitalise on his newly acquired knowledge of mining. Tin and copper deposits were rapidly running out in Cornwall but, he reflected, he had a ready-made force of experienced people to draw on. They could be employed in other parts of the world. He already had shares in a gold mine in South Africa; why not have a team of skilled men operate out there? There was none more highly regarded for expertise in working a mine than a Cornish miner. Hopefully the future held great prospects.

At last he arrived at Liskeard, retrieved his horse and enquired directions from a porter of the whereabouts of Dunterton Woods and the gypsy encampment.

"Thee never didn't want to go theer, my 'andsome! Ye'll get thyself ill wished, gen'lman liken yoursel'. Thass dangerous country round theer, ye stay on't road to Launceston and when ee gets t'markit keep ee hands o'er pockets, 'tis a maze o' rogues gathered theer," he asserted, quite taken aback at the foolishness of this gentleman.

"Thank you for your good advice but I'm looking for

someone who might have taken refuge with gypsies," explained Merrick.

"A Gorgio?" The porter queried in surprise.

"If you mean they are not a gypsy themselves, then yes. A lone woman, a very young woman. One seeking safety where she might not be sought."

"A runaway?"

Merrick nodded. Well she was, wasn't she?

The man drew his breath in through his teeth and shook his head. "They'm won't tell ee diddley. Tell ee what, I got connections wiv the Romanies, how about if my nevvy gads along o' thee, him b'ain't working at mo. Billy knows the tongue on account o' his ma is a gypsy her s'en. Course he'd want payin' fur it seeing it might take a time."

"Naturally." Merrick's tone was dry for he was more than prepared to pay for all the information he could get. He held out money for the porter, who quickly pocketed it.

"That's yours for being helpful, make haste and get your nephew for I've no time to waste. Has he a mount? He needs one to travel across country to get to Launceston."

"Thankee, zurr, you'm a right gen'lman, just give me a minute, I'll fetch ee t'ye." The porter shot off to a cottage opposite the station. Merrick couldn't believe his luck when, after fairly hard negotiating, he and a rather surly young man eventually took the road to Callington, which laid South of Launceston. It was a tiny place of slate-hung stone-built cottages standing on high land between the valleys of the rivers Lynher and Tamar. The men paused briefly to refresh themselves and the horses at a water trough before leaving the main highway to thread their way along narrow paths, ever north towards a wide expanse of woodland in the far distance.

"So, tell I what ee wants me to do when we gets to the camp. Who is the woman? What's she look like?" Billy Bateson had opened up more and lost his surly manner the further they went. Merrick described Linda as best as he could.

"She'm stick out like a sore thumb wiv all them dark'uns, likely they'll 'ave 'idden 'er hair under a wrap. What's 'er name? Course she might not want to be found, y'know?"

Merrick had considered that possibility and thought it most likely. "Suppose I stay back in the trees and you scout around? That way neither she nor any of the gypsies will be forewarned. Can you be casual, visiting your kin maybe? I don't mind going into camp straight off but I've always preferred to reconnoitre strange ground first. It's been the saving of my life many a time. It also saves being beaten at the outset."

"I warn't gonna take ee in anyway, zurr, the Rom ud see me dead afore they trusted me agin." Billy sounded quite positive about that outcome.

"Oh, I see. The trouble is, I must get to her before someone else, or she really will be in danger." Merrick racked his brains for an alternative plan.

"Can I 'ave me money now instead of later?" asked Billy who could see trouble looming ahead. This stranger who seemed so determined could well be one who invited danger for all his brave words of caution.

"Half now and the rest after as we agreed," retorted Merrick grimly. "There will be no skiving off or you'll have me to deal with ultimately, and I guarantee I'll be a lot worse than any of your gypsy brethren. Savvy, my fine young friend?" he said, hardly concealing the menace.

"I won't leave ee," Billy said hastily, not willing to upset the man, while knowing his feeling had been correct. "Now tell I who you'm expectin' to see so's I know who to ask for. Tell ee what, I'll go see my mum's aunt, she's up wiv all the gossip. If there is a girl around, she'll know all about her. Nothing escapes her eye."

They'd been riding for a little over two hours when Billy called a halt and motioned to a distant area of woodland that could be seen some way ahead. "That's the place, zurr; I reckon I leave ee here if'n that sits right wiv thee, my 'andsome?"

"Yes, I'll stay here, but don't be too long at it or I shall come after you. I've never been good at waiting, I'd much rather get on with things. We've no time to waste."

Billy nodded. "I know just what thee means. I'll not be long, trust me." He found Merrick a hiding place, then wandered into the camp. From where he was Merrick saw it was quite large and, as his eye grew keener, he discerned that the area was partitioned into separate units where each small family kept to themselves and their own cooking fire and did not trespass onto another's patch. He had been waiting for over an hour and started to think Billy had thought better of the task and skedaddled when he spotted him sauntering in a seemingly aimless manner towards his hideout.

"She's here! With Serina, would ee believe! She taken 'er up an' she's defending 'er from all comers! Even Matthias!" He looked both awed and stricken at the same time. It was unheard of that anyone messed with the tribal chieftain.

"Who's Matthias?" Merrick was relieved he had found her so easily but wary of further problems. He had pondered uneasily on his next move while he waited on Billy returning from his foray and was no nearer deciding what to do next.

"He's chief! There b'ain't nobody u'll gainsay him. He's a mighty powerful man. He can beat all comers who try to take him on, he can."

"I hope you told your aunt I've come to fetch Linda. Now I have found her I don't want to waste any more time. It's getting dark and there is the problem of getting her safely back to Penzance." Just then an outcry upset the quiet of the woods and they heard a scream that was undoubtedly a woman's. Without stopping to think Merrick ran in the direction of the sound. Unless he was mistaken it was Linda's voice he could hear. He joined others converging on the scene and for a brief moment he was hemmed in by pushing and jostling bodies. When at last he freed himself and found he was at the front of the crowd, he saw Linda caught tightly in Trevarron's grasp. Her scarf had loosened and ripe corn-coloured hair streamed down her back in abandoned curls as she struggled to free herself, but the mine-owner's grip was unshakable.

CHAPTER FORTY-EIGHT

Serina was on her feet, glaring at Trevarron, her arms akimbo; a scowling sneer on her wrinkled face. "So you've come back, you spawn of Satan! Do you think to wreak further harm on an innocent maid? Carry on your evil ways without heed of others?"

"I don't know what you mean, Serina; this is my ward and I've cared for her since she has been small and left an orphan. I've every right to govern her life."

"Leave me alone. I don't want to come with you. I won't ever come back. You are bad! You tried to hurt me! If Aunt Betsy hadn't saved me you would have succeeded." Linda tried once more to wrench herself away but his grasp was unassailable.

"Tell her, Linda, I've never done you any harm," Trevarron begged. "I only want to care for you the rest of your life. You'll be safe with me, I promise."

"So you think to marry her and breed children, eh?" Serina's lip curled with scorn. Merrick gasped unable to contain himself any longer. Instantly the people nearest him realising he was a stranger in their midst, moved away and he was left in an open circle.

"And why not?" retorted Trevarron. "I've as much right as the next man to have an heir and a wife to breed more if I fancy the woman enough. Though it is none of your damned business, I'll have you know. No one interferes with my life or they get what they deserve."

"Your life! Is that all that concerns you? Well, I have a different tale to tell. You haven't the right to crawl on the ground and beg mercy for your life, you rotten despicable creature," Serina taunted. "You got my sister with child then killed her cos it didn't suit you to marry her." After that sally, Serina turned to a huge man standing silent, his arms akimbo warily watching the proceedings from the edge of the crowd. "Matthias! Make him let the gorgio child go; she ain't nowt to do with this scum o' the earth, or us come to it. My nephew u'll take her home. He'll see her to safety away from this devil!"

Before the chief could utter a word Merrick stepped forward and stood on the empty ground facing Matthias. "I'll take her, if I may. I have more right than this man for she is a member of my own family. Her mother was my second cousin."

"You! What the devil are you doing here? You've no right to interfere! You won't take her! She's mine! D'ye hear me. Mine!" Trevarron screeched at Merrick, all sane reason fast fleeing his mind. In spite of the fact that Merrick was in the midst of saving his mine, he envied and hated him with all the poisonous force of his evil nature.

"You'll never be able to father another child again if ye tried between now and kingdom come!" With great satisfaction Serina spat the words out at him.

"What d'ye mean?" A glimmer of doubt flashed for an instant in his eyes. "Why not? Why not? Damn you! What gives you reason to say such a dreadful thing?"

"Cos I gave you a potion to make ye sterile, that's why. You son of a viper." Serina gazed at him mockingly. "Do ee think I'd let ye breed after what you did to my Zelda? Yer not a man, yer a useless eunuch! There is not an ounce o' manhood in that scrawny part between yer legs. I finally saw to that afore you took yourself off. For all your Pikie knowledge of gypsy ways, you don't know everything. All you men think you are masters but you'd do well to be wary of those that possess the wisdom."

With a piercing shriek of rage Trevarron plunged at the old gypsy woman his hands bent into claws to grasp her neck.

Before he managed to reach her throat a massive pain rapidly leached through his chest and he staggered violently, totally unable to bear the awful agony that was tearing at his chest as his heart went into an uncontrollable seizure. Seconds later his anguish was at an end and his life was over. The figure reeled uncontrollably for only a moment then his body dropped at Linda's feet. She had stood stricken whilst fiery words cast violently back and forth, only hearing the words of Merrick Macgregor that she was part of his family. How could this be? Why had this been hidden from her? Whose family did she really belong to?

Merrick leapt forward to her side then immediately he flung himself back as from the corner of his eye he saw a figure race from the trees brandishing a large club.

Linda shrank back in horror as she recognised who it was. "William! Stop! It's milord Macgregor!" Then she screamed in sheer terror, as she saw the murderous look on his face and realised this was a new assault.

"You son o' the devil! You kilt my master, I'll teach un to mess in our affairs! Yer a dead'un fer sure!" He raised the club ready to bring it down on Merrick's head.

Merrick waited until the very last second then neatly sidestepped, swinging one fist straight for William's solar plexus and the other crunching up into his jaw. William instantly dropped to the ground as though pole-axed and lay still. A murmur of approval flew through the crowd and Merrick rubbing his fist to ease the pain in his fingers grinned like a schoolboy. "That was taught me a while ago by a ship's bo'sun. Never knew how useful it could be until now." Then he turned to Linda and took her in his arms while she clutched him thankfully like one who had been saved from an awful fate. Merrick stared across at the proud chieftain who glared back, their eyes drawing sparks like crossed swords.

"Thank you for taking care of her, sir, her safety means a lot to my family. Should you ever wish to camp on my land, you will be more than welcome."

Matthias raised his eyebrows in surprise. "You are most kind, Gorgio, there are few who offer such magnitude. I'll be pleased to learn where your land might be. But for now I bid you welcome at our hearth, we shall eat shortly and we would all be honoured to have you as our guest. Will you stay?" Matthias bowed deeply and gracefully before Merrick.

"I'll be most honoured to stay. Linda? Are you willing to stay a littler longer?"

She raised her eyes, the green depths brimming to overflowing; her long lashes sparkling with teardrops. "Yes, I would like to stay awhile with Serina; she has been so very kind; I don't know what I would have done without her. I've been so scared of all that has happened in the last few days. To be truthful I hardly know where I am. Then to suddenly see Mr Trevarron again was dreadful."

"It's over now, my sweet. Come, dry your eyes, we will dine and stay until tomorrow. Smile or our gracious host will think we are loath to stay and I've a great fancy to make his acquaintance."

Serina looked approvingly at this tall, dark stranger who reminded her of her late husband. Yes, she thought, he would do very well for this young girl she had almost adopted as her daughter. She cast a swift glance at Matthias and caught his eye. She nodded briefly as if to let him know she knew how disappointed he was and he scowled at her, and then gave a bit of a shrug as if to say it was karma. Then a thought struck him and he took her arm. "What wisdom were you referring to, Serina?"

"No more than we all know, Matthias," she said warily. "Twas said to put a right old scare in him and it worked, didn't it? He was more superstitious than he realised."

"What is the poison you spoke of, I know nothing of that," he said sharply.

"Nor I," Serina said. "Twas his bad living and the idea I put in his head that killed him."

CHAPTER FORTY-NINE

Late that night when all save Serina and Merrick were asleep, the two of them lingered by the fire because Serina wanted to talk. Her relief was great as she had successfully diverted Matthias's mind away from the realisation that she possessed more knowledge than he gave her credit for. Compounding everything that had happened that day her curiosity was more roused than she could remember in a long time, especially these last few weeks and she dearly wanted to know what the future held for the girl.

"What do you intend for Linda?" she enquired.

"I'll take her back to my parents in Scotland; they will be delighted to meet her and give her a home. She is part of our family though she doesn't as yet understand it."

"Hmm. And what will you do with yourself?" As she spoke she fetched a pack of cards out of her pocket and began to shuffle them. He was silent for a moment as he watched her then, as she handed him the cards, he held up his hand to reject them.

"I don't need my fortune read. I'll take fate as it comes, not how it's spelt out."

"Just hold them for me, there's a good fellow. 'Tis for my benefit not yours, I've a mind to see where I fit into all this play-acting."

Reluctantly, he took the cards, held them a moment then handed them back. "It won't do any good, you know. I believe everyone makes his own decisions in this life."

She grinned at him showing a gap-toothed mouth then laid the tarot cards in a particular pattern and began to study the configurations. Impatient with her silence and intrigued despite his professed disregard for fortune-telling, he said, "Well, what splendid future have I got? Will I have riches galore, marry a princess, have a dozen children and live happily ever after?"

"I thought you didn't want to know?" she teased. "Yes, you might have all of these, but before the joy there will be sadness, deep sadness and a long, long journey filled with great anxiety. I'm sorry for being the one to tell you but it is written in your fate. But always remember, m'lord, the wheel will spin and grief will turn to gladness if you have forbearance. Now, if you'll forgive me, I must go to bed, these old bones dislike these cold damp nights. Build up the fire and use this blanket, it will not hurt you to sleep out tonight." She flung him a patchwork rug and disappeared inside the caravan before he could reply to her fortune telling.

Despite his beliefs his curiosity had been roused and he had been somewhat taken aback at her prognostications. "Old witch!" he said under his breath. "How can she possibly see the future?" He suddenly found himself upset with her obscure revelations. Furiously he flung a chunk of wood on the fire and lay down beside it, then weary from the early start and the traumatic day he fell asleep. Serina did not. She lay for some time thinking of the fate of these two people. Each ideally suited to one another but still bound for some time to be kept apart by the dark vagaries of fate. Sighing, she knew that she had done her part this day and rid the world of one obstacle for them. The rest was in their hands.

Merrick awakened at dawn next morning and a request to join Matthias in his caravan. Sluicing his face at a nearby stream he donned his jacket and walked over shining dew-laden grass to the chief's Vardas. A mug of steaming hot coffee awaited him as he arrived and, nodding his thanks, he took a deep grateful swallow, enjoying its heat as it warmed his stomach.

"Sit." Matthias pointed the end of his pipe to a nearby chair and Merrick sat down by the fire. "Trevarron's coach is still where his henchman left it. I suggest you take the young miss back to her home in it. Naturally you'll have to hire a coachman but Billy Bateson is willing if that suits you? He will of course appreciate the payment for the task."

"Naturally," acknowledged Merrick. "What about William?"

"He's dead."

"The devil, you say! But surely I didn't hit…?"

"Be easy, you didn't, but we did. He objected…shall we say…to being restrained. In any case we already wanted him for crimes against our folk. His death was justified."

"I'm beginning to realise how confused I am." Merrick frowned in bewilderment.

"Yes, I'm aware you had no idea of the evil connections of these two men. Naturally we have informed the law of course, but could only tell them William was trampled to death by the carriage horses. As for Trevarron, well his heart gave out while he was at the market, nothing to do with us. Neither you nor the girl is implicated. On your return, you will take a route that detours Launceston and any populated part of this locale. It might also interest you to know that previously, Trevarron was one of us, born and bred as a gypsy. He took off after the death of one of our girls, Serina's young sister. It was never proved he killed her or we would have gone for him a long time ago but Serina was sure of it. He did well for himself acquiring an estate from a young lord, no doubt by cheating at cards, but our paths never crossed until today so the rest of his life is mystery. After we found Linda on the moor no doubt he guessed what had happened and came looking for her here. Tell me, sir, in interest only, is she an heiress?"

"Unless Trevarron has any other kin I expect she will inherit his estate and also the mine, though I have the feeling it is running out, nevertheless she'll not lack for money, I'll see to that, never fear. She will be well taken care of from now on."

"And what else will you see to?" Matthias's tone was harsh.

"In what respect?" Merrick was equally curt, but he knew what Matthias hinted.

"Her future. She is a beautiful young woman."

"She is a child, scarce out of the schoolroom." Merrick shrugged the idea away.

"If she were one of us she would be married and have a babe at her breast. I myself was tempted, oh so tempted to keep her here with us, but I am already blessed with a wife and children and they would not have been best pleased had I done so." He chuckled as he saw Merrick's nostrils flare with rage, his fists clench. "You see? She's not a child after all. Already you are full of fire to fight for her." He held out his hand to Merrick. "I think she'll be safe with you, my friend, but take care lest she is not. I will undoubtedly see you again, my lord. Serina has told me you are from Scotland and I have a notion to visit the highlands when the weather is right. We will enjoy talking by a pinewood fire one evening after eating venison. Or do you hang those that fancy deer? In the meantime enjoy your life; may it be a long and fruitful one." Matthias came to his feet and reached out to clasp Merrick's hand firmly.

"You are welcome to the hospitality of our estates but I would suggest you are considerate to those of my neighbours. Strangers are watched with care in the Highlands. We are not far removed from our ancestors." He grinned as he spoke then took his leave and went to fetch Linda who was up and dressed. He explained he was going to take her to his parents after returning to Penzance to take leave of her aunt. "You will be safer with them than anyone."

Linda said goodbye to Serina, surprised how much she hated leaving her. She had found the gypsy way of life an amazing experience and was glad she had met them. Never again would she disparage or fail to help them. They were more honorable than many that professed to live a decent life.

CHAPTER FIFTY

"I think we are far enough away from Launceston to have the blinds drawn, don't you?" Merrick reached over to pull the curtains back from the coach windows as Linda nodded. It allowed her a view of the countryside beyond. "I also think it is time to talk." Stretching out his hand and closing it over hers, folding the small fingers gently in his larger fist. "You still look most apprehensive, my child, I beg you to relax, you are safe now, you know. Why don't you tell me of your life and the real reason you ran from Tregender Hall? It wasn't just because you were frightened by Trevarron, was it?"

"No." Linda sighed heavily, at last admitting to herself that the revelation of her unusual birth had created a desire for a complete change, perhaps travel and a chance to use her brain far from the confines of a rural and deadly boring life. She realised all too clearly now, after Trevarron's insulting but illuminating words, that to have married Richard would have been too stultifying and tedious. As fond as she was of Richard she was not cut out to be a minister's wife. As for marrying Ambrose Trevarron her status would have been raised, but the thought of him having the power to use her as he wished would have been terrifying. Now Lord Macgregor's offer to take her to his family gave her a sight of freedom, bringing a shining vista of adventure and experience she would not find in Cornwall; a chance to make a future for herself. "It is only just a short while ago I found out Jethro and Ellie Barton were not my real parents after all. I am the daughter of Lavinia, who was connected with your family, I believe, also she was a wife to Ambrose Trevarron. She died when I was born, from a fall, so the midwife said. She was barely conscious when she birthed me and said very little to Mrs Bunnion afterwards then died almost immediately."

"So you are Trevarron's daughter?" Merrick frowned, as though waiting for her to reveal her real father, staring at her limpid eyes filled with what he took to be confusion.

"I-I expect so." Suddenly Linda realised if she confessed Ambrose was not her father then this nobleman would scorn her illegitimacy. She must remain silent and keep hidden the letter her mother had given Amy.

Gazing into the deep emerald eyes filled with apprehension, he at once jumped to the conclusion she was not aware the mine-owner was not her father. What a mess, he considered. First, she has the trauma of losing one set of parents and then he would strip her of her dignity by telling her she was illegitimate. He found it was beyond him to cast her down in this way so he said nothing. He thought it was as well that the black-hearted villain had died, for he felt like killing him all over again in sheer revenge!

Leaning over he pressed a kiss on her soft cheek and watched the blush colour her skin. "I'll tell you what you are, besides being adorably lovely, you are my second cousin! And cousins are all bound to kiss and comfort their kin on every possible occasion, most especially when the relation is only seventeen and life has been very cruel to her." Gently he kissed her hand before releasing it.

Unexpectedly she giggled at his words and the delightful peal raised an answering smile from him. "But your mama? How will she feel? And your papa? I am, after all, a complete stranger and not really of your family. Perhaps they will not wish to know me." Linda's face held sudden concern. She did not want to be foisted on people without their wish.

"They won't mind one bit, they will love you very much, you'll see. Come, dry your eyes and lean against me, put your legs upon the seat. You must be tired for you had little rest last night. We must both sleep for it is a long way to Penzance.

Close your eyes, little cousin, I will watch over you." The interior of the chaise was surprisingly roomy and snug, and she leaned back against Merrick with her feet up on the cushions and within moments fell asleep. Lifting his arm he put it around her so her head was cradled against his chest as he wedged himself back against the side of the coach with his legs stretched diagonally across to the opposite seat. Then he too dropped into slumber.

Twilight had fallen when Linda awoke to find she was lying almost completely on top of him. Merrick had shifted their position so that they were both spread entwined on the same seat with Linda wrapped in his arms unable to move anywhere without disturbing him. Carefully lifting her cheek from his chest she peered upwards at him from beneath her long eyelashes. His face was relaxed and softened in sleep. The hard contours that he normally showed to the world less forbiddingly severe, almost youthful and now…aware!

Grey eyes that were hooded and intent, opened and looked down at her, almost as though he did not recognise her. They held an odd perplexity at finding this woman in his arms. Then he smiled, a warm, languid smile, showing amazingly white teeth in the gloom of the coach. "Did you sleep well?"

Linda nodded and tried to move herself upright.

His arms tightened, holding her against his hard body. "Don't go," he whispered. His gaze dropped to her soft lips and lingered on her mouth before lifting to her startled stare a glance that held a question. He wanted her to kiss him, Linda realised. With a surge of pleasure and anticipation, she forgot her commitment to Richard, who had never looked at her in just that slow, sensuous way, enough to cause shivers of erotic anticipation to run through her body.

Shyly, Linda stretched to put her lips on his and felt his hand slide to her back to lift her further up to him. His lips moved lightly against hers, exploring with a gentle touch so that he would not alarm her. As he deepened his kiss, she pouted her lips for him and his tongue teased them open allowing him entry. The sweet offering of her lips dragged a groan from him and he wrenched his mouth away gasping with the racing lust that was possessing his body. "Don't look at my lips unless you want me to kiss you again, my sweet cousin," Merrick whispered, staring down into her glowing green eyes.

Helplessly Linda did just that, wanting, needing the ecstasy of his mouth on hers, unaware that her body was awakening to its destiny. Strong, compelling fingers slid seductively through her hair, caressing the nape of her neck with gentleness, while the other hand continued sensuously, soothingly, stroking her back. He kissed her endlessly, long delicious kisses, his tongue stroking and caressing, shaking her to the core of her being, making her want more until Linda yielded mindlessly to the stormy sensations of his exploring mouth, plunging, retreating, tormenting her until she ventured to touch her own tongue to his. In an instant the kiss flared with passion; his hand moved to curve round her bottom, pulling her tightly against his hardened body while his tongue began thrusting into her mouth in a wildly exciting rhythm that sent jolts of pleasure sweeping through Linda's body.

Not until she felt his hand slide into her bodice to cup her soft breast did she jerk free of the vortex of erotic emotion where she was willingly drowning. Sitting up hastily, she smoothed her tumbled hair from her face before raising an embarrassed gaze to his smouldering grey eyes. "A c-cousinly kiss?" She arched an eyebrow at him, her face grave with concern.

He chuckled wryly, filled with amusement at her volley. "Touché! The occasion did seem to warrant it." Raising his hand he gently smoothed her heated cheek. "So soft, so incredibly innocent," he whispered hoarsely, still caught with the emotion of the moment.

Linda at once interpreted "innocent" to mean childish as she recalled being cuddled like a babe in his arms. She pulled away in mortification. "I must be a dreadful bore for a man of your obvious sophistication, but then, I've never been a 'cousin' before, and I'll have to learn how things are done in your world."

His hands clamped her arms and he hauled her back. "That was a compliment," he retorted, the tense sound of his voice making her wonder if he was angry. Giving her a little shake he clarified his remark. "Innocent - demure, unsullied - and don't let me catch you being anything else, understand?" He shook her again. Suddenly he was concerned at her future in the hands of someone else.

"Perfectly!" Linda flung back with force, then with humorous knowledge, she said disarmingly, "You don't want me to be a 'cousin' to anyone else but you, is that correct?" She watched as his eyes flared in startled comprehension. "I don't think you should worry too much, I am a quick learner and I've learned much these last days."

"Vixen! Nevertheless, you are correct, I took advantage of you. It won't happen again. You have my apologies." His voice was stiff with annoyance at allowing his heated feelings to get the better of him. No longer was there a way he could pretend the urgent, throbbing desire he felt did not exist, or that she was only a child. Matthias was absolutely correct. He wanted her only for himself.

The rest of the journey was conducted with decorum on both their parts, which had a sobering effect on the relationship. Linda's newly awakened senses longed for him to hold her in his arms again but the man she had known earlier had changed into a stranger, back to being the polite gentleman who was keeping a tight clamp on his words which, in turn, served to stifle her spontaneity. She was unaware Merrick knew he would be forever condemned by his parents should he trespass on the chaste virginity of this maiden, so he kept as far away from her as was possible. However not far enough away to avoid the faint perfume of her hair and skin that bathed him continually in lust.

Hell and damnation, he thought. The sooner I am back to London and can have Angelina the better. At least she doesn't keep me in torment without release. Even if she does have a lover I will rid her of him once I am in the city permanently. Except she doesn't have green eyes that melt in passion, or a body that could learn to please, his wayward mind insisted. Instantly another surge of craving warned him he was playing with fire and he directed his thoughts to calmer channels.

Linda, watching the play of emotions across his face, thought how fierce he looked until a blandness replaced what she took to be rage and he began to converse with her of her life as a child drawing out many details she was unaware she possessed. Merrick became more and more interested in her fortitude to this point, which seemed to him had run counter to so much that could have put an end to her existence. That she had managed to survive to become a lovely, educated young woman was a miracle in itself. So the long journey which could have been tedious was passed with pleasure.

CHAPTER FIFTY-ONE

Having heard the rumble of coach wheels Annie had the main door open as the coach drew to a halt outside the Hall that evening. She fully expected Trevarron to emerge and was taken aback when she saw Merrick alight. Then her surprise turned to joy as he helped Linda to step down.

"God save us, child, where have you been? Do you realise how worried we were, why the Master has been gone two days looking for you. Betsy's been fit to be tied since you left. We both thought you'd come to harm setting out on your own."

"Oh, Annie, I'm truly sorry…" Linda's voice became muffled as Annie hugged her.

"Suppose we go inside, Linda? Explanations can wait, don't you think, until we are settled and more relaxed?" said Merrick and turning to Billy, who was replacing the coach steps, he continued quietly, "Stable the horses and feed them, then come to the kitchen for your dinner. I expect you will take over William's quarters but we'll sort it out later, after the explanations."

Billy took his meaning and nodded. "Don't worry, m'lord, things'll work out."

Once inside the huge hall Merrick again took charge and gave orders with the firmness of long command. "Why don't you take the opportunity of changing and make yourself comfortable, Linda? I am sure we can all wait for that. In the meantime I will explain to Annie and your aunt what has happened. By the time you are ready I am sure Mrs Polwen will find us something to eat."

Happy to be once more at home and wishful of delaying her story to Aunt Betsy and Annie, Linda nodded with relief and left.

"Now, Annie, if you will fetch Mrs Polwen, explanations can be disposed of directly." He did not wait for her to reply but went quickly through to the study. A few minutes later the flustered cook and the housekeeper entered the room to find Merrick had taken up a stance before the fireplace. "Come in and sit down both of you. Please, I insist. This might take a while and I would prefer you to be at ease." Embarrassed, the two women did as they were told.

"Firstly," began Merrick, "I have to tell you that Ambrose Trevarron is dead. He had a massive heart attack while at the Launceston Horse Market and did not recover. His coachman, William, is also dead. Regrettably, so I have been told, he fell whilst seeing to the horses and was badly trampled." He paused to allow the two women to express their consternation but not, he saw, much in the way of concern or grief.

"Where was Linda while this was going on? How come you knew where to find 'er?" Betsy burst out, more concerned with her beloved Lindy.

"When she ran away from home she was picked up by gypsies," Merrick continued.

"Gypsies! Oh Lord help us, she'm be ruined."

"Rubbish, woman!" Merrick was terse with the cook. "She has come to no harm in the slightest. On the contrary, they looked after her very well."

"But the whole district knows she was gone, run the Lord knows where, while we was looking all ways. They had a good idea why she run, too. The master had a reputation for – for…well, folks knew what he was like," Annie interjected.

I'll wager you did your share in passing the news, thought Merrick grimly.

"Happen her reputation won't be worth a candle now," the cook continued. "Any chance of her making a decent marriage is gone, an' 'er sweet on Richard, the vicar's boy – his family won't lookit 'er now." Betsy buried her face in her apron and howled. In despair Merrick ran his fingers through his hair and appealed to Annie Gorland.

"Make her see sense, will you. Linda is perfectly all right; she has taken no hurt in the slightest. Dammit, I've just driven all the way back with her, I should know."

Annie stared at him imperviously. "She's right, you know. They'll also point a finger if they get to hear she's been wiv you all day in a coach. She'll never live it down, you bein' a stranger an' all. There's more to consider than the fact you rescued her, which is why you must protect Linda as much as possible. Gossip is a powerful enemy."

Irritated with what he perceived was a lecture he quickly interrupted. "There is more for you to understand concerning past events. Linda's mother was actually Trevarron's wife, Lavinia. Now she is dying, the midwife has suddenly confessed she managed to swap babies when your sister, Mrs Barton, and Lavinia were in labour." If he had thrown a bomb in their midst he couldn't have shocked the women more. The two of them sat mutely stunned at the dramatic news. Merrick also stood silent, his brain working furiously. He had scarcely given any thought on the return journey how the village people or even the Tregender staff would view Linda's disappearance. How their narrow Methodist minds would think the worst of the girl and condemn her without thought of the truth. Considering Trevarron's mine, it would appear there was no heir other than Linda, if it was genuine that Trevarron had legally adopted her. Merrick thought that fact extremely unlikely in view of Trevarron's aim to marry Linda.

However, as partner, there was no problem in him taking over the running of the Hall. He fully intended in any case to pass ownership on to Linda, either on her majority or when she married. Now it was even more obvious because of all the gossip that would arise she could not stay in Cornwall. She would have to remove to Scotland for more than the brief visit he had intended. As far as the future was concerned a potential suitor would want to know her background and her lack of a father would be suspect. He personally did not give a toss of a coin who had fathered her, her sweet nature was an endorsement of the kind of girl she was but others might, indeed would, if their relations had anything to do with it. What a sorry stew he found himself in; just when he thought things had sorted themselves with the combined deaths of Trevarron and William.

It struck him further that when he arranged their journey to Scotland these two old crows would set up a shrieking loud enough to deafen the neighbourhood. He sighed in exasperation; it was no good speculating on Linda's future, or of her chances of making a reasonable marriage with someone who would understand her unusual history. Only one thing he could do to make amends; he would have to offer for her himself.

The cook took her head out of her apron to stare fixedly at Merrick. "I allus knew she were quality. I worked long nuff wiv the late young Lord's family t' know quality. That's why I couldn't bear Ambrose; he was dirt. What's gonna happen t'Annie an' me? Is Tregender going to be sold? We'll have to chance being kept on wi' new owners, won't we?"

"Not if I can help it," replied Merrick at once, seeing an opening to demonstrate his intentions. "I believe I have a good solution to the dilemma. If Linda will marry me as soon as possible, giving her recognised name of Barton and you as her nearest relative, there should be no problem. If we wait for the law to decide who is her formal guardian and who gets the estate then it will be years before things are solved. Meanwhile, Linda will be subject to the notorious press and every blatant falsehood about her past they can dig up. Do you want that to happen? She will never have a chance to take her place in society again. You have done a wonderful job of rearing Linda. She is a credit to you. Anyone who knows her feels this at once. Except now she may have to deal with strangers."

Steady on, Macgregor, you're piling on the agony! Merrick could hardly believe his own words. When he began this discussion marriage was the last thing on his mind - now he was going overboard in an effort to sway the minds of these women. Was this what he really wanted? What about Angelina? All of a sudden she paled beside Linda and he knew there was no contest.

"You're right, m'lord, though what Lindy's gonna say bout it, Lord knows. Almost all her life she's been sweet on Richard Whitely though he's off at the moment studying to become a minister. If the gossip is bad his mother will kick up rough. She's snobbish as they come. For a minister's wife she allus consorted with the social biddies in the place and never took notice of them as needed her help. Lindy will see sense, though, if Annie an' I 'ave anything to do with it. But for now best I go and get dinner. Starving minds are no use to anyone. Come on, Annie. We'm leave his lordship to tell 'er 'isself and we can 'ave our say later."

CHAPTER FIFTY-TWO

Merrick was left to compose his speech to Linda. He had no idea what she would say but he hazarded a guess that she would not be easy to convince. He racked his brains to find a solution that would not convey to her he was marrying out of pity. He sensed it would be the last thing she would want from anyone. In the event, Linda did not join him until dinner was announced. When she emerged, her hair was freshly washed and she was bathed and changed into an apple green dress with matching green ribbons threaded through the puffed sleeves, waist and hem. Similar ties held her hair back from her face to fall in springing curls down her back. She looked refreshingly lovely and his spirits lifted at the prospect of making her his wife. He could do worse, he felt. At least she would give him a base to create a family and if his fancies strayed now and then when he was away on business, did not all men? After they had eaten he rose with her instead of staying to smoke a cigar, and guided her to the study. "Shall you have a tray of tea here? If so I will enjoy a glass of brandy with you."

She nodded her consent. Annie heard and, rather pleased with the change of masters in the house, went to the cellars to find one of Trevarron's finer bottles for his delectation.

"I like this room; it's a cosy place to talk."

"Do you? It still reminds me of him." She shivered suddenly as she recalled the last time she had been in the room then she glanced quickly at him but his face was impassive giving her no hint of his intentions or what he was thinking. His conversation at dinner had been interestingly easy and she had enjoyed the light repartee and teasing wit that had never come her way with Trevarron.

"Well he's gone now and we must look to the future," he began slowly.

"If I may have a moment I'll have a word with Aunt Betsy, she will want to know what happened to me. I must assure her I am…"

"No, Linda, we'll talk first." he said firmly. He did not want Betsy saying anything that would put her on her guard. Things would be hard enough without that. The study was warm, the comfortable fire radiating heat in the evening coolness. Merrick poured himself a brandy and went to stand before it while Linda, a little surprised with his rejection of her wishes, found a chair and helped herself to a cup of tea. While she sipped she thought wryly again of the last time she was in the room facing up to a raging man. Trevarron had horrified her when he had pinned her against the sofa and started tearing at her dress. He was about to beat her, she was sure, though Aunt Betsy had hinted at something worse. How she wished people would be honest, not pretend she was too young to know and make excuses. Now she supposed she was in for a stiff lecture about running away. One of these days when she was old enough she hoped she would be in a position to decide her own future, not do what others wanted.

"You are welcome to join me in a brandy." Merrick tried to break the silence.

She shook her head, surprised at his offer. "I have tried wine but generally it does not suit me. This tea is most welcome."

"This is only to give me Dutch courage." He waved his glass at her. "I find myself lamentably speechless at a time when I need to be talkative."

"Oh? What do you need to confess? I always find I am lost for words if I am guilty of something." She smiled disarmingly. "Come on, 'fess up. You'll feel better afterwards, at least I always do. Aunt Betsy has been a real tyrant at times. She says she loves me and it is all for my own good but I do wonder if she just loves telling me what to do." Her lips puckered in teasing amusement showing an impish humour in her nature.

He chuckled, suddenly realising that he had laughed more in her company than he had done for years. The humorous times had been innocent and guileless but nonetheless most refreshing. Now how would she appraise his words? Well, he would soon find out.

"Linda, will you marry me?" There, it was out in all its baldness.

"Marry you?" Stunned surprise filled her voice. "Oh no! I couldn't."

As her answer came as swiftly and just as baldly as his offer, the humour left her face and stark misgiving replaced it. Slowly she shook her head, her eyes dark and huge with what? Regret? Amusement? Merrick could not read them, so consumed was he with anger. The chit's turned me down! Savagely he took the blow. She had refused him!

He stared at her fiercely but she held his gaze with a bravery that was not echoed inside her. She was glad she was sitting down for she was shaking with fear. "I thank you for your kindness." Linda's voice intruded into his miffed wrath. "But it really won't do, you know. We hardly know each other, and in any case I am promised to someone else. I tried telling him that…Ambrose Trevarron, I mean." How incredible, she thought, three proposals of marriage and from such different characters. "That is when he got furious and attacked me. I could not believe he would act so towards me though the gossip said he was a violent man if crossed."

He interrupted her swiftly. "Well I am not about to do any such thing. Do you mean the minister's son?" With an effort Merrick kept his voice calm trying hard not to let his intense anger show.

She nodded, wondering how he knew about Richard and who could have told him.

He shook his head. "Out of the question." His tone was blunt and final.

"That's what Ambrose said, only he was much ruder. How do you all know? Why won't we suit?" she argued, furious that he was trying to run her life like everyone else.

"Because you are going to marry me." Putting his glass down he took her hands and pulled her up from her chair, bringing her close to him. She gasped and tried to free her hands but he held fast tight to them refusing to let go. Bewildered with the feel of his touch as well as the proposal, she stood trembling, a mere pace away, so close she could see a muscle tighten in his jaw and the glitter of his eyes gazing down at her.

"I know this is sudden but I've travelled the world and never asked a woman to marry me until now. I want you, Linda, with all my heart, I want you." All at once he realised how true it was. The faint perfume that arose from her filled his senses with a longing that was more than just lust. He wanted her in his arms and by his side. He wanted her for his wife. As his deep husky voice assailed her emotions he gently pulled her towards him and slid his arm about her waist while his other hand, cupping the back of her head, drew her close to his waiting lips. Her startled eyes began to darken to a deep chartreuse as, in a daze, she watched his mouth descend on hers and then open her lips in the most passionate kiss she had ever had.

With her brain turned to wool so she could hardly think and her legs to water so she could hardly stand, she slid her hand inside his open jacket to touch his chest to reassure her that indeed she was not dreaming; this was actually happening to her. Gently she smoothed his chest and his muscles clenched with pleasure as she braced herself against his strong body. His kiss deepened, plunging into her mouth in demanding hunger, hands splaying over her back moulding her close to his hardened desire. With a moan of reckless ardour she clung to him, feeling the length of his body that pressed against her own; her senses filled with a pagan longing she had never felt before. Heedless of what he was doing, Merrick forced her to return his sensual urgency, driving his tongue into her mouth until she too ignited in passion.

Shaken to the core with an almost uncontrollable compulsion to take her there and then and with desire pouring along his veins in a hot tidal wave, he tore his mouth from hers and slid his lips across her cheek, while his hand sought her breast to rub gently over the engorged nipple. She flinched in surprise at the unexpected touch; the innocent reaction bringing a further surge of pure lust driving through his body. He knew he had to stop, and stop quickly before things got totally out of hand so with the most supreme effort he had ever made in his life he forced his senses under control and folding his arms around her, held her to his chest staring over her head while he brought his thundering heart to a steadier beat. Until now he had convinced himself she was green, a mere child, the passion erupting between them exaggerated but now he knew this young maiden had the ability to make him lose his mind. Linda stayed in his arms, her flushed cheek pressed against his chest, trembling in the aftermath of the most spectacular feeling she had ever experienced.

Drawing a torturous breath she raised her emerald eyes. "Why me?"

Merrick understood the question. He was asking himself exactly the same thing. How could two people meet and explode in passion like this? Strangers all of their lives and yet suddenly as close as lovers who had known each other forever. "Because it's meant to be, my love. I was right to ask you to be mine, wasn't I? Say yes, please, my darling girl, say yes."

"Where shall we live? What about Aunt Betsy and Annie? I can't leave them without a home. But they wouldn't know a moment's peace to be taken from here."

"Neither shall you uproot them, my sweet. Tregender Hall is yours to do with as you wish and your servants will carry on as they have always done. They will always have a home here for the rest of their lives. Whenever we visit we shall have a warm, comfortable house to welcome us." Thank God it was within his power to grant her this wish.

"Where shall we go?" The impact of hearing she owned the Hall after all the upset that had happened did not register. It was meaningless in the face of this greater shock.

"Firstly to Scotland to introduce you to my family, then wherever you wish to settle. I will show you the world and you can choose where you want to go."

"Shall we be married in Scotland?" All at once a strange curiosity took hold.

"No, we shall marry here in Cornwall. I believe you would prefer to have your aunt attend your wedding. Of course if you want a big affair, it will have to be Scotland."

He tensed as he waited for her reply.

"Oh no, a big affair would be dreadful. I would rather marry quietly, with just the two of us." She had a sudden horrible thought of Richard appearing and stopping the wedding. How embarrassing it would be.

"Does this mean you say yes?" Again he held his breath as he waited on her reply.

"I believe it does. Though how it has come about leaves me quite bewildered. What am I to call you, My Lord? I seem to have so much to learn."

"Call me by my given name, my love, Merrick will suit admirably. Later, you can try darling or even dearest, if you have a mind to and if I please you as much as you please me. I answer to most things except lies and venom."

"Merrick will do very nicely until I know you," she replied primly, a delicate blush creeping over her petal soft skin. Merrick felt an odd sense of unreality as he faced the prospect of teaching a young virginal girl to appreciate the things he liked. What a change from Angelina who, with her worldly experience, had never needed teaching at all. He found he was looking forward to the prospect with keen anticipation.

CHAPTER FIFTY-THREE

A week passed swiftly, during which time Merrick saw the Bishop and purchased a special licence, earning a lasting grudge from the churchman when he was not invited to the wedding. The cleric quite wrongly attributed it to being a coerced marriage to a commoner who was pregnant. Merrick also arranged for Linda to visit the finest dressmaker-cum-lingerie shop in Penzance and virtually bought the whole of her stock, which would fit his bride-to-be. When Linda remonstrated with him he shrugged and told her to throw away anything she did not require but he took immense pains to tell Betsy and Annie to retain certain items he had chosen especially. Merrick returned to his lodgings in Penzance and from there he visited what had become his mines by right of his partnership and made final arrangements for their continuation during his absence.

"I shall be gone some time, Tom. In fact it is difficult at this point to predict when I shall be back in this area, though rest assured my wife and I will definitely return."

"I hope so, m'lord." Tom Spenny was both elated and dismal because the new owner was leaving. Elated because he had been made Mine Captain and was now in full charge of everything to do with the mines and sad because he liked working with the young lord and would miss him. His conscience had taken a drastic dive after Trevarron's disappearance to Launceston and he had racked his brains continuously to find a way out of his servitude to a man he considered to be a devil incarnate. When he heard of Trevarron's death his feeling of relief at his escape was so great he almost collapsed from the sheer shock. Never again would he place himself in such jeopardy. Though, on reflection, Macgregor was not a man who would stoop to such evil, even so Tom knew he would never tread that murderous path again.

"The engineer and his men will fit the new machinery when it is ready but I do not anticipate you will have more than two or three years at most before the deposits run out. In that event no one is to be laid off. I have future plans for my workers and you can tell them they will not be without good employment for the rest of their lives. If there are accidents then the victims must have a pension. In addition, when a situation looks dubious as to further gains from the mine, you are to let me know without fail. Is that clear? I am relying on you to keep things going profitably yet with compassion. It will be a new role for you; do you think you can handle it? Keep control with firmness but fairness. No bullying. You understand me?"

Tom nodded, hardly believing the miracle that was emerging. "Christ yes!" Tom's emotions ran away with him. "Beggin' yer pardon, m'lord, I'll not let ee down, no sir. I've bin waitin' fur a bloody miracle and now it's here I can't find the words to say how wonderful it is. Them miner's u'll work their guts out fur ee, they will. And so will I."

"I truly hope not," replied Merrick with a smile. "Just see to it there is no hardship in the village for my wife-to-be's sake. Some of the profits are to be used to renovate the miner's cottages. I want a healthy crew and that means good living and working conditions to keep them healthy. And, Tom, – I want it be known that Linda is at the bottom of the new arrangements because of her personal associations with the village."

"Aye, I will, sir, and God bless ee and her. I wish ee great happiness," Tom said as they grinned at each other and shook hands on the deal.

The wedding day appeared all too soon as far as Linda was

concerned. She felt she had been busy forever with scarcely a break to rest, ensuring that her old home would carry on without misfortune while she was away. Every now and then, when she had to break off to be fitted with a new gown, her exasperation knew no bounds. "I'm sure I'll be changing from morning to night with all these clothes, Annie. I'll never find the time to wear them. For pity's sake, surely I have enough now?"

"Now hush, Lindy, when ye are in polite society such as m'lord frequents, ye have to do as they do." Annie was in seventh heaven seeing her darling was well equipped.

"Are you sure I'm doing the right thing." Linda sighed heavily. "The future looks so paved with problems. I know I'll never be able to act as I should for him."

"Of course ye are, my lovely. Never fear, you will do everything just like a queen. In any case, he adores ye. Anyone can see that you'll be happy with him."

"I don't know about that, he's scarcely spoken to me in a week and tomorrow I'll be on my own with him. Supposing we run out of conversation and he gets bored with me?"

"Ah yes, I've been meanin' to say somethin' bout that. Ye must do all ee tells ye, understand. Even if it appears a bit strange at first."

"Strange! Don't tell me I'm marrying a madman, for goodness sake!" She laughed hilariously. "If it is too odd then I'll blame it all on you."

Out of her depth, spinster that she was, Annie decided she would leave the telling of the facts of life and how they were interpreted to Lord Macgregor. After all it concerned him the most. Linda forgot the conversation in the rush for she had barely seen Merrick and then only to ask his advice on financial matters with the upkeep of the Estate. Becoming his wife was a vague dream that she was quite sure would vanish like a puff of smoke as soon as she woke but everything proceeded in quick order until all was ready and the day of the wedding arrived and she was faced with reality.

That morning the news reached Merrick that the Launceston inquests on Ambrose Scroggan, his real name, and William Tremor had opened and closed with verdicts of natural death and accidental death respectively. Someone had claimed the bodies and that was the end of that. The note Merrick received was unsigned but he recognised Matthias had sent it. He sighed with relief. At least Linda had been kept away from any damaging publicity and that was all he cared about.

He greeted his bride with quiet courtesy at noon, taking the opportunity to whisper to her that this was not like a normal church wedding, which he would arrange once they reached Scotland for the benefit of his parents. Relieved at the lack of formality, she signed the necessary documents, accepted the well-wishers' congratulations from the few people who attended the short ceremony in Penzance, then decided her nerves and trepidations had been misplaced, for she did not feel married at all.

The unreal situation exploded still further for when they came out of the Registry Office a young lad held out a telegram to Merrick. He opened it, in the expectation of finding yet another goodwill message but Linda saw his face turn completely ashen. A moment later he turned to her, his eyes bright with unshed tears.

"Merrick?" she said anxiously, seeing his distress.

With a huge effort he composed himself and simply said, "I'm sorry, my dear, to spoil your wedding day, but the wire is to say my father has just died."

From then on she scarcely knew what was happening as Merrick cancelled the modest reception that had been going to follow the wedding and sent Billy to the station to book seats on the next train to London. He decided he and Linda would stay one night and then take the train to Edinburgh. He told Annie to pack one case with essentials for his wife and see the rest was sent afterwards. He cancelled the honeymoon trip he had planned, which would have taken them from Hayle to the Moray Firth on one of his ships, then by chaise to Forres and the castle because there was no longer time enough for the voyage.

He did all this like an automaton, holding his grief behind a stern, dark visage, which renewed all Linda's doubts and terrors. When at last they boarded the train she was exhausted from dread and worry. Merrick saw her seated in the private compartment he had booked then beholding her understandable distress he, without more ado, ordered chilled champagne from the dining car.

On its arrival he poured out a glass and handed it to her. "Yes, I know you don't like wine but this is different. It will do you good. Drink up but first may I drink a toast to my new bride? May we be happy and face all troubles with the same degree of fortitude you've displayed today. You've been splendid throughout, my dear. You have helped me to get through a most trying day following the sad news of my father. My deepest regret is that it spoiled your wedding day." He drank deeply then watched while she drank too. The bubbles tickled her nose but she found she quite liked it and did not object when he helped her to some more. His words too had gone a long way towards cheering her and, though the tedious journey passed in a daze for Linda who alternatively napped and watched the passing landscape, her fears began to lessen.

Merrick was busy most of the time with the contents of a briefcase and she hardly dared to interrupt him. She slept deeply overnight in a solitary bed in the London hotel and again at Edinburgh, after which they took another train to Inverness. When they reached the old Scottish town and climbed into the waiting chaise she suddenly recovered.

"Merrick, would you mind very much directing the coachman to a lady's shop, there is s-something quite important I have to buy?" Her eyes, deeply shadowed with tiredness, seemed rather embarrassed and became more so as she added, "Do you have any money? Only I don't seem…"

Directing the coachman to a suitable shop he drawled

carelessly. "My mother shops here, charge it." He paused for an instant before going on. "Charge it to Her Grace, the Duchess of Forres. Don't be long, will you, I'll wait here outside."

The grin he gave her was both sardonic and sad but it did not register. Thanking him, she hurried into the store. With a keen perception of female needs he thought nature had taken her unawares and she was seeking to protect herself. To his complete astonishment she emerged a short while later dressed overall in black. Behind her a woman carried a bag with her clothes. The owner of the store, following on behind, bowed low to Merrick who by this time had stepped out of the coach. "If there is anything more we can do for Her Grace, we are at your service, milord. We will of course attend Her Grace at the castle whenever she requires us to do so." Again he bowed very low.

"Thank you, no; I believe Her Grace has all she wants for the moment. Is that so, darling, or are there any more shops you need to visit?" She shook her head, her face crimson with the knowledge of her new status. "Then, thank you for your help, no doubt she will call on you again when she has need of you." The carriage rolled on leaving the two assistants still bowing in the road. Merrick sat quietly for a moment thinking how he would voice his thoughts, then turned to survey his wife's attire with surprise.

"I am surprised at your choice of new clothes, my dear, though my mother will commend your sentiments. Whatever made you decide to buy attire like that?"

"I could never meet your mother under the present circumstances without showing my respects to her. It will be bad enough me turning up like this when all she will be concerned with will be her grief. I should have stayed behind in Cornwall instead of intruding. And why d-did y-you not tell me I was a Grace or whatever it is." Her eyes shone enormously with unshed tears that suddenly spilled over to splash warmly on his hand as he raised it to stroke her face.

"I'm sorry, Linda, things have happened so fast I've scarcely taken it in myself. Besides what difference does it make? We are still the same people."

"I'd n-never have m-married you if I'd known y-you were going to be a Duke." The tears were running faster and she seemed unable to stop the flow.

Fetching out a large white handkerchief he handed it to her. "Try this. It will be better than that wisp you have in your hand." Gratefully she seized the handkerchief and applied it to her eyes as he said, "As it happens, Linda, you acquired the title of Marchioness when you married me, a title I rarely use. I would have thought you would be pleased you are simply called 'Your Grace'." He sounded quite perturbed.

Looking at his face she decided to say no more. How could she explain how disoriented she felt to be whisked from her own world into his, still not knowing who she really was, or more importantly who had fathered her? However, if she was confused with her status, it was nothing to the stunned emotions she suffered as the carriage turned into the long drive and they bowled rapidly through green manicured parkland towards a fairy-tale castle. She gazed in awe at the cream coloured limestone walls, with ornate corbelled battlements and bartizans; the dark tiling on the roof highlighting the pale walls. A flag hung limply at half-mast to indicate the demise of the late Duke, and the entrance door was amply garlanded in black swathing. Merrick helped her down and turned to encounter Angus Dudwick, the butler, who greeted Merrick with a serious though obviously pleased demeanour.

"This is Dudwick, darling, he knows every inch of the castle so you may rely on him to guide you. My dear wife, Dudwick. An event that is new so there was hardly time to let the castle know. We shall celebrate it later after…" He paused, stricken for a very long moment at the thought of his father dying before he had time to see him again.

"Quite, your Grace, I do understand. M'lady." His bow was

both gracious and hospitable. "May I be the first to welcome you to Forres? May you also be very happy and come to love the place as we all do here."

She smiled shyly and nodded her head. Not expecting her to say anything, he held out his arm to point the way to Linda and led her into the huge entrance hall.

The stone flagged hall, with its vaulted ceiling supported on Romanesque stone pillars was bare of all decoration, save for two enormous carved wooden chests and a huge oaken staircase leading from it. Linda shivered with a sudden chill and was relieved to walk through to a nearby Library filled with hundreds of old books and pictures and, best of all a roaring log fire, where Morag waited to greet them. Linda hung back whilst Merrick enfolded his mother in his arms; Morag shed a quiet tear then hastily dried her eyes.

"I'm glad you've come so quickly, Merrick, the funeral is at two o'clock. I thought you'd not be in time; Cornwall is so very far away. Oh, my dear lassie, I didn't see you standing there!"

Morag swung round to where Linda shyly waited to be seen. "But here I am talking too much and forgetting my manners. I received your telegram, son, and was naturally most surprised but not nearly as much as now. Why, you're a lovely beauty, lassie. Merrick for once is to be commended on his fine taste. Oh welcome, my dear, dear daughter, a thousand times welcome. Come away in by the fire and be warm, the wind has a bite in it today and you'll be chilled and tired from your long journey."

Linda curtsied deeply to her new mother-in-law instantly charmed with her welcome in spite of the overpowering surroundings she stood in. Perhaps things were not so bad after all. "Thank you. I am pleased to be here, though so saddened at your loss," she said shyly. "I hope I'm not intruding at this dreadful time for you. I promise not to get in the way."

Morag smiled. Poor dear child, she thought. What a terrible

time to celebrate one's wedding. She looks dazed but takes time to think of me. Merry has chosen well. "Now, my dears, we've just time get you settled. Are you hungry?" She turned to Dudwick still waiting silently in the doorway for his mistress's orders. "Angus, tell Betty to attend Her Grace and see she has everything she needs. I've put you in the East wing, Merrick; there's not been time to decorate the master suite…" A sob caught in her throat and she held a handkerchief to her face.

Merrick went to her at once. "We shall be perfectly comfortable, Mama. Don't, I beg of you, worry about moving out of your quarters. They're yours as long as you want."

Linda quickly followed the butler out of the room and up the oaken staircase, which led to the many apartments on the first floor. The two grieving people did not need her with them at this time and it might be a long time before they did. Nevertheless she took a crumb of comfort from the kind words of her mother-in-law. At least she did not feel she would be held in dislike for their hasty marriage. Not until, that is, the fact of her illegitimacy came to light. For the time being nothing more gracious could have been said to the lonely, homesick girl than the friendly welcome from Morag. Merrick could have soothed her qualms had he known she was dreading the meeting, but all his life he had been used to his mother's agreeable nature and it did not occur to him. Watching Linda as she relaxed in the warming compassion of his mother's welcome it crossed his mind he had been selfishly expecting her to fit in with his plans without giving a thought to the fact she was a stranger to Scotland and would naturally be very anxious. Not once had she complained of her tiredness from the hasty trip, though he guessed she was drained and weary and, no doubt, missing her old life. Despite it all, she had gone out of her way to honour his dead father and show her respect for his mother. He determined he would make it up to her and ensure she was happy.

CHAPTER FIFTY-FOUR

The ceremonial funeral was over, his father's body interred in the family vault and the many guests at the ensuing feast slowly taking their leave, when Merrick rescued Linda from two elderly ladies who were trying, unsuccessfully, to cross-examine her.

"I hardly understood a word they were saying, My L-Lord, I'm sure they think I'm a complete idiot. It will take me a while to learn the new language."

He smiled humorously and placed his arm around her waist. "A tired idiot, my sweetness. Come, the ceremony is over and we are going to retire. I, for one, could sleep for a week. Look, Betty is waiting to help you. She will ensure you have all you need."

As Linda relaxed in a warm bath, she reflected sleepily that having one's own maid was not so daunting after all. Her clothes had been unpacked, she had been helped to undress and now Betty was waiting with warm towels to dry her. Too sleepy to be embarrassed with her help, she donned the ivory silk nightdress Merrick had selected for her, not aware of the way her breasts were revealed by its low cut or the alluring picture she made with her gown slit to the thigh. She sat down on the dressing stool to have her long hair dried and brushed and, with closed eyes, was luxuriating in the blissful joy of the maid's firm strokes. She was not aware when her husband came silently in from the adjoining bedroom and, with his finger laid on his lips, took the hairbrush from Betty and carried on with the stroking of the brush and running his strong fingers through the blonde tresses. With a tiny smile

Betty gathered up the wet towels and swiftly and silently left the room.

Suddenly aware the brushing had changed its rhythm Linda opened her eyes then gasped with shock as gazing in the mirror before her she met her husband's eyes.

"My Lord, you shouldn't be here! Where is Betty?"

"About her affairs, I should imagine," he said mildly. "I thought to join you for a tiny nightcap. I have some champagne. I recall you enjoyed it before."

"Yes, thank you, I did," she replied doubtfully, her eyes still apprehensive as they gazed at him. Then recalling her nudity she reached for her dressing gown but at once he grasped her hand and drew up her towards him. "You don't need that, my love, it is perfectly warm and you are much too beautiful to be covered." He poured out a glass of champagne and handed it to her. "To my dearest wife. I will honour you all my days."

She held up her glass in a toast before drinking. "To you, My Lord husband - I mean Merrick." She grinned with a cheeky smile. "I hope I'll deserve your honour. Oh dear, this does tickle my nose."

Merrick laughed and took the glass from her. "Enough, I think, my sweet. A tipsy bride I do not need." Pulling her close to him he enfolded her face with his hands then pressed gentle lips to hers, keeping the kisses soft and light for he could feel her begin to quiver with tension. Looking up she gazed into his eyes that unaccountably had changed to a warm smouldering grey then his lips slid down the curve of her cheek and reaching the soft skin of her neck pressed his lips in a lingering kiss. She jumped in alarm.

"You are trembling," he said, warm hands enveloping her shoulders.

"Am I?" she asked nervously. "I don't know why."

"Don't you?" His lips curved humorously. "Perhaps it's because this is truly our wedding night. We have had no time to be together in peace and quiet to relax and enjoy as a married couple ought."

"Oh! Does this mean you are staying in here?"

"No, my darling, you are coming in my bed, it's bigger."

Sliding one hand round her back he swung her up into his arms and held her close to his chest, his mouth immediately taking possession of her lips and then he carried her through the connecting doorway into his own suite where a huge bed waited with the covers already turned down. Her senses awhirl in the stormy kiss Linda slid down his body and realised for the first time he wore only a light robe. As her feet touched the floor his hands went to her nightdress straps pushing them off her shoulders as his mouth nuzzled her neck again. It slid to the floor leaving her naked.

"What are you doing?" she asked worriedly.

"What do you think, my sweet?" Staring into the wide green eyes now filled with sudden apprehension, Merrick knew he would have to curb his fervour and rising desire.

"Undressing me?" she admitted warily.

"Yes, there shouldn't be anything between us to impede my making love to you."

"What do you mean?" The suspicion that there was more to this wedding night than she had previously supposed expanded. She stared back at him and the suspicion increased a thousandfold. What was he going to do? What did he mean by making love? Surely, one either loved or did not.

"Tell me, did Annie speak to you about this? Have you any idea what is to happen between us?" His suspicions were mounting that she was unaware of lovemaking.

She shook her head. "Annie just said I was to do as you told me even if it was strange. To tell you the truth, My Lord, I thought when I was married I would no longer have to be so obedient. I have spent my life so far doing what was required of me." She shook her head in comical dismay. "I really fear I shall never be truly independent after all."

He rewarded her with a deep chuckle, pleased with her

laughing reply. Yes she was nervous, he thought, but handling it well.

"I promise you shall do what you want after this night. Consider me a teacher, darling, and if you wish to practise the lessons - I shall be at your service. You have my word I'll not harm you. You will feel a little pain at first - no - don't fear, it will be over before you know and I shall tell you what to expect. Now get into bed and let your first lesson begin." He held her a moment longer feeling the slightness of her body and would have spent more time dallying with her in his arms but she promptly climbed into bed and hid herself under the sheets in the furthest corner of the bed. Merrick blew out most of the candles then divesting himself of his robe followed her under the sheets. Linda caught a glimpse of him before she shut her eyes and was awed at the wide shoulders and strong muscles of her husband. Apart from a smattering of curling dark hair in the centre of his chest he was brown with the sun. He lay for a moment on his back listening to her rapid breathing then he turned on his side and tenderly stroked her cheek. "Lindy, my love, let me hold you."

His deep, gentle, husky voice did more to allay her fears than anything else did and she turned hesitatingly but obediently towards him. Drawing her into his arms he kissed her slowly and deeply until she responded by opening her mouth to him with warm ardency. Soon her arms went round his neck and then he pulled her tightly against his rigid thighs while his tongue invaded her mouth in a rhythm causing thrills of delight to invade her body. As he felt her press closer he rolled her onto her back, one hand sliding caressingly over her breast, cupping its fullness. When she jumped in helpless surprise he knew he was the first to touch her so and his ardour seethed within him.

Bringing his mouth down to the pale rosebud he teased it lightly before closing his lips firmly over the taut nipple, filling her first with deep shock that he would want to suckle her breast, then to moan in helpless joy as he ignited the flames of need in her body. He trailed his kisses down over her stomach then came back to her mouth and claimed it in another fierce endless ravenous kiss until she drew away gasping for breath.

Tenderly he kissed her closed eyes then whispered in a husky voice, raw with restraint, "Open your eyes, darling, there's nothing to be afraid of, do you like your lessons?" Linda opened her eyes on the face that leaned over her, dark with emotion, his eyes alight with passion. He smiled tenderly as she nodded, her green eyes almost black with unleashed feeling in the dim candlelight.

"I want you. I need you," he whispered yearningly, waiting for her response.

Linda wasn't sure what he meant so she stayed silent; Merrick was immediately unsure for one blinding moment whether she still loved Richard? Had she accepted his caresses like this, or more than this? Jealously, he buried his face in her neck, nuzzling at her soft skin while his fingers slid insistently through curling hair to seek her hot pleasure centre. Linda felt a thrill rush through her body as he touched her. Then instinctively she clasped her legs together, filled with trepidation for her unexpected desire.

"Darling, don't be frightened." Again he was deeply relieved with her reaction, for it reaffirmed the fact she'd known no one else. Then he whispered, "Touch me."

Rising on one elbow she gazed into his eyes then with soft gentle fingers stroked his face for a moment before slipping her hands lightly over his chest. She took his nipple into her mouth sucking on it exactly as he had done to her, watching his chest jump and flinch almost breaking his control. Pleased with his reactions she slowly pursued a path down over his stomach making the taut muscles clench even tighter as the fleeting kisses teased his skin. Before she could reach further he laughed and, grasping her swiftly pulled her back and then, holding her close, moved his hands over her as he took her lips in a fierce kiss.

Linda, beset with feeling, realising rejection would be wrong for all that she was feeling a little scared with unfolding events, forced herself to lie still and soon she was moaning with pleasure as she gave herself up to the intimate stroking. When he finally eased himself between her legs, his penis pressing against her tight entrance he felt her flinch and draw away, then as he lifted her hips to allow him to enter her, she relaxed.

"I'm going to hurt you, darling, I'm sorry, my love, but this is what loving means."

"It's all right, I trust you." She smiled at him tremulously and he felt his heart melt at her words. Easing himself in a little way, he waited for a moment then he took a deep breath and plunged quickly into her before drawing back. She leapt under him and gasped, but the pain vanished so swiftly she hardly noticed it as it was replaced by an unusually rapturous feeling as the penetrating strokes of Merrick filled her body. Guided solely by instinct Linda matched her husband's movements, straining against him, driving Merrick quite completely crazy with desire as he held himself back, determined to give her a fair share of pleasure before he took his own.

Linda could feel a heated surge building up in her body, getting stronger and stronger as Merrick in his turn quickened his thrusts, driving ever deeper inside her. The rush of powerful feeling that exploded through her body took her by surprise and she cried out in surprised ecstasy, shaking with the incredibly throbbing spasms that made her grip Merrick fast.

Immediately he drove into her full length, pouring his seed within her, groaning with effort as his own body convulsed in pleasure. How wonderful! She was not only his woman but she was the best love he had ever known. After taking a moment to recover and afraid his weight would crush her, he rolled over taking Linda with him although still joined to her sweet body. Smoothing her hair from her face, he kissed her lovingly, filled with a delighted joy at finding an ardent bride.

"Am I a good pupil?" she said after a moment, as she tried to smother the laughter in her voice. Startled at her unexpected humour, he laughed happily.

"I don't know if that was one lesson or two or even three," he breathed in her ear. "But you've passed the test with flying colours, my lady. You will be able to teach the teacher shortly." A servant, passing along a nearby corridor, returning polished shoes to guests staying on in the castle, heard the laughter and was glad. The whole of the staff loved the young lord, now become their master and Duke, and he knew, as he passed the word round, how pleased they all were to know milord was finding joy and happiness in his marriage to the young English lady. They gazed on her demureness and wondered at his choice but if he was happy then so were they and they would honour her accordingly.

CHAPTER FIFTY-FIVE

"Good morning, Your Grace, did you sleep well?" Betty was pulling the curtains back on a bright clear day and as Linda stirred she blinked at the encroaching sunlight.

"What time is it?" she asked sleepily as she turned over in bed and tried to snuggle down again vaguely recalling a long night when sleep had been held at bay by champagne and loving, oh so very loving, embraces.

"Eleven o'clock, Your Grace, do you wish to sleep a little longer? I have brought your breakfast in case you felt hungry. I can easily fetch it later. There's no hurry, His Grace said, he thought you'd want to take time with your bath and dressing for the day."

"No, no I'll have breakfast now, and thank you, Betty, for rousing me, I did not know it was so late. Where is my husband?"

"His Grace rose at eight, had breakfast downstairs, then was off with the ghillie, that's Duggie McPherson and David Milton, the steward. He said he would see you later on today. They have gone to view the Estate, I believe. The dowager Duchess is at present in the morning room reviewing her letters."

Betty placed a huge tray on Linda's lap once she was sitting up and she stared at a medley of porridge, eggs, bacon, lightly coloured toast, and tea. An enormous feast.

"Oh," she said blankly, "am I to eat all this?"

"Lord bless you no, Your Grace. It's just that cook had no idea of your appetite or your liking. Have what you want and we can put it right tomorrow."

Linda smiled at her maid. "I think I was too tired yesterday to eat and this looks wonderful. I shall enjoy cook's offering and please thank her for it. Tomorrow I shall eat lightly or I will end up a butterball. But have I time to eat? I don't want to keep the Duchess waiting."

"I don't believe you will, Your Grace, she is always busy with her affairs. But I am sure she will be pleased to see you when you come downstairs. I have laid out your clothes in the dressing room and will be ready to dress you when you have eaten."

"Thank you, Betty, I'm so glad to have you to help me. It is good to have a friend."

"Oh, please don't let the housekeeper hear you say that or I'll be put to other duties. I am a servant and must know my place."

"Then just between us, thank you for being my friend and helping me. This is all rather awesome and I'm sure to make mistakes."

"Don't fret, my lady, everyone has your interests at heart. My Lord Duke is well loved and I'm sure you will be too. Now, if you'll pardon me I shall wait in your dressing room until you are finished then I will run your bath. Call me when you are ready."

When Linda scrambled out of bed and went to the dressing room she found not the black outfit she had worn the previous day but a pale blue dress and matching shawl awaiting her. "Where are my mourning clothes?"

"His Grace gave orders that you were not to wear black, and the dowager agreed. The blue will suit you, I believe. You are, after all, a new bride."

Linda blushed bright pink as she recalled the previous night. Merrick had made love to her at least twice more and each time the event was sweeter and more fulfilling than before. Why she had been terrified of him she could not now imagine. When, at last, she entered the morning room Morag was gathering up some letters she had finished writing. She greeted Linda gently, noting the dark shadows that framed the young girl's eyes. Her son had amused her for he appeared extraordinarily cheerful this morning and she was glad to see the marriage progressing along a pleasing path. She had been aware of his paramour in London from well-meaning friends who mixed in London society and both she and the late Duke had been anxious lest he make the partnership legal. Instead and so surprisingly Merry had brought home this sweet girl to be his wife and Morag truly hoped they could be friends.

"Am I interrupting, Your Grace?"

"No, my dear Linda, not at all, I am about to make my rounds, will you join me?"

Linda nodded with a smile wondering what rounds she was referring to.

"Before we go, shall we settle what you are to call me? To say 'Your Grace' is tedious and besides it is your title now. Mother-in-law is far too long and makes me feel much too old and distant. Have you any preference yourself? I'd welcome a suggestion."

"What does your son call you?"

"Mama, of course. Could you bring yourself to call me the same? I would be honoured, my dear. I have long wished for a daughter, but it was not to be."

"My so-called mama died many years ago and Jethro, her husband, died also. I have a yearning to be a part of a real family again and I know I belong to those that love me."

"My dear child, consider yourself my daughter and your friend. Now before we cry on each other's shoulder let us pursue our domestic duties and I will show you the secrets of Forres and how we conduct ourselves. It's a lot to learn but I have every confidence, now I have met you, that you will do admirably. Come, let me show you around."

At some point on the guided tour Morag was gratified to find that Linda had already acquired considerable domestic knowledge and understood how a big household was run. The reason was easy to understand for Linda had taken over the running of Tregender when Annie was ill and, Ambrose was quick to notice, had accomplished the job with tact and improvement, pleasing him no end. Morag introduced Linda to the various staff controllers then, when one o'clock chimed, led the way to a small dining room where a light luncheon was served.

The afternoon proceeded in like fashion and as evening approached Linda felt more reassured that her life was going to be happy. When Merrick joined the two women for dinner he was delighted to see they had become friends and participated in the happy conversation. After the meal Merrick excused himself and his wife and they retired to their own suite where Linda spent another night joyously engaged in lovemaking.

This went on for several weeks in the same fashion with the Duke hard at work on Estate affairs during the day then with his wife at night. She went round in a rapt dream and her happiness conveyed itself to the staff. She had never been allowed to have missish airs when growing up, never mixed with girls who simpered and sulked because their papas were in a position to spoil them. She acted as Jethro had taught her, to be honest and straightforward with her fellow man.

At first the workforce were standoffish, beginning with the butler, who knew his place and the place of all his underlings, not to mention the places of the gentlefolk for whom he worked. Then, gradually, Linda's genuine interest in the household's welfare made a big impact. Morag had always been greatly respected but she had a brusque, if kindly way with her and the late Duke could be quite irascible and bad-tempered. Merrick, too, was a firm leader and would quell a footman with a lift of his eyebrow. Linda was like a ray of sunshine in the castle, particularly as the Estate was still in mourning for its late Lord. Visiting and activities were curtailed so the household set themselves out to please the beautiful new Duchess and she responded like an opening flower until all were charmed with her pleasing nature.

"Darling, I'm sorry I have to leave for London tomorrow," Merrick murmured to her, after a sweet bout of love. "I can't delay it longer, for not only have I the Estates but there are other interests to see to. I'd take you with me but I shall be so busy I will not have time to escort you or introduce you in society. I would greatly prefer to leave the latter until we have more time."

Linda, though sorry to see him leave, was relieved her debut into society or 'the ton' was delayed. She could not think of a more fearful prospect than to meet those that were entitled the 'upper crust': people high in the social order who regarded those like herself as lower class. She was sure the fact she was called a duchess would make no difference. Still aware of illegitimacy in her background, she was desperately afraid of the truth becoming known. If it were, it would ruin her relationship with her newly found family forever.

CHAPTER FIFTY-SIX

"I am visiting an old friend of the family, Linda, would you like to accompany me?" Morag was aware her daughter-in-law's spirits had visibly dwindled after her son's departure. "He has recently lost his wife and is lonely. With all that has gone on recently it has been difficult to find the time to see him but now I feel would be an excellent opportunity with Merrick away and time on our hands."

"Thank you, I'd love to come. Where does he live?"

"His Estate marches with ours and luckily his house lies on our borders. He attended school with Merrick though a little older than my son and the two boys were great friends. Then there was some trouble in the family before his father's death but, since then, Lucien moved mountains to keep his Estates and care for his mother and his sister. He married not so long ago but sadly things went wrong and now he is a widower."

Lucien! Surely not? A mere coincidence, that was all but how strange it should come up? Abruptly the words in the letter appeared in her mind. No, she was imagining things. The name might be popular in this part of the country. He was a friend of her husband, nothing more. Nevertheless it was with great trepidation Linda undertook the journey with Morag.

Their arrival occasioned a noisy greeting from two pale golden Labradors who had the run of the grounds and considered themselves guardians of the estate. Linda had always loved dogs and showing not the slightest fear was soon petting and scratching their favourite places the moment she stepped from the coach. She was engaged in this when a man appeared from the gateway to the stables and came to an abrupt halt.

"Lavinia! Good God! Lavinia!" She turned slowly as he came towards her his face ashen at her appearance and knew at once that he was her father. How else could he have spoken her mother's name in that fashion? Oh, for pity's sake! Where was Morag? She looked round for her then realised she had gone ahead into the house to find him.

"No. My name is Linda. But I know of whom you speak. Look, please don't say anything to my mother-in-law. Can we possibly meet on our own to talk about Lavinia? Believe me, it is better this way. I can explain everything."

Stunned with her appearance, he mutely agreed, hardly knowing what he was agreeing to. He motioned her into the house and almost immediately Morag was there introducing them to each other in her frank and open way. "This is my daughter-in-law, Linda. She married Merrick just recently and, by an incredible coincidence, is also a cousin of sorts of the family. She is a daughter of Lavinia, the other part of the Forres tribe. They met by chance, would you believe in faraway Cornwall. Now don't tell me blood doesn't call to blood for I'll never have it otherwise after this. But here, I am chattering on and we came to visit you and find out how you are."

"And you, dear Morag, I should be saying the same, after your sad loss. Sadly I couldn't get to the funeral, much as I would have wished, as Mother had one of her bad spells and I daren't leave the house. She is a trifle better now but I think the next episode will be the last. Still, let us not talk of sad things. May I welcome you, daughter of Lavinia, to my home. She was a lovely young woman and you have all her beautiful looks and, I hope, her nature, which was the fairest of spirits. She was a joy to know."

"Oh, did you know her, Lucien? I had the feeling she was only a child when she lived at the Castle." Morag's voice was uninterested. She still retained the angry feelings of her husband when they discovered the depredations of the Estate. She had managed to subdue them knowing she would hurt Merrick if she were to criticise his choice of a wife but she refused to discuss the rest of the family if she could possibly help it.

"Yes, I knew her. A long, long time ago." There was a wealth of meaning in his voice which only Linda perceived and she waited in anxiety for Lucien to confess he had had a part in her birth. However the conversation turned to other topics. Then Morag was gathering up her reticule preparing to leave and still there had been no sign from Lucien about meeting him again at a more convenient time. "My sister will be so disappointed not to meet you, Linda." Her name fell so naturally from his lips that even Morag did not notice he had not been more formal and used her married title. "She is away today visiting her friends. Would tomorrow suit you to pay a visit again? Tell me, do you ride?" She nodded. "You do? That's marvellous, I am sure there's a horse for you in your husband's sizable stables." He smiled at Morag who nodded graciously.

"Good, that is settled, you can ride to our boundary and Jennifer and I will meet you there and show you some wonderful country to explore. My sister is younger than I and shortly expects to be engaged so I am sure you are pining for people of your own age, especially with Merry away. No reflection on you, dear Morag, but the castle can be a bit dreary at times, especially, I would have thought, at this moment."

Morag, who had been about to gently, but firmly veto the meeting, realised Lucien was right. If Linda was to be happy in her marriage she must mix with others of her own age for Merrick would have his hands full at present coping with his responsibilities and would not be able to dance a great deal of attendance on his young wife. She would be selfish indeed if she denied Linda an outing. "I'll send a groom with you, and then you won't get lost."

"That is excellent, Morag. He can return when we have met. Don't worry, Morag, we shall see Linda safely home, and in the meantime give her an enjoyable day."

"Very well, Lucien. Give my best wishes to Jennifer and wish her many felicitations on her forthcoming marriage. Come, Linda, we must depart before the day grows dark."

The two women left in the coach, one reminiscing on her son's youthful friendship with Lucien, the other thinking of the subtle cleverness of the scheme, which would allow Lucien to talk to her. What could she say? Would she accuse him of deserting her mother? How could they converse with his sister there as well? Out of her depth but relieved at last that she knew the identity of her father and he was not the ogre she had imagined, Linda spent part of a wakeful night devising speeches until at last she fell asleep.

The next day Linda set out with the groom who took her along the path that led to Lucien's Estate. They rode through woodland filled with conifer, mountain ash and birch, all taking on a golden hued leaf as autumn approached. The forest was quiet and serene and Linda felt the same peace she had known roaming the moors at Tregender.

Lucien was waiting by an old stone cross on the borderline of the estates and as they approached he rode forward. "My sister is right behind us; she stopped to pick some wild flowers for a vase. Thank you, Simmons, you can return. We shall see Her Grace home safely." The groom politely touched his hat and rode back along the road.

"Oh dear, I shall never get to heaven," Lucien said with a rueful smile. "Jennifer is not here, she returns tomorrow. I thought it best we talked things over on our own as you seemed so very anxious about our meeting. Tell me, what do you know of your mother? I gathered from Morag you are an orphan. Is it true you never knew her?"

"Yes. I've only had my mother's letter to guide me, which was given to me not long ago. I had to let you know, without revealing it to my husband or his mother, that you are actually my father. It's been most upsetting and I don't wish them to be involved."

She handed over her mother's letter, which she had kept hidden from everyone, then walked a short way off to let him read it. He returned in a moment or two mopping his eyes with his kerchief and she could see how upset he was.

"This letter says I'm your father! How can this be possible! For God's sake, Lavinia had a son before she died! Eventually I found out that much, though not before it was too late to do anything about her removal to Cornwall."

Linda began to explain what had happened, frightened at his ashen face, which had paled with shock. "So, you see, I was brought up by Jethro and Ellie Barton. When they died, Betsy and Annie took over. Ambrose Trevarron, who was their master, - well, he paid for my schooling."

"Oh, you poor child, lumped from one person to another; I little thought my appalling cowardice would lead to this. My God, I should be horsewhipped for leaving your mother to face such pain and despair all by herself. I should have had more courage."

"What do you mean – your cowardice?"

"My dear daughter, it should never have happened like this. Sophie, that old harridan of a grandmother, was so determinedly fixed on organising people's lives without recourse to their wishes that she ruined her granddaughter's future, which, to put it bluntly, finally led to her death. I have no compunction about wishing Sophie spent the last years of her life in great misery and loneliness. I have mourned Lavinia since she was taken from me and I can only say how devastated I was to learn of her death. If it had not been that we were so petrified Sophie would find out we were married…"

"Married!" shrieked Linda. "How could you have been married! No one ever told me that! If it's true then my mother's marriage to Trevarron was a great mistake. She should never have been forced to wed him."

"Yes, we married secretly; you would never have been born, had we not. I had too much love and respect for her to behave otherwise. However, my subsequent behaviour is not worth regard. I was derelict in my duty even if I have paid for it ever since and regretted my silence. But, after the event, what could I say that wouldn't get Lavinia into trouble. I could only keep silent and hope nobody would find out and gave her away. She was terribly frightened of Sophie and, unfortunately, so was I."

"Father, do you realise what you've just said?"

"Oh, I do, child. I know only too well I am the lowest cur that ever walked the face of the earth. Deserting your mother like that has left me bereft for all time..."

"But you've made your daughter the happiest person on earth. Do you realise I am not ...not ... illegitimate after all? Incredibly you have put my worst fears to rest at last."

"Of course you are not. Whoever said you were?"

"Oh, father, really! I had to be either Ambrose's daughter or illegitimate. No one knew you were wed and my mother never said anything about it in the letter."

"I'm sorry, Linda, this has all been extremely shocking. I have suddenly acquired a grown-up daughter, who is married to boot and now we have to devise a way to let your husband know, not to mention my family as well. It would tax the mind of a more able person than I to think coherently precisely at this minute. Come, we'll ride and perhaps inspiration will strike me."

Linda nodded, happy to be in the fresh air and free to discuss all the things she had longed to know. They rode over the beautiful countryside until they reached a wide stretch bordering on a lake. There they left the horses to crop while they sauntered along, deep in conversation, both delighted with their sudden relationship.

"At least we can keep up our subterfuge for a while longer. You say Merrick is not due back yet from London?" Lucien said, thinking of how he would broach their news.

"Yes, that is so; I had a letter yesterday telling me he will be delayed for at least another week." She sighed heavily. "I wonder at times if I did the right thing in marrying him. There is nothing cosy about our marriage; the castle is cold and strange and my mother-in-law is – well – she is kind, of course, but I can understand she really wishes to be on her own with her sorrow. She has been extremely welcome towards me but I feel I intrude. Perhaps I should have waited for Richard - I could have married him now without the fear of being illegitimate."

"Who is Richard?"

"A friend I have known all my life. He is training for the church, just like his father. He wanted me to wait for him. I expect he knows now I have let him down. Isn't life difficult at times? I married Merrick knowing I didn't love him and now I am being paid back. But there is no going back now."

Lucien took her in his arms, hugging her, thinking this was the first time he held his own flesh and blood, his own child. She was so like his own beloved Lavinia it was as though his young wife had been created all over again. He felt almost dizzy with joy that the result of their love was standing before him happy in owning him as her father. How he would have loved to have brought her up from babyhood. Still, he must not grumble; she was here at last; his to enjoy for as long as he was on earth. Just as soon as he could, he would tell his mother and sister. He had no doubt Linda would be welcomed lovingly by them as well. It never occurred to him that Merrick would not only be stunned by these new events but may be hurt and angry that his wife had not been honest with him.

CHAPTER FIFTY-SEVEN

When Merrick reached London he went directly to the house in Belgravia which had once belonged to his Aunt Sophie. Although James Walcott had appropriated it for a short time it was now safely a part of the Macgregor Estate once more. Merrick had taken the precaution of sacking all Walcott's servants, installing instead a skeleton staff when he was not in residence, but sufficient to deal with his needs when he was on his own. Indeed, he had known the elderly butler, who took charge in his absence for many years, having sailed with him as first mate on countless voyages. The old salt had given up the sea but Merrick felt there was still a good life to be had in his employ on dry land rather than being washed up with scarce a penny to live in some out of the way coastal harbour. Jem Donovan was grateful for the job and Merrick knew he would guard the house with his life.

"Well, Jem, how are you faring?" he enquired as he handed over his travelling coat, hat and gloves to the butler as they stood on the huge black and white chequered marble floor in a formal hall lit with silver chandeliers. "Is the staff behaving themselves?"

"Under way, cap'n; we're set fair with the wind. Beg pardon, I mean m'lord. Can't get me mind round all the changes." He gazed anxiously at his master who smiled back, amused at being called by a title he had cherished at one time.

"I would not change you for the world, Donovan. It takes me back to my days at sea and that is not a bad thing to do. Sets one's feet on the deck, so to speak, clears the head of worries. These last few weeks have been stormy but we seem to be sailing into fine weather and a safe haven," he said frankly as though he was aboard ship speaking the language of the sea. "I'll be dining at home tonight and retiring early. Tell whoever it is you have taken on for my valet, I will need city clothes first thing tomorrow and to lay out evening wear for tomorrow night for I'll be dining with Lord Keswick." He nodded a dismissal to his butler then went up a short flight of stairs and opened a door to the study.

"Ahem, milord. When shall we have the pleasure of seeing your wife?" Donovan raised his voice from the hall. "And may I congratulate you on splice – er – your nuptials?" he added stuttering with embarrassment, wondering if he should have been so forward.

Merrick grinned and his expression softened. "Soon, Donovan. I shall bring her with me next time. I didn't realise how quickly one gets used to marriage and how one misses a wife."

"Quite, sir. Not that I've had the pleasure –" He coughed, feeling he had said enough on that subject. "Would you prefer rum or brandy, m'lord?"

"Oh, brandy will do. Rum is for a cold sou'wester, running free in the teeth of the wind, is that not so? But there I must not hanker after olden times."

"Aye, sir. 'Tis so, happen we'll never see days like those again, cap'n. Brandy it is."

Donovan was in the hall the next evening when his master came down dressed for his engagement. "Your carriage is waiting, m'lord; no doubt you will be late tonight? May I offer you this as a safeguard?" He handed Merrick a derringer, which was small enough to be concealed in a pocket and an elegant, though wickedly practical, swordstick.

Merrick stared piercingly at him for a moment and then: "You think I need these?"

"I do, cap'n. 'Pears there's a bloke been hanging around for days. Coincidental like he vanished overnight. So I ask meself why and I come up wiv you. If it's that lawyer feller then ye'd best be prepared. Nasty bit o' work! Stick yer ribs easy as pie."

"Thank you, Donovan, for the timely warning. If he is wise he will have left the country. If not, then as you say it's as well to be prepared. Don't wait up for me, I expect to be late." Merrick turned without a further word and went out to his carriage. Donovan was right; there was no one to be seen. He would have to be extra careful, the street was also empty when he returned. Whilst he was not too alarmed at the news of a prowler he also knew Donovan would never have warned him so deliberately had there not been good reason.

The dinner at Lord Keswick's home was a business function and when it finished at an early hour, Merrick went on to another function with some of his companions. The house, owned by a hostess of some vivacious repute, catered for gamblers and fortune hunters that hazarded vast sums on the turn of a card. Merrick, while he enjoyed a game or two of chance, had more respect for his hard-earned money than to waste it on card-sharps. He stood on the sidelines watching the antics of those who had less sense.

"They are even more stupid than usual tonight, Macgregor. By sun-up there will be pockets to let, I'll warrant. All they'll find is piss and wind, there's not a fortune between any of them." Merrick turned to find the Earl of Ashleigh at his side smiling scornfully.

"I suppose you've noticed who is egging them on?" he added with a grin. "I have a notion that, as you are merely watching, you have no particular concern. She has been leading the town fops a merry dance while you have been away."

"Should I have?" Merrick temporised, knowing full well the person to whom Ashleigh was referring. Angelina Vallone was one of the parties and she had not as yet seen him.

"I thought you were sweet on the woman, Macgregor, but it appears not if you can stomach her acting in that crude fashion. Of course, had you consulted me before taking her up, I could have told you a few stories about her tricks..."

"Which I would have found a complete bore, Ashleigh old man," interrupted Merrick. "Do me a favour and talk of something else, if you please. Better still, why don't I take myself off instead. I must be aging rapidly for I find gossiping about these antics just too passé for words."

"I'm inclined to agree, Macgregor. So I take it you are not still sweet on her?" Ashleigh was like a terrier with a bone, reluctant to give it up. This choice titbit of gossip was too good to let go. Maybe he could wheedle some more out of the Duke.

"Do get things right, Ashleigh; neither still sweet nor ever was. You really mustn't confuse accommodation with everlasting friendship. Comprendre?" Merrick was terse.

"Oh, perfectly." Ashleigh swiftly sidled away to pass the gossip to someone else.

Merrick was waiting in the foyer for his topcoat before leaving when Angelina suddenly spotted him. "Merrick darling! When did you dock? I didn't know you were in London. You could have at least warned me." Her lips pouted her displeasure as she frowned at him.

"I came down from Scotland yesterday." His flinty eyes gave nothing away.

"Naughty boy!" She tapped him with her evening fan. "I've been waiting for you."

"So I see." His eyes grew even colder.

"Oh that, take no notice of that," she tittered nervously. "I can't stay in every night."

"Of course not, nor would one would expect you to."

"Merrick?" Her voice was even more uncertain now, perceiving the distant look in his eyes. "Are you coming round to my house later?"

"No, Angelina, I..."

"Macgregor! Congratulations, my friend!" Merrick was suddenly grasped by his shoulders and swung round and his hand shaken fiercely by an old acquaintance. "I only heard today. What's she like? A beauty? Egad if I know you, she must be a beauty! I have never known you put up with less. So you're married at last? Well, who would have believed it? Why didn't you marry in London so we could have joined the celebrations?"

"Yes, she is, as a matter of fact. More of a beauty than I have ever known before." He grinned as another old friend clapped him on the back. "And yes, I have wed her. She is worth every bit of the waiting for, so I had to ensure no one else would get the chance of her. That's why I kept it quiet."

Soon he was surrounded by a bevy of well-wishers and no one saw Angelina quietly sneak away from the gathering. She knew Merrick had guessed she had a lover that day he called on her. Except it was not just one lover; there were more than he could possibly imagine. She had become quite an expert at juggling her men friends and rarely slipped up. His attention had been good while it lasted, she mused, with a tiny feeling of regret for her carelessness but, she shrugged, there would be others.

Merrick marvelled at the lucky escape he had had. Marvelled too that he had gone to Cornwall on a completely different issue, had discovered his love and then found she was a part of his family after all. Who was twisting the strings of fate? All at once he recalled Serina's fortune-telling. She had spoken of grief and that had come true with the death of his father. After that he would know joy and was that not a true fact with his new bride. Maybe he would not deride the old gypsy after all.

There had been a slight mist when Merrick left his house earlier on which now had thickened to a chill fog. He rarely used his own vehicles in town, reluctant to keep his horses or groom waiting around for hours so he motioned to a hansom cab which was waiting outside the club. Giving directions he sat back on the seat thinking of the events of the evening. It came to him that he was bored with London life and the former pastimes that once he had enjoyed. Now most of his business was dealt with he decided his secretary could deal with the rest. He would travel home to Forres a day or two early. Feeling very satisfied with this change of plan he was aware what had caused it. He missed his wife. In fact only now was he aware that, beyond a doubt, he missed her most dreadfully. He had never before felt that a wife would make much difference to his life; presuming that, in the course of time, she would settle in and become an institution like all the rest of his habits. How wrong he was.

The cabby drew to a halt as he peered through the darkness and dense fog to spot the Duke's crest on the front door of his town house. Merrick, more familiar with the street and sensing the cabby's hesitation, called out, "We are almost here, don't worry, I'll get out and walk the rest." Instantly the cabby bent down and opened the door from his high perch. "Thanks, m'lord, my eyes can't glim a thing in this here murk." He caught the coin Merrick threw him and touched his hat. "Much obliged, m'lord. Sleep well." Then he was off, vanishing within seconds into the gloom.

Glancing about Merrick saw he was only a couple of houses away from his own and set out to walk briskly through the dank air, his mind still on his return to Scotland. The sudden rush of feet close by almost caught him by surprise but his instincts were sound and he wheeled instantly and met the onslaught of a man intent on wielding the large dagger he held poised in upraised hand. Bringing his stick round sharply Merrick fended the assault causing the man to yell loudly as the hefty cane struck his wrist. Still holding onto the knife he transferred it to the other hand and came again at Merrick. This time, from the light of a brazier outside a front door, Merrick recognised the attacker.

"Walcott! I thought I made it clear you were to leave the country!"

"And go where or do what? I've had to beg for the very crusts I've eaten these past weeks, since you tossed me out with nary a coin between me and the gutter. My so-called friends, whom I've done favours for in the past, will see me no longer. There's no hope for me but revenge and a squalid death from starvation. Your death will be my revenge and after that I care not what happens to me."

"After the way you treated my cousin you deserve no sympathy but against my better judgement I'll hold out a ray of hope. Here's a guinea to tide you over." He tossed a coin to Walcott, who managed to catch it, dropping the knife as he did so. "Make your way to St Katherine's dock. There you'll find one of my ships ready to sail to the Indies. There will be a letter aboard that will introduce you to my agent in Bombay. He will put you to good use with your legal knowledge and although you will work for me for now, eventually you'll be able to find a niche for yourself and, who knows, maybe make a life. But take warning; work against me and you won't get a second chance."

Walcott stared at him as though he couldn't quite believe his ears. "You mean it? Even though you could easily have killed me. That is a swordstick you hold in your hand?"

Merrick nodded. "I am not in the habit of killing haphazardly; I prefer to settle a matter without resorting to violence."

"I've been all kinds of a fool and yet now you are trying to save me. What can I say?"

"Nothing. I don't want your gratitude. Work hard for me. That's thanks enough."

Walcott bowed, picked up the dagger, stuffed it in a pocket, then bowing once more disappeared into the night without another word. Merrick sighed and turned again to his home.

It might have ended in disaster, he mused. Either he could have been killed or there would have been a body for the authorities to ask questions about.

"All right an' shipshape, m'lord?" Donovan's thick shape loomed up in the mist.

"Where the devil were you hiding, you old reprobate?"

"Close by, m'lord. But you seemed to have everything under

control. There was no call for me to interfere though I'd have done it in a trice. Mind you I'd have thought twice about giving him a job. But then you were ever a generous person."

"Oh he'll have to work at it, never fear, but at least he'll be working in my interests from now on. I'll not have to look over my shoulder for an assassin."

"Ah, but you're a canny man. Now how about we get in out of this dank air and I make you comfortable for the night?"

"Yes, Donovan. I've had all the excitement I want for a very long time. I think it is time I settled down to a peaceful marriage. Talking of which, I'll be returning North in the morning. I can't wait to see my bride again. The future looks to be a happy one, Donovan, so wish me well."

"Aye, captain, I do indeed. And next time you're down I'll be pleased to welcome your lady as well. I wish you both a fair wind and good seas."

Merrick smiled at the old sea dog's turn of phrase and, filled with hope, entered his house little knowing that fate had one or two surprises in store for him yet.

CHAPTER FIFTY-EIGHT

Two days after Linda's meeting with her father, Lucien visited the castle, this time bringing Jennifer. Linda looked at the girl with long brown hair, so very different from her brother, whose hair was like her own, fair, almost ash-blonde, with springy waves and curls, and decided she liked her. Jennifer appeared to be some five years older than her with dancing hazel eyes, which held laughter in their depths and the offer of warmth and companionship in her smile. Within a short time the two young women were at ease with one another, happy to go outside in the gardens to get acquainted. Soon they were on a first name basis and well on their way to becoming firm friends.

"I hope you don't mind," Jennifer said hesitantly when they were alone, "Lucien has told me all about you. I'm very glad you are part of our family. Although he is so much older than me I have always adored my brother and I knew how dreadfully cut up he was when Lavinia vanished. It took him ages to discover where she had gone as the Duchess wouldn't admit him into her house in London for ages. Sadly by then it was far too late."

With a shy smile Linda shook her head. "Of course I don't mind, I feel as if I've found a sister as well as a father, and I am looking forward to meeting my grandmother when she's well enough to see me. Though how I'm going to tell my side of the family, I don't know. I'm sure it will come as a great shock to both Merrick and his mother."

"It shouldn't present a problem, he's your husband after all, and he must love you."

"I'm not sure; perhaps he just married me because he felt sorry for me."

Jennifer gazed at the stunningly lovely face of her companion, her deep emerald eyes holding a hint of woe in their depths and she giggled. "With your face and figure, who wouldn't fall in love with you? I'll have to beware my fiancé, Elliott Mcnairn, whom you'll soon meet, will keep in mind who he is marrying. Besides, surely Merrick has - has - well, you know," she added lamely.

Linda turned bright pink and Jennifer smiled at her embarrassment.

"I haven't tried it myself, of course, but Mama is a most enlightened lady and she says it's a wonderful thing between two people. She and my papa were devoted to one another, even if he was a rogue and nearly cost us our land with his gambling. Lucien isn't nearly so tolerant, but then he had to work like a slave to keep us solvent and then marry an heiress to restore our fortune. After Lavinia, I believe he would have preferred to stay unmarried but Mama wanted a grandson. So he married Belinda ages ago, but she didn't become pregnant until recently, then she died because of it."

Linda put her arm around Jennifer's shoulder. "I'm so sorry," she murmured sadly. "He's had a bad time of things, losing first my mother and then Belinda."

"Well, that's in the past. Now Lucien has found you and he's happy again. Mama, too, is better today. Her heart is not good and she has funny turns so we are very careful with her. Which reminds me - did you know you have the same name as her?"

"So I understand." said Linda, recalling the letter her mother had left. Goodness, she thought, what a small world it is. I come all this way to Scotland and end up with a new mother-in-law, a grandmama, an aunt and a father as well as a husband, all at one and the same time. With a slightly hysterical giggle, causing Jennifer to raise her eyebrows, she explained her surprise at inheriting a newly found family. The two girls went into peals of uncontrollable merriment until the gardens rang with sounds of their laughter. The noise reached Morag and Lucien who were sitting talking in the drawing room. Morag smiled mistily. "She's a lovely girl, isn't she? I'm so glad she has made friends with your sister, she was quite dismal with Merrick having to be absent so long."

"I trust he won't absent himself so much in the future or, if he must, he will take Linda along as well. Too many trips to London will not do." Lucien scowled, having also heard of the lovely Angelina Vallone. Morag did not reply, after all, what was there to say. Her son would go his own way regardless. From that day on Linda spent every moment she could tactfully spare at Heldron House, getting to know her new family and being accepted into their hearts.

CHAPTER FIFTY-NINE

Linda was returning home late one afternoon having spent an enjoyable time with her pleasant grandmother who had been telling her tales of Lucien's youth as well as what she knew of Lavinia and the family history of Linda's husband. Linda sat fascinated as she absorbed the story of the two parts of the family and their beginnings with Murdoch.

"No one appears to have had an easy life at Forres Castle in the past; do you think it's an unlucky place, Grandmama?"

"Some places can be unlucky, child, that is so. But I think it's up to us to see that luck changes for the better. If one endeavours to stay happy then one makes a happy ambience. If we're angry and emotional then I believe that rubs off on our companions and so worsens the situation until nothing is right. You stay as joyful as you can be and always see you live in a happy place. Then you will have merry, contented babies, which hopefully, my dear, will not be long in appearing. Your husband will look for a son, you know."

"Yes, I will be delighted to have a baby too, but most of all I am looking forward to his return. I have missed him very much," she said wistfully.

"And when he's back we shall have a party for you both and celebrate," added her grandmother as Linda took her leave.

Lucien, hearing the last part of the conversation, eagerly concurred. "We shall have a good rowdy celebration to mark a joining of our Estates and a renewal of friendship. Come, young lady, it is time you went back to the castle. Do you wish me to escort you all the way?"

"No, I shall be fine, I promise. I know the way blindfold by now. I have much to think about now I am to have one of your pups." For, to her delight, Lucien had promised her one of his Labrador puppies, which had been born that week and as she watched them grow, she was still undecided which one she would choose. "Perhaps I ought to wait until Merrick sees them before I decide. He might have a preference himself."

"Not at all, it shall be your dog and yours only. They give their loyalty to only one owner you know, even if they tolerate others in a family. Why not let the puppy choose you when the time is right for him to leave the litter?"

"What a good idea. Oh I do love you, Papa, and I'm so glad I've found you. Except I worry …oh I shouldn't, I know, but when Merrick comes home you will be with me when I tell him, won't you?"

"Of course, my darling girl, you must not concern yourself. All will come right. Now are you sure you are comfortable riding the rest of the way by yourself with this mist coming up?"

"You get back to Grandmama, I shall be perfectly all right." She reached up and put her arms round him for his usual kiss and he stayed for a long moment holding her as he gazed down into her smiling eyes.

"You've made all the difference to my life, Linda; you've given me hope for the future instead of despair."

"I'm so glad, Papa, and Merrick will be pleased for you too. His mother said you were good friends when you were young."

"Yes, from long ago, but not for some time. He's been away a long time at sea and I've been struggling for many years to keep this Estate together. He may have forgotten our friendship and me but run along, child, Morag will be anxious for you." With a last hug he let her go and she mounted her horse and rode off into the mist. Neither of them noticed the figure in the trees a short way off from where they stood saying farewell.

* * * * *

Merrick, concluding the last of his business even earlier than he anticipated and eager to get home to Linda, lost no time in leaving London and embarking on the long journey. On his arrival at the castle he asked his butler of his wife's whereabouts.

"Och, she'll still be out riding, m'lord, though wiv the mist comin' up I doubt she'll be much longer. She's generally back about noo," said Dudwick eager to help. "The dowager Duchess is awa' too, for twa, three days, for she's visiting friends in Grantown."

"Does my wife ride often, and where, may I ask?"

"Most days towards Heldron, I believe, m'lord. The Rowleys have made her very welcome and she's settled well here because of it."

"Which groom has gone with her?"

"Oh, naebody, m'lord, she prefers to go on her ain."

"I see. Well, I'll just change to riding gear. Tell them at the stables to saddle my horse, I'll be out shortly." He had set out eagerly to meet his wife, for he could not wait to have her nestled close. Then, near the limit of his property, he caught sight of two figures through the mist. They were standing so near together there was no doubt the woman was being held close in the taller figure's arms. As they parted and one climbed on a horse Merrick could tell at once who she was. So that was why his wife had been off riding every day. To see Lucien Rowley! While he had been gone she had been free to meet with her lover. So my fine lady, the minute my back is turned you cheat on me. But this time you've been found out. I came back too soon for you!

Taking a circuitous route to avoid his wife he drove his horse hard to reach the stables before her. A groom took the horse as he strode off upstairs to their suite where he began to pace back and forth in his room like a caged beast, his temper growing more violent by the minute, cursing his incredulity in thinking she had been waiting anxiously for his return. He heard her enter her room and tell her maid that she would have supper on a tray and go to bed early. "Can I help you with anything else, Your Grace?"

"No, thank you, I will retire when I am ready."

It would seem no one at the stables had informed her he was back. So he would surprise the hussy. It had obviously not taken her long to find another lover in his absence.

CHAPTER SIXTY

Linda began to remove her riding gear when the connecting door between their two rooms squeaked open, startling a scream from her. Then she realised who it was.

"Merrick! Oh my God, you scared me. Why wasn't I told you had returned home? I never expected you tonight and I was about to retire..." Linda was going to say how glad she was to see him but the menacing glitter of ice in his cold grey eyes silenced the very words in her throat. She stared in frightened dismay at his taut graven face, the iron jaw; discerning the furious anger blazing inside him. He had never looked more dangerous even when he had faced Trevarron that day in Launceston. He moved forward and, in spite of herself, she began backing away. He followed after, terrifying her with a lazy misleading stride that covered the floor quite easily. She backed over to her bed then stopped; she had not done anything wrong, so why should she be nervous? He was tired from the journey; perhaps he had been delayed.

"Merrick, I can see you are cross, what's wrong? Don't frighten me so."

"Where the hell have you been?" He stopped stalking and, coming to a halt, stood tautly aggressive in front of her, folding his arms on his chest, as he waited for an answer. Linda opened her mouth to reply but discovered her brain had turned to marshmallow. Words raced around in her head in a jumble of explanations, making no sense to her, let alone trying to explain things to him. If only her father had been with her to lend his weight to the revelations. It would come out about Lavinia and her committing bigamy. Merrick would wonder why she had not shown him the letter, why she had kept it to herself. Perhaps he would think she already knew of her father and pretended she was all alone in the world so he would marry her. As every damming piece fell into place, reasoning fled further and further away till she stood tongue-tied and bright red with confusion.

It was proof enough for Merrick that she was guilty, as he saw the telltale blaze of colour in her cheeks. "I-I was over with the Rowleys."

"Till late afternoon - without a groom?"

"There's n-nothing wrong with that, I-I was riding on our own land. I admit I forgot the time but then how was I to know you were here?"

"When there are better things to do," he sneered.

"I don't need your permission," she exploded with anger. "You've been away a long time, why should you care what I do to amuse myself in your absence?"

"Why indeed," he murmured in a suave voice, as he took off his riding coat and began to undo the buttons on his shirt. "You are my wife, remember? I have the right to know where you are and what you are doing. Now take off your clothes."

Astounded, Linda gaped at him then shook her head in perplexity.

"Don't make me pull them off you or you won't like what happens, I assure you."

"Merrick, what's the matter? What have I done wrong? You are frightening me."

For a moment his instinct told him she was telling the truth, she genuinely did not know what she had done. Then the scene of her with another man flashed through his brain and he seized her roughly and began to strip her naked. She stood completely petrified as he divested himself. He perceived the fear in her gorgeous green eyes but ignored it.

"Get into bed," he growled and she hurriedly obeyed him, then as he slid in beside her she turned quickly to get out the other side. She almost made it to the floor when with a lightning reflex he grabbed her arm and drew her back into bed with him. Holding her hands captive above her head, his mouth came down on hers in a hard, assailing kiss that took her breath away. She wrenched her face to one side and letting go of her he ran his hands over her body then cupped her breast as his mouth came down on her nipple, sucking hard. Liquid heat raced through her veins as he took her lips once more in a devastating kiss that had her moaning in ecstasy. As his tongue plundered her mouth with driving movements tormenting her senses, his hands roamed everywhere over her body, heightening the rapture.

Despite her fright, she found courage in the fact she now knew she loved him and her response was to kiss him passionately back, thus further arousing his rising desire. Wedging her legs apart, his fingers sought and found what they were searching for, making her surrender to his erotic caressing of her moist centre. When his tongue trailed a fiery path down her belly she tried to wriggle furiously away knowing what he intended but he held her fast and by the time he was through with her she had given up all thoughts of escape only wanting him inside her. With a light laugh at her submission Merrick lifted himself over her and stayed poised as he gazed down into pools of velvet green and thick-lashed eyes brimming with tears and passion. "Do you want me, Linda?" He uttered the words in a ragged voice, his eyes still filled with rage.

Dazed, she stared at him, unable to understand. "Why are you like this? Why are you so rough and angry? You have never treated me like this before. I don't understand," she wailed unhappily, aware how different this lovemaking was to what she had known.

"Because I'm jealous. You are mine, understand?" he roared at her. She nodded and then screamed as he thrust himself fully into her, stirring the passion he had taught her into a raging flame that made her circle her hips until he too was white-hot with lust and pleasure. Then he brought her to a wild tumultuous climax before finally allowing himself to drive into her with fierce thrusts until he reached his own riveting fulfilment. After it was over, Merrick lay for a long moment by himself to recover, then, without saying a word, he got out of bed, went into his own room, and shut the door.

Linda stayed where she was; stunned with everything that had happened since Merrick had come into her room. Was he crazy? Had she married a madman? Who was there to ask, for she doubted his mother would tell her? She lay still trying to make sense of things and then she recalled he had been wearing riding clothes, indeed they were still on the floor where he had flung them. Had he had arrived home then gone to find her? Had he seen her with Lucien? Was this what it was all about? In that case she would explain. Tell him he had no need to be jealous.

Leaping out of bed she ran to the connecting door and opened it. "Darling! I know why you're angry. Let me explain!"

He stared at her nude figure framed in the doorway, his senses jolted in spite of himself. With her hair flying in tangled curls over her proud upstanding breasts and her green eyes blazing richly she looked magnificent. Damping down the surge of need that raced once again through his body he eyed her insolently, ignoring her words to say, "I've done with you for now. Goodnight, Linda."

Flinching at his voice as though he had slapped her face and unable to reply, she backed inside her room, shut the door then sank to the floor in a huddle, sobbing bitterly. Had he found out that Lucien was her father? If he had why did not he say? Why treat her like a criminal who had done wrong? Oh, she would never understand him if she were married a lifetime to him. Even the short time had proved a mistake. As Merrick lay on his bed reviewing the resentful words he had said he felt ashamed. Never in his life had he treated a woman that way. Did having a wife cause this violent reaction? He fell asleep and never heard her packing as she prepared to leave him forever.

CHAPTER SIXTY-ONE

It was close on five o'clock the next day when Dudwick knocked on the study door to speak to Merrick. His Grace had been hard at work all day with Estate business and even had a tray of food sent in so that he need not stop. Merrick had barely eaten a thing as he was still raw with the events of the previous evening, though now as his anger had dissipated somewhat he was beginning to feel he had perhaps gone over the top in not allowing her to beg his forgiveness. So she had been with another man? Wasn't the prime society he was a part of just as promiscuous? Hadn't he partaken of someone else's wife without a thought for the husband, merely glad that the wife had seen reason and acceded to their mutual pleasure? He decided he had punished her enough; he would make it up to her and keep her so busy with satisfying him she would not want other lovers.

"Beg pardon, Your Grace, but do you happen to know where Her Grace is, only Betty is anxious to know her whereabouts…"

"Anxious! What the devil do you mean, anxious?" Merrick rose instantly to his feet trepidation twisting his gut uneasily, his expression bleak.

"Well, Your Grace, there are clothes missing and a bag. Not five minutes since, Henry came to tell me her horse has been gone all day. She must've left early well afore the grooms rose. They never heard a thing and it's unlike her to leave so early. In any case she has always got them to saddle up and see her mounted safely."

"Where's her maid? Send her in." Merrick ran his hands

through his hair trying to think. Could she have left him for Lucien? Perfectly possible, he knew. After all, the man was only a bare six years older than him which was nothing out of the way. God blazing almighty, he could kill her! Irritably he massaged the tense muscles at the back of his neck as he recalled she had never said she loved him. He had waited patiently hoping she would say it without him prompting her but it had never happened. He had taken her away from Richard, insisting on her marrying him and last night he had forced her to accept him in that degrading and utterly unkind fashion after she had obviously been with someone else. He was jealous, of course, and had a vile temper when roused but what kind of a selfish monster was he to treat her in that way? He castigated himself unmercifully as he tried to imagine how she had felt.

A knock on the door announced callers and Betty sidled in with Dudwick close behind. She looked and felt quite terrified.

"Tell me why you're worried?" Merrick demanded, careless of her fright.

With quaking knees Betty told him how she had found the supper tray untouched and items of clothing missing. Her Grace's jewellery box was left open and empty and a small valise was gone. "She never told me she was going visiting; mayhap she's with the Rowleys?" She sniffed.

"I don't know where else she could be. She was fine when I saw her last night."

Damn the Rowleys! Did half the castle know what she was up to? Merrick raged to himself before his authoritative voice chilled the two servants. "I shall go myself to see Lord Rowley. Tell the grooms I will need my horse, and have one of them come with me. Oh, and send Browning to me, I'll need my riding gear set out."

The butler made haste to send the valet to his master and word went to the stables to alert them, then he went back to the kitchen to make sure they were not gossiping. He had a very nasty feeling about all this and was only too glad the dowager was still away. He hoped he was not right, because he had taken to the young bride straight off but after all she was English and who knew what they furriners got up to.

It was quite dark by the time Merrick arrived at Hedron House and he waited on the front step impatiently as the door was unbolted and the butler welcomed him inside. Leaving the groom to see to the horses he entered the hallway. The door was ajar to the dining room and hearing the unexpected sound of voices in the hall Lucien emerged to see who had called so late. He and his mother and sister were just finishing dinner and he had not expected guests.

His look of cheerful welcome took Merrick completely by surprise.

"Come away in! I've been waiting for you to return so we can invite you both over here. What an age it is since I've seen you, I've often thought of you. How are you?"

The dog! The treacherous, cheating dog! How dare he act as though all is well?

Lucien took in Merrick's unsmiling fulminating countenance. "What's up, Merry? Is there any trouble? It's not Linda, is it? Is she unwell?"

Merrick shook his head. "Not that I know of," he answered curtly.

"For God's sake, man, come in the study and tell me. You look as though the sky has fallen in on you." When Merrick was seated and had refused the drink Lucien had offered, Lucien said, "Well, tell me then. Bad news is never the better for keeping."

"I thought Linda would be here, but it appears not. If so then she has run away, where I know not," Merrick mumbled, coming to the conclusion that he had erred.

"What do you mean 'it appears not'? I get the impression you don't believe me. Do you wish to search the place? I assure you the last time I saw her was when I escorted her to the boundary between our lands yesterday –" His face blanched. "Hell and damnation, has she been missing since then. Why didn't you come before this?"

"No," Merrick stated baldly. "She arrived home safely last night, but unfortunately we had words and she must have taken off in the early hours of the morning." Words? If only they had just talked. Instead, he had mistreated her in an appalling way. It was his fault. What the hell had he been about? It appeared she was innocent after all.

"She's gone? But where? What the hell is this all about? She was so looking forward to you coming home? She's missed you very much, you know?"

"It was all about you, as a matter of fact."

"ME? What on earth? Oh I see, she told you then?" Lucien enthused.

Merrick's ravaged thoughts hit rock bottom. "Told me what?" he croaked.

"Why, that I'm her father! Isn't it wonderful? I've found out she's actually my own daughter. As well as being your wife, of course. I could have jumped for joy when I read the letter Lavinia left. I have it here, I'll show you."

"Father! Letter?" repeated Merrick feeling he had lost his mind completely.

Lucien began to rummage among the papers on his desk searching for the letter which Linda had left. "Ah yes, here it is." He handed Lavinia's letter to Merrick. "I forgot you hadn't seen it. Lindy …I say, you don't mind me calling her that?" Merrick shook his head. "Well, not long ago she was given this letter. Lavinia wrote it when she was alive, telling me about the expected birth of our baby and Linda was nervous to tell you in case you were cross. She thought you only married her out of pity, as she was illegitimate. When she discovered I had actually married Lavinia first before Trevarron got hold of her you have no idea how overjoyed she was to know she was legitimate after all. But isn't it just like her to be uneasy in case it came out and I was in trouble with the authorities. Actually, it wouldn't have been me in trouble, but Lavinia, for bigamously marrying that swine of a Cornish man. Sadly, she'll never need to worry about it now." He bowed his head sorrowfully.

Merrick shook his head in utter bewilderment. What a shockingly, dreadful, insane situation and it was his fault for not giving her a chance to explain to him. How he must have scared her. She must have thought him a fiend from hell.

Lucien stared penetratingly at him. "You said you quarrelled over me. Why?"

"I saw you kissing her by the cross. I jumped to the wrong conclusions as appears."

"Oh Christ, Merry, you didn't think that we…for pity's sake, you did! And tackled her with it? You really are a complete ass! How could you accuse her so?"

"I didn't quite accuse…" Merrick stammered, thinking of his revenge.

"But you accused her all the same - and now she's taken off. Where? Any ideas?"

Merrick shook his head wearily. "Luce, I can't think. I just can't think. God, I'm such a crass bastard, I was crazy to doubt her, but I thought she didn't love me."

"She loves you, all right, even if she doesn't know it, take it from an expert on other people's emotions. Right, my lad, sit there while I get you a drink then we shall sort this out. I'll just let my family know I'll be busy for a while." He was gone only a moment or two and when he came back Merrick was sitting hunched up in a chair his head in his hands. His face looked grey and totally ravished with despair.

And so it ought, thought his friend. Bloody fool!

"Here drink this and relax. There's nothing that's happened that we can't put right, believe me. Now go over it again and tell me all you know."

Merrick drank the brandy Lucien poured for him as he listened to Lucien tell first Lavinia's life story then go on to what he knew of Linda. The two men went over every clue they could think of to determine where Linda might have gone.

In the end Merrick decided he would make his way to Cornwall and scour every place en route where she might have gone, even track down the gypsies, then if she had not taken refuge with them he would go onto Tregender to see if she had ended up there.

"I'm sorry I can't go with you, Merry, much as I would like to, but I daren't leave my mother. It would be like her to have a heart attack when I wasn't here."

"No, Luce, this is my fault and I must put it right. I only hope she'll forgive me when I do find her. That is if I find her. She could be lying hurt somewhere."

Lucien looked at his bleak face and shook his head. "If you don't have faith, Merry, you'll never find her. You two were meant for one another. Any fool can see that. Find her! You must for both our sakes. I will despair if I cannot see her again. To acquire a daughter and lose her in the space of a couple of weeks would be absolutely devastating. It would also grieve my mother enormously. She has taken to Linda so well that I do believe her health has improved because of it. Merry, you must find her and soon. All our happinesses depend on it."

CHAPTER SIXTY-TWO

Linda eased her horse to a stop and slid from the saddle. She could hear the sound of a stream close by and not only needed to water her mount but was parched herself. She came upon it just off the beaten hill track which she had followed for many weary miles, always wending southwards. She splashed water over her hot face as her horse bent to drink from the icy cold mountain stream. Pausing only to take a few gulps to quench her own thirst she pulled her horse back from the rushing flow lest he drank too much. She needed him to carry her many more miles as yet and a horse, filled with icy water, would suffer wind and gripes before long.

She still marvelled at her escape from the castle. The kitchens were deserted as she helped herself to a slice of cold pie, a couple of chicken legs and half a loaf of bread knowing that lack of food would be fatal if she could find no shelter along the route she meant to travel. The cook might wonder where they had gone but the pantry was so full of food it should not matter.

The big stables were equally silent, all the grooms being abed in various attic accommodations. Harnessing her horse took only moments though she had to hold his nose to prevent him whickering at her as usual. The ready titbit soon soothed him and then, leading him over the more muddy areas of the forecourt instead of the cobblestones so that his hooves would not clatter noisily, she was able to get beyond the immediate compound, mount and be off into the surrounding forest without the alarm being raised. By the time daylight appeared she was many miles away from Forres.

The fascinating talks with Jennifer and her grandmother had been most valuable and, as she expressed her deep interest in the surrounding countryside, had elicited a great deal of information which now stood her in good stead. She had never guessed at that time what purpose it would be used for as she had only wanted to know as much as possible about her adopted country. However, in the light of Merrick's anger and her escape, she was able to keep away from the main roads that he could search forever, never dreaming she was going across country to pick up a conveyance miles away from the route to Inverness which he might expect her to make for. He had yet to learn she was not a stupid woman.

When she eventually reached the town of Grantown she was able to take a local coach to Pitlochry and spend an exhausted night in a small lodging there. The crucial strength that she had started out with seemed to be failing her for some reason and she was conscious of an increasing fatigue that was foreign to her nature. It worried her a little though she supposed it was the quarrel she had had with Merrick and the rigours of the escape plus travelling so many miles on horseback. She tried to get as much rest as she could but the bed was dreadfully lumpy and the room so airless that she ended up sitting on a stool by the window trying to doze.

The next day she was carried on winding roads through mountainous country owing to the kindness of a local farmer who was taking produce to Glasgow. As she alternately drowsed or conversed with the elderly Scot whose conversation consisted solely of his farm, the weather or what he could expect at the market, she was thankful for two things. One: she had managed to arrange for her horse to go back to Forres. She had given the excuse that it was only borrowed, on the condition that this would be done and a small reward awaited whoever took it back. She felt certain her husband would do this if only to gain information as to her route. She was not to know he had already left the castle to pursue her and was now miles away in a different direction. The other thing was the comparative lack of interest in Linda's affairs taken by the Scottish farmer. Of a taciturn nature himself her explanation of being a widow and now heading back to her own family sufficed, he neither needed nor wanted to know more.

Linda felt her story was in part true. She no longer had a husband in one sense and now she was heading for the only family she knew would give her shelter. A wearisome five days later after leaving Forres she appeared on the doorstep of Tregender to be swept back into the care of Betsy and Annie. Within a few short hours of arriving Linda suddenly took ill with severe pains. Sometime later, after calling the doctor to administer to her, Betsy and Annie were informed Linda had lost the baby she had been expecting and would need careful nursing to get her back on her feet. Both the older women were incensed that Merrick had acted in such a dreadful fashion to their ewe lamb and vowed that the man, should he show his face, would never be allowed over their threshold if they had any say in the matter.

Linda was completely distraught over her loss. She alternately berated herself for leaving Forres in that fashion and causing the miscarriage and blaming Merrick for forcing her to do so. Lack of food and fatigue had also taken its toll and for several days she was very ill indeed. When her natural health began to revive and she was able to rise from bed and enjoy sitting in the sunshine she still felt cast down with depression.

What would she do now? She little supposed Merrick would want her back after deserting him like that. Except she told herself, it was his fault in the first place. Blaming her for God knows what? Rack her brains as she might she still had no idea what had caused his furious temper. Perhaps it was a family trait, an illness that only surfaced now and then? If so she was better off away from him but what she would do with the rest of her life was simply unimaginable. Deep down she knew she still loved him with all her heart.

CHAPTER SIXTY-THREE

Merrick, by dint of calling at every inn on the way to Inverness from where he felt she would take a train to London, finally realised, after word reached him that her horse had been brought back, that Linda had ridden to the border and then taken a train from there. He lost all trace after that and though it was a long hard slog decided he would keep his horse with him. It took a further ten days before Merrick, passing through Devon and reaching the borders of Cornwall, gained news of the gypsy tribe. He learned they had moved back into Devon.

Retracing his steps, thoroughly disheartened and tired, at last he rode into their camp to encounter a cheerful Matthias who was pleased to see him, though he at once turned forbidding when he found out the reason for the sudden visit. "No. She is not here, milord. I thought when I let you have her you would have taken better care of her."

His censorious look made Merrick feel like a crass schoolboy again.

"It was a misunderstanding, Matthias, that was all. She had no reason to run. We would have sorted it out given time. I love her very much and need to find her."

"'Twas a serious misunderstanding, methinks, for her to leave you in such a strange fashion. She is like a delicate flower and should be treated with great care; but within her heart she has courage enough to face up to 'mere misunderstandings'."

Merrick sighed, his face grey with fatigue and despair. "Yes, I know," he agreed. "It was my entire fault. I said things that I shouldn't have."

Matthias's face crinkled in a smile. "Excellent." he mocked, "as long as we know where to lay the blame. You do not deserve it, but I am prepared to help you. Stay the night and rest, tomorrow I will tell you where to find her. But on one condition only. You love and care for her with every ounce of your ability from now on; understand?"

Merrick nodded, for once, unable to argue the gypsy's logic. Though he loved her he realised he had not actually been concerned for Linda before. He had left her, a stranger in a foreign place, to his mother, to the servants, or anyone else who cared to make her at ease. Then he had upbraided her because she had found solace. He was disgusted with himself and his arrogant jealousy. Matthias watched his emotions flitting like shadows across Merrick's face and nodded to himself. The young man had learned a valuable lesson. He would not be so proud and sparing of his feelings when he caught up with Linda again. When he saw them once more, no doubt there would be the start of little ones.

"Sleep now; we have a bed for you in a spare Vardas. You will need all the rest you can get as you have a long journey tomorrow. We will speak again over our morning coffee." Merrick fell on the bunk he was given and dropped instantly into a deep sleep. It was the first time since Linda had left him that he had been able to rest easily. Somehow he trusted the gypsy chieftain to set him on the right track. The next morning, rested after a long sleep but still anxious, he joined the gypsy at his welcome fire. It was autumn now and along with the dropping of leaves a heavy mist had collected in the grassy hollows which leached cold into the bones. A light sprinkling of frost on the higher ground foretold winter was on its way.

"You were lucky to find us," began Matthias when he appeared. "We are making for our winter quarters. We disclose this secret place to no one. We need to feel safe and secure away from our enemies. We will stay there until spring and maybe then will we travel north and I shall visit both of you. That is, if you do not mess up your lives again. The next time I shall not help you," he warned. "Now, my friend, you will find her at her home in Cornwall. If I read the signs aright she is like a wounded animal that must return to its lair to mend and become well again. Go on to Tregender and find her but do not tarry for long or she will want to stay forever. Her place is with you, next to your heart or wherever you roam in this world. Understand? I would not leave my Berta behind. She goes with me everywhere; we are kindred souls until death and beyond."

Merrick nodded and thanked the old gypsy for his help then climbed on his horse which one of the tribe had saddled for him. "Then I shall see you in the summer, I trust?" he asked. "Send word if you are coming and I will ready a place." Matthias smiled and nodded his grizzled head. "I will be there, if all goes well."

Merrick turned, saluted and galloped off to find his love. Two days later, he was standing, knocking on the big oak door at Tregender Hall. The place was silent, not a soul to be seen and his heart was already dropping like a stone when the bolt was drawn and Annie stood on the threshold staring, no, on the contrary, glaring fiercely at him.

He took a step forward as though to enter but she barred his way. "Is your mistress at home? May I come in, please?"

She shook her head. "Yer too late, she's gone."

"What do you mean she's gone? What are you babbling about? She can't be gone!"

He pushed roughly past her and entered the huge hall with its magnificent staircase.

Annie nodded. "Ye best be on your way, m'lord. There's nowt fer ee here, she lost the baby. An' we buried 'em day afore yesterday. Go back to where ye came from, we don't want ee here." Annie was unrelentingly grim.

"Baby? What baby? She can't be dead, oh Christ no-oo! Don't tell me this." Merrick stared at her with haggard, bloodshot eyes. She stared back, nervous but still adamant. He stood as though transfixed, hardly able to believe that she was dead. Lost to him forever? His wife, his only love. What a dreadful thing he had done to lose her this way. Tears sprang to his eyes and he shut them, exhausted with the effort of looking on a world where happiness had been lost forever. Suddenly a clear voice rang out from above him.

"Annie! I can't do it! I just can't do it! Merrick, open your eyes! I'm not dead, I'm here!"

CHAPTER SIXTY-FOUR

Dazed at the sound, he opened his eyes and raised his tormented gaze to the top of the stairs where a vision awaited him. She looked exactly like an angel with her fair hair shining in the sunlight streaming through the glass overhead. She wore a long white nightgown, which covered her from head to toe, emphasising the resemblance. The angel spoke.

"Oh, Merry, forgive me, I thought I did not want to see you ever again, but I love you, I can't bear to see you miserable." A sob cut her off as he walked forward to the staircase and began to climb the steps towards her.

"Lindy, my darling love! I've searched everywhere for you!"

She saw sanity return to his eyes as he reached out for her at the top of the stairs. His mouth took hers with a hungry violence, causing her to melt into his arms as though she had never left them, arms that went round her like steel bands, hands splayed across her back, pulling her tight to his body. Back to a place she never expected she would reach again. He had searched for her; did it mean that he had missed her as badly as she had missed him?

Linda reached up to enfold his face between her hands pressing herself so close he could feel her shape with all its voluptuous curves through the thin nightgown. It seemed like forever they stood joined as one to each other then Merrick raised his mouth from hers and looked deep into her shining emerald eyes. She gazed mistily back until suddenly she watched a glowing spark of anger blaze into life in the ice grey of his pupils. Withdrawing her arms from his neck she took a step backwards. "Merrick?" she stammered nervously, aghast that he was going to begin to quarrel all over again. Were they never to make it up and find peace?

"I have ridden through so many counties trying to find you I scarce know where I am at the moment. Have you any idea how much worry you caused me? Now I've found you, my love, I'm going to beat you until you can't sit down."

Linda chuckled uncertainly. "You won't. You can't, not now we're together again, can you?" Suddenly she was not at all sure of him.

"Won't I? Can't I? How much do you bet?"

She squealed as his hand lunged towards her and she scurried back out of reach.

"Merrick! Be reasonable! Don't you love me?"

"Reasonable?" He raised his eyes to the ceiling. "I have scoured half of England searching for you, then when I find you, I'm told you are dead, I'm to go away, and you ask me to be reasonable!" He advanced cat-like as she fell back in dismay, one hand to her throat as she tried to smile placatingly. "I know I frightened you and I'm really sorry."

"Ye-es." Merrick took two steps nearer while she took two steps backwards. "Do go on, my love, your apology gets more interesting."

"But you frightened me, don't forget. You were dreadfully cruel, it serves you right..."

"I think I'm going to enjoy beating you. You are never going to run away again..."

"No! Never! I promise!" She screamed as he came nearer and backed still further away, glancing over her shoulder to see how far her bedroom door lay in order to reach safety.

"There's no escape for you now, you won't stop me!"

Linda saw the ominous glitter in his eyes and taking a chance, raced for safety, pulling up her long gown so it didn't impede her progress. Merrick could see the slim graceful legs beneath and his body raced with lust. He was inches behind her as she reached her bedroom door and tried to close it against him. He pressed against it so hard she was forced to retreat. Giggling helplessly she backed across the room trying to avoid furniture.

"Keep going, my darling, it's in the right direction."

She glanced quickly behind her and saw the bed; at once realising his intentions with great relief. He was not cross after all; he just wanted to love her again. Her legs hit the back of the bed then she flung herself into his arms half laughing and crying with sheer suspense.

Immediately she felt him clasp her to him all the horror and the strain of the days that had elapsed since that dreadful night when he had spurned her, exploded into torrential tears. Merrick held her shaking body, terrified with the force of her grief. He had seen women cry before at various times but never with the anguish of the girl in his arms. Immediately he stopped his jesting.

"Don't cry, my dearest love, I have got you back. You are safe with me, I promise. I didn't mean to scare you, really I didn't; I'll never do it again. Please stop crying." His arms encircled her with overpowering strength, drawing her to his rigid body. "I won't hurt you; you are my life. Everything that I have ever wanted in a woman. I love you and always will." He lifted her chin and pressed a soft kiss to her quivering lips. "Sweetheart, stop weeping, I beg, you are breaking my heart."

With difficulty she controlled herself except for a hiccup or two then whispered sorrowfully, "I lost our baby, Merry, just as I arrived here."

"Don't fret, sweetheart, we shall have another just as soon as you are fit. Have you seen a doctor? If not, we must get one immediately."

She nodded. "He says it sometimes happens with a first baby and not to worry. But it broke my heart. It was the result of our love right at the beginning until…"

"I messed everything up by being jealous and neglecting you," he said soberly. "It won't happen again, Lindy. I realised too well after you left me that of all the things in my life you top the list. It scarcely needed Lucien to tell me the truth of your former life. I knew I'd accused unreasonably. But knowing the true facts devastated me. I didn't realise I was capable of such cruelty. You might find it hard to forgive me but from now on all I want to do is love you."

She glanced at the closed door behind him. "If you lock that, perhaps…" The tiny grin on her still wet face was unmistakable. Gently he wiped her eyes and grinned in return.

"What a fantastic idea."

Downstairs, the housekeeper, cook and parlour maid watched the chase, first with trepidation then with mirth, as they could see how truly their precious girl loved her autocratic husband. "Do you think they're all right?" whispered Betsy, wondering if she ought to go and see why things were so quiet. She had not liked Annie's plan to get rid of Merrick thinking it was tempting fate but Linda was in such a poorly way when she arrived, she had gone along with it. Now she realised it might have caused an even worse tragedy. She hoped all would be well between them, that their love would guide them safely to happiness.

"Course them all right," said Annie stoutly. "All he needed was a push in the right direction.

"I knew she would come round soon as she heard him. As for him, have you ever tried telling Quality what they must or must not do? Come on, Betsy, we m'un eat our dinner. Those two won't rouse fer hours yet."

CHAPTER SIXTY-FIVE

The next few days passed in a flurry of arrangements as Merrick decided to take a long delayed honeymoon on one of his ships. They were due to join the ship in Falmouth and set sail for the West Indies. Linda was excited about the trip and was packed and ready to go on the evening before they sailed. After dinner was over Merrick said firmly, "I think you should retire to bed soon, my love. We have an early start in the morning and you are still not completely as fit as I would like."

"Yes, I will take your advice, I feel my head is so full of things to remember to do before we leave that I shall forget everything if I don't relax." She yawned sleepily then kissed him goodnight.

"I promise I won't wake you when I retire," he said, with a wide grin.

"Promises, promises! And do I promise not to respond when I rouse just a little?" She teased as they grinned at each other like children.

"Maybe a little response," he said, patting her behind as she went out of the door.

Merrick was going through some papers that had to go off in the morning before he sailed when Annie came in the study to say a Mr Richard Whitmore was desirous of seeing him.

"Show him in, please, Annie, and fetch some more brandy." Merrick had a feeling that this might be Linda's young man of her youth. Now what could he want? Annie returned with a tall young man in his early twenties who entered the room looking, Merrick judged, somewhat uneasily hostile. He quickly glanced about the room before nodding curtly at his host.

"Good evening, sir, how may I help you? Come, take a seat and join me in a little refreshment." Merrick's hand hovered over a tray set with sherry, brandy and glasses. "Your preference, sir?" he added, ready to pour out.

"No thank you, I don't drink. I'm of the cloth. I take it you are Linda's husband?"

"That is correct." Hmm, this is not going to be a social visit, thought Merrick.

"Where is she?" Richard Whitmore said bluntly.

"If by she, you mean my wife, not that it is any business of yours, she is resting. Why do you ask?"

"I was first, you know," Richard burst out.

"With what?" Now what skeletons were going to come out?

"Why, asking her to marry me."

"But she didn't accept; she married me instead." Merrick kept his voice steady.

"Yes, well, perhaps she wants to be unmarried," he said sulkily.

"If you mean divorced, I hardly think you're right in assuming that. We are about to leave on an extended honeymoon; for the West Indies, you know. I believe the weather is quite beautiful at this time of year." Young puppy! He was playing with fire if he but knew it.

"I heard she had left you!"

"Goodness! What amazing tales get around! My wife has been a trifle set down a cold perhaps and I'm seeking to remedy it with a sea voyage. Do have a glass of brandy, it is an excellent vintage."

Richard, still concerned with his plan to rescue Linda from the dire clutches of a murderous monster, accepted the glass without thinking and had a deep swallow. Recovering from a violent spate of coughing, he took another sip and decided it was not nearly so bad after all. Why his father made so much fuss about alcohol, he did not know, he thought the taste most enjoyable.

His plan to rescue Linda stemmed from a report related to him by his sister. She, having heard snippets of gossip and being a lover of novels of the most lurid type which would be banned if either her father or mother got to know, had egged him on with the most bizarre of plans to save Linda from a dreadful fate. He was taken aback to learn that her fate was really rather pleasant and what was more he liked the look of her husband.

"It's most gallant of you to care for her well-being but I can truthfully say she is very happy in my company and looking forward to her holiday. But tell me, dear sir, what are your plans for the future, that is, now you are not going to marry my wife?"

Richard took another deep swallow of brandy and Merrick filled up his glass again. He rather liked the look of the young man, thinking it was a pity he was going to waste himself on the church. He had a well-set frame more suited to an energetic country life than that of wearing a cassock and preaching the gospels.

"Continue with the College, I suppose." Richard sighed. "To tell you the truth it was merely to get myself a living to support..." He hesitated, feeling rather foolish over his blunt outburst. Now he had a chance to talk to the man, he really did like the cut of him.

"Linda?" said Merrick helpfully.

"Yes, exactly. I'm not actually very good at it, I'd much rather do something else."

"Would you be any good at looking after a small estate, like this one, for instance? See that it is kept in order, rotate the crops, live in the house - marry a nice girl; have a family?" Merrick was not sure whether the beam on Richard's face and the bright red flush was due to the brandy or the sudden realisation that a job was being presented and that if he did not respond it would be snatched away.

"Do you mean me, sir?"

"Well, there's no one else here, that I can see," Merrick drawled with a teasing grin. "But what about the Church? Don't you have to make vows or something?"

"I haven't as yet. I'm really not suited, if you want the truth."

"Always the truth, Mr Whitmore, I require nothing less. Very well, sir. I shall give you a trial until I return from our honeymoon. I'll inform the housekeeper, Mrs Gorland, and Mrs Polwen that you are now in charge. You are to make sure they are cared for in a proper fashion. My wife needs to know they can stay in this home as long as they are able. See you carry out your responsibilities well and we shall make the job permanent. You may move in when you've notified your college superiors. Good luck to you, Mr Whitmore." Merrick held out his hand and Richard took it with a firm grasp.

"I appreciate the offer, Your Grace. I don't deserve it, under the circumstances."

"Rubbish! You'll laugh about it one of these days when you have your own family at your knees." Merrick saw the young man out and climbed the stairs to bed.

Sliding quietly into bed alongside Linda he wondered what she would make of this unexpected affair but time enough to tell her on the voyage. His hand crept round his sleeping wife and without waking she turned round to be enfolded in his arms. For a moment his mind went to the Estate he planned to buy just outside London so that they could enjoy the best of both worlds, the country and the town, with occasional visits to Scotland and Cornwall then he fell asleep holding his most precious treasure of all.

CHAPTER SIXTY-SIX

Lucien discovered Merrick, one unseasonably hot day in early spring, where he was relaxing under a shady tree in the garden. "Hallo, father-in-law! Come to enjoy the fresh air?" Merrick's voice was a tad mocking as Lucien approached the cluster of lounging chairs.

"Have a heart, Merry, I'm not that much older than you. We played together as boys, remember? I never dreamed then we would be related."

"It seems you got up to more tricks than I did, wouldn't you say, old sir?" Merrick quipped, lazily indicating the empty chair beside him. "Take a seat."

"For which you should be eternally grateful." Lucien laughed as he sat down.

"Do you mean for my wife?"

"No, I meant my daughter."

"Or is she 'our girl' perhaps?" The two men laughed in unison like young schoolboys.

"What are you laughing about?" Linda enquired as she walked towards them.

"A private joke, my darling." Merrick teased her, a smile on his face.

"I see. It's men only today, is it?" She stood with arms akimbo on her hips looking at them, then barely keeping from laughing she announced loudly, "Tea's ready. If Papa and Grandpa would care to join me we shall have it in the drawing room."

She turned and walked back across the grass. For a minute, the two men did not catch on then the garden chairs went over with a crash and both of them took off after Linda with mirthful cheers. Hearing their noisy whoops behind her she began to run towards the house but Merrick's long loping strides took him to her side where he caught her up in his arms and kissed her.

"Is it really true? Are you pregnant?" She nodded tearfully, overcome at his joy. "Then why the hell are you running?" His mock rage made her laugh. "I trust you are not thinking of running away just to get free of us?"

"Darling, of course not." She shuddered wryly. "I'll never do that again. Now be a love and pour the tea out while I fetch Mama Morag and tell her the good news that she is going to be a grandmama." She sighed dramatically, her hand to her head. "When I think of all the efforts I have made to make all of you happy I am amazed at my resilience, despite the fact that some of the ways were rather pleasing on the way." Her eyes twinkled meaningfully at Merrick.

"Only rather?" growled her husband. "Then we shall have to make sure you are entirely pleased, madam. Never let it be said I was lacking in mine own efforts to satisfy. In fact..."

"Merry! Go and pour tea! You will put my father to the blush, I'm sure."

"Lucien? Not him! Haven't you heard? He's going courting again..."

"What's this?" enquired Lucien, as he joined them. "Squabbling again? For goodness sake, I've never known two people to generate such sparks between them."

"Us squabbling? You mistake the ardour, my friend," said Merrick mischievously.

"We were discussing further celebrations. Come, Lucien, tea is getting cold; we shall discuss it in peace. Our days from now on will be beset with babies and their affairs. At least," he murmured softly for Linda's ears only, "we shall have the nights."

SOME MONTHS LATER

Linda stirred sleepily as Merrick came into the room and crossing over to her bed kissed her deeply. "Hello, my darling, how are you feeling?"

Linda stretched lazily, like a cat. "I've just had the best sleep in my life. I feel incredibly flat and wonderfully pleased with myself."

He slid a hand over her tummy and smiled. "Almost, my love. Flat, I mean. We should be able to make the extra plumpness vanish with a little exercise, wouldn't you agree?" His eyes were impish and smiling with tenderness.

"Merry! Not yet! You are insatiable." Nevertheless she smiled lovingly at him.

"And hungry for you, too. But to speak of other matters – I have brought a present for you." Merrick slid a velvet-wrapped parcel into Linda's hands. Surprised, she took out a jewelled necklet with an enormous ruby pendant and gasped in shock.

"Why, this is my great grandmother's locket. I lost it on the Cornish moor. Where did you get it?" Linda swung it gently from side to side watching the scintillating colours flash around her room as the sunlight brought the jewels to life.

"From Trevarron's safe. He must have found it on the moor when he was searching for you. Actually, it belongs to the Forres family estate and Sophie should not have given it away to Lavinia but should have returned it to my father. It was only on loan to her for her lifetime because she produced a son. Murdoch Macgregor, our ancestor, made that very clear in his will. He wanted a dynasty…"

The sound of a crying baby interrupted them and the door opened on a nurse carrying a squalling bundle. She bobbed a curtsy to Merrick and spoke to Linda. "If it pleases you, Your Grace, your son is really hungry. He was getting that cross, he wouldn't be appeased."

"Give him here, Mary, I will soothe his hunger."

The nursery maid handed over the baby and left the room. For some moments there was silence except for the faint sounds of the child at Linda's breast. "Do you wish me to find you a wet-nurse, my love?" Merrick eyed his wife with a quizzical look, which she interpreted easily.

"No. Certainly not. Alastair is mine and I shall feed him myself. Of course, if you are jealous, My Lord, then put your fears at rest…"

"What! Me jealous? Whatever made you think such a thing? Jealous of my son?"

"The look of outrage on your face at another male doing what you want to do."

"Linda! How can you say such a thing?" For a moment Merrick was taken aback at her unusually forward remark and then he saw the laughter in her eyes and chuckled with her. "Of a certainty you are right, my love. I am jealous of my son but I can console myself that he'll not be at your breast forever, it will soon be my turn, then he can take a bottle or whatever young babies have. But to change the subject - the locket is yours."

"Because I've had a son? No thank you, Merrick. I've had a son because I love you; I need no payment for him. Besides, I think the locket is unlucky. Look what has happened to everyone who has had it in their keeping, they have either died or fate has brought them trouble. No, my darling, I thank you for the thought, but give the thing away or sell it or something. Our great, great grandfather may turn in his grave but we need no heirloom to keep our family going, love will do that."

"I somehow thought you would say that and I entirely agree. I've never liked the object myself. Maybe it is the association with the old Duchess. So it is as good as done – however – here is a tiny appreciation of my very deepest love for you." He slid a delicate band of diamonds on her finger and kissed her hand. "Thank you for my son – and maybe the next and the one after!" The grin on his face was huge, his eyes full of mirth.

"Merrick Macgregor! From all I have heard and read you are a veritable throwback to Murdoch – you are quite…quite incorrigible!"

"But of course, my darling. I am a Macgregor!"